PENGUIN CLASSICS

THE STRANGE CASE OF DR JEKYLL AND MR HYDE AND OTHER STORIES

Robert Louis Stevenson was born in Edinburgh in 1850. The son of a prosperous civil engineer, he was expected to follow the family profession but finally was allowed to study law at Edinburgh university. Stevenson reacted violently against the Presbyterian respectability of the city's professional classes and this led to painful clashes with his parents. In his early twenties he became afflicted with a severe respiratory illness from which he was to suffer for the rest of his life, it was at this time that he determined to become a professional writer. The harsh nature of the Scottish climate forced him to spent long periods abroad and he eventually settled in Samoa, where he died on 3 December 1894.

Stevenson's Calvinistic upbringing gave him a preoccupation with predestination and a fascination with the presence of evil. In *Dr Jekyll and Mr Hyde* he explores the darker side of the human psyche, and the character of the Master in *The Master of Ballantrae* (1889) was intended to be 'all I know of the Devil'. Stevenson is well-known for his novels of historical adventure, including *Treasure Island* (1883), *Kidnapped* (1886) and *Catriona* (1893). As Walter Allen in *The English Novel* comments, 'His rediscovery of the art of narrative, of conscious and cunning calculation in telling a story so that the maximum effect of clarity and suspense is achieved, meant the birth of the novel of action as we know it.' But these works also reveal his knowledge and feeling for the Scottish cultural past. During the last years of his life Stevenson's creative range developed considerably and *The Beach of Falesá* brought to fiction the kind of scene now associated with Conrad and Maugham. At the time of his death Robert Louis Stevenson was working on his unfinished masterpiece, *Weir of Hermiston*, which is at once a romantic historical novel and an emotional reworking of one of Stevenson's own most distressing experiences, the conflict between father and son.

•

Jenni Calder was educated at Cambridge University and at the University of London, and has since become both a writer and a teacher. Among her many publications are *Women and Marriage in Victorian Fiction*; a book on Westerns, *There must be a Lone Ranger*; *Heroes: From Byron to Guevara*; *The Victorian Home* and *RLS: A Life Study*. Jenni Calder is the Museum Editor at the Royal Scottish Museum in Edinburgh.

ROBERT LOUIS STEVENSON

THE STRANGE CASE OF
DR JEKYLL AND MR HYDE
AND OTHER STORIES

EDITED WITH
AN INTRODUCTION BY
JENNI CALDER

PENGUIN BOOKS

PENGUIN BOOKS

Published by the Penguin Group
Penguin Books Ltd, 27 Wrights Lane, London W8 5TZ, England
Viking Penguin, a division of Penguin Books USA Inc.
375 Hudson Street, New York, New York 10014, USA
Penguin Books Australia Ltd, Ringwood, Victoria, Australia
Penguin Books Canada Ltd, 2801 John Street, Markham, Ontario, Canada L3R 1B4
Penguin Books (NZ) Ltd, 182–190 Wairau Road, Auckland 10, New Zealand

Penguin Books Ltd, Registered Offices: Harmondsworth, Middlesex, England

The Strange Case of Dr Jekyll and Mr Hyde
first published 1886
The Beach of Falesá
first published under the title *Uma* in the *Illustrated London News* 1892
The Ebb-Tide first published 1893

Published in Penguin Books 1979
15 17 19 20 18 16 14

Printed in England by Clays Ltd, St Ives plc
Set in Linotype Pilgrim

CONTENTS

Introduction	7
A Note on the Texts	25
THE STRANGE CASE OF DR JEKYLL AND MR HYDE	27
THE BEACH OF FALESÁ	99
THE EBB-TIDE	171
Notes	302

INTRODUCTION

ROBERT LOUIS STEVENSON'S career as a successful writer of fiction was brief. It began with the publication of short stories in 1881, and the first instalments of the serial publication of *Treasure Island* at the end of the same year. When he died, in 1894, he was in the middle of two novels, *St Ives* and *Weir of Hermiston*. When Stevenson wrote *The Strange Case of Dr Jekyll and Mr Hyde*, at the end of 1885, he was thirty-five years old and still dependent on his father. *Jekyll and Hyde*, unobtrusively published in January, 1886, was his first really popular book.

He had had a long apprenticeship before this little book came on the scene; a long struggle before he became financially independent. The apprenticeship had been marked by relentless ill health as well as money problems. From early childhood Stevenson had suffered feverish coughs and frequent sickness, and by the time he was thirty tell-tale signs of blood indicated what was generally diagnosed as diseased lungs. 'Bluidy Jack', he called it when he coughed up mouthfuls of blood. His life had always been shaped by the search for health, but the deterioration at this time, brought on to some extent by his desperate journey to California to join his future wife Fanny, inevitably dictated his future. It was no longer possible to spend more than the occasional summer month in his native Scotland; the climate was just not hospitable to his condition. Switzerland, the South of France, the South of England, the Adirondack Mountains in New York State near the Canadian border, and finally the South Pacific and Samoa were the localities where he sought respite from illness.

He was in Bournemouth when he wrote *Jekyll and Hyde*, living in a house given to Fanny as a wedding present by his father, a noted and well-off Edinburgh engineer and lighthouse builder. He called the house Skerryvore after one of the best-known Stevenson lighthouses, built by his uncle Alan Stevenson. He was often ill, often had to do his writing in bed, and was lucky if he was occasionally able to take a gentle stroll around the garden that Fanny lovingly tended. But since his twenty-first year, when he had made it known that he wanted to be a writer, his periods of professional inaction were rare. He began his career as an essayist, and with the help of literary friends in London was publishing in journals in his mid-twenties. His two reflective travel books, *An Inland Voyage* and *Travels with a Donkey*, followed. It is surprising that he took so long to emerge as a writer of fiction. He had tried his hand over the years at a number of stories and novels, but most had been abandoned. He seemed wary of fiction, yet he had been brought up in a tradition of story-telling, and as a child he was unrestrainedly imaginative and inventive. His hours of illness were whiled away with stories, the stories his father wove for him, of pirates and thieves and adventurers, the stories told by his nurse, steeped in uncompromising Calvinist beliefs in sin and coloured by a vivid folk apprehension of the devil, and the stories he told himself, often a strange mixture of both.

Calvinism marked Stevenson's personality and imagination unequivocally. Although as a young man he rebelled against the stern and proper morality of his father, and what he considered to be the genteel hypocrisy of Edinburgh society, it was not easy to shake off the terror of sin, of total evil. The Calvinist imprint stayed with him all his life. And as he grew older experience seemed to confirm at least one aspect of Calvinist teaching: it was impossible to deny that there was evil deep-rooted in the world. At the same time Stevenson believed for many years that his mission as a writer was to please and enliven the spirits of his readers. He had some harsh words for naturalistic writers, particularly the French naturalists of whom Zola was the chief. To drag to the surface the dirt of human experience was not, he felt, the business of the imaginative writer. Fiction, he argued in his essay *A Humble Remonstrance*, 1884, should not be a 'transcript of life', an exact imitation of reality, for that made nonsense of art. The writer needed to 'half-close his eyes against the dazzle and confusion of reality' if he was to bring artistic sensibility to bear on his material.

'Romance' was what Stevenson appeared to want to write, and was encouraged to write by most of his literary friends. Zola pronounced, 'I insist upon the fall of the imagination', but there was growing in Britain at the time a powerful counter-movement to this. Andrew Lang was one of those who was all for romance – 'Romance is permanent,' he said. 'It satisfies a normal and permanent human taste, a taste that survives through all the changing likes and dislikes of critics.' George Saintsbury, another high chieftain of literary taste, condemned what he called 'the domestic and usual novel', and called for a fiction that would enable an escape from drab everyday life.

Stevenson seemed to share this view. He wanted above all to be read and liked, and he considered it the duty of the writer to entertain. But we can find counter-tendencies creeping in at an early stage. Stevenson had strong views on morality, although these views often did not coincide with conventional social and religious attitudes, and his essays are cheerfully full of the expression of these. He maintained a light touch – he tried not to preach – but he had very strong feelings about human behaviour, about man's inhumanity to man in general, and to woman even more. We often find them most nakedly expressed in his letters. 'Romance' for Stevenson did not necessarily mean an escape from thought, even if it did involve an escape from everyday drabness. He talks about the ideal in his essays, a reality that he argues is stronger and more worthwhile than the naturalism of the Zola school. A transcendent reality was what he was after. But perhaps more than anything else he liked a good story, and there had always been, and continued to be, certain aspects of romantic adventure and drama that appealed to him powerfully. They were what he had nourished his youthful imagination on, and his adult imagination required sustenance no less strong.

Stevenson dreamed the essentials of Dr Jekyll and Mr Hyde. One night at Skerryvore Fanny woke him in the middle of a nightmare, and he told her with irritation and excitement that she had disturbed a dream of 'a fine bogy tale'. It was initially the gothic aspect of the story that excited him, and he sat down and rapidly produced a first draft. But Fanny didn't like it. She felt there was potential for more than a mere horror story, that it might have something significant to say about human nature. Stevenson respected his wife's opinion – some would argue her influence was too great, though not, I think, in this case. The first draft went into the fire and a second version was produced with equal rapidity. There erupted into public consciousness a tale that has established itself unshakeably in the British imagination. In Britain, and even more so in America, Stevenson the author had arrived.

There is some irony in the fact that fame came to Stevenson with so frank an exposure of his fascination with evil, for he was loved in his lifetime, and in fact most remembered now – for *Jekyll and Hyde* has become curiously detached from his authorship – as the writer of romantic adventure. Though it is worth remembering that even that wholesome, rattling tale *Treasure Island* contains an ambivalent characterization of evil in the shape of Long John Silver. Not everyone was pleased with Mr Hyde, and many reacted unhappily. His friend and correspondent A. J. Symonds, for instance, was torn. 'You see I am trembling under the magician's wand of your fancy, and rebelling against it with the scorn of a soul that hates to be contaminated with the mere picture of victorious evil. Our only chance seems to me to be to maintain, against all appearances, that evil can never in no way be victorious,' he wrote to Stevenson. And he pinpoints just the ambivalence Stevenson seeks to express in the story. Stevenson suggests that evil is potentially more powerful than good, and if we allow it to come into the open we are in effect allowing it to conquer. But in order to understand evil and to oppose it we must examine it. This was what Symonds couldn't bear, and what Stevenson considered to be a fascinating truth. The evil that the Calvinism and the folk tales of his youth identified was a disguised evil, in the shape of devils and spirits. It is when it takes on human aspect that it becomes terrifying, when the devil removes his tail and horns, those easy aids to identification, and puts on a dress suit, or the spirit enters into the body and soul of an apparently innocent human being. It is the process that Calvinism warns against so violently. The devil may not be as easy to recognize as we think: the potential for evil is within us all.

Inevitably the Calvinist message emerges, which shows how close it was to the Scottish imagination. But more than that, Stevenson shared the Calvinist view to the extent that he considered evil to be a very real presence in human nature and a presence that had to be come to terms with, but what was shocking in *Jekyll and Hyde* was his identification of it. Jekyll is an apparently respectable man who contains within him a potential for profound wickedness, released in the shape of Mr Hyde. Symonds and many others found this chilling to contemplate. And it provided the substance of many a delivery from the pulpit: the two messages were, beware the hidden sin, and beware tampering with nature. But Stevenson did not mean the story to be about the artificial engendering of wickedness, and the dependence on 'the powders' to release Mr Hyde is perhaps the only weakness in the story. The point about Jekyll is not that he is a moral and decent man, but that he has always been leading a double life. And he is leading a double life because he has aimed so high. He wanted respect, honour and distinction, to be highly regarded in society, and thus felt that he had to conceal any irregularities in his life.

> 'Hence it came about that I concealed my pleasures; and that when I reached years of reflection, and began to look round me and take stock of my progress and position in the world, I stood already committed to a profound duplicity of life. Many a man would have blazoned such irregularities as I was guilty of; but from the high views that I had set before me, I regarded and hid them with an almost morbid sense of shame. It was thus rather the exacting nature of my aspirations than any particular degradation in my faults, that made me what I was, and, with even a deeper trench than in the majority of men, severed in me those provinces of good and evil which divide and compound man's dual nature.'

Stevenson is never explicit about these 'irregularities', but knowing something of his own bohemian reaction to Edinburgh middle-class respectability, which involved frequenting the taverns and brothels of Edinburgh's underworld, though he could often afford to do no more than drink beer and look at the women, we can guess what he had in mind. Mr Jekyll's indiscretions would have involved drinking and women, but there is very little sense of any real pleasure these afforded him, in spite of the fact that he talks of his 'gaiety of disposition'. The impression is that he 'plunged in shame' because he knows it is wrong, not because he really enjoys it, and this of course is the other side of the Calvinist coin. The temptation to do what is forbidden *because* it is forbidden is the strongest temptation of all.

It is not until the last phase of the story that Jekyll takes over as narrator and tells us about himself. Up to that point we have seen him through the eyes of his acquaintances. He is seen as a respectable man engaged in a worthy profession. It is interesting and significant that all the characters in the story are in a sense isolated. They have no wives, no families, no close friendships. They have servants and they have acquaintances, but that is all. And there is little sense of a busy city life. Mr Utterson and his friend Enfield clearly have a cool, distant relationship; there is no real intimacy. One of the most striking effects of the story's tone is the juxtaposition of these cool, rather arid characters, isolated and emotionally uncommitted, with the extreme horror and disgust which Hyde and all that is associated with him engenders. The result is more sinister than if the story were built up out of warmer, communal relationships.

The sheer atmosphere of *Jekyll and Hyde* is of course one of its most memorable qualities. The setting is London. But the ambience is without a doubt Edinburgh, the Edinburgh of the Old Town's dark wynds and closes, where the turn of a corner could, in Stevenson's day and even now, abruptly leave behind the world of surface respectability, and the lingering shades of Burke and Hare, the grave-robbers, and Deacon Brodie, cabinet maker by day, criminal by night, still flavoured the atmosphere. Stevenson had absorbed the Deacon Brodie story in his infancy – in fact there was in his own room in his parents' dignified Georgian residence a cabinet Deacon Brodie had himself made.

He was an irresistible symbol of the duality that entered Stevenson's consciousness as a very young child, when he would terrify himself with thoughts of the devil, and reprove himself for the possibility of sin.

Jekyll and Hyde was a popular success, but in exploring the duality of human nature Stevenson was wholly serious. It was a theme he was to come back to repeatedly. The book's popularity was due in part to the incidentals of the story, the atmosphere, the mystery, the horror – it had all the ingredients of what Stevenson himself called 'a good crawler'. But there was more than that to it, more too than the neatness of the idea, and its aptness in terms of human experience. The most serious and fascinating aspect of the story lies in Stevenson's suggestion that the morality that shapes Jekyll's aspirations (and by implication the aspirations of most apparently respectable people) is in fact a terrible burden, a prison, that it imprisons the natural spirit of humanity in an intolerable way. Dr Jekyll, in becoming Mr Hyde, is liberating himself. He experiences a 'solution of the bonds of obligation, an unknown but not an innocent freedom of the soul'. And because Jekyll has tried so hard to be good – he has led a life 'of effort, virtue and control' – the undeveloped, unexercised evil side of his nature is what is set free. The greater the aspirations towards good of Jekyll, the greater the monstrosity of Hyde.

Was Stevenson suggesting that it was dangerous to suppress certain elements of human nature? I think he was, and I think there is a great deal of psychological truth in what he is saying. He had experienced directly the iron grip of Calvinism and of bourgeois morality on human behaviour, and he had recognized that it could be destructive, destructive because it affirmed that good for the majority was something external, artificial, not intrinsic to human nature: men could not be good unless they were told how to be good. Stevenson himself recognized a rather different kind of morality, a morality that came from within, that depended on a sensitive understanding of human relationships and responsibilities, that was flexible, individual, spontaneous. And it was this that made him so attractive, as man and writer, to so many, for at the time he was writing there was a certain weariness with the heavy-handed moral and religious principles of Victorianism. In *Jekyll and Hyde* Stevenson was offering a particularly tantalizing story: the man who sets himself free from moral restraint becomes evil, beast-like, brutish, sub-human it seems. But the freedom itself is irresistibly tempting. Is it inevitable that evil should dominate, or could it happen that the breaking of the bonds might set free the best in human nature?

In the following two stories Stevenson, some years later, was still exploring the same ground. In one, *The Beach of Falesá*, he is suggesting that good *can* be let loose in a situation where a man is free from the conventional rules of behaviour. In *The Ebb-Tide* he is much more equivocal, as he describes characters who remain struggling throughout the story with perceptions of moral restraint. In both stories Stevenson suggests that the concepts of good and evil are highly ambivalent, that they cannot and must not be regarded as absolutes, that absolutes tend to lead to perversion and destruction. We can see him in these stories resisting the dialectic of his upbringing, the dialectic that had impregnated so much of his writing.

In 1887 Stevenson and his wife left England for America. They were never to return. Stevenson's father had died shortly before, and had been his strongest tie to both Scotland and the bourgeois life. America still suggested adventure to Stevenson, although his previous adventures there had nearly killed him. Skerryvore had come to mean an imprisoned existence, imprisoned both by his ill health and the circumstances of ownership. These were things he was desperate to escape from.

The escape from neither was to be wholly possible, but he got as far away from them as he could in the circumstances. After nearly a year in the United States he and Fanny, with an extended family which, though the individuals varied, was never to disperse and remained Stevenson's moral and financial responsibility for the rest of his life, and a great drain on both resources, sailed out of San Francisco harbour on the start of an adventure in the South Pacific which ended only with his death in Samoa six years later. There is no doubt that these experiences clarified Stevenson's vision of life. He was in a position where he could to a great extent choose how he wanted to live, given that he accepted certain obligations. He saw with even greater clarity how meaningless rules of behaviour could be destructive, and equally how, deprived of a moral framework, human beings could deteriorate. He grew furious at the way artificial and often anachronistic standards were imported from Victorian Britain and imposed on the Samoan way of life, and depressed at his encounters throughout the South Seas with white men who had disintegrated under the strain of having to provide their own moral sustenance, or who had seized every opportunity which a confused and fluid situation allowed to exploit and manipulate.

The Beach of Falesá and *The Ebb-Tide* reflect these reactions, and the new experiences and new interests he encountered. Their quality and their substantiality is unquestionable, and it is curious that neither story was ever popular, indeed *Falesá* is here printed in Britain in its original version for the first time. The reason for the submergence of the stories may have something to do with Conrad, who was to explore similar territory himself at much greater length, and whose bulkier genius may have swamped Stevenson's achievement – although Conrad respected and admired what Stevenson had done. But it can also be explained by the fact that these stories did not represent the Stevenson his adulatory public wanted to remember. A story about evil in the idiom of the 'crawler' or an adventure story set in the past was fine, but a story that is direct and contemporary, that treats openly of illicit sexual relations, that demonstrates the least palatable features of human nature, and that does not use its distant and exotic setting to glamourize and entertain is not so likely to be either delightful or exciting.

There were problems with *Falesá*. Stevenson was pleased with the story, felt that he had successfully communicated the feel of things in the South Seas – 'I have got the smell and the look of the thing a good deal,' he wrote to his friend and adviser Sidney Colvin. Other writers had been carried away by the romantic aspect of life in the South Seas, and he was determined to provide a more realistic picture. He had travelled some way in his approach to literature as well as in miles, and the two were connected. At so great a distance from London, where his literary friends were and where it might be said literary taste was shaped, he was able to free himself from certain kinds of literary pressures. Stevenson had always written as a way of coming to terms with contemporary life, whether he was writing adventure stories for boys or amusing essays. For a long time he felt that contemporary life needed diversion, entertainment, reminders that there was more to life than everyday realities. But in his last years of writing he was increasingly concerned to present to his readers the more direct results of his own experience and observations, and increasingly less restrained in doing so.

But there were those who resisted this. Some called *Falesá* 'unwholesome'. Clement Shorter, editor of the *Illustrated London News*, where it was first published, refused to print it as it stood. He insisted on modifying the profanity of some of the dialogue, but more drastically he removed altogether the infamous marriage certificate, which lies at the heart of the story's point, in which John Wiltshire is stated to be 'illegally married' to Uma for one night, and 'is at liberty to send her to hell the next morning'. Shorter removed the direct wording altogether; subsequent editions in Britain have retained the modified 'one week' instead of 'one night'. Stevenson was furious. He had always said that he had felt cautious about tackling 'realistic' subjects because he would not have been able to write what he knew and thought. This episode seemed to prove him right. The story was undermined, for the fact that Wiltshire comes to love and respect the woman he was prepared callously to exploit is central.

The story is written through the persona of Wiltshire, and the consistency of tone achieved is rather remarkable. It is not an easy thing to do, to describe experience through the perceptions of a man of no great sensitivity or intelligence, and to make that experience vivid and telling. Wiltshire is as ready as the next man to take advantage of a situation, and demonstrates the customary attitudes of Europeans in the South Pacific. Certain conventions in business and social behaviour did not need to apply, many considered, when dealing with a people who were gullible and had few means of resisting white manipulation. It was all happening a long way from the obvious sources of ethical behaviour. It was an attitude that disgusted Stevenson. He was keenly aware of the way in which circumstances shaped morality, and this he explores in *Falesá* and *The Ebb-Tide*. Wiltshire is important because he insists on a legal marriage to Uma after the initial fiasco, because he becomes committed to her, to the island and his place there, to his children, and because he risks his life for the island's welfare. He doesn't lose his engrained, white point of view, but he learns commitment to what and where he is.

The profound immorality of this colonial situation is Stevenson's chief concern. Some critics have dismissed the story because of its use of primitive beliefs in devils to convey the extent of domination over the islanders, as this has the appearance of a literary trick. But two features of the story enable Stevenson to carry this off: that he has demonstrated so strongly the fact and the atmosphere of exploitation, partly through Wiltshire's initial cooperation in it, and that he has conveyed tangibly the corruption, suspicion and fear that are a part of the island scene. The relationship between white man and islander is very much on a level of totems and symbols. The white man is there for copra and money, and has to present himself to the islanders in a manner that will bring trade with the least amount of effort and investment. 'I'm a white man, and a British subject, and no end of a big chief at home; and I've come here to do them good, and bring them civilization,' Wiltshire announces when he discovers that a taboo has been laid on him and no one will trade.

The taboo is the natives' only defence against the white man. Wiltshire has always reckoned that 'plain sense and fair dealing', coupled with his rooted belief in native inferiority, brought results. But Case, the arch exploiter, has discovered that instead of relying on the symbols of white civilization to establish a relationship, he can dominate the natives totally by using their own totems – hence the effectiveness of his devils. His power is the result of white technology and native superstition. (The comparison here with Kurtz in Conrad's *Heart of Darkness* is striking.) Wiltshire challenges him not because he suddenly sees himself as a champion of exploited peoples, but because, first, his own survival is being undermined, but also because he is outraged by what he considers to be Case's betrayal of white principles. In a sense he has 'gone native', (his association with the totally deteriorated Randall suggests this) and that renders him highly dubious in the eyes of the conventional white colonialist.

The quality of the story rests not only in its exposition of an imperialist situation, something which simply had not been done at this stage in this way – Conrad was to produce later the most often cited fictional portrayal of the essential corruption of imperialism in *Heart of Darkness*, published in 1899 but arising from an experience of 1890, the year before Stevenson was writing *Falesá*. The achievement has a great deal to do with the character of Wiltshire. For Wiltshire reaches moral status without essentially changing. He resents being under an obligation to Tarleton the missionary to deal fairly with the natives, and is glad when he leaves Falesá and is able to handle things his own way: in other words, he continues to cooperate in exploitation. But he has been involved in circumstances that have released the best in him. He has not taken the easy way out. He is loyal to his wife and to his half-caste children. He is a better man than Case though in some ways not so very different, and Stevenson shows how relativity is very important. He has, in Wiltshire, brought together in a single character, without using the devices of split personality – Wiltshire is very much a whole personality – a moral duality. It is summed up in the masterly final sentences of the story, where he talks of his children. 'But what worries me is the girls. They're only half-castes, of course; I know that as well as you do, and there's nobody thinks less of half-castes than I do; but they're mine, and about all I've got. I can't reconcile my mind to their taking up with Kanakas, and I'd like to know where I'm to find the whites?' Stevenson has quietly and incisively caught a truth of moral ambivalence here which is as arresting as anything he wrote.

Moral ambivalence permeates *The Ebb-Tide*. This long story was begun as a collaborative effort between Stevenson and his step-son Lloyd Osbourne while they were spending some months in Honolulu in 1889. Lloyd was young and eager to learn the writer's craft. Initially he wrote and Stevenson made comments. But the story wasn't completed (they had thought originally in terms of a longish novel) and the early chapters were set aside and forgotten until after the Stevenson entourage was settled in Samoa. There, in Vailima, the house Stevenson built near Apia for himself and his extended family, the early chapters were resuscitated. Stevenson rewrote and completed what Lloyd Osbourne had begun.

It was, Stevenson felt, an uncompromising view of the life of white derelicts in the South Seas. In letters to several friends he mentioned the unpleasantness of the story and the characters. To Henry James he wrote, 'My dear man, the grimness of that story is not to be depicted in words. There are only four characters, to be sure, but they are such a troop of swine! And their behaviour is really so deeply beneath any possible standard, that in retrospect I wonder I have been able to endure them myself until the yarn was finished!' To his friend Sidney Colvin he wrote of the 'grim' and 'hateful' story he had written. Clearly he brooded about it a great deal, and worried about the reception it would get. He was aware that in writing such a story he was moving right out of the character his public expected. Colvin was worried too, and advised that after magazine publication the story should not be published in book form; the book, he said, 'cannot fail to do some harm, more or less, to L's [Louis's] reputation.' It *was* published as a book, and was in fact the last work of Stevenson's to be published in his lifetime.

It is significant that Stevenson was only able to write directly of contemporary experience when he was at a distance from Britain. *Jekyll and Hyde* could be contemporary, but it has a timeless feel about it, and its allegorical qualities lift it out of a contemporary context. The breakthrough that *Falesá* and *The Ebb-Tide* represent was important, for it involved liberating himself from certain confines, which were themselves liable to be contradictory. He had been trapped in Scotland's past, and the unfinished *Weir of Hermiston* might well have been his supreme effort to conquer that. He had been trapped also by the public need for romantic adventure, but he had been able to bring these elements together splendidly in *Kidnapped*, but he could make neither *Catriona* nor *The Master of Ballantrae* work with such success. When he came to write *Weir* it was clear that he no longer felt he should be trying for this. All the signs were that he was moving away from the role of pleasing entertainer (in spite of the fact that in *St Ives*, also unfinished at his death, he was having another attempt – he lost interest and the novel shows it). Finally, in his early forties, the temptation to write about the ambiguities of human character in contemporary and historical contexts became a compulsion. *Weir* is a historical novel about deeply rooted aspects of Scottish character and experience that had confronted Stevenson all his life. It was clearly a very, perhaps dangerously, personal book. *The Ebb-Tide* is about the South Seas that Stevenson himself observed and explored, but it is also about what happens when men are deprived of a moral framework, and have no inner resources, in fact suggests, as Conrad does, that inner resources are part of an outer framework.

Stevenson brings three characters together on a schooner, a self-contained world, surrounded by water. In his use of a ship as an emblem of an isolated society Stevenson may well have been influenced by Melville, whom he admired, but he produces something much starker than the diverse society of Melville's *Pequod*. Stevenson's own experiences on shipboard, many weeks confined with the same company, the flux and the terrors of the sea, the landfalls on islands that were themselves isolated and vulnerable societies, must have been a much greater influence on *The Ebb-Tide*.

His characters are stripped of every support but each other and their own consciences, and the result is devastating; devastating not because deprived of moral restraint Mr Hydes are released in all directions, but because of the dilemma of choice it imposes on Herrick, the central character, in particular. A rigid moral structure that deprives men and women of the possibility of choice limits human potential. But no moral structure at all creates a terrifying void. Herrick, and to a lesser extent Captain Davis, retain some degree of moral sensibility, although self-preservation dominates. In *Jekyll and Hyde* the element of choice is virtually removed; there are forces at work beyond human control. In *Falesá* Wiltshire is in fact aided by circumstances to act in the way he does: self-interest coincides with community interest. But there is little to help Herrick but his own moral awareness, which he struggles painfully to keep alive. It is much easier for Huish, who is totally without restraint, and for Davis, who dulls the painful reminders of his conscience with drink and retains the ability to rationalize his more dubious actions. But Herrick still relates himself to Victorian England and his respectable background. Although he tries to cut himself off from the ties that bind him to a society that is so different from the environment where he now finds himself, he cannot liberate himself. He is bound to his companions too, to Davis and the totally evil Huish, who have helped to rescue him from his derelict state. In Herrick, Stevenson has produced something much more complicated than a straightforward duality. The contrary impulses, the longing to abandon restraint and the clinging to vestiges of morality, are intricately meshed.

The enclosed world of the schooner encounters the enclosed world of Attwater's island. The island is another emblem of an isolated society. In the past Stevenson was able to use islands as symbols of freedom and distance from the restrictions of society, total environments where he could make up his own rules. On Attwater's island Attwater has made up the rules, and gives them added authority by expressing them in terms of certain social symbols. It is on the island that all the currents of ambiguity in the story surface. It first appears as an exotic paradise, 'strange and delicate', sand, coral and breakers, brightly coloured fish and flowers, sea-birds and palm trees – all the tempting ingredients of a restorative, unspoilt escape. Attwater appears at first as the perfect gentleman, upper class, Cambridge educated. Herrick cannot resist the comfort of what seems to be a reconstruction of a familiar moral framework. Attwater is a Christian, a moralist, and serves excellent food and wine, and he seems prepared to accept Herrick as one of his kind. But he is also an exploiter, a tyrant obsessed with power: he will accept Herrick if Herrick accepts his authority. Davis and Huish want to challenge Attwater for the wrong reasons, out of sheer greed for the pearls he has hoarded; Herrick is appalled by the motives and the nakedness of the impulses that now emerge, but resists an alliance with Attwater, whose power and cruelty is no less naked.

It could perhaps be argued that Stevenson makes it too easy for Herrick, for Huish is so totally repellent (it is a much better characterization than Hyde, though) and the vitriol-throwing seems to so unequivocally decide the issue of moral choice. But the terms of the dilemma that faces Herrick mean that in choosing Attwater he is, or thinks he is, eliminating not only Huish but Davis, and a bond of fellowship and sympathy has grown up between Herrick and Davis. Davis in fact survives, but his spirit is annihilated, and it is the survival of the spirit that Stevenson cares about most deeply. In choosing to remain with Attwater, Davis has rediscovered a structure, but it implies a morality that is destructive of the individual. It demands his complete subservience, it takes him out of the world of choice and conflict and challenge, the *real* world, and it involves the renunciation of his wife and children. 'I found peace here, peace in believing,' he says. He trades life for belief. Herrick, it is suggested, chooses life. Although the story ends on so tentative a note there is at least a hint of affirmation.

In terms of Stevenson's own life and career the reverberations of *The Ebb-Tide* are profoundly significant. He had been accused of escaping from the real world by setting up house in Samoa. He knew that this was both true and untrue. He had escaped certain pressures, certain conflicts; he had through this escape gained a perspective on both his own background and the literary scene in London. But he was living in an environment that was both personally and politically challenging. Far from choosing the easy option, Stevenson was, more than was good for his health or his state of mind, leading an involved and committed life. Vailima was no tropical ivory tower.

Stevenson had learnt that duality was too simple a way of representing the ebb and flow of human nature. His years in the South Seas furnished him with fresh images as well as a new

perspective. The sea itself is one of the richest. He has always been drawn to water – *Jekyll and Hyde* is one of his few land-locked stories. He had always seen the sea as a challenge to man, a mystery and a threat. Now he saw it as life itself. He discovered that life required a constant vigilance; there was no escape. Accepting this Stevenson was at the end of his life turning his alert and questing eye on the more immediate areas of his own experience. He remained uneasy about *The Ebb-Tide*, uneasy about a commitment to realism. 'The truth is, I have a little lost my way, and stand bemused at the cross-roads,' he was admitting to Colvin in the summer of 1893. *The Ebb-Tide* was a tale of 'pertinent ugliness and pessimism', he said, and pertinence was perhaps now what he was most after. It seemed to require the loss of the buoyant optimism that had charmed so many and which many admirers of Stevenson still hold to be his chief quality. The signs are that he was willing to let it go.

A NOTE ON THE TEXTS

SHORTLY before Robert Louis Stevenson died in Samoa his friends in Britain were putting into operation a plan to publish a uniform edition of his works. The first volumes were on their way to him when he died on 3 December 1894. The Edinburgh Edition (1894–8), as it was called, was largely the result of hard work on R.L.S.'s behalf by Charles Baxter, an Edinburgh lawyer, and Sidney Colvin, both close friends. R.L.S. himself was minimally involved in the preparation of even the first volumes, partly owing to his great distance from the scene of publication, and also because he was much preoccupied with personal difficulties at this time He relied very much on Colvin's judgement, although he was not happy about some of Colvin's proposals. I have therefore chosen to print from the first edition of *Jekyll and Hyde* (1886), and the first book edition (1894) of *The Ebb-Tide*, which appeared initially in serial form in 1893. In the case of the latter a very few illogicalities in punctuation have been eliminated with reference to the Edinburgh Edition. *The Beach of Falesá*, first published under the title *Uma* in the *Illustrated London News*, July–August, 1892, and then in the volume of stories *Island Nights' Entertainments*, 1893, under its present title, has never been printed in Britain in its complete form. Although the changes that the story's first publisher insisted on were not extensive, amounting to a toning down of some of the dialogue and the changing of the wording on the marriage certificate, R.L.S. was very angry that he was forced to disguise the grossness at the heart of his story. The crucial 'one week' instead of 'one day' (see Introduction) particularly weakened the story, and remained in volume publication. I owe a gratefully acknowledged debt to J C. Furnas's edition, published in the United States in 1956 – the first printing of the story as Stevenson wrote it – in the preparation of the text here printed.

J. C. Furnas has also provided invaluable assistance in elucidating a number of South Pacific terms. I would also like to thank William Kelly of the National Library of Scotland for time spent on my behalf.

THE STRANGE CASE OF
DR JEKYLL AND MR HYDE

To
Katharine de Mattos

It's ill to loose the bands that God decreed to bind;
Still will we be the children of the heather and the wind;
Far away from home, O it's still for you and me
That the broom is blowing bonnie in the north countrie.

Story of the Door

MR UTTERSON the lawyer was a man of a rugged countenance, that was never lighted by a smile; cold, scanty and embarrassed in discourse; backward in sentiment; lean, long, dusty, dreary, and yet somehow lovable. At friendly meetings, and when the wine was to his taste, something eminently human beaconed from his eye; something indeed which never found its way into his talk, but which spoke not only in these silent symbols of the after-dinner face, but more often and loudly in the acts of his life. He was austere with himself; drank gin when he was alone, to mortify a taste for vintages; and though he enjoyed the theatre, had not crossed the doors of one for twenty years. But he had an approved tolerance for others; sometimes wondering, almost with envy, at the high pressure of spirits involved in their misdeeds; and in any extremity inclined to help rather than to reprove. 'I incline to Cain's heresy,' he used to say quaintly: 'I let my brother go to the devil in his own way.' In this character it was frequently his fortune to be the last reputable acquaintance and the last good influence in the lives of down-going men. And to such as these, so long as they came about his chambers, he never marked a shade of change in his demeanour.

No doubt the feat was easy to Mr Utterson; for he was undemonstrative at the best, and even his friendships seemed to be founded in a similar catholicity of good-nature. It is the mark of a modest man to accept his friendly circle ready made from the hands of opportunity; and that was the lawyer's way. His friends were those of his own blood, or those whom he had known the longest; his affections, like ivy, were the growth of time, they implied no aptness in the object. Hence, no doubt, the bond that united him to Mr Richard Enfield, his distant kinsman, the well-known man about town. It was a nut to crack for many, what these two could see in each other, or what subject they could find in common. It was reported by those who encountered them in their Sunday walks, that they said nothing, looked singularly dull, and would hail with obvious relief the appearance of a friend. For all that, the two men put the greatest store by these excursions, counted them the chief jewel of each week, and not only set aside occasions of pleasure, but even resisted the calls of business, that they might enjoy them uninterrupted.

It chanced on one of these rambles that their way led them down a by street in a busy quarter of London. The street was small and what is called quiet, but it drove a thriving trade on the week-days. The inhabitants were all doing well, it seemed, and all emulously hoping to do better still, and laying out the surplus of their gains in coquetry; so that the shop fronts stood along that thoroughfare with an air of invitation, like rows of smiling saleswomen. Even on Sunday, when it veiled its more florid charms and lay comparatively empty of passage, the street shone out in contrast to its dingy neighbourhood, like a fire in a forest; and with its freshly painted shutters, well-polished brasses, and general cleanliness and gaiety of note, instantly caught and pleased the eye of the passenger.

Two doors from one corner, on the left hand going east, the line was broken by the entry of a court; and just at that point, a certain sinister block of building thrust forward its gable on the street. It was two storeys high; showed no window, nothing but a door on the lower storey and a blind forehead of discoloured wall on the upper; and bore in every feature the marks of prolonged and sordid negligence. The door, which was equipped with neither bell nor knocker, was blistered and distained. Tramps slouched into the recess and struck matches on the panels; children kept shop upon the steps; the schoolboy had tried his knife on the mouldings; and for close on a generation no one had appeared to drive away these random visitors or to repair their ravages.

Mr Enfield and the lawyer were on the other side of the by street; but when they came abreast of the entry, the former lifted up his cane and pointed.

'Did you ever remark that door?' he asked; and when his

companion had replied in the affirmative, 'It is connected in my mind,' added he, 'with a very odd story.'

'Indeed!' said Mr Utterson, with a slight change of voice, 'and what was that?'

'Well, it was this way,' returned Mr Enfield: 'I was coming home from some place at the end of the world, about three o'clock of a black winter morning, and my way lay through a part of town where there was literally nothing to be seen but lamps. Street after street, and all the folks asleep – street after street, all lighted up as if for a procession, and all as empty as a church – till at last I got into that state of mind when a man listens and listens and begins to long for the sight of a policeman. All at once, I saw two figures: one a little man who was stumping along eastward at a good walk, and the other a girl of maybe eight or ten who was running as hard as she was able down a cross-street. Well, sir, the two ran into one another naturally enough at the corner; and then came the horrible part of the thing; for the man trampled calmly over the child's body and left her screaming on the ground. It sounds nothing to hear, but it was hellish to see. It wasn't like a man; it was like some damned Juggernaut.[1] I gave a view halloa, took to my heels, collared my gentleman, and brought him back to where there was already quite a group about the screaming child. He was perfectly cool and made no resistance, but gave me one look, so ugly that it brought out the sweat on me like running. The people who had turned out were the girl's own family; and pretty soon the doctor, for whom she had been sent, put in his appearance. Well, the child was not much the worse, more frightened, according to the Sawbones; and there you might have supposed would be an end to it. But there was one curious circumstance. I had taken a loathing to my gentleman at first sight. So had the child's family, which was only natural. But the doctor's case was what struck me. He was the usual cut-and-dry apothecary, of no particular age and colour, with a strong Edinburgh accent, and about as emotional as a bagpipe. Well, sir, he was like the rest of us: every time he looked at my prisoner, I saw that Sawbones turned sick and white with the desire to kill him. I knew what was in his mind, just as he knew what was in mine; and killing being out of the question, we did the next best. We told the man we could and would make such a scandal out of this, as should make his name stink from one end of London to the other. If he had any friends or any credit, we undertook that he should lose them. And all the time, as we were pitching it in red hot, we were keeping the women off him as best we could, for they were as wild as harpies. I never saw a circle of such hateful faces; and there was the man in the middle, with a kind of black sneering coolness – frightened too, I could see that – but carrying it off, sir, really like Satan. "If you choose to make capital out of this accident," said he, "I am naturally helpless. No gentleman but wishes to avoid a scene," says he. "Name your figure." Well, we screwed him up to a hundred pounds for the child's family; he would have clearly liked to stick out; but there was something about the lot of us that meant mischief, and at last he struck. The next thing was to get the money; and where do you think he carried us but to that place with the door? – whipped out a key, went in, and presently came back with the matter of ten pounds in gold and a cheque for the balance on Coutts's, drawn payable to bearer, and signed with a name that I can't mention, though it's one of the points of my story, but it was a name at least very well known and often printed. The figure was stiff; but the signature was good for more than that, if it was only genuine. I took the liberty of pointing out to my gentleman that the whole business looked apocryphal; and that a man does not, in real life, walk into a cellar door at four in the morning and come out of it with another man's cheque for close upon a hundred pounds. But he was quite easy and sneering. "Set your mind at rest," says he; "I will stay with you till the banks open, and cash the cheque myself." So we all set off, the doctor, and the child's father, and our friend and myself, and passed the rest of the night in my chambers; and next day, when we had breakfasted, went in a body to the bank. I gave in the cheque myself, and said I had every reason to believe it was a forgery. Not a bit of it. The cheque was genuine.'

'Tut-tut!' said Mr Utterson.

'I see you feel as I do,' said Mr Enfield. 'Yes, it's a bad story.

For my man was a fellow that nobody could have to do with, a really damnable man; and the person that drew the cheque is the very pink of the proprieties, celebrated too, and (what makes it worse) one of your fellows who do what they call good. Blackmail, I suppose; an honest man paying through the nose for some of the capers of his youth. Blackmail House is what I call that place with the door, in consequence. Though even that, you know, is far from explaining all,' he added; and with the words fell into a vein of musing.

From this he was recalled by Mr Utterson asking rather suddenly: 'And you don't know if the drawer of the cheque lives there?'

'A likely place, isn't it?' returned Mr Enfield. 'But I happen to have noticed his address; he lives in some square or other.'

'And you never asked about – the place with the door?' said Mr Utterson.

'No, sir: I had a delicacy,' was the reply. 'I feel very strongly about putting questions; it partakes too much of the style of the day of judgment. You start a question, and it's like starting a stone. You sit quietly on the top of a hill; and away the stone goes, starting others; and presently some bland old bird (the last you would have thought of) is knocked on the head in his own back garden, and the family have to change their name. No, sir, I make it a rule of mine: the more it looks like Queer Street, the less I ask.'[2]

'A very good rule, too,' said the lawyer.

'But I have studied the place for myself,' continued Mr Enfield. 'It seems scarcely a house. There is no other door, and nobody goes in or out of that one, but, once in a great while, the gentleman of my adventure. There are three windows looking on the court on the first floor; none below; the windows are always shut, but they're clean. And then there is a chimney, which is generally smoking; so somebody must live there. And yet it's not so sure; for the buildings are so packed together about that court, that it's hard to say where one ends and another begins.'

The pair walked on again for a while in silence; and then – 'Enfield,' said Mr Utterson, 'that's a good rule of yours.'

'Yes, I think it is,' returned Enfield.

'But for all that,' continued the lawyer, 'there's one point I want to ask: I want to ask the name of that man who walked over the child.'

'Well,' said Mr Enfield, 'I can't see what harm it would do. It was a man of the name of Hyde.'

'Hm,' said Mr Utterson. 'What sort of a man is he to see?'

'He is not easy to describe. There is something wrong with his appearance; something displeasing, something downright detestable. I never saw a man I so disliked, and yet I scarce know why. He must be deformed somewhere; he gives a strong feeling of deformity, although I couldn't specify the point. He's an extraordinary-looking man, and yet I really can name nothing out of the way. No, sir; I can make no hand of it; I can't describe him. And it's not want of memory; for I declare I can see him this moment.'

Mr Utterson again walked some way in silence, and obviously under a weight of consideration. 'You are sure he used a key?' he inquired at last.

'My dear sir . . .' began Enfield, surprised out of himself.

'Yes, I know,' said Utterson; 'I know it must seem strange. The fact is, if I do not ask you the name of the other party, it is because I know it already. You see, Richard, your tale has gone home. If you have been inexact in any point, you had better correct it.'

'I think you might have warned me,' returned the other, with a touch of sullenness. 'But I have been pedantically exact, as you call it. The fellow had a key; and, what's more, he has it still. I saw him use it, not a week ago.'

Mr Utterson sighed deeply, but said never a word; and the young man presently resumed. 'Here is another lesson to say nothing,' said he. 'I am ashamed of my long tongue. Let us make a bargain never to refer to this again.'

'With all my heart,' said the lawyer. 'I shake hands on that, Richard.'

Search for Mr Hyde

THAT evening Mr Utterson came home to his bachelor house in sombre spirits, and sat down to dinner without relish. It was his custom of a Sunday, when this meal was over, to sit close by the fire, a volume of some dry divinity on his reading-desk, until the clock of the neighbouring church rang out the hour of twelve, when he would go soberly and gratefully to bed. On this night, however, as soon as the cloth was taken away, he took up a candle and went into his business room. There he opened his safe, took from the most private part of it a document endorsed on the envelope as Dr Jekyll's Will, and sat down with a clouded brow to study its contents. The will was holograph; for Mr Utterson, though he took charge of it now that it was made, had refused to lend the least assistance in the making of it; it provided not only that, in case of the decease of Henry Jekyll, M.D., D.C.L., LL.D., F.R.S., &c., all his possessions were to pass into the hands of his 'friend and benefactor Edward Hyde'; but that in case of Dr Jekyll's 'disappearance or unexplained absence for any period exceeding three calendar months,' the said Edward Hyde should step into the said Henry Jekyll's shoes without further delay, and free from any burthen or obligation, beyond the payment of a few small sums to the members of the doctor's household. This document had long been the lawyer's eyesore. It offended him both as a lawyer and as a lover of the sane and customary sides of life, to whom the fanciful was the immodest. And hitherto it was his ignorance of Mr Hyde that had swelled his indignation; now, by a sudden turn, it was his knowledge. It was already bad enough when the name was but a name of which he could learn no more. It was worse when it began to be clothed upon with detestable attributes; and out of the shifting, insubstantial mists that had so long baffled his eye, there leaped up the sudden, definite presentment of a fiend.

'I thought it was madness,' he said, as he replaced the obnoxious paper in the safe; 'and now I begin to fear it is disgrace.'

With that he blew out his candle, put on a great coat, and set forth in the direction of Cavendish Square, that citadel of medicine, where his friend the great Dr Lanyon, had his house and received his crowding patients. 'If any one knows, it will be Lanyon,' he had thought.

The solemn butler knew and welcomed him; he was subjected to no stage of delay, but ushered direct from the door to the dining room, where Dr Lanyon sat alone over his wine. This was a hearty, healthy, dapper, red-faced gentleman, with a shock of hair prematurely white, and a boisterous and decided manner. At sight of Mr Utterson, he sprang up from his chair and welcomed him with both hands. The geniality, as was the way of the man, was somewhat theatrical to the eye; but it reposed on genuine feeling. For these two were old friends, old mates both at school and college, both thorough respecters of themselves and of each other, and, what does not always follow, men who thoroughly enjoyed each other's company.

After a little rambling talk, the lawyer led up to the subject which so disagreeably preoccupied his mind

'I suppose, Lanyon,' he said, 'you and I must be the two oldest friends that Henry Jekyll has?'

'I wish the friends were younger,' chuckled Dr Lanyon. 'But I suppose we are. And what of that? I see little of him now.'

'Indeed!' said Utterson. 'I thought you had a bond of common interest.'

'We had,' was his reply. 'But it is more than ten years since Henry Jekyll became too fanciful for me. He began to go wrong, wrong in mind; and though, of course, I continue to take an interest in him for old sake's sake as they say, I see and I have seen devilish little of the man. Such unscientific balderdash,' added the doctor, flushing suddenly purple, 'would have estranged Damon and Pythias.'[3]

This little spirt of temper was somewhat of a relief to Mr Utterson. 'They have only differed on some point of science,' he thought; and being a man of no scientific passions (except in the matter of conveyancing), he even added: 'It is nothing worse than that!' He gave his friend a few seconds to recover his composure, and then approached the question he had come to put.

'Did you ever come across a *protégé* of his – one Hyde?' he asked.

'Hyde?' repeated Lanyon. 'No. Never heard of him. Since my time.'

That was the amount of information that the lawyer carried back with him to the great, dark bed on which he tossed to and fro until the small hours of the morning began to grow large. It was a night of little ease to his toiling mind, toiling in mere darkness and besieged by questions.

Six o'clock struck on the bells of the church that was so conveniently near to Mr Utterson's dwelling, and still he was digging at the problem. Hitherto it had touched him on the intellectual side alone; but now his imagination also was engaged, or rather enslaved; and as he lay and tossed in the gross darkness of the night and the curtained room, Mr Enfield's tale went by before his mind in a scroll of lighted pictures. He would be aware of the great field of lamps of a nocturnal city; then of the figure of a man walking swiftly; then of a child running from the doctor's; and then these met, and that human Juggernaut trod the child down and passed on regardless of her screams. Or else he would see a room in a rich house, where his friend lay asleep, dreaming and smiling at his dreams; and then the door of that room would be opened, the curtains of the bed plucked apart, the sleeper recalled, and, lo! there would stand by his side a figure to whom power was given, and even at that dead hour he must rise and do its bidding. The figure in these two phases haunted the lawyer all night; and if at any time he dozed over, it was but to see it glide more stealthily through sleeping houses, or move the more swiftly, and still the more swiftly, even to dizziness, through wider labyrinths of lamp-lighted city, and at every street corner crush a child and leave her screaming. And still the figure had no face by which he might know it; even in his dreams it had no face, or one that baffled him and melted before his eyes; and thus it was that there sprang up and grew apace in the lawyer's mind a singularly strong, almost an inordinate, curiosity to behold the features of the real Mr Hyde. If he could but once set eyes on him, he thought the mystery would lighten and perhaps roll altogether away, as was the habit of mysterious things when well examined. He might see a reason for his friend's strange preference or bondage (call it which you please), and even for the startling clauses of the will. And at least it would be a face worth seeing: the face of a man who was without bowels of mercy: a face which had but to show itself to raise up, in the mind of the unimpressionable Enfield, a spirit of enduring hatred.

From that time forward, Mr Utterson began to haunt the door in the by street of shops. In the morning before office hours, at noon when business was plenty and time scarce, at night under the face of the fogged city moon, by all lights and at all hours of solitude or concourse, the lawyer was to be found on his chosen post.

'If he be Mr Hyde,' he had thought, 'I shall be Mr Seek.'

And at last his patience was rewarded. It was a fine dry night; frost in the air; the streets as clean as a ball-room floor; the lamps, unshaken by any wind, drawing a regular pattern of light and shadow. By ten o'clock, when the shops were closed, the by street was very solitary, and, in spite of the low growl of London from all around, very silent. Small sounds carried far; domestic sounds out of the houses were clearly audible on either side of the roadway; and the rumour of the approach of any passenger preceded him by a long time. Mr Utterson had been some minutes at his post when he was aware of an odd light footstep drawing near. In the course of his nightly patrols he had long grown accustomed to the quaint effect with which the footfalls of a single person, while he is still a great way off, suddenly spring out distinct from the vast hum and clatter of the city. Yet his attention had never before been so sharply and decisively arrested; and it was with a strong, superstitious prevision of success that he withdrew into the entry of the court.

The steps drew swiftly nearer, and swelled out suddenly louder as they turned the end of the street. The lawyer, looking forth from the entry, could soon see what manner of man he had to deal with. He was small, and very plainly dressed; and the look of him, even at that distance, went somehow strongly against the watcher's inclination. But he made straight for the door, crossing the roadway to save time; and as he came, he drew a key from his pocket, like one approaching home.

Mr Utterson stepped out and touched him on the shoulder as he passed. 'Mr Hyde, I think?'

Mr Hyde shrank back with a hissing intake of the breath. But his fear was only momentary; and though he did not look the lawyer in the face, he answered coolly enough: 'That is my name. What do you want?'

'I see you are going in,' returned the lawyer. 'I am an old friend of Dr Jekyll's – Mr Utterson, of Gaunt Street – you must have heard my name; and meeting you so conveniently, I thought you might admit me.'

'You will not find Dr Jekyll; he is from home,' replied Mr Hyde, blowing in the key. And then suddenly, but still without looking up, 'How did you know me?' he asked.

'On your side,' said Mr Utterson, 'will you do me a favour?'

'With pleasure,' replied the other. 'What shall it be?'

'Will you let me see your face?' asked the lawyer.

Mr Hyde appeared to hesitate; and then, as if upon some sudden reflection, fronted about with an air of defiance; and the pair stared at each other pretty fixedly for a few seconds. 'Now I shall know you again,' said Mr Utterson. 'It may be useful.'

'Yes,' returned Mr Hyde, 'it is as well we have met; and *à propos*, you should have my address.' And he gave a number of a street in Soho.

'Good God!' thought Mr Utterson, 'can he too have been thinking of the will?' But he kept his feelings to himself, and only grunted in acknowledgment of the address.

'And now,' said the other, 'how did you know me?'

'By description,' was the reply.

'Whose description?'

'We have common friends,' said Mr Utterson.

'Common friends!' echoed Mr Hyde, a little hoarsely. 'Who are they?'

'Jekyll, for instance,' said the lawyer.

'He never told you,' cried Mr Hyde, with a flush of anger. 'I did not think you would have lied.'

'Come,' said Mr Utterson, 'that is not fitting language.'

The other snarled aloud into a savage laugh; and the next moment, with extraordinary quickness, he had unlocked the door and disappeared into the house.

The lawyer stood awhile when Mr Hyde had left him, the picture of disquietude. Then he began slowly to mount the street, pausing every step or two, and putting his hand to his brow like a man in mental perplexity. The problem he was thus debating as he walked was one of a class that is rarely solved. Mr Hyde was pale and dwarfish; he gave an impression of deformity without any namable malformation, he had a displeasing smile, he had borne himself to the lawyer with a sort of murderous mixture of timidity and boldness, and he spoke with a husky, whispering and somewhat broken voice, – all these were points against him; but not all of these together could explain the hitherto unknown disgust, loathing and fear with which Mr Utterson regarded him. 'There must be something else,' said the perplexed gentleman. 'There *is* something more, if I could find a name for it. God bless me, the man seems hardly human! Something troglodytic, shall we say? or can it be the old story of Dr Fell? or is it the mere radiance of a foul soul that thus transpires through, and transfigures, its clay continent? The last, I think; for, O my poor old Harry Jekyll, if ever I read Satan's signature upon a face, it is on that of your new friend!'

Round the corner from the by street there was a square of ancient, handsome houses, now for the most part decayed from their high estate, and let in flats and chambers to all sorts and conditions of men: map-engravers, architects, shady lawyers, and the agents of obscure enterprises. One house, however, second from the corner, was still occupied entire; and at the door of this, which wore a great air of wealth and comfort, though it was now plunged in darkness except for the fan-light, Mr Utterson stopped and knocked. A well-dressed, elderly servant opened the door.

'Is Dr Jekyll at home, Poole?' asked the lawyer.

'I will see, Mr Utterson,' said Poole, admitting the visitor, as he spoke, into a large, low-roofed, comfortable hall, paved with flags, warmed (after the fashion of a country house) by a bright, open fire, and furnished with costly cabinets of oak. 'Will you wait here by the fire, sir? or shall I give you a light in the dining-room?'

'Here, thank you,' said the lawyer; and he drew near and leaned on the tall fender. This hall, in which he was now left alone, was a pet fancy of his friend the doctor's; and Utterson himself was wont to speak of it as the pleasantest room in London. But to-night there was a shudder in his blood; the face of Hyde sat heavy on his memory; he felt (what was rare in him) a nausea and distaste of life; and in the gloom of his spirits, he seemed to read a menace in the flickering of the firelight on the polished cabinets and the uneasy starting of the shadow on the roof. He was ashamed of his relief when Poole presently returned to announce that Dr Jekyll was gone out.

'I saw Mr Hyde go in by the old dissecting-room door, Poole,' he said. 'Is that right, when Dr Jekyll is from home?'

'Quite right, Mr Utterson, sir,' replied the servant. 'Mr Hyde has a key.'

'Your master seems to repose a great deal of trust in that young man, Poole,' resumed the other, musingly.

'Yes, sir, he do indeed,' said Poole. 'We have all orders to obey him.'

'I do not think I ever met Mr Hyde?' asked Utterson.

'O dear no, sir. He never *dines* here,' replied the butler. 'Indeed, we see very little of him on this side of the house; he mostly comes and goes by the laboratory.'

'Well, good-night, Poole.'

'Good-night, Mr Utterson.'

And the lawyer set out homeward with a very heavy heart. 'Poor Harry Jekyll,' he thought, 'my mind misgives me he is in deep waters! He was wild when he was young; a long while ago, to be sure; but in the law of God there is no statute of limitations. Ah, it must be that; the ghost of some old sin, the cancer of some concealed disgrace; punishment coming, *pede claudo*, years after memory has forgotten and self-love condoned the fault.'[4] And the lawyer, scared by the thought, brooded awhile on his own past, groping in all the corners of memory, lest by chance some Jack-in-the-Box of an old iniquity should leap to light there. His past was fairly blameless; few men could read the rolls of their life with less apprehension; yet he was humbled to the dust by the many ill things he had done, and raised up again into a sober and fearful gratitude by the many that he had come so near to doing, yet avoided. And then by a return on his former subject, he conceived a spark of hope. 'This Master Hyde, if he were studied,' thought he, 'must have secrets of his own: black secrets, by the look of him; secrets compared to which poor Jekyll's worst would be like sunshine. Things cannot continue as they are. It turns me quite cold to think of this creature stealing like a thief to Harry's bedside; poor Harry, what a wakening! And the danger of it! for if this Hyde suspects the existence of the will, he may grow impatient to inherit. Ay, I must put my shoulder to the wheel – if Jekyll will but let me,' he added, 'if Jekyll will only let me.' For once more he saw before his mind's eye, as clear as a transparency, the strange clauses of the will.

Dr Jekyll was Quite at Ease

A FORTNIGHT later, by excellent good fortune, the doctor gave one of his pleasant dinners to some five or six old cronies, all intelligent reputable men, and all judges of good wine; and Mr Utterson so contrived that he remained behind after the others had departed. This was no new arrangement, but a thing that had befallen many scores of times. Where Utterson was liked, he was liked well. Hosts loved to detain the dry lawyer, when the light-hearted and the loose-tongued had already their foot on the threshold; they liked to sit awhile in his unobtrusive company, practising for solitude, sobering their minds in the man's rich silence, after the expense and strain of gaiety. To this rule Dr Jekyll was no exception; and as he now sat on the opposite side of the fire – a large, well-made, smooth-faced man of fifty, with something of a slyish cast perhaps, but every mark of capacity and kindness – you could see by his looks that he cherished for Mr Utterson a sincere and warm affection.

'I have been wanting to speak to you, Jekyll,' began the latter. 'You know that will of yours?'

A close observer might have gathered that the topic was distasteful; but the doctor carried it off gaily. 'My poor Utterson,' said he, 'you are unfortunate in such a client. I never saw a man so distressed as you were by my will; unless it were that hide-bound pedant, Lanyon, at what he called my scientific heresies. O, I know he's a good fellow – you needn't frown – an excellent fellow, and I always mean to see more of him; but a hide-bound pedant for all that; an ignorant, blatant pedant. I was never more disappointed in any man than Lanyon.'

'You know I never approved of it,' pursued Utterson, ruthlessly disregarding the fresh topic.

'My will? Yes, certainly, I know that,' said the doctor, a trifle sharply. 'You have told me so.'

'Well, I tell you so again,' continued the lawyer. 'I have been learning something of young Hyde.'

The large handsome face of Dr Jekyll grew pale to the very lips, and there came a blackness about his eyes. 'I do not care to hear more,' said he. 'This is a matter I thought we had agreed to drop.'

'What I heard was abominable,' said Utterson.

'It can make no change. You do not understand my position,' returned the doctor, with a certain incoherency of manner. 'I am painfully situated, Utterson; my position is a very strange – a very strange one. It is one of those affairs that cannot be mended by talking.'

'Jekyll,' said Utterson, 'you know me: I am a man to be trusted. Make a clean breast of this in confidence; and I make no doubt I can get you out of it.'

'My good Utterson,' said the doctor, 'this is very good of you, this is downright good of you, and I cannot find words to thank you in. I believe you fully; I would trust you before any man alive, ay, before myself, if I could make the choice; but indeed it isn't what you fancy; it is not so bad as that; and just to put your good heart at rest, I will tell you one thing: the moment I choose, I can be rid of Mr Hyde. I give you my hand upon that; and I thank you again and again; and I will just add one little word, Utterson, that I'm sure you'll take in good part: this is a private matter, and I beg of you to let it sleep.'

Utterson reflected a little, looking in the fire.

'I have no doubt you are perfectly right,' he said at last, getting to his feet.

'Well, but since we have touched upon this business, and for the last time, I hope,' continued the doctor, 'there is one point I should like you to understand. I have really a very great interest in poor Hyde. I know you have seen him; he told me so; and I fear he was rude. But I do sincerely take a great, a very great interest in that young man; and if I am taken away, Utterson, I wish you to promise me that you will bear with him and get his rights for him. I think you would, if you knew all; and it would be a weight off my mind if you would promise.'

'I can't pretend that I shall ever like him,' said the lawyer.

'I don't ask that,' pleaded Jekyll, laying his hand upon the other's arm; 'I only ask for justice; I only ask you to help him for my sake, when I am no longer here.'

Utterson heaved an irrepressible sigh. 'Well,' said he, 'I promise.'

The Carew Murder Case

NEARLY a year later, in the month of October, 18——, London was startled by a crime of singular ferocity, and rendered all the more notable by the high position of the victim. The details were few and startling. A maid-servant living alone in a house not far from the river had gone upstairs to bed about eleven. Although a fog rolled over the city in the small hours, the early part of the night was cloudless, and the lane, which the maid's window overlooked, was brilliantly lit by the full moon. It seems she was romantically given; for she sat down upon her box, which stood immediately under the window, and fell into a dream of musing. Never (she used to say, with streaming tears, when she narrated that experience), never had she felt more at peace with all men or thought more kindly of the world. And as she so sat she became aware of an aged and beautiful gentleman with white hair drawing near along the lane; and advancing to meet him, another and very small gentleman, to whom at first she paid less attention. When they had come within speech (which was just under the maid's eyes) the older man bowed and accosted the other with a very pretty manner of politeness. It did not seem as if the subject of his address were of great importance; indeed, from his pointing, it sometimes appeared as if he were only inquiring his way; but the moon shone on his face as he spoke, and the girl was pleased to watch it, it seemed to breathe such an innocent and old-world kindness of disposition, yet with something high too, as of a well-founded self-content. Presently her eye wandered to the other, and she was surprised to recognise in him a certain Mr Hyde, who had once visited her master and for whom she had conceived a dislike. He had in his hand a heavy cane, with which he was trifling; but he answered never a word, and seemed to listen with an ill-contained impatience. And then all of a sudden he broke out in a great flame of anger, stamping with his foot, brandishing the cane, and carrying on (as the maid described it) like a madman. The old gentleman took a step back, with the air of one very much surprised and a trifle hurt; and at that Mr Hyde broke out of all bounds, and clubbed him to the earth. And next moment, with ape-like fury, he was trampling his victim under foot, and hailing down a storm of blows, under which the bones were audibly shattered and the body jumped upon the roadway. At the horror of these sights and sounds, the maid fainted.

It was two o'clock when she came to herself and called for the police. The murderer was gone long ago; but there lay his victim in the middle of the lane, incredibly mangled. The stick with which the deed had been done, although it was of some rare and very tough and heavy wood, had broken in the middle under the stress of this insensate cruelty; and one splintered half had rolled in the neighbouring gutter – the other, without doubt, had been carried away by the murderer. A purse and a gold watch were found upon the victim; but, no cards or papers, except a sealed and stamped envelope, which he had been probably carrying to the post, and which bore the name and address of Mr Utterson.

This was brought to the lawyer the next morning, before he was out of bed; and he had no sooner seen it, and been told the circumstances, than he shot out a solemn lip. 'I shall say nothing till I have seen the body,' said he; 'this may be very serious. Have the kindness to wait while I dress.' And with the same grave countenance, he hurried through his breakfast and drove to the police station, whither the body had been carried. As soon as he came into the cell, he nodded.

'Yes,' said he, 'I recognise him. I am sorry to say that this is Sir Danvers Carew.'

'Good God, sir!' exclaimed the officer, 'is it possible?' And the next moment his eye lighted up with professional ambition. 'This will make a deal of noise,' he said. 'And perhaps you can help us to the man.' And he briefly narrated what the maid had seen, and showed the broken stick.

Mr Utterson had already quailed at the name of Hyde; but

when the stick was laid before him, he could doubt no longer: broken and battered as it was, he recognised it for one that he had himself presented many years before to Henry Jekyll.

'Is this Mr Hyde a person of small stature?' he inquired.

'Particularly small and particularly wicked-looking, is what the maid calls him,' said the officer.

Mr Utterson reflected; and then, raising his head, 'If you will come with me in my cab,' he said, 'I think I can take you to his house.'

It was by this time about nine in the morning, and the first fog of the season. A great chocolate-coloured pall lowered over heaven, but the wind was continually charging and routing these embattled vapours; so that as the cab crawled from street to street, Mr Utterson beheld a marvellous number of degrees and hues of twilight; for here it would be dark like the back-end of evening; and there would be a glow of a rich, lurid brown, like the light of some strange conflagration; and here, for a moment, the fog would be quite broken up, and a haggard shaft of daylight would glance in between the swirling wreaths. The dismal quarter of Soho seen under these changing glimpses, with its muddy ways, and slatternly passengers, and its lamps, which had never been extinguished or had been kindled afresh to combat this mournful reinvasion of darkness, seemed, in the lawyer's eyes, like a district of some city in a nightmare. The thoughts of his mind, besides, were of the gloomiest dye; and when he glanced at the companion of his drive, he was conscious of some touch of that terror of the law and the law's officers which may at times assail the most honest.

As the cab drew up before the address indicated, the fog lifted a little and showed him a dingy street, a gin palace, a low French eating-house, a shop for the retail of penny numbers and two-penny salads, many ragged children huddled in the doorways, and many women of many different nationalities passing out, key in hand, to have a morning glass; and the next moment the fog settled down again upon that part, as brown as umber, and cut him off from his blackguardly surroundings. This was the home of Henry Jekyll's favourite; of a man who was heir to a quarter of a million sterling.

An ivory-faced and silvery-haired old woman opened the door. She had an evil face, smoothed by hypocrisy; but her manners were excellent. Yes, she said, this was Mr Hyde's, but he was not at home; he had been in that night very late, but had gone away again in less than an hour: there was nothing strange in that; his habits were very irregular, and he was often absent; for instance, it was nearly two months since she had seen him till yesterday.

'Very well then, we wish to see his rooms,' said the lawyer; and when the woman began to declare it was impossible, 'I had better tell you who this person is,' he added. 'This is Inspector Newcomen of Scotland Yard.'

A flash of odious joy appeared upon the woman's face. 'Ah!' said she, 'he is in trouble! What has he done?'

Mr Utterson and the inspector exchanged glances. 'He don't seem a very popular character,' observed the latter. 'And now, my good woman, just let me and this gentleman have a look about us.'

In the whole extent of the house, which but for the old woman remained otherwise empty, Mr Hyde had only used a couple of rooms; but these were furnished with luxury and good taste. A closet was filled with wine; the plate was of silver, the napery elegant; a good picture hung upon the walls, a gift (as Utterson supposed) from Henry Jekyll, who was much of a connoisseur; and the carpets were of many plies and agreeable in colour. At this moment, however, the rooms bore every mark of having been recently and hurriedly ransacked; clothes lay about the floor, with their pockets inside out; lockfast drawers stood open; and on the hearth there lay a pile of grey ashes, as though many papers had been burned. From these embers the inspector disinterred the butt end of a green cheque book, which had resisted the action of the fire; the other half of the stick was found behind the door; and as this clinched his suspicions, the officer declared himself delighted. A visit to the bank, where several thousand pounds were found to be lying to the murderer's credit, completed his gratification.

'You may depend upon it, sir,' he told Mr Utterson. 'I have him in my hand. He must have lost his head, or he never would have left the stick or, above all, burned the cheque book. Why, money's life to the man. We have nothing to do but wait for him at the bank, and get out the handbills.'

This last, however, was not so easy of accomplishment; for Mr Hyde had numbered few familiars – even the master of the servant-maid had only seen him twice; his family could nowhere be traced; he had never been photographed; and the few who could describe him differed widely, as common observers will. Only on one point were they agreed; and that was the haunting sense of unexpressed deformity with which the fugitive impressed his beholders.

Incident of the Letter

It was late in the afternoon when Mr Utterson found his way to Dr Jekyll's door, where he was at once admitted by Poole, and carried down by the kitchen offices and across a yard which had once been a garden, to the building which was indifferently known as the laboratory or the dissecting-rooms. The doctor had bought the house from the heirs of a celebrated surgeon; and his own tastes being rather chemical than anatomical, had changed the destination of the block at the bottom of the garden. It was the first time that the lawyer had been received in that part of his friend's quarters; and he eyed the dingy windowless structure with curiosity, and gazed round with a distasteful sense of strangeness as he crossed the theatre, once crowded with eager students and now lying gaunt and silent, the tables laden with chemical apparatus, the floor strewn with crates and littered with packing straw, and the light falling dimly through the foggy cupola. At the further end, a flight of stairs mounted to a door covered with red baize; and through this Mr Utterson was at last received into the doctor's cabinet. It was a large room, fitted round with glass presses, furnished, among other things, with a cheval-glass and a business table, and looking out upon the court by three dusty windows barred with iron. The fire burned in the grate; a lamp was set lighted on the chimney-shelf, for even in the houses the fog began to lie thickly; and there, close up to the warmth, sat Dr Jekyll, looking deadly sick. He did not rise to meet his visitor, but held out a cold hand and bade him welcome in a changed voice.

'And now,' said Mr Utterson, as soon as Poole had left them, 'you have heard the news?'

The doctor shuddered. 'They were crying it in the square,' he said. 'I heard them in my dining room.'

'One word,' said the lawyer. 'Carew was my client, but so

are you; and I want to know what I am doing. You have not been mad enough to hide this fellow?'

'Utterson, I swear to God,' cried the doctor, 'I swear to God I will never set eyes on him again. I bind my honour to you that I am done with him in this world. It is all at an end. And indeed he does not want my help; you do not know him as I do; he is safe, he is quite safe; mark my words, he will never more be heard of.'

The lawyer listened gloomily; he did not like his friend's feverish manner. 'You seem pretty sure of him,' said he; 'and for your sake, I hope you may be right. If it came to a trial, your name might appear.'

'I am quite sure of him,' replied Jekyll; 'I have grounds for certainty that I cannot share with any one. But there is one thing on which you may advise me. I have – I have received a letter; and I am at a loss whether I should show it to the police. I should like to leave it in your hands, Utterson; you would judge wisely, I am sure; I have so great a trust in you.'

'You fear, I suppose, that it might lead to his detection?' asked the lawyer.

'No,' said the other. 'I cannot say that I care what becomes of Hyde; I am quite done with him. I was thinking of my own character, which this hateful business has rather exposed.'

Utterson ruminated awhile; he was surprised at his friend's selfishness, and yet relieved by it. 'Well,' said he, at last, 'let me see the letter.'

The letter was written in an odd, upright hand, and signed 'Edward Hyde': and it signified, briefly enough, that the writer's benefactor, Dr Jekyll, whom he had long so unworthily repaid for a thousand generosities, need labour under no alarm for his safety as he had means of escape on which he placed a sure dependence. The lawyer liked this letter well enough; it put a better colour on the intimacy than he had looked for, and he blamed himself for some of his past suspicions.

'Have you the envelope?' he asked.

'I burned it,' replied Jekyll, 'before I thought what I was about. But it bore no postmark. The note was handed in.'

'Shall I keep this and sleep upon it?' asked Utterson.

'I wish you to judge for me entirely,' was the reply. 'I have lost confidence in myself.'

'Well, I shall consider,' returned the lawyer. 'And now one word more: it was Hyde who dictated the terms in your will about that disappearance?'

The doctor seemed seized with a qualm of faintness; he shut his mouth tight and nodded.

'I knew it,' said Utterson. 'He meant to murder you. You have had a fine escape.'

'I have had what is far more to the purpose,' returned the doctor solemnly: 'I have had a lesson – O God, Utterson, what a lesson I have had!' And he covered his face for a moment with his hands.

On his way out, the lawyer stopped and had a word or two with Poole. 'By the by,' said he, 'there was a letter handed in today: what was the messenger like?' But Poole was positive nothing had come except by post; 'and only circulars by that,' he added.

This news sent off the visitor with his fears renewed. Plainly the letter had come by the laboratory door; possibly, indeed, it had been written in the cabinet; and, if that were so, it must be differently judged, and handled with the more caution. The news boys, as he went, were crying themselves hoarse along the footways: 'Special edition. Shocking murder of an M.P.' That was the funeral oration of one friend and client; and he could not help a certain apprehension lest the good name of another should be sucked down in the eddy of the scandal. It was, at least, a ticklish decision that he had to make; and, self-reliant as he was by habit, he began to cherish a longing for advice. It was not to be had directly; but perhaps, he thought, it might be fished for.

Presently after, he sat on one side of his own hearth, with Mr Guest, his head clerk, upon the other, and midway between, at a nicely calculated distance from the fire, a bottle of a particular old wine that had long dwelt unsunned in the foundations of his house. The fog still slept on the wing above the drowned city, where the lamps glimmered like carbuncles; and through the muffle and smother of these fallen clouds, the procession of the town's life was still rolling in through the great arteries with a sound as of a mighty wind. But the room was gay with firelight. In the bottle the acids were long ago resolved; the imperial dye had softened with time, as the colour grows richer in stained windows; and the glow of hot autumn afternoons on hillside vineyards was ready to be set free and to disperse the fogs of London. Insensibly the lawyer melted. There was no man from whom he kept fewer secrets than Mr Guest; and he was not always sure that he kept as many as he meant. Guest had often been on business to the doctor's; he knew Poole; he could scarce have failed to hear of Mr Hyde's familiarity about the house; he might draw conclusions: was it not as well, then, that he should see a letter which put that mystery to rights? and above all, since Guest, being a great student and critic of handwriting, would consider the step natural and obliging? The clerk, besides, was a man of counsel; he would scarce read so strange a document without dropping a remark; and by that remark Mr Utterson might shape his future course.

'This is a sad business about Sir Danvers,' he said.

'Yes, sir, indeed. It has elicited a great deal of public feeling,' returned Guest. 'The man, of course, was mad.'

'I should like to hear your views on that,' replied Utterson. 'I have a document here in his handwriting; it is between ourselves, for I scarce know what to do about it; it is an ugly business at the best. But there it is; quite in your way: a murderer's autograph.'

Guest's eyes brightened, and he sat down at once and studied it with passion. 'No, sir,' he said; 'not mad; but it is an odd hand.'

'And by all accounts a very odd writer,' added the lawyer.

Just then the servant entered with a note.

'Is that from Dr Jekyll, sir?' inquired the clerk. 'I thought I knew the writing. Anything private, Mr Utterson?'

'Only an invitation to dinner. Why? Do you want to see it?'

'One moment. I thank you, sir'; and the clerk laid the two sheets of paper alongside and sedulously compared their contents. 'Thank you, sir,' he said at last, returning both; 'it's a very interesting autograph.'

There was a pause, during which Mr Utterson struggled with himself. 'Why did you compare them, Guest?' he inquired suddenly.

'Well, sir,' returned the clerk, 'there's a rather singular resemblance; the two hands are in many points identical; only differently sloped.'

'Rather quaint,' said Utterson.

'It is, as you say, rather quaint,' returned Guest.

'I wouldn't speak of this note, you know,' said the master.

'No, sir,' said the clerk. 'I understand.'

But no sooner was Mr Utterson alone that night than he locked the note into his safe, where it reposed from that time forward. 'What!' he thought. 'Henry Jekyll forge for a murderer!' And his blood ran cold in his veins.

Remarkable Incident of Dr Lanyon

TIME ran on; thousands of pounds were offered in reward, for the death of Sir Danvers was resented as a public injury; but Mr Hyde had disappeared out of the ken of the police as though he had never existed. Much of his past was unearthed, indeed, and all disreputable: tales came out of the man's cruelty, at once so callous and violent, of his vile life, of his strange associates, of the hatred that seemed to have surrounded his career; but of his present whereabouts, not a whisper. From the time he had left the house in Soho on the morning of the murder, he was simply blotted out; and gradually, as time drew on, Mr Utterson began to recover from the hotness of his alarm, and to grow more at quiet with himself. The death of Sir Danvers was, to his way of thinking, more than paid for by the disappearance of Mr Hyde. Now that that evil influence had been withdrawn, a new life began for Dr Jekyll. He came out of his seclusion, renewed relations with his friends, became once more their familiar guest and entertainer; and whilst he had always been known for charities, he was now no less distinguished for religion. He was busy, he was much in the open air, he did good; his face seemed to open and brighten, as if with an inward consciousness of service; and for more than two months the doctor was at peace.

On the 8th of January Utterson had dined at the doctor's with a small party; Lanyon had been there; and the face of the host had looked from one to the other as in the old days when the trio were inseparable friends. On the 12th, and again on the 14th, the door was shut against the lawyer. 'The doctor was confined to the house,' Poole said, 'and saw no one.' On the 15th he tried again, and was again refused; and having now been used for the last two months to see his friend almost daily, he found this return of solitude to weigh upon his spirits. The fifth night he had in Guest to dine with him; and the sixth he betook himself to Dr Lanyon's.

There at least he was not denied admittance; but when he came in, he was shocked at the change which had taken place in the doctor's appearance. He had his death-warrant written legibly upon his face. The rosy man had grown pale; his flesh had fallen away; he was visibly balder and older; and yet it was not so much these tokens of a swift physical decay that arrested the lawyer's notice, as a look in the eye and quality of manner that seemed to testify to some deep-seated terror of the mind. It was unlikely that the doctor should fear death; and yet that was what Utterson was tempted to suspect. 'Yes,' he thought; 'he is a doctor, he must know his own state and that his days are counted; and the knowledge is more than he can bear.' And yet when Utterson remarked on his ill looks, it was with an air of great firmness that Lanyon declared himself a doomed man.

'I have had a shock,' he said, 'and I shall never recover. It is a question of weeks. Well, life has been pleasant; I liked it; yes, sir, I used to like it. I sometimes think if we knew all, we should be more glad to get away.'

'Jekyll is ill, too,' observed Utterson. 'Have you seen him?'

But Lanyon's face changed, and he held up a trembling hand. 'I wish to see or hear no more of Dr Jekyll,' he said, in a loud, unsteady voice. 'I am quite done with that person; and I beg that you will spare me any allusion to one whom I regard as dead.'

'Tut, tut,' said Mr Utterson; and then, after a considerable pause, 'Can't I do anything?' he inquired. 'We are three very old friends, Lanyon; we shall not live to make others.'

'Nothing can be done,' returned Lanyon; 'ask himself.'

'He will not see me,' said the lawyer.

'I am not surprised at that,' was the reply. 'Some day, Utterson, after I am dead, you may perhaps come to learn the right and wrong of this. I cannot tell you. And in the meantime, if you can sit and talk with me of other things, for God's sake, stay and do so; but if you cannot keep clear of this accursed topic, then, in God's name, go, for I cannot bear it.'

As soon as he got home, Utterson sat down and wrote to

Jekyll, complaining of his exclusion from the house, and asking the cause of this unhappy break with Lanyon; and the next day brought him a long answer, often very pathetically worded, and sometimes darkly mysterious in drift. The quarrel with Lanyon was incurable. 'I do not blame our old friend,' Jekyll wrote, 'but I share his view that we must never meet. I mean from henceforth to lead a life of extreme seclusion; you must not be surprised, nor must you doubt my friendship, if my door is often shut even to you. You must suffer me to go my own dark way. I have brought on myself a punishment and a danger that I cannot name. If I am the chief of sinners, I am the chief of sufferers also. I could not think that this earth contained a place for sufferings and terrors so unmanning; and you can do but one thing, Utterson, to lighten this destiny, and that is to respect my silence.' Utterson was amazed; the dark influence of Hyde had been withdrawn, the doctor had returned to his old tasks and amities; a week ago, the prospect had smiled with every promise of a cheerful and an honoured age; and now in a moment, friendship and peace of mind and the whole tenor of his life were wrecked. So great and unprepared a change pointed to madness; but in view of Lanyon's manner and words, there must lie for it some deeper ground.

A week afterwards Dr Lanyon took to his bed, and in something less than a fortnight he was dead. The night after the funeral, at which he had been sadly affected, Utterson locked the door of his business room, and sitting there by the light of a melancholy candle, drew out and set before him an envelope addressed by the hand and sealed with the seal of his dead friend. 'PRIVATE: for the hands of J. G. Utterson ALONE, and in case of his predeccase *to be destroyed unread*,' so it was emphatically superscribed; and the lawyer dreaded to behold the contents. 'I have buried one friend to-day,' he thought: 'what if this should cost me another?' And then he condemned the fear as a disloyalty, and broke the seal. Within there was another enclosure, likewise sealed, and marked upon the cover as 'not to be opened till the death or disappearance of Dr Henry Jekyll.' Utterson could not trust his eyes. Yes, it was disappearance; here again, as in the mad will, which he had long ago restored to its author, here again were the idea of a disappearance and the name of Henry Jekyll bracketed. But in the will, that idea had sprung from the sinister suggestion of the man Hyde; it was set there with a purpose all too plain and horrible. Written by the hand of Lanyon, what should it mean? A great curiosity came to the trustee, to disregard the prohibition and dive at once to the bottom of these mysteries; but professional honour and faith to his dead friend were stringent obligations; and the packet slept in the inmost corner of his private safe.

It is one thing to mortify curiosity, another to conquer it; and it may be doubted if, from that day forth, Utterson desired the society of his surviving friend with the same eagerness. He thought of him kindly; but his thoughts were disquieted and fearful. He went to call indeed; but he was perhaps relieved to be denied admittance; perhaps, in his heart, he preferred to speak with Poole upon the doorstep, and surrounded by the air and sounds of the open city, rather than to be admitted into that house of voluntary bondage, and to sit and speak with its inscrutable recluse. Poole had, indeed, no very pleasant news to communicate. The doctor, it appeared, now more than ever confined himself to the cabinet over the laboratory, where he would sometimes even sleep; he was out of spirits, he had grown very silent, he did not read; it seemed as if he had something on his mind. Utterson became so used to the unvarying character of these reports, that he fell off little by little in the frequency of his visits.

Incident at the Window

IT chanced on Sunday, when Mr Utterson was on his usual walk with Mr Enfield, that their way lay once again through the by street; and that when they came in front of the door, both stopped to gaze on it.

'Well,' said Enfield, 'that story's at an end, at least. We shall never see more of Mr Hyde.'

'I hope not,' said Utterson. 'Did I ever tell you that I once saw him, and shared your feeling of repulsion?'

'It was impossible to do the one without the other,' returned Enfield. 'And, by the way, what an ass you must have thought me, not to know that this was a back way to Dr Jekyll's! It was partly your own fault that I found it out, even when I did.'

'So you found it out, did you?' said Utterson. 'But if that be so, we may step into the court and take a look at the windows. To tell you the truth, I am uneasy about poor Jekyll; and even outside, I feel as if the presence of a friend might do him good.'

The court was very cool and a little damp, and full of premature twilight, although the sky, high up overhead, was still bright with sunset. The middle one of the three windows was half way open; and sitting close beside it, taking the air with an infinite sadness of mien, like some disconsolate prisoner, Utterson saw Dr Jekyll.

'What! Jekyll!' he cried. 'I trust you are better.'

'I am very low, Utterson,' replied the doctor drearily; 'very low. It will not last long, thank God.'

'You stay too much indoors,' said the lawyer. 'You should be out, whipping up the circulation like Mr Enfield and me. (This is my cousin – Mr Enfield – Dr Jekyll.) Come, now; get your hat and take a quick turn with us.'

'You are very good,' sighed the other. 'I should like to very much; but no, no, no, it is quite impossible; I dare not. But indeed, Utterson, I am very glad to see you; this is really a great pleasure. I would ask you and Mr Enfield up, but the place is really not fit.'

'Why then,' said the lawyer, good-naturedly, 'the best thing we can do is to stay down here, and speak with you from where we are.'

'That is just what I was about to venture to propose,' returned the doctor, with a smile. But the words were hardly uttered, before the smile was struck out of his face and succeeded by an expression of such abject terror and despair, as froze the very blood of the two gentlemen below. They saw it but for a glimpse, for the window was instantly thrust down; but that glimpse had been sufficient, and they turned and left the court without a word. In silence, too, they traversed the by street; and it was not until they had come into a neighbouring thoroughfare, where even upon a Sunday there were still some stirrings of life, that Mr Utterson at last turned and looked at his companion. They were both pale; and there was an answering horror in their eyes.

'God forgive us! God forgive us!' said Mr Utterson.

But Mr Enfield only nodded his head very seriously, and walked on once more in silence.

The Last Night

MR UTTERSON was sitting by his fireside one evening after dinner, when he was surprised to receive a visit from Poole.

'Bless me, Poole, what brings you here?' he cried; and then, taking a second look at him, 'What ails you?' he added; 'is the doctor ill?'

'Mr Utterson,' said the man, 'there is something wrong.'

'Take a seat, and here is a glass of wine for you,' said the lawyer. 'Now, take your time, and tell me plainly what you want.'

'You know the doctor's ways, sir,' replied Poole, 'and how he shuts himself up. Well, he's shut up again in the cabinet; and I don't like it, sir – I wish I may die if I like it. Mr Utterson, sir, I'm afraid.'

'Now, my good man,' said the lawyer, 'be explicit. What are you afraid of?'

'I've been afraid for about a week,' returned Poole, doggedly disregarding the question, 'and I can bear it no more.'

The man's appearance amply bore out his words; his manner was altered for the worse; and except for the moment when he had first announced his terror, he had not once looked the lawyer in the face. Even now, he sat with the glass of wine untasted on his knee, and his eyes directed to a corner of the floor. 'I can bear it no more,' he repeated.

'Come,' said the lawyer, 'I see you have some good reason, Poole; I see there is something seriously amiss. Try to tell me what it is.'

'I think there's been foul play,' said Poole, hoarsely.

'Foul play!' cried the lawyer, a good deal frightened, and rather inclined to be irritated in consequence. 'What foul play? What does the man mean?'

'I daren't say, sir,' was the answer; 'but will you come along with me and see for yourself?'

Mr Utterson's only answer was to rise and get his hat and great coat; but he observed with wonder the greatness of the relief that appeared upon the butler's face, and perhaps with no less, that the wine was still untasted when he set it down to follow.

It was a wild, cold, seasonable night of March, with a pale moon, lying on her back as though the wind had tilted her, and a flying wrack of the most diaphanous and lawny texture. The wind made talking difficult, and flecked the blood into the face. It seemed to have swept the streets unusually bare of passengers, besides; for Mr Utterson thought he had never seen that part of London so deserted. He could have wished it otherwise; never in his life had he been conscious of so sharp a wish to see and touch his fellow-creatures; for, struggle as he might, there was borne in upon his mind a crushing anticipation of calamity. The square, when they got there, was all full of wind and dust, and the thin trees in the garden were lashing themselves along the railing. Poole, who had kept all the way a pace or two ahead, now pulled up in the middle of the pavement, and in spite of the biting weather, took off his hat and mopped his brow with a red pocket-handkerchief. But for all the hurry of his coming, these were not the dews of exertion that he wiped away, but the moisture of some strangling anguish; for his face was white, and his voice, when he spoke, harsh and broken.

'Well, sir,' he said, 'here we are, and God grant there be nothing wrong.'

'Amen, Poole,' said the lawyer.

Thereupon the servant knocked in a very guarded manner; the door was opened on the chain; and a voice asked from within, 'Is that you, Poole?'

'It's all right,' said Poole. 'Open the door.'

The hall, when they entered it, was brightly lighted up; the fire was built high; and about the hearth the whole of the servants, men and women, stood huddled together like a flock of sheep. At the sight of Mr Utterson, the housemaid broke into hysterical whimpering; and the cook, crying out, 'Bless God! it's Mr Utterson,' ran forward as if to take him in her arms.

'What, what? Are you all here?' said the lawyer, peevishly. 'Very irregular, very unseemly : your master would be far from pleased.'

'They're all afraid,' said Poole.

Blank silence followed, no one protesting; only the maid lifted up her voice and now wept loudly.

'Hold your tongue!' Poole said to her, with a ferocity of accent that testified to his own jangled nerves; and indeed when the girl had so suddenly raised the note of her lamentation, they had all started and turned towards the inner door with faces of dreadful expectation. 'And now,' continued the butler, addressing the knife-boy, 'reach me a candle, and we'll get this through hands at once.' And then he begged Mr Utterson to follow him, and led the way to the back garden.

'Now, sir,' said he, 'you come as gently as you can. I want you to hear, and I don't want you to be heard. And see here, sir, if by any chance he was to ask you in, don't go.'

Mr Utterson's nerves, at this unlooked-for termination, gave a jerk that nearly threw him from his balance; but he recollected his courage, and followed the butler into the laboratory building and through the surgical theatre, with its lumber of crates and bottles, to the foot of the stair. Here Poole motioned him to stand on one side and listen; while he himself, setting down the candle and making a great and obvious call on his resolution, mounted the steps, and knocked with a somewhat uncertain hand on the red baize of the cabinet door.

'Mr Utterson, sir, asking to see you,' he called; and even as he did so, once more violently signed to the lawyer to give ear.

A voice answered from within : 'Tell him I cannot see any one,' it said, complainingly.

'Thank you, sir,' said Poole, with a note of something like triumph in his voice; and taking up his candle, he led Mr Utterson back across the yard and into the great kitchen, where the fire was out and the beetles were leaping on the floor.

'Sir,' he said, looking Mr Utterson in the eyes, 'was that my master's voice?'

'It seems much changed,' replied the lawyer, very pale, but giving look for look.

'Changed? Well, yes, I think so,' said the butler. 'Have I been twenty years in this man's house, to be deceived about his voice? No, sir; master's made away with; he was made away with eight days ago, when we heard him cry out upon the name of God; and *who's* in there instead of him, and *why* it stays there, is a thing that cries to Heaven, Mr Utterson!'

'This is a very strange tale, Poole; this is rather a wild tale, my man,' said Mr Utterson, biting his finger. 'Suppose it were as you suppose, supposing Dr Jekyll to have been – well, murdered, what could induce the murderer to stay? That won't hold water; it doesn't commend itself to reason.'

'Well, Mr Utterson, you are a hard man to satisfy, but I'll do it yet,' said Poole. 'All this last week (you must know) him, or it, or whatever it is that lives in that cabinet, has been crying night and day for some sort of medicine and cannot get it to his mind. It was sometimes his way – the master's, that is – to write his orders on a sheet of paper and throw it on the stair. We've had nothing else this week back; nothing but papers, and a closed door, and the very meals left there to be smuggled in when nobody was looking. Well, sir, every day, ay, and twice and thrice in the same day, there have been orders and complaints, and I have been sent flying to all the wholesale chemists in town. Every time I brought the stuff back, there would be another paper telling me to return it, because it was not pure, and another order to a different firm. This drug is wanted bitter bad, sir, whatever for.'

'Have you any of these papers?' asked Mr Utterson.

Poole felt in his pocket and handed out a crumpled note, which the lawyer, bending nearer to the candle, carefully examined. Its contents ran thus: 'Dr Jekyll presents his compliments to Messrs Maw. He assures them that their last sample is impure and quite useless for his present purpose. In the year 18——, Dr J. purchased a somewhat large quantity from Méssrs M. He now begs them to search with the most sedulous care, and should any of the same quality be left, to forward it to him at once. Expense is no consideration. The importance of this to Dr

J. can hardly be exaggerated.' So far the letter had run composedly enough; but here, with a sudden splutter of the pen, the writer's emotion had broken loose. 'For God's sake,' he had added, 'find me some of the old.'

'This is a strange note,' said Mr Utterson; and then sharply, 'How do you come to have it open?'

'The man at Maw's was main angry, sir, and he threw it back to me like so much dirt,' returned Poole.

'This is unquestionably the doctor's hand, do you know?' resumed the lawyer.

'I thought it looked like it,' said the servant, rather sulkily; and then, with another voice, 'But what matters hand of write?' he said. 'I've seen him!'

'Seen him?' repeated Mr Utterson. 'Well?'

'That's it!' said Poole. 'It was this way. I came suddenly into the theatre from the garden. It seems he had slipped out to look for this drug, or whatever it is; for the cabinet door was open, and there he was at the far end of the room digging among the crates. He looked up when I came in, gave a kind of cry, and whipped upstairs into the cabinet. It was but for one minute that I saw him, but the hair stood upon my head like quills. Sir, if that was my master, why had he a mask upon his face? If it was my master, why did he cry out like a rat and run from me? I have served him long enough. And then ...' the man paused and passed his hand over his face.

'These are all very strange circumstances,' said Mr Utterson, 'but I think I begin to see daylight. Your master, Poole, is plainly seized with one of those maladies that both torture and deform the sufferer; hence, for aught I know, the alteration of his voice; hence the mask and his avoidance of his friends; hence his eagerness to find this drug, by means of which the poor soul retains some hope of ultimate recovery – God grant that he be not deceived! There is my explanation; it is sad enough, Poole, ay, and appalling to consider; but it is plain and natural, hangs well together and delivers us from all exorbitant alarms.'

'Sir,' said the butler, turning to a sort of mottled pallor, 'that thing was not my master, and there's the truth. My master' – here he looked round him, and began to whisper – 'is a tall fine build of a man, and this was more of a dwarf.' Utterson attempted to protest. 'O, sir,' cried Poole, 'do you think I do not know my master after twenty years? do you think I do not know where his head comes to in the cabinet door, where I saw him every morning of my life? No, sir, that thing in the mask was never Dr Jekyll – God knows what it was, but it was never Dr Jekyll; and it is the belief of my heart that there was murder done.'

'Poole,' replied the lawyer, 'if you say that, it will become my duty to make certain. Much as I desire to spare your master's feelings, much as I am puzzled about this note, which seems to prove him to be still alive, I shall consider it my duty to break in that door.'

'Ah, Mr Utterson, that's talking!' cried the butler.

'And now comes the second question,' resumed Utterson: 'Who is going to do it?'

'Why, you and me, sir,' was the undaunted reply.

'That is very well said,' returned the lawyer; 'and whatever comes of it, I shall make it my business to see you are no loser.'

'There is an axe in the theatre,' continued Poole; 'and you might take the kitchen poker for yourself.'

The lawyer took that rude but weighty instrument into his hand, and balanced it. 'Do you know, Poole,' he said, looking up, 'that you and I are about to place ourselves in a position of some peril?'

'You may say so, sir, indeed,' returned the butler.

'It is well, then, that we should be frank,' said the other. 'We both think more than we have said; let us make a clean breast. This masked figure that you saw, did you recognise it?'

'Well, sir, it went so quick, and the creature was so doubled up, that I could hardly swear to that,' was the answer. 'But if you mean, was it Mr Hyde? – why, yes, I think it was! You see, it was much of the same bigness; and it had the same quick light way with it; and then who else could have got in by the laboratory door? You have not forgot, sir, that at the time of the murder he had still the key with him? But that's not all. I don't know, Mr Utterson, if ever you met this Mr Hyde?'

'Yes,' said the lawyer, 'I once spoke with him.'

'Then you must know, as well as the rest of us, that there was something queer about that gentleman – something that gave a man a turn – I don't know rightly how to say it, sir, beyond this : that you felt in your marrow – kind of cold and thin.'

'I own I felt something of what you describe,' said Mr Utterson.

'Quite so, sir,' returned Poole. 'Well, when that masked thing like a monkey jumped up from among the chemicals and whipped into the cabinet, it went down my spine like ice. O, I know it's not evidence, Mr Utterson; I'm book-learned enough for that; but a man has his feelings; and I give you my bible-word it was Mr Hyde!'

'Ay, ay,' said the lawyer. 'My fears incline to the same point. Evil, I fear, founded – evil was sure to come – of that connection. Ay, truly, I believe you; I believe poor Harry is killed; and I believe his murderer (for what purpose, God alone can tell) is still lurking in his victim's room. Well, let our name be vengeance. Call Bradshaw.'

The footman came at the summons, very white and nervous.

'Pull yourself together, Bradshaw,' said the lawyer. 'This suspense, I know, is telling upon all of you; but it is now our intention to make an end of it. Poole, here, and I are going to force our way into the cabinet. If all is well, my shoulders are broad enough to bear the blame. Meanwhile, lest anything should really be amiss, or any malefactor seek to escape by the back, you and the boy must go round the corner with a pair of good sticks, and take your post at the laboratory door. We give you ten minutes, to get to your stations.'

As Bradshaw left, the lawyer looked at his watch. 'And now, Poole, let us get to ours,' he said; and taking the poker under his arm, he led the way into the yard. The scud had banked over the moon, and it was now quite dark. The wind, which only broke in puffs and draughts into that deep well of building, tossed the light of the candle to and fro about their steps, until they came into the shelter of the theatre, where they sat down silently to wait. London hummed solemnly all around; but nearer at hand, the stillness was only broken by the sound of a footfall moving to and fro along the cabinet floor.

'So it will walk all day, sir,' whispered Poole; 'ay, and the better part of the night. Only when a new sample comes from the chemist, there's a bit of a break. Ah, it's an ill conscience that's such an enemy to rest! Ah, sir, there's blood foully shed in every step of it! But hark again, a little closer – put your heart in your ears Mr Utterson, and tell me, is that the doctor's foot?'

The steps fell lightly and oddly, with a certain swing, for all they went so slowly; it was different indeed from the heavy creaking tread of Henry Jekyll. Utterson sighed. 'Is there never anything else?' he asked.

Poole nodded. 'Once,' he said. 'Once I heard it weeping!'

'Weeping? how that?' said the lawyer, conscious of a sudden chill of horror.

'Weeping like a woman or a lost soul,' said the butler. 'I came away with that upon my heart, that I could have wept too.'

But now the ten minutes drew to an end. Poole disinterred the axe from under a stack of packing straw; the candle was set upon the nearest table to light them to the attack; and they drew near with bated breath to where the patient foot was still going up and down, up and down in the quiet of the night.

'Jekyll,' cried Utterson, with a loud voice, 'I demand to see you.' He paused a moment, but there came no reply. 'I give you fair warning, our suspicions are aroused, and I must and shall see you,' he resumed; 'if not by fair means, then by foul – if not of your consent, then by brute force!'

'Utterson,' said the voice, 'for God's sake, have mercy!'

'Ah, that's not Jekyll's voice – it's Hyde's!' cried Utterson. 'Down with the door, Poole!'

Poole swung the axe over his shoulder; the blow shook the building, and the red baize door leaped against the lock and hinges. A dismal screech, as of mere animal terror, rang from the cabinet. Up went the axe again, and again the panels crashed and the frame bounded; four times the blow fell; but the wood was tough and the fittings were of excellent workmanship; and it was not until the fifth that the lock burst in sunder, and the wreck of the door fell inwards on the carpet.

The besiegers, appalled by their own riot and the stillness that had succeeded, stood back a little and peered in. There lay the cabinet before their eyes in the quiet lamplight, a good fire glowing and chattering on the hearth, the kettle singing its thin strain, a drawer or two open, papers neatly set forth on the business table, and nearer the fire, the things laid out for tea; the quietest room, you would have said, and, but for the glazed presses full of chemicals, the most commonplace that night in London.

Right in the midst there lay the body of a man sorely contorted and still twitching. They drew near on tiptoe, turned it on its back, and beheld the face of Edward Hyde. He was dressed in clothes far too large for him, clothes of the doctor's bigness; the cords of his face still moved with a semblance of life, but life was quite gone; and by the crushed phial in the hand and the strong smell of kernels that hung upon the air, Utterson knew that he was looking on the body of a self-destroyer.

'We have come too late,' he said sternly, 'whether to save or punish. Hyde is gone to his account; and it only remains for us to find the body of your master.'

The far greater proportion of the building was occupied by the theatre, which filled almost the whole ground storey, and was lighted from above, and by the cabinet, which formed an upper storey at one end and looked upon the court. A corridor joined the theatre to the door on the by street; and with this, the cabinet communicated separately by a second flight of stairs. There were besides a few dark closets and a spacious cellar. All these they now thoroughly examined. Each closet needed but a glance, for all they were empty and all, by the dust that fell from their doors, had stood long unopened. The cellar, indeed, was filled with crazy lumber, mostly dating from the times of the surgeon who was Jekyll's predecessor; but even as they opened the door, they were advertised of the uselessness of further search by the fall of a perfect mat of cobweb which had for years sealed up the entrance. Nowhere was there any trace of Henry Jekyll, dead or alive.

Poole stamped on the flags of the corridor. 'He must be buried here,' he said, hearkening to the sound.

'Or he may have fled,' said Utterson, and he turned to examine the door in the by street. It was locked; and lying near by on the flags, they found the key, already stained with rust.

'This does not look like use,' observed the lawyer.

'Use!' echoed Poole. 'Do you not see, sir, it is broken? much as if a man had stamped on it.'

'Ah,' continued Utterson, 'and the fractures, too, are rusty.' The two men looked at each other with a scare. 'This is beyond me, Poole,' said the lawyer. 'Let us go back to the cabinet.'

They mounted the stair in silence, and still, with an occasional awestruck glance at the dead body, proceeded more thoroughly to examine the contents of the cabinet. At one table, there were traces of chemical work, various measured heaps of some white salt being laid on glass saucers, as though for an experiment in which the unhappy man had been prevented.

'That is the same drug that I was always bringing him,' said Poole; and even as he spoke, the kettle with a startling noise boiled over.

This brought them to the fireside, where the easy chair was drawn cosily up, and the tea things stood ready to the sitter's elbow, the very sugar in the cup. There were several books on a shelf; one lay beside the tea things open, and Utterson was amazed to find it a copy of a pious work for which Jekyll had several times expressed a great esteem, annotated, in his own hand, with startling blasphemies.

Next, in the course of their review of the chamber, the searchers came to the cheval-glass, into whose depth they looked with an involuntary horror. But it was so turned as to show them nothing but the rosy glow playing on the roof, the fire sparkling in a hundred repetitions along the glazed front of the presses, and their own pale and fearful countenances stooping to look in.

'This glass has seen some strange things, sir,' whispered Poole.

'And surely none stranger than itself,' echoed the lawyer, in the same tone. 'For what did Jekyll' – he caught himself up at the word with a start, and then conquering the weakness: 'what could Jekyll want with it?' he said.

'You may say that!' said Poole.

Next they turned to the business table. On the desk, among the neat array of papers, a large envelope was uppermost, and bore, in the doctor's hand, the name of Mr Utterson. The lawyer unsealed it, and several enclosures fell to the floor. The first was a will, drawn in the same eccentric terms as the one which he had returned six months before, to serve as a testament in case of death and as a deed of gift in case of disappearance; but in place of the name of Edward Hyde, the lawyer, with indescribable amazement, read the name of Gabriel John Utterson. He looked at Poole, and then back at the papers, and last of all at the dead malefactor stretched upon the carpet.

'My head goes round,' he said. 'He has been all these days in possession; he had no cause to like me; he must have raged to see himself displaced; and he has not destroyed this document.'

He caught the next paper; it was a brief note in the doctor's hand and dated at the top. 'O Poole!' the lawyer cried, 'he was alive and here this day. He cannot have been disposed of in so short a space; he must be still alive, he must have fled! And then, why fled? and how? and in that case can we venture to declare this suicide? O, we must be careful. I foresee that we may yet involve your master in some dire catastrophe.'

'Why don't you read it, sir?' asked Poole.

'Because I fear,' replied the lawyer, solemnly. 'God grant I have no cause for it!' And with that he brought the paper to his eyes, and read as follows:

MY DEAR UTTERSON, – When this shall fall into your hands, I shall have disappeared, under what circumstances I have not the penetration to foresee, but my instinct and all the circumstances of my nameless situation tell me that the end is sure and must be early. Go then, and first read the narrative which Lanyon warned me he was to place in your hands; and if you care to hear more, turn to the confession of

Your unworthy and unhappy friend,

HENRY JEKYLL

'There was a third enclosure,' asked Utterson.

'Here, sir,' said Poole, and gave into his hands a considerable packet sealed in several places.

The lawyer put it in his pocket. 'I would say nothing of this paper. If your master has fled or is dead, we may at least save his credit. It is now ten; I must go home and read these documents in quiet; but I shall be back before midnight, when we shall send for the police.'

They went out, locking the door of the theatre behind them; and Utterson, once more leaving the servants gathered about the fire in the hall, trudged back to his office to read the two narratives in which this mystery was now to be explained.

Dr Lanyon's Narrative

ON the ninth of January, now four days ago, I received by the evening delivery a registered envelope, addressed in the hand of my colleague and old school-companion, Henry Jekyll. I was a good deal surprised by this; for we were by no means in the habit of correspondence; I had seen the man, dined with him, indeed, the night before; and I could imagine nothing in our intercourse that should justify the formality of registration. The contents increased my wonder; for this is how the letter ran:

10th December 18—

DEAR LANYON, – You are one of my oldest friends; and although we may have differed at times on scientific questions, I cannot remember, at least on my side, any break in our affection. There was never a day when, if you had said to me, "Jekyll, my life, my honour, my reason, depend upon you," I would not have sacrificed my fortune or my left hand to help you. Lanyon, my life, my honour, my reason, are all at your mercy; if you fail me to-night, I am lost. You might suppose, after this preface, that I am going to ask you for something dishonourable to grant. Judge for yourself.

I want you to postpone all other engagements for to-night – ay, even if you were summoned to the bedside of an emperor; to take a cab, unless your carriage should be actually at the door; and, with this letter in your hand for consultation, to drive straight to my house. Poole, my butler, has his orders; you will find him waiting your arrival with a locksmith. The door of my cabinet is then to be forced; and you are to go in alone; to open the glazed press (letter E) on the left hand, breaking the lock if it be shut; and to draw out, *with all its contents as they stand*, the fourth drawer from the top or (which is the same thing) the third from the bottom. In my extreme distress of mind, I have a morbid fear of misdirecting you; but even if I am in error, you may know the right drawer by its contents: some powders, a phial, and a paper book. This drawer I beg of you to carry back with you to Cavendish Square exactly as it stands.

That is the first part of the service: now for the second. You should be back, if you set out at once on the receipt of this, long before midnight; but I will leave you that amount of margin, not only in the fear of one of those obstacles that can neither be prevented nor foreseen, but because an hour when your servants are in bed is to be preferred for what will then remain to do. At midnight, then, I have to ask you to be alone in your consulting-room, to admit with your own hand into the house a man who will present himself in my name, and to place in his hands the drawer that you will have brought with you from my cabinet. Then you will have played your part and earned my gratitude completely. Five minutes afterwards, if you insist upon an explanation, you will have understood that these arrangements are of capital importance; and that by the neglect of one of them, fantastic as they must appear, you might have charged your conscience with my death or the shipwreck of my reason.

Confident as I am that you will not trifle with this appeal, my heart sinks and my hand trembles at the bare thought of such a possibility. Think of me at this hour, in a strange place, labouring under a blackness of distress that no fancy can exaggerate, and yet well aware that, if you will but punctually serve me, my troubles will roll away like a story that is told. Serve me, my dear Lanyon, and save

Your friend,

H. J.

PS. — I had already sealed this up when a fresh terror struck upon my soul. It is possible that the post office may fail me, and this letter not come into your hands until to-morrow morning. In that case, dear Lanyon, do my errand when it shall be most convenient for you in the course of the day; and once more expect my messenger at midnight. It may then already be too late; and if that night passes without event, you will know that you have seen the last of Henry Jekyll.

Upon the reading of this letter, I made sure my colleague was insane; but till that was proved beyond the possibility of doubt, I felt bound to do as he requested. The less I understood of this farrago, the less I was in a position to judge of its importance; and an appeal so worded could not be set aside without a grave responsibility. I rose accordingly from table, got into a hansom, and drove straight to Jekyll's house. The butler was awaiting my arrival; he had received by the same post as mine a registered letter of instruction, and had sent at once for a locksmith and a carpenter. The tradesmen came while we were yet speaking; and we moved in a body to old Dr Denman's surgical theatre, from which (as you are doubtless aware) Jekyll's private cabinet is most conveniently entered. The door was very strong, the lock excellent; the carpenter avowed he would have great trouble, and have to do much damage, if force were to be used; and the locksmith was near despair. But this last was a handy fellow, and after two hours' work, the door stood open. The press marked E was unlocked; and I took out the drawer, had it filled up with straw and tied in a sheet, and returned with it to Cavendish Square.

Here I proceeded to examine its contents. The powders were neatly enough made up, but not with the nicety of the dispensing chemist; so that it was plain they were of Jekyll's private manufacture; and when I opened one of the wrappers, I found what seemed to me a simple crystalline salt of a white colour. The phial, to which I next turned my attention, might have been about half-full of a blood-red liquor, which was highly pungent to the sense of smell, and seemed to me to contain phosphorus and some volatile ether. At the other ingredients I could make no guess. The book was an ordinary version book, and contained little but a series of dates. These covered a period of many years, but I observed that the entries ceased nearly a year ago and quite abruptly. Here and there a brief remark was appended to a date, usually no more than a single word: 'double' occurring perhaps six times in a total of several hundred entries; and once very early in the list and followed by several marks of exclamation, 'total failure!!!' All this, though it whetted my curiosity, told me little that was definite. Here were a phial of some tincture, a paper of some salt, and the record of a series of experiments that had led (like too many of Jekyll's investigations) to no end of practical usefulness. How could the presence of these articles in my house affect either the honour, the sanity, or the life of my flighty colleague? If his messenger could go to one place, why could he not go to another? And even granting some impediment, why was this gentleman to be received by me in secret? The more I reflected, the more convinced I grew that I was dealing with a case of cerebral disease; and though I dismissed my servants to bed, I loaded an old revolver, that I might be found in some posture of self-defence.

Twelve o'clock had scarce rung out over London, ere the knocker sounded very gently on the door. I went myself at the summons, and found a small man crouching against the pillars of the portico.

'Are you come from Dr Jekyll?' I asked.

He told me 'yes' by a constrained gesture; and when I had bidden him enter, he did not obey me without a searching backward glance into the darkness of the square. There was a policeman not far off, advancing with his bull's eye open; and at the sight, I thought my visitor started and made greater haste.

These particulars struck me, I confess, disagreeably; and as I followed him into the bright light of the consulting-room, I kept my hand ready on my weapon. Here, at last, I had a chance of clearly seeing him. I had never set eyes on him before, so much was certain. He was small, as I have said; I was struck besides with the shocking expression of his face, with his remarkable combination of great muscular activity and great apparent debility of constitution, and – last but not least – with the odd, subjective disturbance caused by his neighbourhood. This bore some resemblance to incipient rigor, and was accompanied by a marked sinking of the pulse. At the time, I set it down to some idiosyncratic, personal distaste, and merely wondered at the acuteness of the symptoms; but I have since had reason to believe the cause to lie much deeper in the nature of man, and to turn on some nobler hinge than the principle of hatred.

This person (who had thus, from the first moment of his entrance, struck in me what I can only describe as a disgustful curiosity) was dressed in a fashion that would have made an ordinary person laughable; his clothes, that is to say, although they were of rich and sober fabric, were enormously too large for him in every measurement – the trousers hanging on his legs and rolled up to keep them from the ground, the waist of the coat below his haunches, and the collar sprawling wide upon his shoulders. Strange to relate, this ludicrous accoutrement was far from moving me to laughter. Rather, as there was something abnormal and misbegotten in the very essence of the creature that now faced me – something seizing, surprising and revolting – this fresh disparity seemed but to fit in with and to reinforce it; so that to my interest in the man's nature and character there was added a curiosity as to his origin, his life, his fortune and status in the world.

These observations, though they have taken so great a space to be set down in, were yet the work of a few seconds. My visitor was, indeed, on fire with sombre excitement.

'Have you got it?' he cried. 'Have you got it?' And so lively was his impatience that he even laid his hand upon my arm and sought to shake me.

I put him back conscious at his touch of a certain icy pang along my blood. 'Come, sir,' said I. 'You forget that I have not yet the pleasure of your acquaintance. Be seated, if you please.' And I showed him an example, and sat down myself in my customary seat and with as fair an imitation of my ordinary manner to a patient, as the lateness of the hour, the nature of my pre-occupations, and the horror I had of my visitor would suffer me to muster.

'I beg your pardon, Dr Lanyon,' he replied, civilly enough. 'What you say is very well founded; and my impatience has shown its heels to my politeness. I come here at the instance of your colleague, Dr Henry Jekyll, on a piece of business of some moment; and I understood . . .' he paused and put his hand to his throat, and I could see, in spite of his collected manner, that he was wrestling against the approaches of the hysteria – 'I understood, a drawer . . .'

But here I took pity on my visitor's suspense, and some perhaps on my own growing curiosity.

'There it is, sir,' said I, pointing to the drawer where it lay on the floor behind a table, and still covered with the sheet.

He sprang to it, and then paused, and laid his hand upon his heart; I could hear his teeth grate with the convulsive action of his jaws; and his face was so ghastly to see that I grew alarmed both for his life and reason.

'Compose yourself,' said I.

He turned a dreadful smile to me, and, as if with the decision of despair, plucked away the sheet. At sight of the contents, he uttered one loud sob of such immense relief that I sat petrified. And the next moment, in a voice that was already fairly well under control, 'Have you a graduated glass?' he asked.

I rose from my place with something of an effort, and gave him what he asked.

He thanked me with a smiling nod, measured out a few minims of the red tincture and added one of the powders. The mixture, which was at first of a reddish hue, began, in proportion as the crystals melted, to brighten in colour, to effervesce audibly, and to throw off small fumes of vapour. Suddenly, and at the same moment, the ebullition ceased, and the compound changed to a dark purple, which faded again more slowly to a watery green. My visitor, who had watched these metamorphoses with a keen eye, smiled, set down the glass upon the table, and then turned and looked upon me with an air of scrutiny.

'And now,' said he, 'to settle what remains. Will you be wise? will you be guided? will you suffer me to take this glass in my hand, and to go forth from your house without further parley? or has the greed of curiosity too much command of you? Think before you answer, for it shall be done as you decide. As you decide, you shall be left as you were before, and neither richer nor wiser, unless the sense of service rendered to a man in mortal distress may be counted as a kind of riches of the soul. Or, if you shall so prefer to choose, a new province of knowledge and new avenues to fame and power shall be laid open to you, here, in this room, upon the instant; and your sight shall be blasted by a prodigy to stagger the unbelief of Satan.'

'Sir,' said I, affecting a coolness that I was far from truly possessing, 'you speak enigmas, and you will perhaps not wonder that I hear you with no very strong impression of belief. But I have gone too far in the way of inexplicable services to pause before I see the end.'

'It is well,' replied my visitor. 'Lanyon, you remember your vows: what follows is under the seal of our profession. And now, you who have so long been bound to the most narrow and material views, you who have denied the virtue of transcendental medicine, you who have derided your superiors – behold!'

He put the glass to his lips, and drank at one gulp. A cry followed; he reeled, staggered, clutched at the table and held on, staring with injected eyes, gasping with open mouth; and as I looked, there came, I thought, a change – he seemed to swell – his face became suddenly black, and the features seemed to melt and alter – and the next moment I had sprung to my feet and leaped back against the wall, my arm raised to shield me from that prodigy, my mind submerged in terror.

'O God!' I screamed, and 'O God!' again and again; for there before my eyes – pale and shaken, and half fainting, and groping before him with his hands, like a man restored from death – there stood Henry Jekyll!

What he told me in the next hour I cannot bring my mind to set on paper. I saw what I saw, I heard what I heard, and my soul sickened at it; and yet, now when that sight has faded from my eyes, I ask myself if I believe it, and I cannot answer. My life is shaken to its roots; sleep has left me; the deadliest terror sits by me at all hours of the day and night; I feel that my days are numbered, and that I must die; and yet I shall die incredulous. As for the moral turpitude that man unveiled to me, even with tears of penitence, I cannot, even in memory, dwell on it without a start of horror. I will say but one thing, Utterson, and that (if you can bring your mind to credit it) will be more than enough. The creature who crept into my house that night was, on Jekyll's own confession, known by the name of Hyde and hunted for in every corner of the land as the murderer of Carew.

HASTIE LANYON

Henry Jekyll's Full Statement of the Case

I WAS born in the year 18—— to a large fortune, endowed besides with excellent parts, inclined by nature to industry, fond of the respect of the wise and good among my fellow-men, and thus, as might have been supposed, with every guarantee of an honourable and distinguished future. And indeed, the worst of my faults was a certain impatient gaiety of disposition, such as has made the happiness of many, but such as I found it hard to reconcile with my imperious desire to carry my head high, and wear a more than commonly grave countenance before the public. Hence it came about that I concealed my pleasures; and that when I reached years of reflection, and began to look round me and take stock of my progress and position in the world, I stood already committed to a profound duplicity of life. Many a man would have even blazoned such irregularities as I was guilty of; but from the high views that I had set before me, I regarded and hid them with an almost morbid sense of shame. It was thus rather the exacting nature of my aspirations, than any particular degradation in my faults, that made me what I was and, with even a deeper trench than in the majority of men, severed in me those provinces of good and ill which divide and compound man's dual nature. In this case, I was driven to reflect deeply and inveterately on that hard law of life which lies at the root of religion, and is one of the most plentiful springs of distress. Though so profound a double-dealer, I was in no sense a hypocrite; both sides of me were in dead earnest; I was no more myself when I laid aside restraint and plunged in shame, than when I laboured, in the eye of day, at the furtherance of knowledge or the relief of sorrow and suffering. And it chanced that the direction of my scientific studies, which led wholly towards the mystic and the transcendental, reacted and shed a strong light on this consciousness of the perennial war among my members. With every day, and from both sides of my intelligence, the moral and the intellectual, I thus drew steadily nearer to that truth by whose partial discovery I have been doomed to such a dreadful shipwreck: that man is not truly one, but truly two. I say two, because the state of my own knowledge does not pass beyond that point. Others will follow, others will outstrip me on the same lines; and I hazard the guess that man will be ultimately known for a mere polity of multifarious, incongruous and independent denizens. I, for my part, from the nature of my life, advanced infallibly in one direction and in one direction only. It was on the moral side, and in my own person, that I learned to recognise the thorough and primitive duality of man; I saw that, of the two natures that contended in the field of my consciousness, even if I could rightly be said to be either, it was only because I was radically both; and from an early date, even before the course of my scientific discoveries had begun to suggest the most naked possibility of such a miracle, I had learned to dwell with pleasure, as a beloved day-dream, on the thought of the separation of these elements. If each, I told myself, could but be housed in separate identities, life would be relieved of all that was unbearable; the unjust might go his way, delivered from the aspirations and remorse of his more upright twin; and the just could walk steadfastly and securely on his upward path, doing the good things in which he found his pleasure, and no longer exposed to disgrace and penitence by the hands of this extraneous evil. It was the curse of mankind that these incongruous faggots were thus bound together – that in the agonised womb of consciousness these polar twins should be continuously struggling. How, then, were they dissociated?

I was so far in my reflections when, as I have said, a side light began to shine upon the subject from the laboratory table. I began to perceive more deeply than it has ever yet been stated, the trembling immateriality, the mist-like transience, of this seemingly so solid body in which we walk attired. Certain agents I found to have the power to shake and to pluck back that fleshly vestment, even as a wind might toss the curtains of a pavilion.

For two good reasons, I will not enter deeply into this scientific branch of my confession. First, because I have been made to learn that the doom and burthen of our life is bound for ever on man's shoulders; and when the attempt is made to cast it off, it but returns upon us with more unfamiliar and more awful pressure. Second, because, as my narrative will make, alas! too evident, my discoveries were incomplete. Enough, then, that I not only recognised my natural body for the mere aura and effulgence of certain of the powers that made up my spirit, but managed to compound a drug by which these powers should be dethroned from their supremacy, and a second form and countenance substituted, none the less natural to me because they were the expression, and bore the stamp, of lower elements in my soul.

I hesitated long before I put this theory to the test of practice. I knew well that I risked death; for any drug that so potently controlled and shook the very fortress of identity, might by the least scruple of an overdose or at the least inopportunity in the moment of exhibition, utterly blot out that immaterial tabernacle which I looked to it to change. But the temptation of a discovery so singular and profound at last overcame the suggestions of alarm. I had long since prepared my tincture; I purchased at once, from a firm of wholesale chemists, a large quantity of a particular salt, which I knew, from my experiments, to be the last ingredient required; and, late one accursed night, I compounded the elements, watched them boil and smoke together in the glass, and when the ebullition had subsided, with a strong glow of courage, drank off the potion.

The most racking pangs succeeded: a grinding in the bones, deadly nausea, and a horror of the spirit that cannot be exceeded at the hour of birth or death. Then these agonies began swiftly to subside, and I came to myself as if out of a great sickness. There was something strange in my sensations, something indescribably new and, from its very novelty, incredibly sweet. I felt younger, lighter, happier in body; within I was conscious of a heady recklessness, a current of disordered sensual images running like a mill race in my fancy, a solution of the bonds of obligation, an unknown but not an innocent freedom of the soul.

I knew myself, at the first breath of this new life, to be more wicked, tenfold more wicked, sold a slave to my original evil; and the thought, in that moment, braced and delighted me like wine. I stretched out my hands, exulting in the freshness of these sensations; and in the act, I was suddenly aware that I had lost in stature.

There was no mirror, at that date, in my room; that which stands beside me as I write was brought there later on, and for the very purpose of those transformations. The night, however, was far gone into the morning – the morning, black as it was, was nearly ripe for the conception of the day – the inmates of my house were locked in the most rigorous hours of slumber; and I determined, flushed as I was with hope and triumph, to venture in my new shape as far as to my bedroom. I crossed the yard, wherein the constellations looked down upon me, I could have thought, with wonder, the first creature of that sort that their unsleeping vigilance had yet disclosed to them; I stole through the corridors, a stranger in my own house; and coming to my room, I saw for the first time the appearance of Edward Hyde.

I must here speak by theory alone, saying not that which I know, but that which I suppose to be most probable. The evil side of my nature, to which I had now transferred the stamping efficacy, was less robust and less developed than the good which I had just deposed. Again, in the course of my life, which had been, after all, nine-tenths a life of effort, virtue and control, it had been much less exercised and much less exhausted. And hence, as I think, it came about that Edward Hyde was so much smaller, slighter, and younger than Henry Jekyll. Even as good shone upon the countenance of the one, evil was written broadly and plainly on the face of the other. Evil besides (which I must still believe to be the lethal side of man) had left on that body an imprint of deformity and decay. And yet when I looked upon that ugly idol in the glass, I was conscious of no repugnance, rather of a leap of welcome. This, too, was myself. It seemed natural and human. In my eyes it bore a livelier image of the spirit, it seemed more express and single, than the imperfect and divided countenance, I had been hitherto accustomed to call mine. And in so far I was doubtless right. I have observed that when I wore the semblance of Edward Hyde, none could come near to me at first without a visible misgiving of the flesh. This, as I take it, was because all human beings, as we meet them, are commingled out of good and evil: and Edward Hyde, alone, in the ranks of mankind, was pure evil.

I lingered but a moment at the mirror: the second and conclusive experiment had yet to be attempted; it yet remained to be seen if I had lost my identity beyond redemption and must flee before daylight from a house that was no longer mine; and hurrying back to my cabinet, I once more prepared and drank the cup, once more suffered the pangs of dissolution, and came to myself once more with the character, the stature, and the face of Henry Jekyll.

That night I had come to the fatal cross roads. Had I approached my discovery in a more noble spirit, had I risked the experiment while under the empire of generous or pious aspirations, all must have been otherwise, and from these agonies of death and birth I had come forth an angel instead of a fiend. The drug had no discriminating action; it was neither diabolical nor divine; it but shook the doors of the prisonhouse of my disposition; and, like the captives of Philippi, that which stood within ran forth. At that time my virtue slumbered; my evil, kept awake by ambition, was alert and swift to seize the occasion; and the thing that was projected was Edward Hyde. Hence, although I had now two characters as well as two appearances, one was wholly evil, and the other was still the old Henry Jekyll, that incongruous compound of whose reformation and improvement I had already learned to despair. The movement was thus wholly toward the worse.

Even at that time, I had not yet conquered my aversion to the dryness of a life of study. I would still be merrily disposed at times; and as my pleasures were (to say the least) undignified, and I was not only well known and highly considered, but growing towards the elderly man, this incoherency of my life was daily growing more unwelcome. It was on this side that my new power tempted me until I fell in slavery. I had but to drink the cup, to doff at once the body of the noted professor, and to assume, like a thick cloak, that of Edward Hyde. I smiled at the notion; it seemed to me at the time to be humorous; and I made my preparations with the most studious care. I took and furnished that house in Soho to which Hyde was tracked by the police; and engaged as housekeeper a creature whom I well knew to be silent and unscrupulous. On the other side, I announced to my servants that a Mr Hyde (whom I described) was to have full liberty and power about my house in the square; and, to parry mishaps, I even called and made myself a familiar object in my second character. I next drew up that will to which you so much objected; so that if anything befell me in the person of Dr Jekyll, I could enter on that of Edward Hyde without pecuniary loss. And thus fortified, as I supposed, on every side, I began to profit by the strange immunities of my position.

Men have before hired bravos to transact their crimes, while their own person and reputation sat under shelter. I was the first that ever did so for his pleasures. I was the first that could thus plod in the public eye with a load of genial respectability, and in a moment, like a schoolboy, strip off these lendings and spring headlong into the sea of liberty. But for me, in my impenetrable mantle, the safety was complete. Think of it – I did not even exist! Let me but escape into my laboratory door, give me but a second or two to mix and swallow the draught that I had always standing ready; and, whatever he had done, Edward Hyde would pass away like the stain of breath upon a mirror; and there in his stead, quietly at home, trimming the midnight lamp in his study, a man who could afford to laugh at suspicion, would be Henry Jekyll.

The pleasures which I made haste to seek in my disguise were, as I have said, undignified; I would scarce use a harder term. But in the hands of Edward Hyde they soon began to turn towards the monstrous. When I would come back from these excursions, I was often plunged into a kind of wonder at my vicarious depravity. This familiar that I called out of my own soul, and sent forth alone to do his good pleasure, was a being inherently malign and villainous; his every act and thought centred on self; drinking pleasure with bestial avidity from any degree of torture to another; relentless like a man of stone.

Henry Jekyll stood at times aghast before the acts of Edward Hyde; but the situation was apart from ordinary laws, and insidiously relaxed the grasp of conscience. It was Hyde, after all, and Hyde alone, that was guilty. Jekyll was no worse; he woke again to his good qualities seemingly unimpaired; he would even make haste, where it was possible, to undo the evil done by Hyde. And thus his conscience slumbered.

Into the details of the infamy at which I thus connived (for even now I can scarce grant that I committed it) I have no design of entering. I mean but to point out the warnings and the successive steps with which my chastisement approached. I met with one accident which, as it brought on no consequence, I shall no more than mention. An act of cruelty to a child aroused against me the anger of a passerby, whom I recognised the other day in the person of your kinsman; the doctor and the child's family joined him; there were moments when I feared for my life; and at last, in order to pacify their too just resentment, Edward Hyde had to bring them to the door, and pay them in a cheque drawn in the name of Henry Jekyll. But this danger was easily eliminated from the future by opening an account at another bank in the name of Edward Hyde himself; and when, by sloping my own hand backwards, I had supplied my double with a signature, I thought I sat beyond the reach of fate.

Some two months before the murder of Sir Danvers, I had been out for one of my adventures, had returned at a late hour, and woke the next day in bed with somewhat odd sensations. It was in vain I looked about me; in vain I saw the decent furniture and tall proportions of my room in the square; in vain that I recognised the pattern of the bed curtains and the design of the mahogany frame; something still kept insisting that I was not where I was, that I had not wakened where I seemed to be, but in the little room in Soho where I was accustomed to sleep in the body of Edward Hyde. I smiled to myself, and, in my psychological way, began lazily to inquire into the elements of this illusion, occasionally, even as I did so, dropping back into a comfortable morning doze. I was still so engaged when, in one of my more wakeful moments, my eye fell upon my hand. Now, the hand of Henry Jekyll (as you have often remarked) was professional in shape and size; it was large, firm, white and comely. But the hand which I now saw, clearly enough in the yellow light of a mid-London morning, lying half shut on the bed-clothes, was lean, corded, knuckly, of a dusky pallor, and thickly shaded with a swart growth of hair. It was the hand of Edward Hyde.

I must have stared upon it for near half a minute, sunk as I was in the mere stupidity of wonder, before terror woke up in my breast as sudden and startling as the crash of cymbals; and bounding from my bed, I rushed to the mirror. At the sight that met my eyes, my blood was changed into something exquisitely thin and icy. Yes, I had gone to bed Henry Jekyll, I had awakened Edward Hyde. How was this to be explained? I asked myself; and then, with another bound of terror – how was it to be remedied? It was well on in the morning; the servants were up; all my drugs were in the cabinet – a long journey, down two pairs of stairs, through the back passage, across the open court and through the anatomical theatre, from where I was then standing horror-struck. It might indeed be possible to cover my face; but of what use was that, when I was unable to conceal the alteration in my stature? And then, with an overpowering sweetness of relief, it came back upon my mind that the servants were already used to the coming and going of my second self. I had soon dressed, as well as I was able, in clothes of my own size; had soon passed through the house, where Bradshaw stared and drew back at seeing Mr Hyde at such an hour and in such a strange array; and ten minutes later, Dr Jekyll had returned to his own shape and was sitting down, with a darkened brow, to make a feint of breakfasting.

Small indeed was my appetite. This inexplicable incident, this reversal of my previous experience, seemed, like the Babylonian finger on the wall, to be spelling out the letters of my judgment; and I began to reflect more seriously than ever before on the issues and possibilities of my double existence. That part of me which I had the power of projecting had lately been much exercised and nourished; it had seemed to me of late as though the body of Edward Hyde had grown in stature, as though (when I wore that form) I were conscious of a more generous tide of blood; and I began to spy a danger that, if this were much prolonged, the balance of my nature might be permanently overthrown, the power of voluntary change be forfeited, and the character of Edward Hyde become irrevocably mine. The power of the drug had not been always equally displayed. Once, very early in my career, it had totally failed me; since then I had been obliged on more than one occasion to double, and once, with infinite risk of death, to treble the amount; and these rare uncertainties had cast hitherto the sole shadow on my contentment. Now, however, and in the light of that morning's accident, I was led to remark that whereas, in the beginning, the difficulty had been to throw off the body of Jekyll, it had of late gradually but decidedly transferred itself to the other side. All things therefore seemed to point to this: that I was slowly losing hold of my original and better self, and becoming slowly incorporated with my second and worse.

Between these two I now felt I had to choose. My two natures had memory in common, but all other faculties were most unequally shared between them. Jekyll (who was a composite) now with the most sensitive apprehensions, now with a greedy gusto, projected and shared in the pleasures and adventures of Hyde; but Hyde was indifferent to Jekyll, or but remembered him as the mountain bandit remembers the cavern in which he conceals himself from pursuit. Jekyll had more than a father's interest; Hyde had more than a son's indifference. To cast in my lot with Jekyll was to die to those appetites which I had long secretly indulged and had of late begun to pamper. To cast it in with Hyde was to die to a thousand interests and aspirations, and to become, at a blow and for ever, despised and friendless. The bargain might appear unequal; but there was still another consideration in the scales; for while Jekyll would suffer smartingly in the fires of abstinence, Hyde would be not even conscious of all that he had lost. Strange as my circumstances were, the terms of this debate are as old and commonplace as man; much the same inducements and alarms cast the die for any tempted and trembling sinner; and it fell out with me, as it falls with so vast a majority of my fellows, that I chose the better part and was found wanting in the strength to keep to it.

Yes, I preferred the elderly and discontented doctor, surrounded by friends and cherishing honest hopes; and bade a resolute farewell to the liberty, the comparative youth, the light step, leaping pulses and secret pleasures, that I had enjoyed in the disguise of Hyde. I made this choice perhaps with some unconscious reservation, for I neither gave up the house in Soho, nor destroyed the clothes of Edward Hyde, which still lay ready in my cabinet. For two months, however, I was true to my determination; for two months I led a life of such severity as I had never before attained to, and enjoyed the compensations of an approving conscience. But time began at last to obliterate the freshness of my alarm; the praises of conscience began to grow into a thing of course; I began to be tortured with throes and longings, as of Hyde struggling after freedom; and at last, in an hour of moral weakness, I once again compounded and swallowed the transforming draught.

I do not suppose that when a drunkard reasons with himself upon his vice, he is once out of five hundred times affected by the dangers that he runs through his brutish physical insensibility; neither had I, long as I had considered my position made enough allowance for the complete moral insensibility and insensate readiness to evil which were the leading characters of Edward Hyde. Yet it was by these that I was punished. My devil had been long caged, he came out roaring. I was conscious, even when I took the draught, of a more unbridled, a more furious propensity to ill. It must have been this, I suppose, that stirred in my soul that tempest of impatience with which I listened to the civilities of my unhappy victim; I declare at least, before God, no man morally sane could have been guilty of that crime upon so pitiful a provocation; and that I struck in no more reasonable spirit than that in which a sick child may break a plaything. But I had voluntarily stripped myself of all those balancing instincts by which even the worst of us continues to walk with some degree of steadiness among temptations; and in my case, to be tempted, however slightly, was to fall.

Instantly the spirit of hell awoke in me and raged. With a transport of glee, I mauled the unresisting body, tasting delight from every blow; and it was not till weariness had begun to succeed that I was suddenly, in the top fit of my delirium, struck through the heart by a cold thrill of terror. A mist dispersed; I saw my life to be forfeit; and fled from the scene of these excesses, at once glorying and trembling, my lust of evil gratified and stimulated, my love of life screwed to the topmost peg. I ran to the house in Soho, and (to make assurance doubly sure) destroyed my papers; thence I set out through the lamplit streets, in the same divided ecstasy of mind, gloating on my crime, light-headedly devising others in the future, and yet still hastening and still harkening in my wake for the steps of the avenger. Hyde had a song upon his lips as he compounded the draught, and as he drank it pledged the dead man. The pangs of transformation had not done tearing him, before Henry Jekyll, with streaming tears of gratitude and remorse, had fallen upon his knees and lifted his clasped hand to God. The veil of self-indulgence was rent from head to foot, I saw my life as a whole: I followed it up from the days of childhood, when I had walked with my father's hand, and through the self-denying toils of my professional life, to arrive again and again, with the same sense of unreality, at the damned horrors of the evening. I could have screamed aloud; I sought with tears and prayers to smother down the crowd of hideous images and sounds with which my memory swarmed against me; and still, between the petitions, the ugly face of my iniquity stared into my soul. As the acuteness of this remorse began to die away, it was succeeded by a sense of joy. The problem of my conduct was solved. Hyde was henceforth impossible; whether I would or not, I was now confined to the better part of my existence; and, oh, how I rejoiced to think it! with what willing humility I embraced anew the restrictions of natural life! with what sincere renunciation I locked the door by which I had so often gone and come, and ground the key under my heel!

The next day came the news that the murder had been overlooked, that the guilt of Hyde was patent to the world, and that the victim was a man high in public estimation. It was not only a crime, it had been a tragic folly. I think I was glad to know it; I think I was glad to have my better impulses thus buttressed and guarded by the terrors of the scaffold. Jekyll was now my city of refuge; let but Hyde peep out an instant, and the hands of all men would be raised to take and slay him.

I resolved in my future conduct to redeem the past; and I can say with honesty that my resolve was fruitful of some good. You know yourself how earnestly in the last months of last year I laboured to relieve suffering; you know that much was done for others, and that the days passed quietly, almost happily for myself. Nor can I truly say that I wearied of this beneficent and innocent life; I think instead that I daily enjoyed it more completely; but I was still cursed with my duality of purpose; and as the first edge of my penitence wore off, the lower side of me, so long indulged, so recently chained down, began to growl for licence. Not that I dreamed of resuscitating Hyde; the bare idea of that would startle me to frenzy: no, it was in my own person that I was once more tempted to trifle with my conscience; and it was as an ordinary secret sinner that I at last fell before the assaults of temptation.

There comes an end to all things; the most capacious measure is filled at last; and this brief condescension to my evil finally destroyed the balance of my soul. And yet I was not alarmed; the fall seemed natural, like a return to the old days before I had made my discovery. It was a fine, clear January day, wet under foot where the frost had melted, but cloudless overhead; and the Regent's Park was full of winter chirrupings and sweet with Spring odours. I sat in the sun on a bench; the animal within me licking the chops of memory; the spiritual side a little drowsed, promising subsequent penitence, but not yet moved to begin. After all, I reflected, I was like my neighbours; and then I smiled, comparing myself with other men, comparing my active goodwill with the lazy cruelty of their neglect. And at the very moment of that vainglorious thought, a qualm came over me, a horrid nausea and the most deadly shuddering. These passed away, and left me faint; and then as in its turn the faintness subsided, I began to be aware of a change in the temper of my thoughts, a greater boldness, a contempt of danger, a solution of the bonds of obligation. I looked down; my clothes hung formlessly on my shrunken limbs; the hand that lay on my knee was corded and hairy. I was once more Edward

Hyde. A moment before I had been safe of all men's respect, wealthy, beloved – the cloth laying for me in the dining-room at home; and now I was the common quarry of mankind, hunted, houseless, a known murderer, thrall to the gallows.

My reason wavered, but it did not fail me utterly. I have more than once observed that, in my second character, my faculties seemed sharpened to a point and my spirits more tensely elastic; thus it came about that, where Jekyll perhaps might have succumbed, Hyde rose to the importance of the moment. My drugs were in one of the presses of my cabinet: how was I to reach them? That was the problem that (crushing my temples in my hands) I set myself to solve. The laboratory door I had closed. If I sought to enter by the house, my own servants would consign me to the gallows. I saw I must employ another hand, and thought of Lanyon. How was he to be reached? how persuaded? Supposing that I escaped capture in the streets, how was I to make my way into his presence? and how should I, an unknown and displeasing visitor, prevail on the famous physician to rifle the study of his colleague, Dr Jekyll? Then I remembered that of my original character, one part remained to me: I could write my own hand; and once I had conceived that kindling spark, the way that I must follow became lighted up from end to end.

Thereupon, I arranged my clothes as best I could, and summoning a passing hansom, drove to an hotel in Portland Street, the name of which I chanced to remember. At my appearance (which was indeed comical enough, however tragic a fate these garments covered) the driver could not conceal his mirth. I gnashed my teeth upon him with a gust of devilish fury; and the smile withered from his face – happily for him – yet more happily for myself, for in another instant I had certainly dragged him from his perch. At the inn, as I entered, I looked about me with so black a countenance as made the attendants tremble; not a look did they exchange in my presence; but obsequiously took my orders, led me to a private room, and brought me wherewithal to write. Hyde in danger of his life was a creature new to me: shaken with inordinate anger, strung to the pitch of murder, lusting to inflict pain. Yet the creature was astute;

mastered his fury with a great effort of the will; composed his two important letters, one to Lanyon and one to Poole, and, that he might receive actual evidence of their being posted, sent them out with directions that they should be registered.

Thenceforward, he sat all day over the fire in the private room, gnawing his nails; there he dined, sitting alone with his fears, the waiter visibly quailing before his eye; and thence, when the night was fully come, he set forth in the corner of a closed cab, and was driven to and fro about the streets of the city. He, I say – I cannot say, I. That child of Hell had nothing human; nothing lived in him but fear and hatred. And when at last, thinking the driver had begun to grow suspicious, he discharged the cab and ventured on foot, attired in his misfitting clothes, an object marked out for observation, into the midst of the nocturnal passengers, these two base passions raged within him like a tempest. He walked fast, hunted by his fears, chattering to himself, skulking through the less frequented thoroughfares, counting the minutes that still divided him from midnight. Once a woman spoke to him, offering, I think, a box of lights. He smote her in the face, and she fled.

When I came to myself at Lanyon's, the horror of my old friend perhaps affected me somewhat: I do not know; it was at least but a drop in the sea to the abhorrence with which I looked back upon these hours. A change had come over me. It was no longer the fear of the gallows, it was the horror of being Hyde that racked me. I received Lanyon's condemnation partly in a dream; it was partly in a dream that I came home to my own house and got into bed. I slept after the prostration of the day, with a stringent and profound slumber which not even the nightmares that wrung me could avail to break. I awoke in the morning shaken, weakened, but refreshed. I still hated and feared the thought of the brute that slept within me, and I had not of course forgotten the appalling dangers of the day before; but I was once more at home, in my own house and close to my drugs; and gratitude for my escape shone so strong in my soul that it almost rivalled the brightness of hope.

I was stepping leisurely across the court after breakfast, drinking the chill of the air with pleasure, when I was seized again with those indescribable sensations that heralded the change; and I had but the time to gain the shelter of my cabinet, before I was once again raging and freezing with the passions of Hyde. It took on this occasion a double dose to recall me to myself; and alas, six hours after, as I sat looking sadly in the fire, the pangs returned, and the drug had to be re-administered. In short, from that day forth it seemed only by a great effort as of gymnastics, and only under the immediate stimulation of the drug, that I was able to wear the countenance of Jekyll. At all hours of the day and night I would be taken with the premonitory shudder; above all, if I slept, or even dozed for a moment in my chair, it was always as Hyde that I awakened. Under the strain of this continually impending doom and by the sleeplessness to which I now condemned myself, ay, even beyond what I had thought possible to man, I became, in my own person, a creature eaten up and emptied by fever, languidly weak both in body and mind, and solely occupied by one thought: the horror of my other self. But when I slept, or when the virtue of the medicine wore off, I would leap almost without transition (for the pangs of transformation grew daily less marked) into the possession of a fancy brimming with images of terror, a soul boiling with causeless hatreds, and a body that seemed not strong enough to contain the raging energies of life. The powers of Hyde seemed to have grown with the sickliness of Jekyll. And certainly the hate that now divided them was equal on each side. With Jekyll, it was a thing of vital instinct. He had now seen the full deformity of that creature that shared with him some of the phenomena of consciousness, and was co-heir with him to death: and beyond these links of community, which in themselves made the most poignant part of his distress, he thought of Hyde, for all his energy of life, as of something not only hellish but inorganic. This was the shocking thing; that the slime of the pit seemed to utter cries and voices; that the amorphous dust gesticulated and sinned; that what was dead, and had no shape, should usurp the offices of life. And this again, that that insurgent horror was knit to him closer than a wife, closer than an eye; lay caged in his flesh, where he heard it mutter and felt it struggle to be born; and at every hour of weakness, and in the confidences of slumber, prevailed against him, and deposed him out of life. The hatred of Hyde for Jekyll was of a different order. His terror of the gallows drove him continually to commit temporary suicide, and return to his subordinate station of a part instead of a person; but he loathed the necessity, he loathed the despondency into which Jekyll was now fallen, and he resented the dislike with which he was himself regarded. Hence the ape-like tricks that he would play me, scrawling in my own hand blasphemies on the pages of my books, burning the letters and destroying the portrait of my father; and indeed, had it not been for his fear of death, he would long ago have ruined himself in order to involve me in the ruin. But his love of life is wonderful; I go further: I, who sicken and freeze at the mere thought of him, when I recall the abjection and passion of this attachment, and when I know how he fears my power to cut him off by suicide, I find it in my heart to pity him.

It is useless, and the time awfully fails me, to prolong this description; no one has ever suffered such torments, let that suffice; and yet even to these, habit brought – no, not alleviation – but a certain callousness of soul, a certain acquiescence of despair; and my punishment might have gone on for years, but for the last calamity which has now fallen, and which has finally severed me from my own face and nature. My provision of the salt, which had never been renewed since the date of the first experiment, began to run low. I sent out for a fresh supply, and mixed the draught; the ebullition followed, and the first change of colour, not the second; I drank it, and it was without efficiency. You will learn from Poole how I have had London ransacked; it was in vain; and I am now persuaded that my first supply was impure, and that it was that unknown impurity which lent efficacy to the draught.

About a week has passed, and I am now finishing this statement under the influence of the last of the old powders. This, then, is the last time, short of a miracle, that Henry Jekyll can think his own thoughts or see his own face (now how sadly altered!) in the glass. Nor must I delay too long to bring my writing to an end; for if my narrative has hitherto escaped destruction, it has been by a combination of great prudence and great good luck. Should the throes of change take me in the act of writing it, Hyde will tear it in pieces; but if some time shall have elapsed after I have laid it by, his wonderful selfishness and circumscription to the moment will probably save it once again from the action of his ape-like spite. And indeed the doom that is closing on us both has already changed and crushed him. Half an hour from now, when I shall again and for ever reindue that hated personality, I know how I shall sit shuddering and weeping in my chair, or continue, with the most strained and fearstruck ecstasy of listening, to pace up and down this room (my last earthly refuge) and give ear to every sound of menace. Will Hyde die upon the scaffold? or will he find the courage to release himself at the last moment? God knows; I am careless; this is my true hour of death, and what is to follow concerns another than myself. Here, then, as I lay down the pen, and proceed to seal up my confession, I bring the life of that unhappy Henry Jekyll to an end.

THE BEACH OF FALESÁ

A South-Sea Bridal

I SAW that island first when it was neither night nor morning. The moon was to the west, setting, but still broad and bright. To the east, and right amidships of the dawn, which was all pink, the day-star sparkled like a diamond. The land breeze blew in our faces, and smelt strong of wild lime and vanilla; other things besides, but these were the most plain; and the chill of it set me sneezing. I should say I had been for years on a low island near the line, living for the most part solitary among natives. Here was a fresh experience; even the tongue would be quite strange to me; and the look of these woods and mountains, and the rare smell of them, renewed my blood.

The captain blew out the binnacle-lamp.[1]

'There!' said he, 'there goes a bit of smoke, Mr Wiltshire, behind the break of the reef. That's Falesá,[2] where your station is, the last village to the east; nobody lives to windward – I don't know why. Take my glass, and you can make the houses out.'

I took the glass; and the shores leaped nearer, and I saw the tangle of the woods and the breach of the surf, and the brown roofs and the black insides of houses peeped among the trees.

'Do you catch a bit of white there to the east'ard?' the captain continued. 'That's your house. Coral built, stands high, veranda you could walk on three abreast; best station in the South Pacific. When old Adams saw it, he took and shook me by the hand. 'I've dropped into a soft thing here,' says he. 'So you have,' says I, 'and time too!' Poor Johnny! I never saw him again but the once, and then he had changed his tune – couldn't get on with the natives, or the whites, or something; and the next time we came around there, he was dead and buried. I took and put up a bit of a stick to him: "John Adams, *obit* eighteen and sixty-eight. Go thou and do likewise." I missed that man. I could never see much harm in Johnny.'

'What did he die of?' I inquired.

'Some kind of sickness,' says the captain. 'It appears it took him sudden. Seems he got up in the night, and filled up on Pain-Killer and Kennedy's Discovery. No go – he was booked beyond Kennedy. Then he had tried to open a case of gin. No go again – not strong enough. Then he must have turned to and run out on the veranda, and capsized over the rail. When they found him, the next day, he was clean crazy – carried on all the time about somebody watering his copra.[3] Poor John!'

'Was it thought to be the island?' I asked.

'Well, it was thought to be the island, or the trouble, or something,' he replied. 'I never could hear but what it was a healthy place. Our last man, Vigours, never turned a hair. He left because of the beach – said he was afraid of Black Jack and Case and Whistling Jimmie, who was still alive at the time, but got drowned soon afterward when drunk.[4] As for old Captain Randall, he's been here any time since eighteen-forty, forty-five. I never could see much harm in Billy, nor much change. Seems as if he might live to be Old Kafoozleum. No, I guess it's healthy.'

'There's a boat coming now,' said I. 'She's right in the pass; looks to be a sixteen-foot whale; two white men in the stern-sheets.'

'That's the boat that drowned Whistling Jimmie!' cried the captain; 'let's see the glass. Yes, that's Case, sure enough, and the darkie. They've got a gallows bad reputation, but you know what a place the beach is for talking. My belief, that Whistling Jimmie was the worst of the trouble; and he's gone to glory, you see. What'll you bet they ain't after gin? Lay you five to two they take six cases.'

When these two traders came aboard I was pleased with the looks of them at once, or, rather, with the looks of both, and the speech of one. I was sick for white neighbours after my four years at the line, which I always counted years of prison; getting tabooed, and going down to the Speak House to see and get it taken off; buying gin and going on a break, and then repenting; sitting in the house at night with the lamp for company; or walking on the beach and wondering what kind of a fool to call myself for being where I was. There were no other whites upon my island, and when I sailed to the next, rough customers made the most of the society. Now to see these two when they came aboard was a pleasure. One was a Negro, to be sure; but they were both rigged out smart in striped pyjamas and straw hats, and Case would have passed muster in a city. He was yellow and smallish, had a hawk's nose to his face, pale eyes, and his beard trimmed with scissors. No man knew his country, beyond he was of English speech; and it was clear he came of a good family and was splendidly educated. He was accomplished too; played the accordion first rate; and give him a piece of string or a cork or a pack of cards, and he could show you tricks equal to any professional. He could speak, when he chose, fit for a drawing-room; and when he chose he could blaspheme worse than a Yankee boatswain, and talk smart to sicken a Kanaka.[5] The way he thought would pay best at the moment, that was Case's way, and it always seemed to come natural, and like as if he was born to it. He had the courage of a lion and the cunning of a rat; and if he's not in hell to-day, there's no such place. I know but one good point to the man – that he was fond of his wife, and kind to her. She was a Samoa woman, and dyed her hair red – Samoa style; and when he came to die (as I have to tell of) they found one strange thing – that he had made a will, like a Christian, and the widow got the lot; all this, they said, and all Black Jack's, and the most of Billy Randall's in the bargain, for it was Case that kept the books. So she went off home in the schooner Manu'a, and does the lady to this day in her own place.

But of all this on that first morning I knew no more than a fly. Case used me like a gentleman and like a friend, made me welcome to Falesá, and put his services at my disposal, which was the more helpful from my ignorance of the natives. All the better part of the day we sat drinking better acquaintance in the cabin, and I never heard a man talk more to the point. There was no smarter trader, and none dodgier, in the islands. I thought Falesá seemed to be the right kind of a place; and the more I drank the lighter my heart. Our last trader had fled the place at half an hour's notice, taking a chance passage in a labour ship from up west. The captain, when he came, had found the station closed, the keys left with the native pastor, and a letter from the runaway, confessing he was fairly frightened of his life. Since then the firm had not been represented, and of course there was no cargo. The wind, besides, was fair, the captain hoped he could make his next island by dawn, with a good tide, and the business of landing my trade was gone about lively. There was no call for me to fool with it, Case said; nobody would touch my things, everyone was honest in Falesá, only about chickens or an odd knife or an odd stick of tobacco; and the best I could do was to sit quiet till the vessel left, then come straight to his house, see old Captain Randall, the father of the beach, take pot-luck, and go home to sleep when it got dark. So it was high noon, and the schooner was under way before I set my foot on shore at Falesá.

I had a glass or two on board; I was just off a long cruise, and the ground heaved under me like a ship's deck. The world was like all new painted; my foot went along to music; Falesá might have been Fiddler's Green, if there is such a place, and more's the pity if there isn't! It was good to foot the grass, to look aloft at the green mountains, to see the men with their green wreaths and the women in their bright dresses, red and blue. On we went, in the strong sun and the cool shadow, liking both; and all the children in the town came trotting after with their shaven heads and their brown bodies, and raising a thin kind of a cheer in our wake, like crowing poultry.

'By the bye,' says Case, 'we must get you a wife.'

'That's so,' said I; 'I had forgotten.'

There was a crowd of girls about us, and I pulled myself up and looked among them like a bashaw. They were all dressed out for the sake of the ship being in; and the women of Falesá are a handsome lot to see. If they have a fault, they are a trifle broad in the beam; and I was just thinking so when Case touched me.

'That's pretty,' says he.

I saw one coming on the other side alone. She had been fishing; all she wore was a chemise, and it was wetted through. She was young and very slender for an island maid, with a long face, a high forehead, and a shy, strange, blindish look between a cat's and a baby's.

'Who's she?' said I. 'She'll do.'

'That's Uma,' said Case, and he called her up and spoke to her in the native. I didn't know what he said; but when he was in the midst she looked up at me quick and timid, like a child dodging a blow, then down again, and presently smiled. She had a wide mouth, the lips and the chin cut like any statue's; and the smile came out for a moment and was gone. Then she stood with her head bent, and heard Case to an end, spoke back in the pretty Polynesian voice, looking him full in the face, heard him again in answer, and then with an obeisance started off. I had just a share of the bow, but never another shot of her eye, and there was no more word of smiling.

'I guess it's all right,' said Case. 'I guess you can have her. I'll make it square with the old lady. You can have your pick of the lot for a plug of tobacco,' he added, sneering.

I suppose it was the smile stuck in my memory, for I spoke back sharp. 'She doesn't look that sort,' I cried.

'I don't know that she is,' said Case. 'I believe she's as right as the mail. Keeps to herself, don't go round with the gang, and that. Oh, no, don't you misunderstand me – Uma's on the square.' He spoke eager, I thought, and that surprised and pleased me. 'Indeed,' he went on, 'I shouldn't make so sure of getting her, only she cottoned to the cut of your jib. All you have to do is to keep dark and let me work the mother my own way; and I'll bring the girl round to the captain's for the marriage.'

I didn't care for the word marriage, and I said so.

'Oh, there's nothing to hurt in the marriage,' says he. 'Black Jack's the chaplin.'

By this time we had come in view of the house of these three white men; for a Negro is counted a white man, and so is a Chinese! A strange idea, but common in the islands. It was a board house with a strip of rickety veranda. The store was to the front, with a counter, scales, and the finest possible display of trade: a case or two of tinned meats; a barrel of hard bread, a few bolts of cotton stuff, not to be compared with mine; the only thing well represented being the contraband firearms and liquor. 'If these are my only rivals,' thinks I, 'I should do well in Falesá.' Indeed, there was only the one way they could touch me, and that was with the guns and drink.

In the back room was old Captain Randall, squatting on the floor native fashion, fat and pale, naked to the waist, grey as a badger, and his eyes set with drink. His body was covered with grey hair and crawled over by flies; one was in the corner of his eye – he never heeded; and the mosquitoes hummed about the man like bees. Any clean-minded man would have had the creature out at once and buried him; and to see him, and think he was seventy, and remember he had once commanded a ship, and come ashore in his smart togs, and talked big in bars and consulates, and sat in club verandas, turned me sick and sober.

He tried to get up when I came in, but that was hopeless; so he reached me a hand instead, and stumbled out some salutation.

'Papa's pretty full this morning,' observed Case. 'We've had an epidemic here; and Captain Randall takes gin for a prophylactic – don't you, papa?'

'Never took such a thing in my life!' cried the captain, indignantly. 'Take gin for my health's sake, Mr Wha's-ever-your-name—'s a precautionary measure.'

'That's all right, papa,' said Case. 'But you'll have to brace up. There's going to be a marriage – Mr Wiltshire here is going to get spliced.'

The old man asked to whom.

'To Uma,' said Case.

'Uma!' cried the captain. 'Wha's he want Uma for? 's he come here for his health, anyway? Wha' 'n hell's he want Uma for?'

'Dry up, papa,' said Case. ''Tain't you that's to marry her. I guess you're not her godfather and godmother. I guess Mr Wiltshire's going to please himself.'

With that he made an excuse to me that he must move about the marriage, and left me alone with the poor wretch that was his partner and (to speak truth) his gull. Trade and station belonged both to Randall; Case and the Negro were parasites; they crawled and fed upon him like the flies, he none the wiser. Indeed, I have no harm to say of Billy Randall beyond the fact that my gorge rose at him, and the time I now passed in his company was like a nightmare.

The room was stifling hot and full of flies; for the house was dirty and low and small, and stood in a bad place, behind the village, in the borders of the bush, and sheltered from the trade. The three men's beds were on the floor, and a litter of pans and dishes. There was no standing furniture; Randall, when he was violent, tearing it to laths. There I sat and had a meal which was served us by Case's wife; and there I was entertained all day by that remains of man, his tongue stumbling among low old jokes and long old stories, and his own wheezy laughter always ready, so that he had no sense of my depression. He was nipping gin all the while. Sometimes he fell asleep and awoke again, whimpering and shivering, and every now and again he would ask me why I wanted to marry Uma. 'My friend,' I was telling myself all day, 'you must not come to be an old gentleman like this.'

It might be four in the afternoon, perhaps, when the back door was thrust slowly open, and a strange old native woman crawled into the house almost on her belly. She was swathed in black stuff to her heels; her hair was grey in swatches; her face was tattooed, which was not the practice in that island; her eyes big and bright and crazy. These she fixed upon me with a rapt expression that I saw to be part acting. She said no plain word, but smacked and mumbled with her lips, and hummed aloud, like a child over its Christmas pudding. She came straight across the house, heading for me, and, as soon as she was alongside, caught up my hand and purred and crooned over it like a great cat. From this she slipped into a kind of song.

'Who the devil's this?' cried I, for the thing startled me.

'It's Faavao,' says Randall; and I saw he had hitched along the floor into the farthest corner.

'You ain't afraid of her?' I cried.

'Me 'fraid?' cried the captain. 'My dear friend, I defy her! I don't let her put her foot in here, only I suppose 's different to-day for the marriage. 's Uma's mother.'

'Well, suppose it is; what's she carrying on about?' I asked, more irritated, perhaps more frightened, than I cared to show; and the captain told me she was making up a quantity of poetry in my praise because I was to marry Uma. 'All right, old lady,' says I, with rather a failure of a laugh, 'anything to oblige. But when you're done with my hand, you might let me know.'

She did as though she understood; the song rose into a cry, and stopped; the woman crouched out of the house, the same way that she came in, and must have plunged straight into the bush, for when I followed her to the door she had already vanished.

'These are rum manners,' said I.

''S a rum crowd,' said the captain, and, to my surprise, he made the sign of the cross on his bare bosom.

'Hillo!' says I, 'are you a Papist?'

He repudiated the idea with contempt. 'Hard-shell Baptis',' said he. 'But, my dear friend, the Papists got some good ideas too; and th' 's one of 'em. You take my advice, and whenever you come across Uma or Faavao or Vigours, or any of that crowd, you take a leaf out o' the priests, and do what I do. Savvy?' says he, repeated the sign, and winked his dim eye at me. 'No, *sir*!' he broke out again, 'no Papists here!' and for a long time entertained me with his religious opinions.

I must have been taken with Uma from the first, or I should certainly have fled from that house, and got into the clean air, and the clean sea, or some convenient river – though, it's true, I was committed to Case; and, besides, I could never have held my head up in that island if I had run from a girl upon my wedding-night.

The sun was down, the sky all on fire, and the lamp had been some time lighted, when Case came back with Uma and the Negro. She was dressed and scented; her kilt was of fine tapa,[6] looking richer in the folds than any silk; her bust, which was of the colour of dark honey, she wore bare, only for some half a dozen necklaces of seeds and flowers; and behind her ears and in her hair she had the scarlet flowers of the hibiscus. She showed the best bearing for a bride conceivable, serious and still; and I thought shame to stand up with her in that mean house and before that grinning Negro. I thought shame, I say; for the mountebank was dressed with a big paper collar, the book he made believe to read from was an odd volume of a novel, and the words of his service not fit to be set down. My conscience smote me when we joined hands; and when she got her certificate I was tempted to throw up the bargain and confess. Here is the document. It was Case that wrote it, signatures and all, in a leaf out of the ledger:

This is to certify that *Uma*, daughter of *Faavao*, of Falesá, island of ——, is illegally married to *Mr John Wiltshire* for one night, and Mr. John Wiltshire is at liberty to send her to hell next morning.

JOHN BLACKAMOAR,
Chaplain to the Hulks

Extracted from the register
by William T. Randall,
Master Mariner

A nice paper to put in a girl's hand and see her hide away like gold. A man might easily feel cheap for less. But it was the practice in these parts, and (as I told myself) not the least the fault of us white men, but of the missionaries. If they had let the natives be, I had never needed this deception, but taken all the wives I wished, and left them when I pleased, with a clear conscience.

The more ashamed I was, the more hurry I was in to be gone; and our desires thus jumping together, I made the less remark of a change in the traders. Case had been all eagerness to keep me; now, as though he had attained a purpose, he seemed all eagerness to have me go. Uma, he said, could show me to my house, and the three bade us farewell indoors.

The night was nearly come; the village smelt of trees and flowers and the sea and bread-fruit-cooking; there came a fine roll of sea from the reef, and from a distance, among the woods and houses, many pretty sounds of men and children. It did me good to breathe free air; it did me good to be done with the captain, and see, instead, the creature at my side. I felt for all the world as though she were some girl at home in the Old Country, and forgetting myself for the minute, took her hand to walk with. Her fingers nestled into mine, I heard her breathe deep and quick, and all at once she caught my hand to her face and pressed it there. 'You good!' she cried, and ran ahead of me, and stopped and looked back and smiled, and ran ahead of me again, thus guiding me through the edge of the bush, and by a quiet way to my own house.

The truth is, Case had done the courting for me in style – told her I was mad to have her, and cared nothing for the consequences; and the poor soul, knowing that which I was still ignorant of, believed it, every word, and had her head nigh turned with vanity and gratitude. Now, of all this I had no guess; I was one of the most opposed to any nonsense about native women, having seen so many whites eaten up by their wives' relatives, and made fools of into the bargain; and I told myself I must make a stand at once, and bring her to her bearings. But she looked so quaint and pretty as she ran away and then awaited me, and the thing was done so like a child or a kind dog, that the best I could do was just to follow her whenever she went on, to listen for the fall of her bare feet, and to watch in the dusk for the shining of her body. And there was another thought came in my head. She played kitten with me now when we were alone; but in the house she had carried it the way a countess might, so proud and humble. And what with her dress – for all there was so little of it, and that native enough – what with her fine tapa and fine scents, and her red flowers and seeds, that were quite as bright as jewels, only larger – it came over me she was a kind of countess really, dressed to hear great singers at a concert, and no even mate for a poor trader like myself.

She was the first in the house; and while I was still without I saw a match flash and the lamplight kindle in the windows. The station was a wonderful fine place, coral built, with quite a wide veranda, and the main room high and wide. My chests and cases had been piled in, and made rather of a mess; and there, in the thick of the confusion, stood Uma by the table, awaiting me. Her shadow went all the way up behind her into the hollow of the iron roof; she stood against it bright, the lamplight shining on her skin. I stopped in the door, and she looked at me, not speaking, with eyes that were eager and yet daunted; then she touched herself on the bosom.

'Me – your wifie,' she said. It had never taken me like that before; but the want of her took and shook all through me, like the wind in the luff of a sail.

I could not speak if I had wanted; and if I could, I would not. I was ashamed to be so much moved about a native, ashamed of the marriage too, and the certificate she had treasured in her kilt; and I turned aside and made believe to rummage among my cases. The first thing I lighted on was a case of gin, the only one that I had brought; and partly for the girl's sake, and partly for horror of the recollections of old Randall, took a sudden resolve. I pried the lid off. One by one I drew the bottles with a pocket corkscrew, and sent Uma out to pour the stuff from the veranda.

She came back after the last, and looked at me puzzled like.

'No good,' said I, for I was now a little better master of my tongue. 'Man he drink, he no good.'

She agreed with this, but kept considering. 'Why you bring him?' she asked, presently. 'Suppose you no want drink, you no bring him, I think.'

'That's all right,' said I. 'One time I want drink too much; now no want. You see, I no savvy, I get one little wifie. Suppose I drink gin, my little wifie be 'fraid.'

To speak to her kindly was about more than I was fit for; I had made my vow I would never let on to weakness with a native, and I had nothing for it but to stop.

She stood looking gravely down at me where I sat by the open case. 'I think you good man,' she said. And suddenly she had fallen before me on the floor. 'I belong you all-e-same pig!' she cried.

The Ban

I CAME on the veranda just before the sun rose on the morrow. My house was the last on the east; there was a cape of woods and cliffs behind that hid the sunrise. To the west, a swift, cold river ran down, and beyond was the green of the village, dotted with cocoa-palms and bread-fruits and houses. The shutters were some of them down and some open; I saw the mosquito bars still stretched, with shadows of people new-awakened sitting up inside; and all over the green others were stalking silent, wrapped in their many-coloured sleeping clothes, like Bedouins in Bible pictures. It was mortal still and solemn and chilly, and the light of the dawn on the lagoon was like the shining of a fire.

But the thing that troubled me was nearer hand. Some dozen young men and children made a piece of a half-circle, flanking my house: the river divided them, some were on the near side, some on the far, and one on a boulder in the midst; and they all sat silent, wrapped in their sheets, and stared at me and my house as straight as pointer dogs. I thought it strange as I went out. When I had bathed and come back again, and found them all there, and two or three more along with them, I thought it stranger still. What could they see to gaze at in my house I wondered, and went in.

But the thought of these starers stuck in my mind, and presently I came out again. The sun was now up, but it was still behind the cape of woods. Say a quarter of an hour had come and gone. The crowd was greatly increased, the far bank of the river was lined for quite a way – perhaps thirty grown folk, and of children twice as many, some standing, some squatted on the ground, and all staring at my house. I have seen a house in a South-Sea village thus surrounded, but then a trader was thrashing his wife inside, and she singing out. Here was nothing – the stove was alight, the smoke coming up in a Christian manner; all was shipshape and Bristol fashion. To be sure, there was a stranger come, but they had a chance to see that stranger yesterday, and took it quiet enough. What ailed them now? I leaned my arms on the rail and stared back. Devil a wink they had in them! Now and then I could see the children chatter, but they spoke so low not even the hum of their speaking came my length. The rest were like graven images: they stared at me, dumb and sorrowful, with their bright eyes; and it came upon me things would look not much different if I were on the platform of the gallows, and these good folk had come to see me hanged.

I felt I was getting daunted, and began to be afraid I looked it, which would never do. Up I stood, made believe to stretch myself, came down the veranda stair, and strolled toward the river. There went a short buzz from one to the other, like what you hear in theatres when the curtain goes up; and some of the nearest gave back the matter of a pace. I saw a girl lay one hand on a young man and make a gesture upward with the other; at the same time she said something in the native with a gasping voice. Three little boys sat beside my path, where I must pass within three feet of them. Wrapped in their sheets, with their shaved heads and bits of topknots, and queer faces, they looked like figures on a chimney-piece. Awhile they sat their ground, solemn as judges. I came up hand over fist, doing my five knots, like a man that meant business; and I thought I saw a sort of a wink and gulp in the three faces. Then one jumped up (he was the farthest off) and ran for his mammy. The other two, trying to follow suit, got foul, came to the ground together bawling, wriggled right out of their sheets, and in a moment there were all three of them scampering for their lives mother-naked and singing out like pigs. The natives, who would never let a joke slip, even at a burial, laughed and let up, as short as a dog's bark.

They say it scares a man to be alone. No such thing. What scares him in the dark or the high bush is that he can't make sure, and there might be an army at his elbow. What scares him worst is to be right in the midst of a crowd, and have no guess of what they're driving at. When that laugh stopped, I stopped too. The boys had not yet made their offing, they were still on the full stretch going the one way, when I had already gone about ship and was sheering off the other. Like a fool I had come out, doing my five knots; like a fool I went back again. It must have been the funniest thing to see, and what knocked me silly, this time no one laughed; only one old woman gave a kind of pious moan, the way you have heard Dissenters in their chapels at the sermon.

'I never saw such dam-fool fools of Kanakas as your people here,' I said once to Uma, glancing out of the window at the starers.

'Savvy nothing,' says Uma, with a kind of disgusted air that she was good at.

And that was all the talk we had upon the matter, for I was put out, and Uma took the thing so much as a matter of course that I was fairly ashamed.

All day, off and on, now fewer and now more, the fools sat about the west end of my house and across the river, waiting for the show, whatever that was – fire to come down from heaven, I suppose, and consume me, bones and baggage. But by evening, like real islanders, they had wearied of the business, and got away, and had a dance instead in the big house of the village, where I heard them singing and clapping hands till, maybe, ten at night, and the next day it seemed they had forgotten I existed. If fire had come down from heaven or the earth opened and swallowed me, there would have been nobody to see the sport or take the lesson, or whatever you like to call it. But I was to find they hadn't forgot either, and kept an eye lifting for phenomena over my way.

I was hard at it both these days getting my trade in order and taking stock of what Vigours had left. This was a job that made me pretty sick, and kept me from thinking on much else. Ben had taken stock the trip before – I knew I could trust Ben – but it was plain somebody had been making free in the meantime. I found I was out by what might easily cover six months' salary and profit, and I could have kicked myself all around the village to have been such a blamed ass, sitting boozing with that Case instead of attending to my own affairs and taking stock.

However, there's no use crying over spilt milk. It was done now, and couldn't be undone. All I could do was to get what was left of it, and my own stuff (my own choice) in order, to go round and get after the rats and cockroaches, and to fix up that store regular Sydney style. A fine show I made of it; and the third morning, when I had lit my pipe and stood in the doorway and looked in, and turned and looked far up the mountain and saw the cocoa-mats waving and posted up the tons of copra, and over the village green and saw the island dandies and reckoned up the yards of print they wanted for their kilts and dresses, I felt as if I was in the right place to make a fortune, and go home again and start a public-house. There was I, sitting in that veranda, in as handsome a piece of scenery as you could find, a splendid sun, and a fine, fresh, healthy trade that stirred up a man's blood like sea-bathing; and the whole thing was clean gone from me, and I was dreaming England, which is, after all, a nasty, cold, muddy hole, with not enough light to see to read by; and dreaming the looks of my public, by a cant of a broad high-road like an avenue and with the sign on a green tree.

So much for the morning, but the day passed and the devil anyone looked near me, and from all I knew of natives in other islands I thought this strange. People laughed a little at our firm and their fine stations, and at this station of Falesá in particular; all the copra in the district wouldn't pay for it (I had heard them say) in fifty years, which I supposed was an exaggeration. But when the day went, and no business came at all, I began to get downhearted; and, about three in the afternoon, I went out for a stroll to cheer me up. On the green I saw a white man coming with a cassock on, by which and by the face of him I knew he was a priest. He was a good-natured old soul to look at, gone a little grizzled, and so dirty you could have written with him on a piece of paper.

'Good-day, sir,' said I.

He answered me eagerly in native.

'Don't you speak any English?' said I.

'French,' says he.

'Well,' said I, 'I'm sorry, but I can't do anything there.'

He tried me a while in the French, and then again in native, which he seemed to think was the best chance. I made out he was after more than passing the time of day with me, but had something to communicate, and I listened the harder. I heard the names of Adams and Case and of Randall – Randall the oftenest – and the word 'poison', or something like it, and a native word that he said very often. I went home, repeating it to myself.

'What does fussy-ocky mean?' I asked of Uma, for that was as near as I could come to it.

'Make dead,' said she.

'The devil it does!' says I. 'Did ever you hear that Case had poisoned Johnny Adams?'

'Every man he savvy that,' says Uma, scornful-like. 'Give him white sand – bad sand. He got the bottle still. Suppose he give you gin, you no take him.'

Now I had heard much the same sort of story in other islands, and the same white powder always to the front, which made me think the less of it. For all that, I went over to Randall's place to see what I could pick up, and found Case on the doorstep, cleaning a gun.

'Good shooting here?' says I.

'A-1,' says he. 'The bush is full of all kinds of birds. I wish copra was as plenty,' says he – I thought, slyly – 'but there don't seem anything doing.'

I could see Black Jake in the store, serving a customer.

'That looks like business, though,' said I.

'That's the first sale we've made in three weeks,' said he.

'You don't tell me?' says I. 'Three weeks? Well, well.'

'If you don't believe me,' he cries, a little hot, 'you can go and look at the copra-house. It's half empty to this blessed hour.'

'I shouldn't be much the better for that, you see,' says I. 'For all I can tell, it might have been whole empty yesterday.'

'That's so,' says he, with a bit of a laugh.

'By the by,' I said, 'what sort of a party is that priest? Seems rather a friendly sort.'

At this Case laughed right out loud. 'Ah!' says he, 'I see what ails you now. Galuchet's been at you.' *Father Galoshes* was the name he went by most, but Case always gave it the French quirk, which was another reason we had for thinking him above the common.

'Yes, I have seen him,' I says. 'I made out he didn't think much of your Captain Randall.'

'That he don't!' says Case. 'It was the trouble about poor Adams. The last day, when he lay dying, there was young Buncombe round. Ever met Buncombe?'

I told him no.

'He's a cure, is Buncombe!' laughs Case. 'Well, Buncombe took it in his head that, as there was no other clergyman about, bar Kanaka pastors, we ought to call in Father Galuchet, and have the old man administered and take the sacrament. It was all the same to me, you may suppose; but I said I thought Adams was the fellow to consult. He was jawing away about watered copra and a sight of foolery. 'Look here,' I said, 'you're pretty sick. Would you like to see Galoshes?' He sat right up on his elbow. 'Get the priest,' says he, 'get the priest; don't let me die here like a dog!' He spoke kind of fierce and eager, but sensible enough. There was nothing to say against that, so we went and asked Galuchet if he would come. You bet he would. He jumped in his dirty linen at the thought of it. But we had reckoned without Papa. He's a hard-shelled Baptist, is Papa; no Papists need apply. And he took and locked the door. Buncombe told him he was bigoted, and I thought he would have had a fit. 'Bigoted!' he says. 'Me bigoted? Have I lived to hear it from a jackanapes like you?' And he made for Buncombe, and I had to hold them apart; and there was Adams in the middle, gone luny again, and carrying on about copra like a born fool. It was good as the play, and I was about knocked out of time with laughing, when all of a sudden Adams sat up, clapped his hands to his chest, and went into the horrors. He died hard, did John Adams,' says Case, with a kind of a sudden sternness.

'And what became of the priest?' I asked.

'The priest?' says Case. 'Oh! he was hammering on the door outside, and crying on the natives to come and beat it in, and singing out it was a soul he wished to save, and that. He was in a rare taking, was the priest. But what would you have? Johnny had slipped his cable; no more Johnny in the market; and the administration racket clean played out. Next thing, word came to Randall that the priest was praying upon Johnny's grave. Papa was pretty full, and got a club, and lit out straight for the place, and there was Galoshes on his knees, and a lot of natives looking on. You wouldn't think Papa cared that much about anything, unless it was liquor; but he and the priest stuck to it two hours, slanging each other in native, and every time Galoshes tried to kneel down Papa went for him with the club. There never were such larks in Falesá. The end of it was that Captain Randall knocked over with some kind of a fit or stroke, and the priest got in his goods after all. But he was the angriest priest you ever heard of, and complained to the chiefs about the outrage, as he called it. There was no account, for our chiefs are Protestant here; and, anyway, he had been making trouble about the drum for morning school, and they were glad to give him a wipe. Now he swears old Randall gave Adams poison or something, and when the two meet they grin at each other like baboons.'

He told this story as natural as could be, and like a man that enjoyed the fun; though now I come to think of it after so long, it seems rather a sickening yarn. However, Case never set up to be soft, only to be square and hearty, and a man all round; and, to tell the truth, he puzzled me entirely.

I went home and asked Uma if she were a Popey, which I made out to be the native word for Catholics.

'*E le ai!*' says she. She always used the native when she meant 'no' more than usually strong, and, indeed, there's more of it. 'No good Popey,' she added.

Then I asked her about Adams and the priest, and she told me much the same yarn in her own way. So that I was left not much farther on, but inclined, upon the whole, to think the bottom of the matter was the row about the sacrament, and the poisoning only talk.

The next day was a Sunday, when there was no business to be looked for. Uma asked me in the morning if I was going to 'pray'; I told her she bet not, and she stopped home herself, with no more words. I thought this seemed unlike a native, and a native woman, and a woman that had new clothes to show off; however, it suited me to the ground, and I made the less of it. The queer thing was that I came next door to going to church after all, a thing I'm little likely to forget. I had turned out for a stroll, and heard the hymn tune up. You know how it is. If you hear folk singing, it seems to draw you; and pretty soon I found myself alongside the church. It was a little, long, low place, coral built, rounded off at both ends like a whale-boat, a big native roof on the top of it, windows without sashes and doorways without doors. I stuck my head into one of the windows, and the sight was so new to me – for things went quite different in the islands I was acquainted with – that I stayed and looked on. The congregation sat on the floor on mats, the women on one side, the men on the other, all rigged out to kill – the women with dresses and trade hats, the men in white jackets and shirts. The hymn was over; the pastor, a big buck Kanaka, was in the pulpit, preaching for his life; and by the way he wagged his hand, and worked his voice, and made his points, and seemed to argue with the folk, I made out he was a gun at the business. Well, he looked up suddenly and caught my eye, and I give you my word he staggered in the pulpit; his eyes bulged out of his head, his hand rose and pointed at me like as if against his will, and the sermon stopped right there.

It isn't a fine thing to say for yourself, but I ran away; and, if the same kind of a shock was given me, I should run away again to-morrow. To see that palavering Kanaka struck all of a heap at the mere sight of me gave me a feeling as if the bottom had dropped out of the world. I went right home, and stayed there, and said nothing. You might think I would tell Uma, but that was against my system. You might have thought I would have gone over and consulted Case; but the truth was I was ashamed to speak of such a thing, I thought everyone would blurt out laughing in my face. So I held my tongue, and thought all the more; and the more I thought, the less I liked the business.

By Monday night I got it clearly in my head I must be tabooed. A new store to stand open two days in a village and not a man or woman come to see the trade, was past believing.

'Uma,' said I, 'I think I'm tabooed.'

'I think so,' said she.

I thought a while whether I should ask her more, but it's a bad idea to set natives up with any notion of consulting them, so I went to Case. It was dark, and he was sitting alone, as he did mostly, smoking on the stairs.

'Case,' said I, 'here's a queer thing. I'm tabooed.'

'Oh, fudge!' says he; ''tain't the practice in these islands.'

'That may be, or it mayn't,' said I. 'It's the practice where I was before. You can bet I know what it's like; and I tell you for a fact, I'm tabooed.'

'Well,' said he, 'what have you been doing?'

'That's what I want to find out,' said I.

'Oh, you can't be,' said he; 'it ain't possible. However, I'll tell you what I'll do. Just to put your mind at rest, I'll go round and find out for sure. Just you waltz in and talk to Papa.'

'Thank you,' I said, 'I'd rather stay right out here on the veranda. Your house is so close.'

'I'll call Papa out here, then,' says he.

'My dear fellow,' I says, 'I wish you wouldn't. The fact is, I don't take to Mr Randall.'

Case laughed, took a lantern from the store, and set out into the village. He was gone perhaps a quarter of an hour, and he looked mighty serious when he came back.

'Well,' said he, clapping down the lantern on the veranda steps, 'I would never have believed it. I don't know where the impudence of these Kanakas 'll go next; they seem to have lost all idea of respect for whites. What we want is a man-of-war – a German, if we could – they know how to manage Kanakas.'

'I *am* tabooed, then?' I cried.

'Something of the sort,' said he. 'It's the worst thing of the kind I've heard of yet. But I'll stand by you, Wiltshire, man to man. You come round here to-morrow about nine, and we'll have it out with the chiefs. They're afraid of me, or they used to be; but their heads are so big by now, I don't know what to think. Understand me, Wiltshire; I don't count this your quarrel,' he went on, with a great deal of resolution, 'I count it all of our quarrel, I count it the White Man's Quarrel, and I'll stand to it through thick and thin, and there's my hand on it.'

'Have you found out what's the reason?' I asked.

'Not yet,' said Case. 'But we'll fire them down to-morrow.'

Altogether I was pretty well pleased with his attitude, and almost more the next day, when we met to go before the chiefs, to see him so stern and resolved. The chiefs awaited us in one of their big oval houses, which was marked out to us from a long way off by the crowd about the eaves, a hundred strong if there was one – men, women, and children. Many of the men were on their way to work and wore green wreaths, and it put me in thoughts of the first of May at home. This crowd opened and buzzed about the pair of us as we went in, with a sudden angry animation. Five chiefs were there; four mighty, stately men, the fifth old and puckered. They sat on mats in their white kilts and jackets; they had fans in their hands, like fine ladies; and two of the younger ones wore Catholic medals, which gave me matter of reflection. Our place was set, and the mats laid for us over against these grandees, on the near side of the house; the midst was empty; the crowd, close at our backs, murmured and craned and jostled to look on, and the shadows of them tossed in front of us on the clean pebbles of the floor. I was just a hair put out by the excitement of the commons, but the quiet, civil appearance of the chiefs reassured me, all the more when their spokesman began and made a long speech in a low tone of voice, sometimes waving his hand toward Case, sometimes towards me, and sometimes knocking with his knuckles on the mat. One thing was clear: there was no sign of anger in the chiefs.

'What's he been saying?' I asked, when he had done.

'Oh, just that they're glad to see you, and they understand by me you wish to make some kind of complaint, and you're to fire away, and they'll do the square thing.'

'It took a precious long time to say that,' said I.

'Oh, the rest was sawder and *bonjour* and that,' said Case.[7] 'You know what Kanakas are.'

'Well, they don't get much *bonjour* out of me,' said I. 'You tell them who I am. I'm a white man, and a British subject, and no end of a big chief at home; and I've come here to do them good, and bring them civilization; and no sooner have I got my trade sorted out than they go and taboo me, and no one dare come near my place! Tell them I don't mean to fly in the face of anything legal; and if what they want's a present, I'll do what's fair. I don't blame any man looking out for himself, tell them, for that's human nature; but if they think they're going to come any of their native ideas over me, they'll find themselves mistaken. And tell them plain that I demand the reason of this treatment as a white man and a British subject.'

That was my speech. I knew how to deal with Kanakas: give them plain sense and fair dealing, and – I'll do them that much justice – they knuckle under every time. They haven't any real government or any real law, that's what you've got to knock into their heads; and even if they had, it would be a good joke if it was to apply to a white man. It would be a strange thing if we came all this way and couldn't do what we pleased. The mere idea has always put my monkey up, and I rapped my speech out pretty big. Then Case translated it – or made believe to, rather – and the first chief replied, and then a second, and a third, all in the same style – easy and genteel, but solemn underneath. Once a question was put to Case, and he answered it, and all hands (both chiefs and commons) laughed out aloud, and looked at me. Last of all, the puckered old fellow and the big young chief that spoke first started in to put Case through a kind of catechism. Sometimes I made out that Case was trying to fence, and they stuck to him like hounds, and the sweat ran down his face, which was no very pleasant sight to me, and at some of his answers the crowd moaned and murmured, which was a worse hearing. It's a cruel shame I knew no native, for (as I now believe) they were asking Case about my marriage, and he must have had a tough job of it to clear his feet. But leave Case alone; he had the brains to run a parliament.

'Well, is that all?' I asked, when a pause came.

'Come along,' says he, mopping his face; 'I'll tell you outside.'

'Do you mean they won't take the taboo off?' I cried.

'It's something queer,' said he. 'I'll tell you outside. Better come away.'

'I won't take it at their hands,' cried I. 'I ain't that kind of a man. You don't find me turn my back on a parcel of Kanakas.'

'You'd better,' said Case.

He looked at me with a signal in his eye; and the five chiefs looked at me civilly enough, but kind of pointed; and the people looked at me and craned and jostled. I remembered the folks that watched my house, and how the pastor had jumped in his pulpit at the bare sight of me; and the whole business seemed so out of the way that I rose and followed Case. The crowd opened again to let us through, but wider than before, the children on the skirts running and singing out, and as we two white men walked away they all stood and watched us.

'And now,' said I, 'what is all this about?'

'The truth is I can't rightly make it out myself. They have a down on you,' says Case.

'Taboo a man because they have a down on him!' I cried. 'I never heard the like.'

'It's worse than that, you see,' said Case. 'You ain't tabooed – I told you that couldn't be. The people won't go near you, Wiltshire, and there's where it is.'

'They won't go near me? What do you mean by that? Why won't they go near me?' I cried.

Case hesitated. 'Seems they're frightened,' says he, in a low voice.

I stopped dead short. 'Frightened?' I repeated. 'Are you gone crazy, Case? What are they frightened of?'

'I wish I could make out,' Case answered, shaking his head. 'Appears like one of their tomfool superstitions. That's what I don't cotton to,' he said. 'It's like the business about Vigours.'

'I'd like to know what you mean by that, and I'll trouble you to tell me,' says I.

'Well, you know, Vigours lit out and left all standing,' said he. 'It was some superstition business – I never got the hang of it; but it began to look bad before the end.'

'I've heard a different story about that,' said I, 'and I had better tell you so. I heard he ran away because of you.'

'Oh! well, I suppose he was ashamed to tell the truth,' says Case; 'I guess he thought it silly. And it's a fact that I packed him off. "What would you do, old man?" says he. "Get," says I, "and not think twice about it." I was the gladdest kind of man to see him clear away. It ain't my notion to turn my back on a mate when he's in a tight place, but there was that much trouble in the village that I couldn't see where it might likely end. I was a fool to be so much about with Vigours. They cast it up to me to-day. Didn't you hear Maea – that's the young chief, the big one – ripping out about "Vika"? That was him they were after. They don't seem to forget it, somehow.'

'This is all very well,' said I, 'but don't tell me what's wrong; it don't tell me what they're afraid of – what their idea is.'

'Well, I wish I knew,' said Case. 'I can't say fairer than that.'

'You might have asked, I think,' says I.

'And so I did,' says he. 'But you must have seen for yourself, unless you're blind, that the asking got the other way. I'll go as far as I dare for another white man; but when I find I'm in the scrape myself, I think first of my own bacon. The loss of me is I'm too good-natured. And I'll take the freedom of telling you you show a queer kind of gratitude to a man who's got into all this mess along of your affairs.'

'There's a thing I'm thinking of,' said I. 'You were a fool to be so much about with Vigours. One comfort, you haven't been much about with me. I notice you've never been inside my house. Own up now; you had word of this before?'

'It's a fact I haven't been,' said he. 'It was an oversight, and I'm sorry for it, Wiltshire. But about coming now, I'll be quite plain.'

'You mean you won't?' I asked.

'Awfully sorry, old man, but that's the size of it,' says Case.

'In short, you're afraid?' says I.

'In short, I'm afraid,' says he.

'And I'm still to be tabooed for nothing?' I asked.

'I tell you you're not tabooed,' said he. 'The Kanakas won't go near you, that's all. And who's to make 'em? We traders have a lot of gall, I must say; we make these poor Kanakas take back their laws, and take up their taboos, and that, whenever it happens to suit us. But you don't mean to say you expect a law obliging people to deal in your store whether they want to or not? You don't mean to tell me you've got the gall for that? And if you had, it would be a queer thing to propose to me. I would just like to point out to you, Wiltshire, that I'm a trader myself.'

'I don't think I would talk of gall if I was you,' said I. 'Here's about what it comes to, as well as I can make out: None of the people are to trade with me, and they're all to trade with you. You're to have the copra, and I'm to go to the devil and shake myself. And I don't know any native, and you're the only man here worth mention that speaks English, and you have the gall to up and hint to me my life's in danger, and all you've got to tell me is you don't know why!'

'Well, it *is* all I have to tell you,' said he. 'I don't know – I wish I did.'

'And so you turn your back and leave me to myself! Is that the position?' says I.

'If you like to put it nasty,' says he. 'I don't put it so. I say merely, "I'm going to keep clear of you; or, if I don't, I'll get in danger for myself." '

'Well,' says I, 'you're a nice kind of a white man!'

'Oh, I understand; you're riled,' said he. 'I would be myself. I can make excuses.'

'All right,' I said, 'go and make excuses somewhere else. Here's my way, there's yours!'

With that we parted, and I went straight home, in a hot temper, and found Una trying on a lot of trade goods like a baby.

'Here,' I said, 'you quit that foolery! Here's a pretty mess to have made, as if I wasn't bothered enough anyway! And I thought I told you to get dinner!'

And then I believe I gave her the rough side of my tongue, as she deserved. She stood up at once, like a sentry to his officer; for I must say she was always well brought up, and had a great respect for whites.

'And now,' says I, 'you belong round here, you're bound to understand that. What am I tabooed for, anyway? Or, if I ain't tabooed, what makes the folks afraid of me?'

She stood and looked at me with eyes like saucers.

'You no savvy?' she gasps at last.

'No,' said I. 'How would you expect me to? We don't have any such craziness where I come from.'

'Ese no tell you?' she asked again.

(*Ese* was the name the natives had for Case; it may mean foreign, or extraordinary; or it might mean a mummy-apple; but most like it was only his own name misheard and put in a Kanaka spelling.)

'Not much,' said I.

'Damn Ese!' she cried.

You might think it funny to hear this Kanaka girl come out with a big swear. No such thing. There was no swearing in her – no, nor anger; she was beyond anger, and meant the word simple and serious. She stood there straight as she said it. I cannot justly say that I ever saw a woman look like that before or after, and it struck me mum. Then she made a kind of an obeisance, but it was the proudest kind, and threw her hands out open.

'I 'shamed,' she said. 'I think you savvy. Ese he tell me you savvy, he tell me you no mind, tell me you love me too much. Taboo belong me,' she said, touching herself on the bosom, as she had done upon our wedding-night. 'Now I go 'way, taboo he go 'way too. Then you get too much copra. You like more better, I think. Tofá, alii,' says she in the native – 'Farewell, chief!'

'Hold on!' I cried. 'Don't be in such a hurry.'

She looked at me sidelong with a smile. 'You see, you get copra,' she said, the same as you might offer candies to a child.

'Uma,' said I, 'hear reason. I didn't know, and that's a fact; and Case seems to have played it pretty mean upon the pair of us. But I do know now, and I don't mind; I love you too much. You no go 'way, you no leave me, I too much sorry.'

'You no love me,' she cried, 'you talk me bad words!' And she threw herself in a corner of the floor, and began to cry.

Well, I'm no scholar, but I wasn't born yesterday, and I thought the worst of that trouble was over. However, there she lay – her back turned, her face to the wall – and shook with sobbing like a little child, so that her feet jumped with it. It's strange how it hits a man when he's in love; for there's no use mincing things; Kanaka and all, I was in love with her, or just as good. I tried to take her hand, but she would have none of that. 'Uma,' I said, 'there's no sense in carrying on like that. I want you to stop here, I want my little wifie, I tell you true.'

'No tell me true,' she sobbed.

'All right,' says I, 'I'll wait till you're through with this.' And I sat right down beside her on the floor, and set to smooth her hair with my hand. At first she wriggled away when I touched her; then she seemed to notice me no more; then her sobs grew gradually less, and presently stopped; and the next thing I knew, she raised her face to mine.

'You tell me true? You like me stop?' she asked.

'Uma,' I said, 'I would rather have you than all the copra in the South Seas,' which was a very big expression, and the strangest thing was that I meant it.

She threw her arms about me, sprang close up, and pressed her face to mine in the island way of kissing, so that I was all wetted with her tears, and my heart went out to her wholly. I never had anything so near me as this little brown bit of a girl. Many things went together, and all helped to turn my head. She was pretty enough to eat; it seemed she was my only friend in that queer place; I was ashamed that I had spoken rough to her: and she was a woman, and my wife, and a kind of a baby besides that I was sorry for; and the salt of her tears was in my mouth. And I forgot Case and the natives; and I forgot that I knew nothing of the story, or only remembered it to banish the remembrance; and I forgot that I was to get no copra, and so could make no livelihood; and I forgot my employers, and the strange kind of service I was doing them, when I preferred my fancy to their business; and I forgot even that Uma was no true wife of mine, but just a maid beguiled, and that in a pretty shabby style. But that is to look too far on. I will come back to that part of it next.

It was late before we thought of getting dinner. The stove was out, and gone stone-cold; but we fired up after a while, and cooked each a dish, helping and hindering each other, and making a play of it like children. I was so greedy of her nearness that I sat down to dinner with my lass upon my knee, made sure of her with one hand, and ate with the other. Ay, and more than that. She was the worst cook I suppose God made; the things she set her hand to, it would have sickened an honest horse to eat of; yet I made my meal that day on Uma's cookery, and can never call to mind to have been better pleased.

I didn't pretend to myself, and I didn't pretend to her. I saw I was clean gone; and if she was to make a fool of me, she must. And I suppose it was this that set her talking, for now she made sure that we were friends. A lot she told me, sitting in my lap and eating my dish, as I ate hers, from foolery – a lot about herself and her mother and Case, all of which would be very tedious, and fill sheets if I set it down in Beach de Mar, but which I must give a hint of in plain English, and one thing about myself, which had a very big effect on my concerns, as you are soon to hear.

It seems she was born in one of the Line Islands;[8] had been only two or three years in these parts, where she had come with a white man, who was married to her mother and then died; and only the one year in Falesá. Before that they had been a good deal on the move, trekking about after the white man, who was one of those rolling stones that keep going round after a soft job. They talk about looking for gold at the end of a rainbow; but if a man wants an employment that'll last him till he dies, let him start out on the soft-job hunt. There's meat and drink in it too, and beer and skittles, for you never hear of them starving, and rarely see them sober; and as for steady sport, cock-fighting isn't in the same county with it. Anyway, this beachcomber carried the woman and her daughter all over the shop, but mostly to out-of-the-way islands, where there were no police, and he thought, perhaps, the soft job hung out. I've my own view of this old party; but I was just as glad he had kept Uma clear of Apia and Papeete and these flash towns.[9] At last he struck Fale-alii on this island, got some trade – the Lord knows how! – muddled it all away in the usual style, and died worth next to nothing, bar a bit of land at Falesá that he had got for a bad debt, which was what put it in the minds of the mother and daughter to come there and live. It seems Case encouraged them all he could, and helped to get their house built. He was very kind those days, and gave Uma trade, and there is no doubt he had his eye on her from the beginning. However, they had scarce settled, when up turned a young man, a native, and wanted to marry her. He was a small chief, and had some fine mats and old songs in his family, and was 'very pretty', Uma said; and, altogether, it was an extraordinary match for a penniless girl and an out-islander.

At the first word of this I got downright sick with jealousy.

'And you mean to say you would have married him?' I cried.

'Ioe, yes,' said she. 'I like too much!'

'Well!' I said. 'And suppose I had come round after?'

'I like you more better now,' said she. 'But suppose I marry Ioane, I one good wife. I no common Kanaka. Good girl!' says she.

Well, I had to be pleased with that; but I promise you I didn't care about the business one little bit. And I liked the end of that yarn no better than the beginning. For it seems this proposal of marriage was the start of all the trouble. It seems, before that, Uma and her mother had been looked down upon, of course, for kinless folk and out-islanders, but nothing to hurt; and, even when Ioane came forward, there was less trouble at first than might have been looked for. And then, all of a sudden, about six months before my coming, Ioane backed out and left that part of the island, and from that day to this Uma and her mother had found themselves alone. None called at their house – none spoke to them on the roads. If they went to church, the other women drew their mats away and left them in a clear place by themselves. It was a regular excommunication, like what you read of in the Middle Ages; and the cause or sense of it beyond guessing. It was some *talo pepelo*, Uma said, some lie, some calumny; and all she knew of it was that the girls who had been jealous of her luck with Ioane used to twit her with his desertion, and cry out, when they met her alone in the woods, that she would never be married. 'They tell me no man he marry me. He too much 'fraid,' she said.

The only soul that came about them after this desertion was Master Case. Even he was chary of showing himself, and turned up mostly by night; and pretty soon he began to table his cards and make up to Uma. I was still sore about Ioane, and when

Case turned up in the same line of business I cut up downright rough.

'Well,' I said, sneering, 'and I suppose you thought Case "very pretty" and "liked too much"?'

'Now you talk silly,' said she. 'White man, he come here, I marry him all-e-same Kanaka; very well! then, he marry all-e-same white woman. Suppose he no marry, he go 'way, woman he stop. All-e-same thief, empty hand, Tonga-heart – no can love! Now you come marry me. You big heart – you no 'shamed island-girl. That thing I love you far too much. I proud.'

I don't know that ever I felt sicker all the days of my life. I laid down my fork, and I put away 'the island-girl'; I didn't seem somehow to have any use for either, and I went and walked up and down in the house, and Uma followed me with her eyes, for she was troubled, and small wonder! But troubled was no word for it with me. I so wanted, and so feared, to make a clean breast of the sweep that I had been.[10]

And just then there came a sound of singing out of the sea; it sprang up suddenly clear and near, as the boat turned the headland, and Uma, running to the window, cried out it was 'Misi' come upon his rounds.

I thought it was a strange thing I should be glad to have a missionary; but, if it was strange, it was still true.

'Uma,' said I, 'you stop here in this room, and don't budge a foot out of it till I come back.'

The Missionary

As I came out on the veranda, the mission-boat was shooting for the mouth of the river. She was a long whale-boat painted white; a bit of an awning astern; a native pastor crouched on the wedge of poop, steering; some four-and-twenty paddles flashing and dipping, true to the boat-song; and the missionary under the awning, in his white clothes, reading in a book; and set him up! It was pretty to see and hear; there's no smarter sight in the islands than a missionary-boat with a good crew and a good pipe to them; and I considered it for half a minute, with a bit of envy perhaps, and then strolled down towards the river.

From the opposite side there was another man aiming for the same place, but he ran and got there first. It was Case; doubtless his idea was to keep me apart from the missionary, who might serve me as interpreter; but my mind was upon other things. I was thinking how he had jockeyed us about the marriage, and tried his hand on Uma before; and at the sight of him rage flew into my nostrils.

'Get out of that, you low, swindling thief!' I cried.

'What's that you say?' says he.

I gave him the word again, and rammed it down with a good oath. 'And if ever I catch you within six fathoms of my house,' I cried, 'I'll clap a bullet in your measly carcass.'

'You must do as you like about your house,' said he, 'where I told you I have no thought of going; but this is a public place.'

'It's a place where I have private business,' said I. 'I have no idea of a hound like you eavesdropping, and I give you notice to clear out.'

'I don't take it, though,' says Case.

'I'll show you, then,' said I.

'We'll have to see about that,' said he.

He was quick with his hands, but he had neither the height

nor the weight, being a flimsy creature alongside a man like me, and, besides, I was blazing to that height of wrath that I could have bit into a chisel. I gave him first the one and then the other, so that I could hear his head rattle and crack, and he went down straight.

'Have you had enough?' cries I. But he only looked up white and blank, and the blood spread upon his face like wine upon a napkin. 'Have you had enough?' I cried again. 'Speak up, and don't lie malingering there, or I'll take my feet to you.'

He sat up at that, and held his head – by the look of him you could see it was spinning – and the blood poured on his pyjamas.

'I've had enough for this time,' says he, and he got up staggering, and went off by the way that he had come.

The boat was close in; I saw the missionary had laid his book to one side, and I smiled to myself. 'He'll know I'm a man, anyway,' thinks I.

This was the first time, in all my years in the Pacific, I had ever exchanged two words with any missionary, let alone asked one for a favour. I didn't like the lot, no trader does; they look down upon us, and make no concealment; and, besides, they're partly Kanakaized, and suck up with natives instead of with other white men like themselves. I had on a rig of clean, striped pyjamas – for, of course, I had dressed decent to go before the chiefs; but when I saw the missionary step out of this boat in the regular uniform, white duck clothes, pith helmet, white shirt and tie, and yellow boots to his feet, I could have bunged stones at him. As he came nearer, queering me pretty curious (because of the fight, I suppose), I saw he looked mortal sick, for the truth was he had a fever on, and had just had a chill in the boat.

'Mr Tarleton, I believe?' says I, for I had got his name.

'And you, I suppose, are the new trader?' says he.

'I want to tell you first that I don't hold with missions,' I went on, 'and that I think you and the likes of you do a sight of harm, filling up the natives with old wives' tales and bumptiousness.'

'You are perfectly entitled to your opinions,' says he, looking a bit ugly, 'but I have no call to hear them.'

'It so happens that you've got to hear them,' I said. 'I'm no missionary, nor missionary lover; I'm no Kanaka, nor favourer of Kanakas – I'm just a trader; I'm just a common, low God-damned white man and British subject, the sort you would like to wipe your boots on. I hope that's plain!'

'Yes, my man,' said he. 'It's more plain than creditable. When you are sober, you'll be sorry for this.'

He tried to pass on, but I stopped him with my hand. The Kanakas were beginning to growl. Guess they didn't like my tone, for I spoke to that man as free as I would to you.

'Now, you can't say I've deceived you,' said I, 'and I can go on. I want a service – I want two services, in fact; and, if you care to give me them, I'll perhaps take more stock in what you call your Christianity.'

He was silent for a moment. Then he smiled. 'You are rather a strange sort of man,' says he.

'I'm the sort of man God made me,' says I. 'I don't set up to be a gentleman,' I said.

'I am not quite so sure,' said he. 'And what can I do for you, Mr ——?'

'Wiltshire,' I says, 'though I'm mostly called Welsher; but Wiltshire is the way it's spelt, if the people on the beach could only get their tongues about it. And what do I want? Well, I'll tell you the first thing. I'm what you call a sinner – what I call a sweep – and I want you to help me make it up to a person I've deceived.'

He turned and spoke to his crew in the native. 'And now I am at your service,' said he, 'but only for the time my crew are dining. I must be much farther down the coast before night. I was delayed at Papa-malulu till this morning, and I have an engagement in Fale-alii to-morrow night.'

I led the way to my house in silence, and rather pleased with myself for the way I had managed the talk, for I like a man to keep his self-respect.

'I was sorry to see you fighting,' says he.

'Oh, that's part of the yarn I want to tell you,' I said. 'That's service number two. After you've heard it you'll let me know whether you're sorry or not.'

We walked right in through the store, and I was surprised to find Uma had cleared away the dinner things. This was so unlike her ways that I saw she had done it out of gratitude, and liked her the better. She and Mr Tarleton called each other by name, and he was very civil to her seemingly. But I thought little of that; they can always find civility for a Kanaka, it's us white men they lord it over. Besides, I didn't want much Tarleton just then. I was going to do my pitch.

'Uma,' said I, 'give us your marriage certificate.' She looked put out. 'Come,' said I, 'you can trust me. Hand it up.'

She had it about her person, as usual; I believe she thought it was a pass to heaven, and if she had died without having it handy she would go to hell. I couldn't see where she put it the first time, I couldn't see now where she took it from; it seemed to jump into her hand like that Blavatsky business in the papers.[11] But it's the same way with all island women, and I guess they're taught it when young.

'Now,' said I, with the certificate in my hand, 'I was married to this girl by Black Jack, the Negro. The certificate was wrote by Case, and it's a dandy piece of literature, I promise you. Since then I've found that there's a kind of cry in the place against this wife of mine, and so long as I keep her I cannot trade. Now, what would any man do in my place, if he was a man?' I said. 'The first thing he would do is this, I guess.' And I took and tore up the certificate and bunged the pieces on the floor.

'Aue!'* cried Uma, and began to clap her hands; but I caught one of them in mine.

'And the second thing that he would do,' said I, 'if he was what I would call a man and you would call a man, Mr Tarleton, is to bring the girl right before you or any other missionary, and to up and say: "I was wrong married to this wife of mine, but I think a heap of her, and now I want to be married to her right." Fire away, Mr Tarleton. And I guess you'd better do it in native; it'll please the old lady,' I said, giving her the proper name of a man's wife upon the spot.

So we had in two of the crew for to witness, and were spliced in our own house; and the parson prayed a good bit, I must say

*Alas!

– but not so long as some – and shook hands with the pair of us.

'Mr Wiltshire,' he says, when he had made out the lines and packed off the witnesses, 'I have to thank you for a very lively pleasure. I have rarely performed the marriage ceremony with more grateful emotions.'

That was what you would call talking. He was going on, besides, with more of it, and I was ready for as much taffy as he had in stock, for I felt good. But Uma had been taken up with something half through the marriage, and cut straight in.

'How your hand he get hurt?' she asked.

'You ask Case's head, old lady,' says I.

She jumped with joy, and sang out.

'You haven't made much of a Christian of this one,' says I to Mr Tarleton.

'We didn't think her one of our worst,' says he, 'when she was at Fale-alii; and if Uma bears malice I shall be tempted to fancy she has good cause.'

'Well, there we are at service number two,' said I. 'I want to tell you our yarn, and see if you can let a little daylight in.'

'Is it long?' he asked.

'Yes,' I cried; 'it's a goodish bit of a yarn!'

'Well, I'll give you all the time I can spare,' says he, looking at his watch. 'But I must tell you fairly, I haven't eaten since five this morning, and, unless you can let me have something, I am not likely to eat again before seven or eight to-night.'

'By God, we'll give you dinner!' I cried.

I was a little caught up at my swearing, just when all was going straight; and so was the missionary, I suppose, but he made believe to look out of the window, and thanked us.

So we ran him up a bit of a meal. I was bound to let the old lady have a hand in it, to show off, so I deputized her to brew the tea. I don't think I ever met such tea as she turned out. But that was not the worst, for she got round with the salt-box, which she considered an extra European touch, and turned my stew into sea-water. Altogether, Mr Tarleton had a devil of a dinner of it; but he had plenty of entertainment by the way, for all the while that we were cooking, and afterward, when he was making believe to eat, I kept posting him up on Master Case and the beach of Falesá, and he putting questions that showed he was following close.

'Well,' said he at last, 'I am afraid you have a dangerous enemy. This man Case is very clever and seems really wicked. I must tell you I have had my eye on him for nearly a year, and have rather had the worst of our encounters. About the time when the last representative of your firm ran so suddenly away, I had a letter from Namu, the native pastor, begging me to come to Falesá at my earliest convenience, as his flock were all "adopting Catholic practices". I had great confidence in Namu; I fear it only shows how easily we are deceived. No one could hear him preach and not be persuaded he was a man of extraordinary parts. All our islanders easily acquire a kind of eloquence, and can roll out and illustrate, with a great deal of vigour and fancy, second-hand sermons; but Namu's sermons are his own, and I cannot deny that I have found them means of grace. Moreover, he has a keen curiosity in secular things, does not fear work, is clever at carpentering, and has made himself so much respected among the neighbouring pastors that we call him, in a jest which is half serious, the Bishop of the East. In short, I was proud of the man; all the more puzzled by his letter, and took an occasion to come this way. The morning before my arrival, Vigours had been sent on board the *Lion*, and Namu was perfectly at his ease, apparently ashamed of his letter, and quite unwilling to explain it. This, of course, I could not allow, and he ended by confessing that he had been much concerned to find his people using the sign of the cross, but since he had learned the explanation his mind was satisfied. For Vigours had the Evil Eye, a common thing in a country of Europe called Italy, where men were often struck dead by that kind of devil, and it appeared the sign of the cross was a charm against its power.

'"And I explain it, Misi," said Namu, "in this way: the country in Europe is a Popey country, and the devil of the Evil Eye may be a Catholic devil, or, at least, used to Catholic ways. So then I reasoned thus: if this sign of the cross were used in a Popey manner it would be sinful, but when it is used only to protect men from a devil, which is a thing harmless in itself, the sign too must be harmless. For the sign is neither good nor bad, even as a bottle is neither good nor bad. But if the bottle be full of gin, the gin is bad; and if the sign made in idolatry be bad, so is the idolatry." And, very like a native pastor, he had a text apposite about the casting out of devils.

'"And who has been telling you about the Evil Eye?" I asked.

'He admitted it was Case. Now, I am afraid you will think me very narrow, Mr Wiltshire, but I must tell you I was displeased, and cannot think a trader at all a good man to advise or have an influence upon my pastors. And, besides, there had been some flying talk in the country of old Adams and his being poisoned, to which I had paid no great heed; but it came back to me at this moment.

'"And is this Case a man of sanctified life?" I asked.

'He admitted he was not; for, though he did not drink, he was profligate with women, and had no religion.

'"Then," said I, "I think the less you have to do with him the better."

'But it is not easy to have the last word with a man like Namu. He was ready in a moment with an illustration. "Misi," said he, "you have told me there were wise men, not pastors, not even holy, who knew many things useful to be taught – about trees, for instance, and beasts, and to print books, and about the stones that are burned to make knives of. Such men teach you in your college, and you learn from them, but take care not to learn to be unholy. Misi, Case is my college."

'I knew not what to say. Mr Vigours had evidently been driven out of Falesá by the machinations of Case and with something not very unlike the collusion of my pastor. I called to mind it was Namu who had reassured me about Adams and traced the rumour to the ill-will of the priest. And I saw I must inform myself more thoroughly from an impartial source. There is an old rascal of a chief here, Faiaso, whom I dare say you saw to-day at the council; he has been all his life turbulent and sly, a great fomenter of rebellions, and a thorn in the side of the mission and the island. For all that he is very shrewd, and, except in politics or about his own misdemeanours, a teller of the truth. I went to his house, told him what I had heard, and besought him to be frank. I do not think I had ever a more painful interview. Perhaps you will understand me, Mr Wiltshire, if I tell you that I am perfectly serious in these old wives' tales with which you reproached me, and as anxious to do well for these islands as you can be to please and to protect your pretty wife. And you are to remember that I thought Namu a paragon, and was proud of the man as one of the first ripe fruits of the mission. And now I was informed that he had fallen in a sort of dependence upon Case. The beginning of it was not corrupt; it began, doubtless, in fear and respect, produced by trickery and pretence; but I was shocked to find that another element had been lately added, that Namu helped himself in the store, and was believed to be deep in Case's debt. Whatever the trader said, that Namu believed with trembling. He was not alone in this; many in the village lived in a similar subjection; but Namu's case was the most influential, it was through Namu that Case had wrought most evil; and with a certain following among the chiefs, and the pastor in his pocket, the man was as good as master of the village. You know something of Vigours and Adams, but perhaps you have never heard of old Underhill, Adams's predecessor. He was a quiet, mild old fellow, I remember, and we were told he had died suddenly: white men die very suddenly in Falesá. The truth, as I now heard it, made my blood run cold. It seems he was struck with a general palsy, all of him dead but one eye, which he continually winked. Word was started that the helpless old man was now a devil, and this vile fellow Case worked upon the natives' fears, which he professed to share, and pretended he durst not go into the house alone. At last a grave was dug, and the living body buried at the far end of the village. Namu, my pastor, whom I helped to educate, offered up a prayer at the hateful scene.

'I felt myself in a very difficult position. Perhaps it was my duty to have denounced Namu and had him deposed. Perhaps I think so now, but at the time it seemed less clear. He had a great influence, it might prove greater than mine. The natives are prone to superstition; perhaps by stirring them up I might but ingrain and spread these dangerous fancies. And Namu besides, apart from this novel and accursed influence, was a good pastor, an able man, and spiritually minded. Where should I look for a better? How was I to find as good? At that moment, with Namu's failure fresh in my view, the work of my life appeared a mockery; hope was dead in me. I would rather repair such tools as I had than go abroad in quest of others that must certainly prove worse; and a scandal is, at the best, a thing to be avoided when humanly possible. Right or wrong, then, I determined on a quiet course. All that night I denounced and reasoned with the erring pastor, twitting him with his ignorance and want of faith, twitted him with his wretched attitude, making clean the outside of the cup and platter, callously helping at a murder, childishly flying in excitement about a few childish, unnecessary, and inconvenient gestures; and long before day I had him on his knees and bathed in tears of what seemed a genuine repentance. On Sunday I took the pulpit in the morning, and preached from First Kings, nineteenth, on the fire, the earthquake, and the voice, distinguishing the true spiritual power, and referring with such plainness as I dared to recent events in Falesá. The effect produced was great, and it was much increased when Namu rose in his turn and confessed that he had been wanting in faith and conduct, and was convinced of sin. So far, then, all was well; but there was one unfortunate circumstance. It was nearing the time of our "May" in the island, when the native contributions to the missions are received; it fell in my duty to make a notification on the subject, and this gave my enemy his chance, by which he was not slow to profit.

'News of the whole proceedings must have been carried to Case as soon as church was over, and the same afternoon he made an occasion to meet me in the midst of the village. He came up with so much intentness and animosity that I felt it would be damaging to avoid him.

' "So," says he, in native, "here is the holy man. He has been preaching against me, but that was not in his heart. He has been preaching upon the love of God; but that was not in his heart, it was between his teeth. Will you know what was in his heart?" cries he. "I will show it to you!" And, making a snatch at my hand, he made believe to pluck out a dollar, and held it in the air.

'There went that rumour through the crowd with which Polynesians receive a prodigy. As for myself, I stood amazed. The thing was a common conjuring trick, which I have seen performed at home a score of times; but how was I to convince the villagers of that? I wished I had learned legerdemain instead of Hebrew, that I might have paid the fellow out with his own coin. But there I was; I could not stand there silent, and the best I could find to say was weak.

'"I will trouble you not to lay hands on me again," said I.

'"I have no such thought," said he, "nor will I deprive you of your dollar. Here it is," he said, and flung it at my feet. I am told it lay where it fell three days.'

'I must say it was well played,' said I.

'Oh! he is clever,' said Mr Tarleton, 'and you can now see for yourself how dangerous. He was a party to the horrid death of the paralytic; he is accused of poisoning Adams; he drove Vigours out of the place by lies that might have led to murder; and there is no question but he has now made up his mind to rid himself of you. How he means to try we have no guess; only be sure, it's something new. There is no end to his readiness and invention.'

'He gives himself a sight of trouble,' says I. 'And after all, what for?'

'Why, how many tons of copra may they make in this district?' asked the missionary.

'I dare say as much as sixty tons,' says I.

'And what is the profit to the local trader?' he asked.

'You may call it three pounds,' said I.

'Then you can reckon for yourself how much he does it for,' said Mr Tarleton. 'But the more important thing is to defeat him. It is clear he spread some report against Uma, in order to isolate and have his wicked will of her. Failing of that, and seeing a new rival come upon the scene, he used her in a different way. Now, the first point to find out is about Namu. Uma, when people began to leave you and your mother alone, what did Namu do?'

'Stop away all-e-same,' says Uma.

'I fear the dog has returned to his vomit,' said Mr Tarleton.

'And now what am I to do for you? I will speak to Namu, I will warn him he is observed; it will be strange if he allow anything to go on amiss when he is put upon his guard. At the same time, this precaution may fail, and then you must turn elsewhere. You have two people at hand to whom you might apply. There is, first of all, the priest, who might protect you by the Catholic interest; they are a wretchedly small body, but they count two chiefs. And then there is old Faiaso. Ah! if it had been some years ago you would have needed no one else; but his influence is much reduced, it has gone into Maea's hands, and Maea, I fear, is one of Case's jackals. In fine, if the worst comes to the worst, you must send up or come yourself to Fale-alii, and, though I am not due at this end of the island for a month, I will just see what can be done.'

So Mr Tarleton said farewell; and half an hour later the crew were singing and the paddles flashing in the missionary-boat.

Devil-work

NEAR a month went by without much doing. The same night of our marriage Galoshes called round, and made himself mighty civil, and got into the habit of dropping in about dark and smoking his pipe with the family. He could talk to Uma, of course, and started to teach me native and French at the same time. He was a kind old buffer, though the dirtiest you would wish to see, and he muddled me up with foreign languages worse than the Tower of Babel.

That was one employment we had, and it made me feel less lonesome; but there was no profit in the thing, for though the priest came and sat and yarned, none of his folks could be enticed into my store, and if it hadn't been for the other occupation I struck out, there wouldn't have been a pound of copra in the house. This was the idea: Faavao (Uma's mother) had a score of bearing-trees. Cf course we could get no labour, being all as good as tabooed, and the two women and I turned to and made copra with our own hands. It was copra to make your mouth water when it was done – I never understood how much the natives cheated me till I had made that four hundred pounds of my own hand – and it weighed so light I felt inclined to take and water it myself.

When we were at the job a good many Kanakas used to put in the best of the day looking on, and once that nigger turned up. He stood back with the natives and laughed and did the big don and the funny dog, till I began to get riled.

'Here, you nigger!' says I.

'I don't address myself to you, Sah,' says the nigger. 'Only speak to gen'le'um.'

'I know,' says I, 'but it happens I was addressing myself to you Mr Black Jack. And all I want to know is just this: did you see Case's figure-head about a week ago?'

'No, Sah,' says he.

'That's all right, then,' says I; 'for I'll show you the own brother to it, only black, in the inside of about two minutes.'

And I began to walk toward him, quite slow, and my hands down; only there was trouble in my eye, if anybody took the pains to look.

'You're a low, obstropulous fellow, Sah,' says he.

'You bet!' says I.

By that time he thought I was about as near as convenient, and lit out so it would have done your heart good to see him travel. And that was all I saw of that precious gang until what I am about to tell you.

It was one of my chief employments these days to go pot-hunting in the woods, which I found (as Case had told me) very rich in game. I have spoken of the cape which shut up the village and my station from the east. A path went about the end of it, and led into the next bay. A strong wind blew here daily, and as the line of the barrier reef stopped at the end of the cape, a heavy surf ran on the shores of the bay. A little cliffy hill cut the valley in two parts, and stood close on the beach; and at high water the sea broke right on the face of it, so that all passage was stopped. Woody mountains hemmed the place all round; the barrier to the east was particularly steep and leafy, the lower parts of it, along the sea, falling in sheer black cliffs streaked with cinnabar; the upper part lumpy with the tops of the great trees. Some of the trees were bright green, and some red, and the sand of the beach as black as your shoes. Many birds hovered round the bay, some of them snow-white; and the flying-fox (or vampire) flew there in broad daylight, gnashing its teeth.

For a long while I came as far as this shooting, and went no farther. There was no sign of any path beyond, and the cocoa-palms in the front of the foot of the valley were the last this way. For the whole 'eye' of the island, as natives call the windward end, lay desert. From Falesá round about to Papa-malulu, there was neither house, nor man, nor planted fruit-tree; and the reef being mostly absent, and the shores bluff, the sea beat direct among crags, and there was scarce a landing-place.

I should tell you that after I began to go in the woods, although no one appeared to come near my store, I found people willing enough to pass the time of day with me where nobody could see them; and as I had begun to pick up native, and most of them had a word or two of English, I began to hold little odds and ends of conversation, not to much purpose, to be sure, but they took off the worst of the feeling, for it's a miserable thing to be made a leper of.

It chanced one day, toward the end of the month, that I was sitting in this bay in the edge of the bush, looking east, with a Kanaka. I had given him a fill of tobacco, and we were making out to talk as best we could; indeed, he had more English than most.

I asked him if there was a road going eastward.

'One time one road,' said he. 'Now he dead.'

'Nobody he go there?' I asked.

'No good,' said he. 'Too much devil he stop there.'

'Oho!' says I, 'got-um plenty devil, that bush?'

'Man devil, woman devil; too much devil,' said my friend. 'Stop there all-e-time. Man he go there, no come back.'

I thought if this fellow was so well posted on devils and spoke of them so free, which is not common, I had better fish for a little information about myself and Uma.

'You think me one devil?' I asked.

'No think devil,' said he, soothingly. 'Thing all-e-same fool.'

'Uma, she devil?' I asked again.

'No, no; no devil. Devil stop bush,' said the young man.

I was looking in front of me across the bay, and I saw the hanging front of the woods pushed suddenly open, and Case, with a gun in his hand, step forth into the sunshine on the black beach. He was got up in light pyjamas, near white, his gun sparkled, he looked mighty conspicuous; and the land-crabs scuttled from all round him to their holes.

'Hullo, my friend!' says I, 'you no talk all-e-same true. Ese he go, he come back.'

'Ese no all-e-same; Ese *Tiapolo*,' says my friend; and, with a 'Good-bye,' slunk off among the trees.

I watched Case all around the beach, where the tide was low;

and let him pass me on the homeward way to Falesá. He was in deep thought, and the birds seemed to know it, trotting quite near him on the sand, or wheeling and calling in his ears. When he passed me I could see by the working of his lips that he was talking to himself, and what pleased me mightily, he had still my trade-mark on his brow. I tell you the plain truth: I had a mind to give him a gunful in his ugly mug, but I thought better of it.

All this time, and all the time I was following home, I kept repeating that native word, which I remembered by 'Polly, put the kettle on and make us all some tea,' tea-a-pollo.

'Uma,' says I, when I got back, 'what does *Tiapolo* mean?'

'Devil,' says she.

'I thought *aitu* was the word for that,' I said.

'*Aitu* 'nother kind of devil,' said she; 'stop bush, eat Kanaka. Tiapolo big chief devil, stop home; all-e-same Christian devil.'

'Well, then,' said I, 'I'm no further forward. How can Case be Tiapolo?'

'No all-e-same,' said she. 'Ese belong Tiapolo. Tiapolo too much like; Ese all-e-same his son. Suppose Ese he wish something, Tiapolo he make him.'

'That's mighty convenient for Ese,' says I. 'And what kind of things does he make for him?'

Well, out came a rigmarole for all sorts of stories, many of which (like the dollar he took from Mr Tarleton's head) were plain enough to me, but others I could make nothing of; and the thing that most surprised the Kanakas was what surprised me least – namely, that he would go in the desert among all the *aitus*. Some of the boldest, however, had accompanied him, and had heard him speak with the dead and give them orders, and, safe in his protection, had returned unscathed. Some said he had a church there, where he worshipped Tiapolo, and Tiapolo appeared to him; others swore that there was no sorcery at all, that he performed his miracles by the power of prayer, and the church was no church, but a prison, in which he had confined a dangerous *aitu*. Namu had been in the bush with him once, and returned glorifying God for these wonders. Altogether, I began to have a glimmer of the man's position, and the means by which he had acquired it, and though I saw he was a tough nut to crack, I was noways cast down.

'Very well,' said I, 'I'll have a look at Master Case's place of worship myself, and we'll see about the glorifying.'

At this Uma fell in a terrible taking; if I went in the high bush I should never return; none could go there but by the protection of Tiapolo.

'I'll chance it on God's,' said I. 'I'm a good sort of a fellow, Uma, as fellows go, and I guess God'll con me through.'

She was silent for a while. 'I think,' said she, mighty solemn – and then, presently – 'Victoreea, he big chief?'

'You bet!' said I.

'He like you too much?' she asked again.

I told her, with a grin, I believed the old lady was rather partial to me.

'All right,' said she. 'Victoreea he big chief, like you too much. No can help you here in Falesá; no can do – too far off. Maea he be small chief – stop here. Suppose he like you – make you all right. All-e-same God and Tiapolo. God he big chief – got too much work. Tiapolo he small chief – he like too much make-see, work very hard.'

'I'll have to hand you over to Mr Tarleton,' said I. 'Your theology's out of its bearings, Uma.'

However, we stuck to this business all the evening, and, with the stories she told me of the desert and its dangers, she came near frightening herself into a fit. I don't remember half a quarter of them, of course, for I paid little heed; but two came back to me kind of clear.

About six miles up the coast there is a sheltered cove they call *Fanga-anaana* – 'the haven full of caves'. I've seen it from the sea myself, as near as I could get my boys to venture in; and it's a little strip of yellow sand, black cliffs overhang it, full of the black mouths of caves; great trees overhang the cliffs, and dangle-down lianas; and in one place, about the middle, a big brook pours over in a cascade. Well, there was a boat going by here, with six young men of Falesá, 'all very pretty,' Uma said, which was the loss of them. It blew strong, there was a heavy head sea, and by the time they opened Fanga-anaana, and saw the white cascade and the shady beach, they were all tired and thirsty, and their water had run out. One proposed to land and get a drink, and, being reckless fellows, they were all of the same mind except the youngest. Lotu was his name; he was a very good young gentleman, and very wise; and he held out that they were crazy, telling them the place was given over to spirits and devils and the dead, and there were no living folk nearer than six miles the one way, and maybe twelve the other. But they laughed at his words, and, being five to one, pulled in, beached the boat, and landed. It was a wonderful pleasant place, Lotu said, and the water excellent. They walked round the beach, but could see nowhere any way to mount the cliffs, which made them easier in their mind; and at last they sat down to make a meal on the food they had brought with them. They were scarce set, when there came out of the mouth of one of the black caves six of the most beautiful ladies ever seen; they had flowers in their hair, and the most beautiful breasts, and necklaces of scarlet seeds; and began to jest with these young gentlemen, and the young gentlemen to jest back with them, all but Lotu. As for Lotu, he saw there could be no living woman in such a place, and ran, and flung himself in the bottom of the boat, covered his face, and prayed. All the time the business lasted Lotu made one clean break of prayer, and that was all he knew of it, until his friends came back, and made him sit up, and they put to sea again out of the bay, which was now quite desert, and no word of the six ladies. But, what frightened Lotu most, not one of the five remembered anything of what had passed, but they were all like drunken men, and sang and laughed in the boat, and skylarked. The wind freshened and came squally, and the sea rose extraordinary high; it was such weather as any man in the islands would have turned his back to and fled home to Falesá; but these five were like crazy folk, and cracked on all sail and drove their boat into the seas. Lotu went to the bailing; none of the others thought to help him, but sang and skylarked and carried on, and spoke singular things beyond a man's comprehension, and laughed out loud when they said them. So the rest of the day Lotu bailed for his life in the bottom of the boat, and was all drenched with sweat and cold sea-water; and none heeded him. Against all expectation, they came safe in a dreadful tempest to Papa-malulu, where the palms were singing out, and the cocoanuts flying like cannon-balls about the village green; and the same night the five young gentlemen sickened, and spoke never a reasonable word until they died.

'And do you mean to tell me you can swallow a yarn like that?' I asked.

She told me the thing was well known, and with handsome young men alone it was even common; but this was the only case where five had been slain the same day and in a company by the love of the woman-devils; and it had made a great stir in the island, and she would be crazy if she doubted.

'Well, anyway,' says I, 'you needn't be frightened about me. I've no use for the women-devils. You're all the women I want, and all the devil too, old lady.'

To this she answered there were other sorts, and she had seen one with her own eyes. She had gone one day alone to the next bay, and, perhaps, got too near the margin of the bad place. The boughs of the high bush overshadowed her from the cant of the hill, but she herself was outside on a flat place, very stony and growing full of young mummy-apples four and five feet high. It was a dark day in the rainy season, and now there came squalls that tore off the leaves and sent them flying, and now it was all still as in a house. It was in one of these still times that a whole gang of birds and flying-foxes came pegging out of the bush like creatures frightened. Presently after she heard a rustle nearer hand, and saw, coming out of the margin of the trees, among the mummy-apples, the appearance of a lean grey old boar. It seemed to think as it came, like a person; and all of a sudden, as she looked at it coming, she was aware it was no boar, but a thing that was a man with a man's thoughts. At that she ran, and the pig after her, and as the pig ran it holla'd aloud, so that the place rang with it.

'I wish I had been there with my gun,' said I. 'I guess that pig would have holla'd so as to surprise himself.'

But she told me a gun was of no use with the like of these, which were the spirits of the dead.

Well, this kind of talk put in the evening, which was the best of it; but of course it didn't change my notion, and the next day, with my gun and a good knife, I set off upon a voyage of discovery. I made, as near as I could, for the place where I had seen Case come out; for if it was true he had some kind of establishment in the bush I reckoned I should find a path. The beginning of the desert was marked off by a wall, to call it so, for it was more of a long mound of stones. They say it reaches right across the island, but how they know it is another question, for I doubt if any one has made the journey in a hundred years, the natives sticking chiefly to the sea and their little colonies along the coast, and that part being mortal high and steep and full of cliffs. Up to the west side of the wall the ground has been cleared, and there are cocoa-palms and mummy-apples and guavas, and lots of sensitive.[12] Just across, the bush begins outright; high bush at that, trees going up like the masts of ships, and ropes of liana hanging down like a ship's rigging, and nasty orchids growing in the forks like funguses. The ground where there was no underwood looked to be a heap of boulders. I saw many green pigeons which I might have shot, only I was there with a different idea. A number of butterflies flopped up and down along the ground like dead leaves; sometimes I would hear a bird calling, sometimes the wind overhead, and always the sea along the coast.

But the queerness of the place it's more difficult to tell of, unless to one who has been alone in the high bush himself. The brightest kind of a day it is always dim down there. A man can see to the end of nothing; whichever way he looks the wood shuts up, one bough folding with another like the fingers of your hand; and whenever he listens he hears always something new – men talking, children laughing, the strokes of an axe a far way ahead of him, and sometimes a sort of a quick, stealthy scurry near at hand that makes him jump and look to his weapons. It's all very well for him to tell himself that he's alone, bar trees and birds; he can't make out to believe it; whichever way he turns the whole place seems to be alive and looking on. Don't think it was Uma's yarns that put me out; I don't value native talk a fourpenny-piece; it's a thing that's natural in the bush, and that's the end of it.

As I got near the top of the hill, for the ground of the wood goes up in this place steep as a ladder, the wind began to sound straight on, and the leaves to toss and switch open and let in the sun. This suited me better; it was the same noise all the time, and nothing to startle. Well, I had got to a place where there was an underwood of what they call wild cocoanut – mighty pretty with its scarlet fruit – when there came the sound of singing in the wind that I thought I had never heard the like of. It was all very fine to tell myself it was the branches; I knew better. It was all very fine to tell myself it was a bird; I knew never a bird that sang like that. It rose and swelled, and died away and swelled again; and now I thought it was like someone weeping, only prettier; and now I thought it was like harps; and there was one thing I made sure of, it was a sight too sweet to be wholesome in a place like that. You may laugh if you like; but I declare I called to mind the six young ladies that came, with their scarlet necklaces, out of the cave at Fanga-anaana, and wondered if they sang like that. We laugh at the natives and their superstitions; but see how many traders take them up, splendidly educated white men, that have been book-keepers (some of them) and clerks in the old country. It's my belief a superstition grows up in a place like the different kinds of weeds; and as I stood there and listened to that wailing I twittered in my shoes.

You may call me a coward to be frightened; I thought myself brave enough to go on ahead. But I went mighty carefully, with my gun cocked, spying all about me like a hunter, fully expecting to see a handsome young woman sitting somewhere in the bush, and fully determined (if I did) to try her with a charge of duck-shot. And sure enough, I had not gone far when I met with a queer thing. The wind came on the top of the wood in a strong puff, the leaves in front of me burst open, and I saw for a second something hanging in a tree. It was gone in a wink, the puff blowing by and the leaves closing. I tell you the truth: I had made up my mind to see an *aitu*; and if the thing had looked like a pig or a woman, it wouldn't have given me the same turn. The trouble was that it seemed kind of square, and the idea of a square thing that was alive and sang knocked me sick and silly. I must have stood quite a while; and I made pretty certain it was right out of the same tree that the singing came. Then I began to come to myself a bit.

'Well,' says I, 'if this is really so, if this is a place where there are square things that sing, I'm gone up anyway. Let's have my fun for my money.'

But I thought I might as well take the off-chance of a prayer being any good; so I plumped on my knees and prayed out loud; and all the time I was praying the strange sounds came out of the tree, and went up and down, and changed, for all the world like music, only you could see it wasn't human – there was nothing there that you could whistle.

As soon as I had made an end in proper style, I laid down my gun, stuck my knife between my teeth, walked right up to that tree and began to climb. I tell you my heart was like ice. But presently, as I went up, I caught another glimpse of the thing, and that relieved me, for I thought it seemed like a box; and when I got right up to it I near fell out of the tree with laughing.

A box it was, sure enough, and a candle-box at that, with the brand upon the side of it; and it had banjo-strings stretched so as to sound when the wind blew. I believe they call the thing a Tyrolean * harp, whatever that may mean.

'Well, Mr Case,' said I, 'you frightened me once, but I defy you to frighten me again,' I says, and slipped down the tree, and set out again to find my enemy's head office, which I guessed would not be far away.

The undergrowth was thick in this part; I couldn't see before my nose, and must burst my way through by main force and ply the knife as I went, slicing the cords of the lianas and slashing down whole trees at a blow. I call them trees for the bigness, but in truth they were just big weeds, and sappy to cut through like carrot. From all this crowd and kind of vegetation, I was just thinking to myself, the place might have

*Eolian.

once been cleared, when I came on my nose over a pile of stones, and saw in a moment it was some kind of a work of man. The Lord knows when it was made or when deserted, for this part of the island has lain undisturbed since long before the whites came. A few steps beyond I hit into the path I had been always looking for. It was narrow, but well beaten, and I saw that Case had plenty of disciples. It seems, indeed it was, a piece of fashionable boldness to venture up here with the trader, and a young man scarce reckoned himself grown till he had got his breech tattooed, for one thing, and seen Case's devils for another. This is mighty like Kanakas: but, if you look at it another way, it's mighty like white folks too.

A bit along the path I was brought to a clear stand, and had to rub my eyes. There was a wall in front of me, the path passing it by a gap; it was tumbledown and plainly very old, but built of big stones very well laid; and there is no native alive to-day upon that island that could dream of such a piece of building! Along all the top of it was a line of queer figures, idols or scarecrows, or what not. They had carved and painted faces ugly to view, their eyes and teeth were of shell, their hair and their bright clothes blew in the wind, and some of them worked with the tugging. There are islands up west where they make these kind of figures till to-day; but if ever they were made in this island, the practice and the very recollection of it are now long forgotten. And the singular thing was that all these bogies were as fresh as toys out of a shop.

Then it came in my mind that Case had let out to me the first day that he was a good forger of island curiosities – a thing by which so many traders turn an honest penny. And with that I saw the whole business, and how this display served the man a double purpose: first of all, to season his curiosities, and then to frighten those that came to visit him.

But I should tell you (what made the thing more curious) that all the time the Tyrolean harps were hanging round me in the trees, and even while I looked, a green-and-yellow bird (that, I suppose, was building) began to tear the hair off the head of one of the figures.

A little farther on I found the best curiosity of the museum.

The first I saw of it was a longish mound of earth with a twist to it. Digging off the earth with my hands, I found underneath tarpaulin stretched on boards, so that this was plainly the roof of a cellar. It stood right on the top of the hill, and the entrance was on the far side, between two rocks, like the entrance to a cave. I went as far in as the bend, and, looking round the corner, saw a shining face. It was big and ugly, like a pantomime mask, and the brightness of it waxed and dwindled, and at times it smoked.

'Oho!' says I, 'luminous paint!'

And I must say I rather admired the man's ingenuity. With a box of tools and a few mighty simple contrivances he had made out to have a devil of a temple. Any poor Kanaka brought up here in the dark, with the harps whining all round him, and shown that smoking face in the bottom of a hole, would make no kind of doubt but he had seen and heard enough devils for a lifetime. It's easy to find out what Kanakas think. Just go back to yourself anyway round from ten to fifteen years old, and there's an average Kanaka. There are some pious, just as there are pious boys; and most of them, like the boys again, are middling honest and yet think it rather larks to steal, and are easy scared, and rather like to be so. I remember a boy I was at school with at home who played the Case business. He didn't know anything, that boy; he couldn't do anything; he had no luminous paint and no Tyrolean harps; he just boldly said he was a sorcerer, and frightened us out of our boots, and we loved it. And then it came in my mind how the master had once flogged that boy, and the surprise we were all in to see the sorcerer catch it and hum like anybody else. Thinks I to myself: 'I must find some way of fixing it so for Master Case.' And the next moment I had my idea.

I went back by the path, which, when once you had found it, was quite plain and easy walking; and when I stepped out on the black sands, who should I see but Master Case himself. I cocked my gun and held it handy, and we marked up and passed without a word, each keeping the tail of his eye on the other; and no sooner had we passed than we each wheeled round like fellows drilling, and stood face to face. We had each taken the same notion in his head, you see, that the other fellow might give him the load of his gun in the stern.

'You've shot nothing,' says Case.

'I'm not on the shoot to-day,' said I.

'Well, the devil go with you for me,' says he.

'The same to you,' says I.

But we stuck just the way we were; no fear of either of us moving.

Case laughed. 'We can't stop here all day, though,' said he.

'Don't let me detain you,' says I.

He looked again. 'Look here, Wiltshire, do you think me a fool?' he asked.

'More of a knave, if you want to know,' says I.

'Well, do you think it would better me to shoot you here, on this open beach?' said he. 'Because I don't. Folks come fishing every day. There may be a score of them up the valley now, making copra; there might be half a dozen on the hill behind you, after pigeons; they might be watching us this minute, and I shouldn't wonder. I give you my word I don't want to shoot you. Why should I? You don't hinder me any. You haven't got one pound of copra but what you made with your own hands, like a Negro slave. You're vegetating – that's what I call it – and I don't care where you vegetate, nor yet how long. Give me your word you don't mean to shoot me, and I'll give you a lead and walk away.'

'Well,' said I, 'you're frank and pleasant, ain't you? And I'll be the same. I don't mean to shoot you to-day. Why should I? This business is beginning; it ain't done yet, Mr Case. I've given you one turn already. I can see the marks of my knuckles on your head to this blooming hour, and I've more cooking for you. I'm not a paralee, like Underhill. My name ain't Adams, and it ain't Vigours; and I mean to show you that you've met your match.'

'This is a silly way to talk,' said he. 'This is not the talk to make me move on with.'

'All right,' said I, 'stay where you are. I ain't in any hurry, and you know it. I can put in a day on this beach and never mind. I ain't got any copra to bother with. I ain't got any luminous paint to see to.'

I was sorry I said that last, but it whipped out before I knew. I could see it took the wind out of his sails, and he stood and stared at me with his brow drawn up. Then I suppose he made up his mind he must get to the bottom of this.

'I take you at your word,' says he, and turned his back, and walked right into the devil's bush.

I let him go, of course, for I had passed my word. But I watched him as long as he was in sight, and after he was gone lit out for cover as lively as you would want to see, and went the rest of the way home under the bush, for I didn't trust him sixpence worth. One thing I saw, I had been ass enough to give him warning, and that which I meant to do I must do at once.

You would think I had had about enough excitement for one morning, but there was another turn waiting me. As soon as I got far enough round the cape to see my house I made out there were strangers there; a little farther, and no doubt about it. There was a couple of armed sentinels squatting at my door. I could only suppose the trouble about Uma must have come to a head, and the station been seized. For aught I could think, Uma was taken up already, and these armed men were waiting to do the like with me.

However, as I came nearer, which I did at top speed, I saw there was a third native sitting on the veranda like a guest, and Uma was talking with him like a hostess. Nearer still I made out it was the big young chief, Maea, and that he was smiling away and smoking. And what was he smoking? None of your European cigarettes fit for a cat, not even the genuine big, knock-me-down native article that a fellow can really put in the time with if his pipe is broke – but a cigar, and one of my Mexicans at that, that I could swear to. At sight of this my heart started beating, and I took a wild hope in my head that the trouble was over, and Maea had come round.

Uma pointed me out to him as I came up, and he met me at the head of my own stairs like a thorough gentleman.

'Vilivili,' said he, which was the best they could make of my name, 'I pleased.'

There is no doubt when an island chief wants to be civil he can do it. I saw the way things were from the word go. There was no call for Uma to say to me: 'He no 'fraid Ese now, come bring copra.' I tell you I shook hands with that Kanaka like as if he was the best white man in Europe.

The fact was, Case and he had got after the same girl, or Maea suspected it, and concluded to make hay of the trader on the chance. He had dressed himself up, got a couple of his retainers cleaned and armed to kind of make the thing more public, and, just waiting till Case was clear of the village, came round to put the whole of his business my way. He was rich as well as powerful. I suppose that man was worth fifty thousand nuts per annum. I gave him the price of the beach and a quarter cent better, and as for credit, I would have advanced him the inside of the store and the fittings besides, I was so pleased to see him. I must say he bought like a gentleman: rice and tins and biscuits enough for a week's feast, and stuffs by the bolt. He was agreeable besides; he had plenty fun to him; and we cracked jests together, mostly through the interpreter, because he had mighty little English, and my native was still off colour. One thing I made out: he could never really have thought much harm of Uma; he could never have been really frightened, and must just have made believe from dodginess, and because he thought Case had a strong pull in the village and could help him on.

This set me thinking that both he and I were in a tightish place. What he had done was to fly in the face of the whole village, and the thing might cost him his authority. More than that, after my talk with Case on the beach, I thought it might very well cost me my life. Case had as good as said he would pot me if ever I got any copra; he would come home to find the best business in the village had changed hands, and the best thing I thought I could do was to get in first with the potting.

'See here, Uma,' says I, 'tell him I'm sorry I made him wait, but I was up looking at Case's Tiapolo store in the bush.'

'He want savvy if you no 'fraid?' translated Uma.

I laughed out. 'Not much!' says I. 'Tell him the place is a

blooming toy-shop! Tell him in England we give these things to the kid to play with.'

'He want savvy if you hear devil sing?' she asked next.

'Look here,' I said, 'I can't do it now, because I've got no banjo-strings in stock; but the next time the ship comes round I'll have one of these same contraptions right here in my veranda, and he can see for himself how much devil there is to it. Tell him, as soon as I can get the strings I'll make one for his picaninnies. The name of the concern is a Tyrolean harp; and you can tell him the name means in English that nobody but dam-fools give a cent for it.'

This time he was so pleased he had to try his English again. 'You talk true?' says he.

'Rather!' said I. 'Talk all-e-same Bible. Bring out a Bible here, Uma, if you've such a thing, and I'll kiss it. Or, I'll tell you what's better still,' says I, taking a header, 'ask him if he's afraid to go up there himself by day.'

It appeared he wasn't; he could venture as far as that by day and in company.

'That's the ticket, then!' said I. 'Tell him the man's a fraud and the place foolishness, and if he'll go up there to-morrow he'll see all that's left of it. But tell him this, Uma, and mind he understands it: If he gets talking it's bound to come to Case, and I'm a dead man! I'm playing his game, tell him, and if he says one word my blood will be at his door and be the damnation of him here and after.'

She told him, and he shook hands with me up to the hilt, and, says he: 'No talk. Go up to-mollow. You my friend?'

'No, sir,' says I, 'no such foolishness. I've come here to trade, tell him, and not to make friends. But, as to Case, I'll send that man to glory!'

So off Maea went, pretty well pleased, as I could see.

Night in the Bush

WELL, I was committed now; Tiapolo had to be smashed up before next day, and my hands were pretty full, not only with preparations, but with argument. My house was like a mechanics' debating society. Uma was so made up that I shouldn't go into the bush by night, or that, if I did, I was never to come back again. You know her style of arguing: you've had a specimen about Queen Victoria and the devil; and I leave you to fancy if I was tired of it before dark.

At last I had a good idea. 'What was the use of casting my pearls before her?' I thought; some of her own chopped hay would be likelier to do the business.

'I'll tell you what, then,' said I. 'You fish out your Bible, and I'll take that up along with me. That'll make me right.'

She swore a Bible was no use.

'That's just your Kanaka ignorance,' said I. 'Bring the Bible out.'

She brought it, and I turned to the title-page, where I thought there would likely be some English, and so there was. 'There!' said I. 'Look at that! "*London: Printed for the British and Foreign Bible Society, Blackfriars*," and the date, which I can't read, owing to its being in these X's. There's no devil in hell can look near the Bible Society, Blackfriars. Why, you silly,' I said, 'how do you suppose we get along with our own *aitus* at home! All Bible Society!'

'I think you no got any,' said she. 'White man, he tell me you no got.'

'Sounds likely, don't it?' I asked. 'Why would these islands all be chock full of them and none in Europe?'

'Well, you no got bread-fruit,' said she.

I could have torn my hair. 'Now, look here, old lady,' said I, 'you dry up, for I'm tired of you. I'll take the Bible, which'll put me as straight as the mail, and that's the last word I've got to say.'

The night fell extraordinary dark, clouds coming up with sundown and overspreading all; not a star showed; there was only an end of a moon, and that not due before the small hours. Round the village, what with the lights and the fires in the open houses, and the torches of many fishers moving on the reef, it kept as gay as an illumination; but the sea and the mountains and woods were all clean gone. I suppose it might be eight o'clock when I took the road, laden like a donkey. First there was that Bible, a book as big as your head, which I had let myself in for by my own tomfoolery. Then there was my gun, and knife, and lantern, and patent matches, all necessary. And then there was the real plant of the affair in hand, a mortal weight of gunpowder, a pair of dynamite fishing-bombs, and two or three pieces of slow match that I had pulled out of the tin cases and spliced together the best way I could; for the match was only trade stuff, and a man would be crazy that trusted it. Altogether, you see, I had the materials of a pretty good blow-up! Expense was nothing to me; I wanted that thing done right.

As long as I was in the open, and had the lamp in my house to steer by, I did well. But when I got to the path, it fell so dark I could make no headway, walking into trees and swearing there, like a man looking for the matches in his bed-room. I knew it was risky to light up, for my lantern would be visible all the way to the point of the cape, and as no one went there after dark, it would be talked about, and come to Case's ears. But what was I to do? I had either to give the business over and lose caste with Maea, or light up, take my chance, and get through the thing the smartest I was able.

As long as I was on the path I walked hard, but when I came to the black beach I had to run. For the tide was now nearly flowed; and to get through with my powder dry between the surf and the steep hill, took all the quickness I possessed. As it was, even the wash caught me to the knees, and I came near falling on a stone. All this time the hurry I was in, and the free air and smell of the sea, kept my spirits lively; but when I was once in the bush and began to climb the path I took it easier.

The fearsomeness of the wood had been a good bit rubbed off for me by Master Case's banjo-strings and graven images, yet I thought it was a dreary walk, and guessed, when the disciples went up there, they must be badly scared. The light of the lantern, striking among all these trunks and forked branches and twisted rope-ends of lianas, made the whole place, or all that you could see of it, a kind of a puzzle of turning shadows. They came to meet you, solid and quick like giants, and then spun off and vanished; they hove up over your head like clubs, and flew away into the night like birds. The floor of the bush glimmered with dead wood, the way the match-box used to shine after you had struck a lucifer. Big, cold drops fell on me from the branches overhead like sweat. There was no wind to mention; only a little icy breath of a land breeze that stirred nothing; and the harps were silent.

The first landfall I made was when I got through the bush of wild cocoanuts, and came in view of the bogies on the wall. Mighty queer they looked by the shining of the lantern, with their painted faces and shell eyes, and their clothes, and their hair hanging. One after another I pulled them all up and piled them in a bundle on the cellar roof, so as they might go to glory with the rest. Then I chose a place behind one of the big stones at the entrance, buried my powder and the two shells, and arranged my match along the passage. And then I had a look at the smoking head, just for good-bye. It was doing fine.

'Cheer up,' says I. 'You're booked.'

It was my first idea to light up and be getting homeward; for the darkness and the glimmer of the dead wood and the shadows of the lantern made me lonely. But I knew where one of the harps hung; it seemed a pity it shouldn't go with the rest; and at the same time I couldn't help letting on to myself that I was mortal tired of my employment, and would like best to be at home and have the door shut. I stepped out of the cellar and argued it fore and back. There was a sound of the sea far down below me on the coast; nearer hand not a leaf stirred; I might have been the only living creature this side of Cape Horn. Well, as I stood there thinking, it seemed the bush woke and became full of little noises. Little noises they were, and nothing to hurt;

a bit of a crackle, a bit of a rush; but the breath jumped right out of me and my throat went as dry as a biscuit. It wasn't Case I was afraid of, which would have been common-sense; I never thought of Case; what took me, as sharp as the colic, was the old wives' tales – the devil-women and the man-pigs. It was the toss of a penny whether I should run; but I got a purchase on myself, and stepped out, and held up the lantern (like a fool) and looked all round.

In the direction of the village and the path there was nothing to be seen; but when I turned inland it's a wonder to me I didn't drop. There, coming right up out of the desert and the bad bush – there, sure enough, was a devil-woman, just as the way I had figured she would look. I saw the light shine on her bare arms and her bright eyes, and there went out of me a yell so big that I thought it was my death.

'Ah! No sing out!' says the devil-woman, in a kind of a high whisper. 'Why you talk big voice? Put out light! Ese he come.'

'My God Almighty, Uma, is that you?' says I.

'*Ioe*,'* says she. 'I come quick. Ese here soon.'

'You come alone?' I asked. 'You no 'fraid?'

'Ah, too much 'fraid!' she whispered, clutching me. 'I think die.'

'Well,' says I, with a kind of a weak grin, 'I'm not the one to laugh at you, Mrs Wiltshire, for I'm about the worst scared man in the South Pacific myself.'

She told me in two words what brought her. I was scarce gone, it seems, when Faavao came in, and the old woman had met Black Jack running as hard as he was fit from our house to Case's. Uma neither spoke nor stopped, but lit right out to come and warn me. She was so close at my heels that the lantern was her guide across the beach, and afterwards, by the glimmer of it in the trees, she got her line uphill. It was only when I had got to the top or was in the cellar that she wandered – Lord knows where! – and lost a sight of precious time, afraid to call out lest Case was at the heels of her, and falling in the bush, so that she was all knocked and bruised. That must have been when she got too far to the southward, and how she came to take me in

*Yes.

the flank at last and frighten me beyond what I've got the words to tell of.

Well, anything was better than a devil-woman, but I thought her yarn serious enough. Black Jack had no call to be about my house, unless he was set there to watch; and it looked to me as if my tomfool word about the paint, and perhaps some chatter of Maea's, had got us all in a clove hitch. One thing was clear: Uma and I were here for the night; we daren't try to go home before day, and even then it would be safer to strike round up the mountain and come in by the back of the village, or we might walk into an ambuscade. It was plain, too, that the mine should be sprung immediately, or Case might be in time to stop it.

I marched into the tunnel, Uma keeping tight hold of me, opened my lantern and lit the match. The first length of it burned like a spill of paper, and I stood stupid, watching it burn, and thinking we were going aloft with Tiapolo, which was none of my views. The second took to a better rate, though faster than I cared about; and at that I got my wits again, hauled Uma clear of the passage, blew out and dropped the lantern, and the pair of us groped our way into the bush until I thought it might be safe, and lay down together by a tree.

'Old lady,' I said, 'I won't forget this night. You're a trump, and that's what's wrong with you.'

She bumped herself close up to me. She had run out the way she was, with nothing on her but her kilt; and she was all wet with the dews and the sea on the black beach, and shook straight on with cold and the terror of the dark and the devils.

'Too much 'fraid,' was all she said.

The far side of Case's hill goes down near as steep as a precipice into the next valley. We were on the very edge of it, and I could see the dead wood shine and hear the sea sound far below. I didn't care about the position, which left me no retreat, but I was afraid to change. Then I saw I had made a worse mistake about the lantern, which I should have left lighted, so that I could have had a crack at Case when he stepped into the shine of it. And since I hadn't had the wit to do that, it seemed a senseless thing to leave the good lantern to blow up with the graven images. The thing belonged to me, after all, and was worth money, and might come in handy. If I could have trusted the match, I might have run in still and rescued it. But who was going to trust to the match? You know what trade is. The stuff was good enough for Kanakas to go fishing with, where they've got to look lively anyway, and the most they risk is only to have their hand blown off. But for anyone that wanted to fool around a blow-up like mine that match was rubbish.

Altogether the best I could do was to lie still, see my shot-gun handy, and wait for the explosion. But it was a solemn kind of a business. The blackness of the night was like solid; the only thing you could see was the nasty bogy glimmer of the dead wood, and that showed you nothing but itself; and as for sounds, I stretched my ears till I thought I could have heard the match burn in the tunnel, and that bush was as silent as a coffin. Now and then there was a bit of a crack; but whether it was near or far, whether it was Case stubbing his toes within a few yards of me, or a tree breaking miles away, I knew no more than the babe unborn.

And then, all of a sudden, Vesuvius went off. It was a long time coming; but when it came (though I say it that shouldn't) no man could ask to see a better. At first it was just a son of a gun of a row, and a spout of fire, and the wood lighted up so that you could see to read. And then the trouble began. Uma and I were half buried under a wagonful of earth, and glad it was no worse, for one of the rocks at the entrance of the tunnel was fired clean into the air, fell within a couple of fathoms of where we lay, and bounded over the edge of the hill, and went pounding down into the next valley. I saw I had rather under-calculated our distance, or over-done the dynamite and powder, which you please.

And presently I saw I had made another slip. The noise of the thing began to die off, shaking the island; the dazzle was over; and yet the night didn't come back the way I expected. For the whole wood was scattered with red coals and brands from the explosion; they were all round me on the flat, some had fallen below in the valley, and some stuck and flared in the tree-tops. I had no fear of fire, for these forests are too wet to kindle. But the trouble was that the place was all lit up – not very bright, but good enough to get shot by; and the way the coals were scattered, it was just as likely Case might have the advantage as myself. I looked all round for his white face, you may be sure; but there was not a sign of him. As for Uma, the life seemed to have been knocked right out of her by the bang and blaze of it.

There was one bad point in my game. One of the blessed graven images had come down all afire, hair and clothes and body, not four yards away from me. I cast a mighty noticing glance all round; there was still no Case, and I made up my mind I must get rid of that burning stick before he came, or I should be shot there like a dog.

It was my first idea to have crawled, and then I thought speed was the main thing, and stood half up to make a rush. The same moment, from somewhere between me and the sea, there came a flash and a report, and a rifle-bullet screeched in my ear. I swung straight round and up with my gun, but the brute had a Winchester, and before I could as much as see him his second shot knocked me over like a ninepin. I seemed to fly in the air, then came down by the run and lay half a minute, silly; and then I found my hands empty, and my gun had flown over my head as I fell. It makes a man mighty wide awake to be in the kind of box that I was in. I scarcely knew where I was hurt, or whether I was hurt or not, but turned right over on my face to crawl after my weapon. Unless you have tried to get about with a smashed leg you don't know what pain is, and I let out a howl like a bullock's.

This was the unluckiest noise that ever I made in my life. Up to then Uma had stuck to her tree like a sensible woman, knowing she would be only in the way; but as soon as she heard me sing out she ran forward. The Winchester cracked again, and down she went.

I had sat up, leg and all, to stop her; but when I saw her tumble I clapped down again where I was, lay still, and felt the handle of my knife. I had been scurried and put out before. No more of that for me. He had knocked over my girl, I had to fix him for it; and I lay there and gritted my teeth, and footed up the chances. My leg was broke, my gun was gone. Case had still ten shots in his Winchester. It looked a kind of hopeless business. But I never despaired nor thought upon despairing: that man had got to go.

For a goodish bit not one of us let on. Then I heard Case begin to move nearer in the bush, but mighty careful. The image had burned out, there were only a few coals left here and there, and the wood was main dark, but had a kind of low glow in it like a fire on its last legs. It was by this that I made out Case's head looking at me over a big tuft of ferns, and at the same time the brute saw me and shouldered his Winchester. I lay quite still, and as good as looked into the barrel: it was my last chance, but I thought my heart would have come right out of its bearings. Then he fired. Lucky for me it was no shot-gun, for the bullet struck within an inch of me and knocked the dirt in my eyes.

Just you try and see if you can lie quiet, and let a man take a sitting shot at you and miss you by a hair. But I did, and lucky, too. A while Case stood with the Winchester at the port-arms; then he gave a little laugh to himself and stepped round the ferns.

'Laugh!' thought I. 'If you had the wit of a louse you would be praying!'

I was all as taut as a ship's hawser or the spring of a watch, and as soon as he came within reach of me I had him by the ankle, plucked the feet right out from under him, laid him out, and was upon the top of him, broken leg and all, before he breathed. His Winchester had gone the same road as my shot-gun; it was nothing to me – I defied him now. I'm a pretty strong man anyway, but I never knew what strength was till I got hold of Case. He was knocked out of time by the rattle he came down with, and threw up his hands together, more like a frightened woman, so that I caught both of them with my left. This wakened him up, and he fastened his teeth in my fore-arm like a weasel. Much I cared. My leg gave me all the pain I had any use for, and I drew my knife and got it in the place.

'Now,' said I, 'I've got you; and you're gone up, and a good job too! Do you feel the point of that? That's for Underhill!

And there's for Adams! And now here's for Uma, and that's going to knock your blooming soul right out of you!'

With that I gave him the cold steel for all I was worth. His body kicked under me like a spring sofa; he gave a dreadful kind of a long moan, and lay still.

'I wonder if you're dead? I hope so!' I thought, for my head was swimming. But I wasn't going to take chances; I had his own example too close before me for that; and I tried to draw the knife out to give it him again. The blood came over my hands, I remember, hot as tea; and with that I fainted clean away, and fell with my head on the man's mouth.

When I came to myself it was pitch dark; the cinders had burned out; there was nothing to be seen but the shine of the dead wood, and I couldn't remember where I was nor why I was in such pain, nor what I was all wetted with. Then it came back, and the first thing I attended to was to give him the knife again a half a dozen times up to the handle. I believe he was dead already, but it did him no harm and did me good.

'I bet you're dead now,' I said, and then I called to Uma.

Nothing answered, and I made a move to go and grope for her, fouled my broken leg, and fainted again.

When I came to myself the second time the clouds had all cleared away, except a few that sailed there, white as cotton. The moon was up – a tropic moon. The moon at home turns a wood black, but even this old butt-end of a one showed up that forest as green as by day. The night birds – or, rather, they're a kind of early morning bird – sang out with their long, falling notes like nightingales. And I could see the dead man, that I was still half resting on, looking right up into the sky with his eyes open, no paler than when he was alive; and a little way off Uma tumbled on her side. I got over to her the best way I was able, and when I got there she was broad awake and crying, and sobbing to herself with no more noise than an insect. It appears she was afraid to cry out loud, because of the *aitus*. Altogether she was not much hurt, but scared beyond belief; she had come to her senses a long while ago, cried out to me, heard nothing in reply, made out we were both dead, and had lain there ever since, afraid to budge a finger. The ball had ploughed up her shoulder, and she had lost a main quantity of blood; but I soon had that tied up the way it ought to be with the tail of my shirt and a scarf I had on, got her head on my sound knee and my back against a trunk, and settled down to wait for morning. Uma was for neither use nor ornament, and could only clutch hold of me and shake and cry. I don't suppose there was ever anybody worse scared, and, to do her justice, she had had a lively night of it. As for me, I was in a good bit of pain and fever, but not so bad when I sat still; and every time I looked over to Case I could have sung and whistled. Talk about meat and drink! To see that man lying there dead as a herring filled me full.

The night birds stopped after a while; and then the light began to change, the east came orange, the whole wood began to whirr with singing like a musical box, and there was the broad day.

I didn't expect Maea for a long while yet; and, indeed, I thought there was an off-chance he might go back on the whole idea and not come at all. I was the better pleased when, about an hour after daylight, I heard sticks smashing and a lot of Kanakas laughing and singing out to keep their courage up. Uma sat up quite brisk at the first word of it; and presently we saw a party come stringing out of the path, Maea in front, and behind a white man in a pith helmet. It was Mr Tarleton, who had turned up late last night in Falesá, having left his boat and walked the last stage with a lantern.

They buried Case upon the field of glory, right in the hole where he had kept the smoking head. I waited till the thing was done; and Mr Tarleton prayed, which I thought tomfoolery, but I'm bound to say he gave a pretty sick view of the dear departed's prospects, and seemed to have his own ideas of hell. I had it out with him afterward, told him he had scamped his duty, and what he had ought to have done was to up like a man and tell the Kanakas plainly Case was damned, and a good riddance; but I never could get him to see it my way. Then they made me a litter of poles and carried me down to the station. Mr Tarleton set my leg, and made a regular missionary splice of it, so that I limp to this day. That done, he took down my evidence, and Uma's, and Maea's, wrote it all out fine, and had us sign it; and then he got the chiefs and marched over to Papa Randall's to seize Case's papers.

All they found was a bit of a diary, kept for a good many years, and all about the price of copra, and chickens being stolen, and that; and the books of the business and the will I told you of in the beginning, by both of which the whole thing (stock, lock, and barrel) appeared to belong to the Samoa woman. It was I that bought her out at a mighty reasonable figure, for she was in a hurry to get home. As for Randall and the black, they had to tramp; got into some kind of a station on the Papa-malulu side; did very bad business, for the truth is neither of the pair was fit for it, and lived mostly on fish, which was the means of Randall's death. It seems there was a nice shoal in one day, and papa went after them with the dynamite; either the match burned too fast, or papa was full, or both, but the shell went off (in the usual way) before he threw it, and where was papa's hand? Well, there's nothing to hurt in that; the islands up north are all full of one-handed men, like the parties in the 'Arabian Nights'; but either Randall was too old, or he drank too much, and the short and the long of it was that he died. Pretty soon after, the nigger was turned out of the island for stealing from white men, and went off to the west, where he found men of his own colour, in case he liked that, and the men of his own colour took and ate him at some kind of a corro-borree, and I'm sure I hope he was to their fancy!

So there was I, left alone in my glory at Falesá; and when the schooner came round I filled her up, and gave her a deck cargo half as high as the house. I must say Mr Tarleton did the right thing by us; but he took a meanish kind of a revenge.

'Now, Mr Wiltshire,' said he, 'I've put you all square with every-body here. It wasn't difficult to do, Case being gone; but I have done it, and given my pledge besides that you will deal fairly with the natives. I must ask you to keep my word.'

Well, so I did. I used to be bothered about my balances, but I reasoned it out this way. We all have queerish balances, and the natives all know it and water their copra in a proportion so that it's fair all round; but the truth is, it did use to bother me, and, though I did well in Falesá, I was half glad when the firm moved me on to another station, where I was under no kind of a pledge and could look my balances in the face.

As for the old lady, you know her as well as I do. She's only the one fault. If you don't keep your eye lifting she would give away the roof off the station. Well, it seems it's natural in Kanakas. She's turned a powerful big woman now, and could throw a London bobby over her shoulder. But that's natural in Kanakas too, and there's no manner of doubt that she's an A-1 wife.

Mr Tarleton's gone home, his trick being over. He was the best missionary I ever struck, and now, it seems, he's parsonising down Somerset way. Well, that's best for him; he'll have no Kanakas there to get luny over.

My public-house? Not a bit of it, nor ever likely. I'm stuck here, I fancy. I don't like to leave the kids, you see: and – there's no use talking – they're better here than what they would be in a white man's country, though Ben took the eldest up to Auckland, where he's being schooled with the best. But what bothers me is the girls. They're only half-castes, of course; I know that as well as you do, and there's nobody thinks less of half-castes than I do; but they're mine, and about all I've got. I can't reconcile my mind to their taking up with Kanakas, and I'd like to know where I'm to find the whites?

THE EBB-TIDE

PART I

THE TRIO

Night on the Beach

THROUGHOUT the island world of the Pacific, scattered men of many European races and from almost every grade of society carry activity and disseminate disease. Some prosper, some vegetate. Some have mounted the steps of thrones and owned islands and navies. Others again must marry for a livelihood; a strapping, merry, chocolate-coloured dame supports them in sheer idleness; and, dressed like natives, but still retaining some foreign element of gait or attitude, still perhaps with some relic (such as a single eye-glass) of the officer and gentleman, they sprawl in palm-leaf verandahs and entertain an island audience with memoirs of the music-hall. And there are still others, less pliable, lass capable, less fortunate, perhaps less base, who continue, even in these isles of plenty, to lack bread.

At the far end of the town of Papeete, three such men were seated on the beach under a *purao*-tree.

It was late. Long ago the band had broken up and marched musically home, a motley troop of men and women, merchant clerks and navy officers, dancing in its wake, arms about waist and crowned with garlands. Long ago darkness and silence had gone from house to house about the tiny pagan city. Only the streetlamps shone on, making a glow-worm halo in the umbrageous alleys or drawing a tremulous image on the waters of the port. A sound of snoring ran among the piles of lumber by the Government pier. It was wafted ashore from the graceful clipper-bottomed schooners, where they lay moored close in like dinghies, and their crews were stretched upon the deck under the open sky or huddled in a rude tent amidst the disorder of merchandise.

But the men under the *purao* had no thought of sleep. The

same temperature in England would have passed without remark in summer; but it was bitter cold for the South Seas. Inanimate nature knew it, and the bottle of cocoanut oil stood frozen in every bird-cage house about the island; and the men knew it, and shivered. They wore flimsy cotton clothes, the same they had sweated in by day and run the gauntlet of the tropic showers; and to complete their evil case, they had no breakfast to mention, less dinner, and no supper at all.

In the telling South Sea phrase, these three men were *on the beach*.[1] Common calamity had brought them acquainted, as the three most miserable English-speaking creatures in Tahiti; and beyond their misery, they knew next to nothing of each other, not even their true names. For each had made a long apprenticeship in going downward; and each, at some stage of the descent, had been shamed into the adoption of an *alias*. And yet none of them had figured in a court of justice; two were men of kindly virtues; and one, as he sat and shivered under the *purao*, had a tattered Virgil in his pocket.

Certainly, if money could have been raised upon the book, Robert Herrick would long ago have sacrified that last possession; but the demand for literature, which is so marked a feature in some parts of the South Seas, extends not so far as the dead tongues; and the Virgil, which he could not exchange against a meal, had often consoled him in his hunger. He would study it, as he lay with tightened belt on the floor of the old calaboose, seeking favourite passages and finding new ones only less beautiful because they lacked the consecration of remembrance. Or he would pause on random country walks; sit on the path-side, gazing over the sea on the mountains of Eimeo[2]; and dip into the *Aeneid*, seeking *sortes*.[3] And if the oracle (as is the way of oracles) replied with no very certain nor encouraging voice, visions of England at least would throng upon the exile's memory: the busy schoolroom, the green playing-fields, holidays at home, and the perennial roar of London, and the fireside, and the white head of his father. For it is the destiny of those grave, restrained, and classic writers, with whom we make enforced and often painful acquaintanceship at school, to pass into the blood and become native in the memory; so that a phrase of Virgil speaks not so much of Mantua or Augustus, but of English places and the student's own irrevocable youth.

Robert Herrick was the son of an intelligent, active, and ambitious man, small partner in a considerable London house. Hopes were conceived of the boy; he was sent to a good school, gained there an Oxford scholarship, and proceeded in course to the Western University. With all his talent and taste (and he had much of both) Robert was deficient in consistency and intellectual manhood, wandered in bypaths of study, worked at music or at metaphysics when he should have been at Greek, and took at last a paltry degree. Almost at the same time, the London house was disastrously wound up; Mr Herrick must begin the world again as a clerk in a strange office, and Robert relinquish his ambitions and accept with gratitude a career that he detested and despised. He had no head for figures, no interest in affairs, detested the constraint of hours, and despised the aims and the success of merchants. To grow rich was none of his ambitions; rather to do well. A worse or a more bold young man would have refused the destiny; perhaps tried his future with his pen; perhaps enlisted. Robert, more prudent, possibly more timid, consented to embrace that way of life in which he could most readily assist his family. But he did so with a mind divided; fled the neighbourhood of former comrades; and chose, out of several positions placed at his disposal, a clerkship in New York.

His career thenceforth was one of unbroken shame. He did not drink, he was exactly honest, he was never rude to his employers, yet was everywhere discharged. Bringing no interest to his duties, he brought no attention; his day was a tissue of things neglected and things done amiss; and from place to place, and from town to town, he carried the character of one thoroughly incompetent. No man can bear the word applied to him without some flush of colour, as indeed there is none other that so emphatically slams in a man's face the door of self-respect. And to Herrick, who was conscious of talents and acquirements, who looked down upon those humble duties in which he was found wanting, the pain was the more exquisite. Early in his fall he had ceased to be able to make remittances; shortly after, having nothing but failure to communicate, he ceased writing home; and about a year before this tale begins, turned suddenly upon the streets of San Francisco by a vulgar and infuriated German Jew, he had broken the last bonds of self-respect, and, upon a sudden impulse, changed his name and invested his last dollar in a passage on the mail brigantine, the *City of Papeete*. With what expectation he had trimmed his flight for the South Seas, Herrick perhaps scarcely knew. Doubtless there were fortunes to be made in pearl and copra; doubtless others not more gifted than himself had climbed in the island world to be queen's consorts and king's ministers. But if Herrick had gone there with any manful purpose, he would have kept his father's name: the *alias* betrayed his moral bankruptcy; he had struck his flag; he entertained no hope to reinstate himself or help his straitened family; and he came to the islands (where he knew the climate to be soft, bread cheap, and manners easy) a skulker from life's battle and his own immediate duty. Failure, he had said, was his portion: let it be a pleasant failure.

It is fortunately not enough to say 'I will be base.' Herrick continued in the islands his career of failure; but in the new scene and under the new name, he suffered no less sharply than before. A place was got, it was lost in the old style; from the long-suffering of the keepers of restaurants he fell to more open charity upon the wayside; as time went on, good-nature became weary and, after a repulse or two, Herrick became shy. There were women enough who would have supported a far worse and a far uglier man; Herrick never met or never knew them : or if he did both, some manlier feeling would revolt, and he preferred starvation. Drenched with rains, broiling by day, shivering by night, a disused and ruinous prison for a bedroom, his diet begged or pilfered out of rubbish heaps, his associates two creatures equally outcast with himself, he had drained for months the cup of penitence. He had known what it was to be resigned, what it was to break forth in a childish fury of rebellion against fate, and what it was to sink into the coma of despair. The time had changed him. He told himself no longer tales of an easy and perhaps agreeable declension; he read his nature otherwise; he had proved himself incapable of rising, and he now learned by experience that he could not stoop to fall. Something that was scarcely pride or strength, that was perhaps only refinement, withheld him from capitulation; but he looked on upon his own misfortune with a growing rage, and sometimes wondered at his patience.

It was now the fourth month completed, and still there was no change or sign of change. The moon, racing through a world of flying clouds of every size and shape and density, some black as inkstains, some delicate as lawn, threw the marvel of her southern brightness over the same lovely and detested scene: the island mountains crowned with the perennial island cloud, the embowered city studded with rare lamps, the masts in the harbour, the smooth mirror of the lagoon, and the mole of the barrier reef on which the breakers whitened. The moon shone too, with bull's-eye sweeps, on his companions; on the stalwart frame of the American who called himself Brown, and was known to be a master-mariner in some disgrace; and on the dwarfish person, the pale eyes and toothless smile of a vulgar and bad-hearted cockney clerk. Here was society for Robert Herrick! The Yankee skipper was a man at least: he had sterling qualities of tenderness and resolution; he was one whose hand you could take without a blush. But there was no redeeming grace about the other, who called himself sometimes Hay and sometimes Tomkins, and laughed at the discrepancy; who had been employed in every store in Papeete, for the creature was able in his way; who had been discharged from each in turn, for he was wholly vile; who had alienated all his old employers so that they passed him in the street as if he were a dog, and all his old comrades so that they shunned him as they would a creditor.

Not long before, a ship from Peru had brought an influenza, and it now raged in the island, and particularly in Papeete. From all round the *purao* arose and fell a dismal sound of men coughing, and strangling as they coughed. The sick natives, with the islander's impatience of a touch of fever, had crawled from their houses to be cool and, squatting on the shore or on the beached canoes, painfully expected the new day. Even as the crowing of cocks goes about the country in the night from farm to farm, accesses of coughing arose, and spread, and died in the distance, and sprang up again. Each miserable shiverer caught the suggestion from his neighbour, was torn for some minutes by that cruel ecstasy, and left spent and without voice or courage when it passed. If a man had pity to spend, Papeete beach, in that cold night and in that infected season, was a place to spend it on. And of all the sufferers perhaps the least deserving, but surely the most pitiable, was the London clerk. He was used to another life, to houses, beds, nursing, and the dainties of the sickroom; he lay here now, in the cold open, exposed to the gusting of the wind, and with an empty belly. He was besides infirm; the disease shook him to the vitals; and his companions watched his endurance with surprise. A profound commiseration filled them, and contended with and conquered their abhorrence. The disgust attendant on so ugly a sickness magnified this dislike; at the same time, and with more than compensating strength, shame for a sentiment so inhuman bound them the more straitly to his service; and even the evil they knew of him swelled their solicitude, for the thought of death is always the least supportable when it draws near to the merely sensual and selfish. Sometimes they held him up; sometimes, with mistaken helpfulness, they beat him between the shoulders; and when the poor wretch lay back ghastly and spent after a paroxysm of coughing, they would sometimes peer into his face, doubtfully exploring it for any mark of life. There is no one but has some virtue: that of the clerk was courage; and he would make haste to reassure them in a pleasantry not always decent.

'I'm all right, pals,' he gasped once: 'this is the thing to strengthen the muscles of the larynx.'

'Well, you take the cake!' cried the captain.

'O, I'm good, plucked enough,' pursued the sufferer with a broken utterance. 'But it do seem bloomin' hard to me, that I should be the only party down with this form of vice, and the only one to do the funny business. I think one of you other parties might wake up. Tell a fellow something.'

'The trouble is we've nothing to tell, my son,' returned the captain.

'I'll tell you, if you like, what I was thinking,' said Herrick.

'Tell us anything,' said the clerk, 'I only want to be reminded that I ain't dead.'

Herrick took up his parable, lying on his face and speaking slowly and scarce above his breath, not like a man who has anything to say, but like one talking against time.

'Well, I was thinking this,' he began: 'I was thinking I lay on Papeete beach one night – all moon and squalls and fellows coughing – and I was cold and hungry, and down in the mouth, and was about ninety years of age, and had spent two hundred and twenty of them on Papeete beach. And I was thinking I wished I had a ring to rub, or had a fairy godmother, or could raise Beelzebub. And I was trying to remember how you did it. I knew you made a ring of skulls, for I had seen that in the *Freischütz*:[4] and that you took off your coat and turned up your sleeves, for I had seen Formes do that when he was playing Kaspar,[5] and you could see (by the way he went about it) it was a business he had studied; and that you ought to have something to kick up a smoke and a bad smell, I daresay a cigar might do, and that you ought to say the Lord's Prayer backwards. Well, I wondered if I could do that; it seemed rather a feat, you see. And then I wondered if I would say it forward, and I thought I did. Well, no sooner had I got to *world without end*, than I saw a man in a *pariu*, and with a mat under his arm, come along the beach from the town. He was rather a hard-favoured old party, and he limped and crippled, and all the time he kept coughing. At first I didn't cotton to his looks, I thought, and then I got sorry for the old soul because he coughed so hard. I remembered that we had some of that cough mixture the American Consul gave the captain for Hay. It never did Hay a ha'porth of service, but I thought it might do the old gentleman's business for him, and stood up. "*Yorana!*" says I. "*Yorana!*" says he. "Look here," I said, "I've got some first-rate stuff in a bottle; it'll fix your cough, savvy? *Harry my** and I'll measure you a tablespoonful in the palm of my hand, for all our plate is at the bankers." So I thought the old party came up, and the nearer he came the less I took to him. But I had passed my word, you see.'

*Come here.

'Wot is this bloomin' drivel?' interrupted the clerk. 'It's like the rot there is in tracts.'

'It's a story; I used to tell them to the kids at home,' said Herrick. 'If it bores you, I'll drop it.'

'O, cut along!' returned the sick man irritably. 'It's better than nothing.'

'Well,' continued Herrick, 'I had no sooner given him the cough mixture than he seemed to straighten up and change, and I saw he wasn't a Tahitian after all, but some kind of Arab, and had a long beard on his chin. "One good turn deserves another," says he. "I am a magician out of the *Arabian Nights*, and this mat that I have under my arm is the original carpet of Mohammed Ben Somebody-or-other. Say the word, and you can have a cruise upon the carpet." "You don't mean to say this is the Travelling Carpet?" I cried. "You bet I do," said he. "You've been to America since last I read the *Arabian Nights*," said I, a little suspicious. "I should think so," said he. "Been everywhere. A man with a carpet like this isn't going to moulder in a semi-detached villa." Well, that struck me as reasonable. "All right," I said; "and do you mean to tell me I can get on that carpet and go straight to London, England?" I said "London, England," captain, because he seemed to have been so long in your part of the world. "In the crack of a whip," said he. I figured up the time. 'What is the difference between Papeete and London, captain?'

'Taking Greenwich and Point Venus,[6] nine hours, odd minutes and seconds,' replied the mariner.

'Well, that's about what I made it,' resumed Herrick, 'about nine hours. Calling this three in the morning, I made out I would drop into London about noon; and the idea tickled me immensely. "There's only one bother," I said, "I haven't a copper cent. It would be a pity to go to London and not buy the morning *Standard*." "O!" said he, "you don't realise the conveniences of this carpet. You see this pocket? you've only got to stick your hand in, and you pull it out filled with sovereigns." '

'Double-eagles, wasn't it?' inquired the captain.

'That was what it was!' cried Herrick. 'I thought they seemed unusually big, and I remember now I had to go to the money-changers at Charing Cross and get English silver.'

'O, you went there?' said the clerk. 'Wot did you do? Bet you had a B and S!'[7]

'Well, you see, it was just as the old boy said – like the cut of a whip,' said Herrick. 'The one minute I was here on the beach at three in the morning, the next I was in front of the Golden Cross at midday. At first I was dazzled, and covered my eyes, and there didn't seem the smallest change; the roar of the Strand and the roar of the reef were like the same: hark to it now, and you can hear the cabs and 'buses rolling and the streets resound! And then at last I could look about, and there was the old place, and no mistake! With the statues in the square, and St Martin's-in-the-Fields, and the bobbies, and the sparrows, and the hacks; and I can't tell you what I felt like. I felt like crying, I believe, or dancing, or jumping clean over the Nelson Column. I was like a fellow caught up out of Hell and flung down into the dandiest part of Heaven. Then I spotted for a hansom with a spanking horse. "A shilling for yourself if you're there in twenty minutes!" said I to the jarvey. He went a good pace, though of course it was a trifle to the carpet; and in nineteen minutes and a half I was at the door.'

'What door?' asked the captain.

'O, a house I know of,' returned Herrick.

'But it was a public-house!' cried the clerk – only these were not his words. 'And w'y didn't you take the carpet there instead of trundling in a growler?'[8]

'I didn't want to startle a quiet street,' said the narrator. 'Bad form. And, besides, it was a hansom.'

'Well, and what did you do next?' inquired the captain.

'O, I went in,' said Herrick.

'The old folks?' asked the captain.

'That's about it,' said the other, chewing a grass.

'Well, I think you are about the poorest 'and at a yarn!' cried the clerk. 'Crikey, it's like *Ministering Children*! I can tell you there would be more beer and skittles about my little jaunt. I would go and have a B-and-S for luck. Then I would get a big ulster[9] with astrakhan fur, and take my cane and do the la-de-da down Piccadilly. Then I would go to a slap-up restaurant, and have green peas, and a bottle of fizz, and a chump chop – O! and

I forgot, I'd 'ave some devilled whitebait first – and green gooseberry tart, and 'ot coffee, and some of that form of vice in big bottles with a seal – Benedictine – that's the bloomin' nyme! Then I'd drop into a theatre, and pal on with some chappies, and do the dancing rooms and bars, and that, and wouldn't go 'ome till morning, till daylight doth appear. And the next day I'd have water-cresses, 'am, muffin, and fresh butter; wouldn't I just, O my!'

The clerk was interrupted by a fresh attack of coughing.

'Well, now, I'd tell you what I would do,' said the captain: 'I would have none of your fancy rigs with the man driving from the mizzen cross-trees, but a plain fore-and-aft hack cab of the highest registered tonnage. First of all, I would bring up at the market and get a turkey and a sucking-pig. Then I'd go to a wine-merchant's and get a dozen of champagne, and a dozen of some sweet wine, rich and sticky and strong, something in the port or madeira line, the best in the store. Then I'd bear up for a toy-store, and lay out twenty dollars in assorted toys for the piccaninnies; and then to a confectioner's and take in cakes and pies and fancy bread, and that stuff with the plums in it; and then to a news-agency and buy all the papers, all the picture ones for the kids, and all the story papers for the old girl about the Earl discovering himself to Anna-Mariar and the escape of Lady Maude from the private madhouse; and then I'd tell the fellow to drive home.'

'There ought to be some syrup for the kids,' suggested Herrick; 'they like syrup.'

'Yes, syrup for the kids, red syrup at that!' said the captain. 'And those things they pull at, and go pop, and have measly poetry inside. And then I tell you we'd have a thanksgiving-day and Christmas-tree combined. Great Scott, but I would like to see the kids! I guess they would light right out of the house when they saw daddy driving up. My little Adar ...'

The captain stopped sharply.

'Well, keep it up!' said the clerk.

'The damned thing is, I don't know if they ain't starving!' cried the captain.

'They can't be worse off than we are, and that's one comfort,' returned the clerk. 'I defy the devil to make me worse off.'

It seemed as if the devil heard him. The light of the moon had been some time cut off and they had talked in darkness. Now there was heard a roar, which drew impetuously nearer; the face of the lagoon was seen to whiten; and before they had staggered to their feet, a squall burst in rain upon the outcasts. The rage and volume of that avalanche one must have lived in the tropics to conceive; a man panted in its assault as he might pant under a shower-bath; and the world seemed whelmed in night and water.

They fled, groping for their usual shelter – it might be almost called their home – in the old calaboose; came drenched into its empty chambers; and lay down, three sops of humanity, on the cold coral floors, and presently, when the squall was overpast, the others could hear in the darkness the chattering of the clerk's teeth.

'I say, you fellows,' he wailed, 'for God's sake, lie up and try to warm me. I'm blymed if I don't think I'll die else!'

So the three crept together into one wet mass, and lay until day came, shivering and dozing off, and continually reawakened to wretchedness by the coughing of the clerk.

Morning on the Beach – the Three Letters

THE clouds were all fled, the beauty of the tropic day was spread upon Papeete; and the wall of breaking seas upon the reef, and the palms upon the islet, already trembled in the heat. A French man-of-war was going out, homeward bound; she lay in the middle distance of the port, an ant-heap of activity. In the night a schooner had come in, and now lay far out, hard by the passage; and the yellow flag, the emblem of pestilence, flew on her. From up the coast, a long procession of canoes headed round the point and towards the market, bright as a scarf with the many-coloured clothing of the natives and the piles of fruit. But not even the beauty and the welcome warmth of the morning, not even these naval movements, so interesting to sailors and to idlers, could engage the attention of the outcasts. They were still cold at heart, their mouths sour from the want of sleep, their steps rambling from the lack of food; and they strung like lame geese along the beach in a disheartened silence. It was towards the town they moved; towards the town whence smoke arose, where happier folk were breakfasting; and as they went, their hungry eyes were upon all sides, but they were only scouting for a meal.

A small and dingy schooner lay snug against the quay, with which it was connected by a plank. On the forward deck, under a spot of awning, five Kanakas who made up the crew, were squatted round a basin of fried feis,* and drinking coffee from tin mugs.

'Eight bells: knock off for breakfast!' cried the captain, with a miserable heartiness. 'Never tried this craft before; positively my first appearance; guess I'll draw a bumper house.'

He came close up to where the plank rested on the grassy

*Fei is the hill banana.

quay; turned his back upon the schooner, and began to whistle that lively air, 'The Irish Washerwoman.' It caught the ears of the Kanaka seamen like a preconcerted signal; with one accord they looked up from their meal and crowded to the ship's side, fei in hand and munching as they looked. Even as a poor brown Pyrenean bear dances in the streets of English towns under his master's baton; even so, but with how much more of spirit and precision, the captain footed it in time to his own whistling, and his long morning shadow capered beyond him on the grass. The Kanakas smiled on the performance; Herrick looked on heavy-eyed, hunger for the moment conquering all sense of shame; and a little farther off, but still hard by, the clerk was torn by the seven devils of the influenza.

The captain stopped suddenly, appeared to perceive his audience for the first time, and represented the part of a man surprised in his private hour of pleasure.

'Hello!' said he.

The Kanakas clapped hands and called upon him to go on.

'No, *sir*!' said the captain. 'No eat, no dance. Savvy?'

'Poor old man!' returned one of the crew. 'Him no eat?'

'Lord, no!' said the captain. 'Like-um too much eat. No got.'

'All right. Me got,' said the sailor; 'you tome here. Plenty toffee, plenty fei. Nutha man him tome too.'

'I guess we'll drop right in,' observed the captain; and he and his companions hastened up the plank. They were welcomed on board with the shaking of hands; place was made for them round the basin; a sticky demijohn of molasses was added to the feast in honour of company, and an accordion brought from the forecastle and significantly laid by the performer's side.

'*Ariana*,'* said he lightly, touching the instrument as he spoke; and he fell to on a long savoury fei, made an end of it, raised his mug of coffee, and nodded across at the spokesman of the crew. 'Here's your health, old man; you're a credit to the South Pacific,' said he.

With the unsightly greed of hounds they glutted themselves with the hot food and coffee; and even the clerk revived and

*By-and by.

the colour deepened in his eyes. The kettle was drained, the basin cleaned; their entertainers, who had waited on their wants throughout with the pleased hospitality of Polynesians, made haste to bring forward a dessert of island tobacco and rolls of pandanus leaf to serve as paper; and presently all sat about the dishes puffing like Indian Sachems.[10]

'When a man 'as breakfast every day, he don't know what it is,' observed the clerk.

'The next point is dinner,' said Herrick; and then with a passionate utterance: 'I wish to God I was a Kanaka!'

'There's one thing sure,' said the captain. 'I'm about desperate; I'd rather hang than rot here much longer.' And with the word he took the accordion and struck up 'Home, sweet Home.'

'O, drop that!' cried Herrick, 'I can't stand that.'

'No more can I,' said the captain. 'I've got to play something though: got to pay the shot, my son.' And he struck up 'John Brown's Body' in a fine sweet baritone: 'Dandy Jim of Carolina' came next; 'Rorin the Bold,' 'Swing low, Sweet Chariot,' and 'The Beautiful Land' followed. The captain was paying his shot with usury, as he had done many a time before; many a meal had he bought with the same currency from the melodious-minded natives, always, as now, to their delight.

He was in the middle of 'Fifteen Dollars in the Inside Pocket,' singing with dogged energy, for the task went sore against the grain, when a sensation was suddenly to be observed among the crew.

'*Tapena Tom harry my*,'* said the spokesman, pointing.

And the three beachcombers, following his indication, saw the figure of a man in pyjama trousers and a white jumper approaching briskly from the town.

'That's Tapena Tom, is it?' said the captain, pausing in his music. 'I don't seem to place the brute.'

'We'd better cut,' said the clerk. ''E's no good.'

'Well,' said the musician deliberately, 'one can't most generally always tell. I'll try it on, I guess. Music has charms to

*'Captain Tom is coming.'

soothe the savage Tapena, boys. We might strike it rich; it might amount to iced punch in the cabin.'

'Hiced punch? O my!' said the clerk. 'Give him something 'ot, captain. "Way down the Swannee River"; try that.'

'No, *sir*! Looks Scots,' said the captain; and he struck, for his life, into 'Auld Lang Syne.'

Captain Tom continued to approach with the same business-like alacrity; no change was to be perceived in his bearded face as he came swinging up the plank: he did not even turn his eyes on the performer.

> 'We twa hae paidled in the burn,
> Frae morning tide till dine,'[11]

went the song.

Captain Tom had a parcel under his arm, which he laid on the house roof, and then turning suddenly to the strangers: 'Here, you!' he bellowed, 'be off out of that!'

The clerk and Herrick stood not on the order of their going, but fled incontinently by the plank. The performer, on the other hand, flung down the instrument and rose to his full height slowly.

'What's that you say?' he said. 'I've half a mind to give you a lesson in civility.'

'You set up any more of your gab to me,' returned the Scotsman, 'and I'll show ye the wrong side of a jyle. I've heard tell of the three of ye. Ye're not long for here, I can tell you that. The Government has their eyes upon ye. They make short work of damned beachcombers, I'll say that for the French.'

'You wait till I catch you off your ship!' cried the captain: and then, turning to the crew, 'Good-bye, you fellows!' he said. 'You're gentlemen, anyway! The worst nigger among you would look better upon a quarter-deck than that filthy Scotsman.'

Captain Tom scorned to reply; he watched with a hard smile the departure of his guests, and as soon as the last foot was off the plank, turned to the hands to work cargo.

The beachcombers beat their inglorious retreat along the shore; Herrick first, his face dark with blood, his knees trembling under him with the hysteria of rage. Presently, under the same *purao* where they had shivered the night before, he cast himself down, and groaned aloud, and ground his face into the sand.

'Don't speak to me, don't speak to me. I can't stand it,' broke from him.

The other two stood over him perplexed.

'Wot can't he stand now?' said the clerk. ''Asn't he 'ad a meal? *I'm* lickin' my lips.'

Herrick reared up his wild eyes and burning face. 'I can't beg!' he screamed, and again threw himself prone.

'This thing's got to come to an end,' said the captain, with an intake of breath.

'Looks like signs of an end, don't it?' sneered the clerk.

'He's not so far from it, and don't you deceive yourself,' replied the captain. – 'Well,' he added in a livelier voice, 'you fellows hang on here, and I'll go and interview my representative.'

Whereupon he turned on his heel, and set off at a swinging sailor's walk towards Papeete.

It was some half-hour later when he returned. The clerk was dozing with his back against the tree: Herrick still lay where he had flung himself; nothing showed whether he slept or waked.

'See, boys!' cried the captain, with that artificial heartiness of his which was at times so painful, 'here's a new idea.' And he produced note-paper, stamped envelopes, and pencils, three of each. 'We can all write home by the mail brigantine; the consul says I can come over to his place and ink up the addresses.

'Well, that's a start, too,' said the clerk. 'I never thought of that.'

'It was that yarning last night about going home that put me up to it,' said the captain.

'Well, 'and over,' said the clerk. 'I'll 'ave a shy,' and he retired a little distance to the shade of a canoe.

The others remained under the *purao*. Now they would write a word or two, now scribble it out; now they would sit biting at the pencil end and staring seaward; now their eyes would rest on the clerk, where he sat propped on the canoe, leering and coughing, his pencil racing glibly on the paper.

'I can't do it,' said Herrick suddenly. 'I haven't got the heart.'

'See here,' said the captain, speaking with unwonted gravity; 'it may be hard to write, and to write lies at that; and God knows it is; but it's the square thing. It don't cost anything to say you're well and happy, and sorry you can't make a remittance this mail; and if you don't I'll tell you what I think it is – I think it's about the high-water mark of being a brute beast.'

'It's easy to talk,' said Herrick. 'You don't seem to have written much yourself, I notice.'

'What do you bring in me for?' broke from the captain. His voice was indeed scarce raised above a whisper, but emotion clanged in it. 'What do you know about me? If you had commanded the finest barque that ever sailed from Portland;[12] if you had been drunk in your berth when she struck the breakers in Fourteen Island Group, and hadn't had the wit to stay there and drown, but came on deck, and given drunken orders, and lost six lives – I could understand your talking then! There,' he said more quietly, 'that's my yarn, and now you know it. It's a pretty one for the father of a family. Five men and a woman murdered. Yes, there was a woman on board, and hadn't no business to be either. Guess I sent her to Hell, if there is such a place. I never dared go home again; and the wife and the little ones went to England to her father's place. I don't know what's come to them,' he added, with a bitter shrug.

'Thank you, captain,' said Herrick. 'I never liked you better.'

They shook hands, short and hard, with eyes averted, tenderness swelling in their bosoms.

'Now, boys! to work again at lying!' said the captain.

'I'll give my father up,' returned Herrick with a writhen smile. 'I'll try my sweetheart instead for a change of evils.'

And here is what he wrote:

Emma, I have scratched out the beginning to my father, for I think I can write more easily to you. This is my last farewell to all, the last you will ever hear or see of an unworthy friend and son. I have failed in life; I am quite broken down and disgraced. I pass under a false name; you will have to tell my father that with all your kindness. It is my own fault. I know, had I chosen, that I might have done well; and yet I swear to you I tried to choose. I could not bear that you should think I did not try. For I loved you all; you must never doubt me in that, you least of all. I have always unceasingly loved, but what was my love worth? and what was I worth? I had not the manhood of a common clerk; I could not work to earn you; I have lost you now, and for your sake I could be glad of it. When you first came to my father's house – do you remember those days? I want you to – you saw the best of me then, all that was good in me. Do you remember the day I took your hand and would not let it go – and the day on Battersea Bridge, when we were looking at a barge, and I began to tell you one of my silly stories, and broke off to say I loved you? That was the beginning, and now here is the end. When you have read this letter, you will go round and kiss them all good-bye, my father and mother, and the children, one by one, and poor uncle; and tell them all to forget me, and forget me yourself. Turn the key in the door; let no thought of me return; be done with the poor ghost that pretended he was a man and stole your love. Scorn of myself grinds in me as I write. I should tell you I am well and happy, and want for nothing. I do not exactly make money, or I should send a remittance; but I am well cared for, have friends, live in a beautiful place and climate, such as we have dreamed of together, and no pity need be wasted on me. In such places, you understand, it is easy to live, and live well, but often hard to make sixpence in money. Explain this to my father, he will understand. I have no more to say; only linger, going out, like an unwilling guest. God in heaven bless you. Think of me at the last, here, on a bright beach, the sky and sea immoderately blue, and the great breakers roaring outside on a barrier reef, where a little isle sits green with palms. I am well and strong. It is a more pleasant way to die than if you were crowding about me on a sick-bed. And yet I am dying. This is my last kiss. Forgive, forget the unworthy.

So far he had written, his paper was all filled, when there returned a memory of evenings at the piano, and that song, the masterpiece of love, in which so many have found the expression of their dearest thoughts. *'Einst, O Wunder!'* [13] he added. More was not required; he knew that in his love's heart the context would spring up, escorted with fair images and harmony;

of how all through life her name should tremble in his ears, her name be everywhere repeated in the sounds of nature; and when death came, and he lay dissolved, her memory lingered and thrilled among his elements.

> Once, O wonder! once from the ashes of my heart
> Arose a blossom –

Herrick and the captain finished their letters about the same time; each was breathing deep, and their eyes met and were averted as they closed the envelopes.

'Sorry I write so big,' said the captain gruffly. 'Came all of a rush, when it did come.'

'Same here,' said Herrick. 'I could have done with a ream when I got started; but it's long enough for all the good I had to say.'

They were still at the addresses when the clerk strolled up, smirking and twirling his envelope, like a man well pleased. He looked over Herrick's shoulder.

'Hullo,' he said, 'you ain't writing 'ome.'

'I am, though,' said Herrick; 'she lives with my father. – O, I see what you mean,' he added. 'My real name is Herrick. No more Hay' – they had both used the same *alias* – 'no more Hay than yours, I daresay.'

'Clean bowled in the middle stump!' laughed the clerk. 'My name's 'Uish, if you want to know. Everybody has a false nyme in the Pacific. Lay you five to three the captain 'as.'

'So I have too,' replied the captain; 'and I've never told my own since the day I tore the title-page out of my Bowditch and flung the damned thing into the sea. But I'll tell it to you, boys. John Davis is my name. I'm Davis of the *Sea Ranger*.'

'Dooce you are!' said Huish. 'And what was she? a pirate or a slyver?'

'She was the fastest barque out of Portland, Maine,' replied the captain; 'and for the way I lost her, I might as well have bored a hole in her side with an auger.'

'O, you lost her, did you?' said the clerk. ''Ope she was insured?'

No answer being returned to this sally, Huish, still brimming over with vanity and conversation, struck into another subject.

'I've a good mind to read you my letter,' said he. 'I've a good fist with a pen when I choose, and this is a prime lark. She was a barmaid I ran across in Northampton; she was a spanking fine piece, no end of style; and we cottoned at first sight like parties in the play. I suppose I spent the chynge of a fiver on that girl. Well, I 'appened to remember her nyme, so I wrote to her, and told her 'ow I had got rich, and married a queen in the Hislands, and lived in a blooming palace. Such a sight of crammers! I must read you one bit about my opening the nigger parliament in a cocked 'at. It's really prime.'

The captain jumped to his feet. 'That's what you did with the paper that I went and begged for you?' he roared.

It was perhaps lucky for Huish – it was surely in the end unfortunate for all – that he was seized just then by one of his prostrating accesses of cough; his comrades would have deserted him, so bitter was their resentment. When the fit had passed, the clerk reached out his hand, picked up the letter, which had fallen to the earth, and tore it into fragments, stamp and all.

'Does that satisfy you?' he asked sullenly.

'We'll say no more about it,' replied Davis.

The Old Calaboose – Destiny at the Door

THE old calaboose, in which the waifs had so long harboured, is a low, rectangular enclosure of building at the corner of a shady western avenue and a little townward of the British consulate. Within was a grassy court, littered with wreckage and the traces of vagrant occupation. Six or seven cells opened from the court: the doors, that had once been locked on mutinous whalermen, rotting before them in the grass. No mark remained of their old destination, except the rusty bars upon the windows.

The floor of one of the cells had been a little cleared; a bucket (the last remaining piece of furniture of the three caitiffs) stood full of water by the door, a half cocoanut shell beside it for a drinking-cup; and on some ragged ends of mat Huish sprawled asleep, his mouth open, his face deathly. The glow of the tropic afternoon, the green of sunbright foliage, stared into that shady place through door and window; and Herrick, pacing to and fro on the coral floor, sometimes paused and laved his face and neck with tepid water from the bucket. His long arrears of suffering, the night's vigil, the insults of the morning, and the harrowing business of the letter, had strung him to that point when pain is almost pleasure, time shrinks to a mere point, and death and life appear indifferent. To and fro he paced like a caged brute; his mind whirling through the universe of thought and memory; his eyes, as he went, skimming the legends on the wall. The crumbling whitewash was all full of them: Tahitian names, and French, and English, and rude sketches of ships under sail and men at fisticuffs.

It came to him of a sudden that he too must leave upon these walls the memorial of his passage. He paused before a clean space, took the pencil out, and pondered. Vanity, so hard to dislodge, awoke in him. We call it vanity at least; perhaps unjustly. Rather it was the bare sense of his existence prompted him; the sense of his life, the one thing wonderful, to which he scarce clung with a finger. From his jarred nerves there came a strong sentiment of coming change; whether good or ill he could not say: change, he knew no more – change with inscrutable veiled face, approaching noiseless. With the feeling came the vision of a concert room, the rich hues of instruments, the silent audience, and the loud voice of the symphony. 'Destiny knocking at the door,' he thought; drew a stave on the plaster, and wrote in the famous phrase from the Fifth Symphony.[14] 'So,' thought he, 'they will know that I loved music and had classical tastes. They? He, I suppose: the unknown, kindred spirit that shall come some day and read my *memor querela*.[15] Ha, he shall have Latin too!' And he added: *terque quaterque beati Queis ante ora patrum*.

He turned again to his uneasy pacing, but now with an irrational and supporting sense of duty done. He had dug his grave that morning; now he had carved his epitaph; the folds of the toga were composed, why should he delay the insignificant trifle that remained to do? He paused and looked long in the face of the sleeping Huish, drinking disenchantment and distaste of life. He nauseated himself with that vile countenance. Could the thing continue? What bound him now? Had he no rights? – only the obligation to go on, without discharge or furlough, bearing the unbearable? *Ich trage unerträgliches*,[16] the quotation rose in his mind; he repeated the whole piece, one of the most perfect of the most perfect of poets; and a phrase struck him like a blow: *Du, stolzes Herz, du hast es ja gewollt*.[17] Where was the pride of his heart? And he raged against himself, as a man bites on a sore tooth, in a heady sensuality of scorn. 'I have no pride, I have no heart, no manhood,' he thought, 'or why should I prolong a life more shameful than the gallows? Or why should I have fallen to it? No pride, no capacity, no force. Not even a bandit! and to be starving here with worse than banditti – with this trivial hell-hound!' His rage against his comrade rose and flooded him, and he shook a trembling fist at the sleeper.

A swift step was audible. The captain appeared upon the threshold of the cell, panting and flushed, and with a foolish face of happiness. In his arms he carried a loaf of bread and bottles of beer; the pockets of his coat were bulging with cigars. He rolled his treasures on the floor, grasped Herrick by both hands, and crowed with laughter.

'Broach the beer!' he shouted. 'Broach the beer, and glory hallelujah!'

'Beer?' repeated Huish, struggling to his feet.

'Beer it is!' cried Davis. 'Beer, and plenty of it. Any number of persons can use it (like Lyon's tooth-tablet) with perfect propriety and neatness. Who's to officiate?'

'Leave me alone for that,' said the clerk. He knocked the necks off with a lump of coral, and each drank in succession from the shell.

'Have a weed,' said Davis. 'It's all in the bill.'

'What is up?' asked Herrick.

The captain fell suddenly grave. 'I'm coming to that,' said he. 'I want to speak with Herrick here. You, Hay – or Huish, or whatever your name is – you take a weed and the other bottle, and go and see how the wind is down by the *purao*. I'll call you when you're wanted!'

'Hey? Secrets? That ain't the ticket,' said Huish.

'Look here, my son,' said the captain, 'this is business, and don't you make any mistake about it. If you're going to make trouble, you can have it your own way and stop right here. Only get the thing right: if Herrick and I go, we take the beer. Savvy?'

'O, I don't want to shove my oar in,' returned Huish. 'I'll cut right enough. Give me the swipes. You can jaw till you're blue in the face for what I care. I don't think it's the friendly touch, that's all.' And he shambled grumbling out of the cell into the staring sun.

The captain watched him clear of the courtyard; then turned to Herrick.

'What is it?' asked Herrick thickly.

'I'll tell you,' said Davis. 'I want to consult you. It's a chance we've got. – What's that?' he cried, pointing to the music on the wall.

'What?' said the other. 'O, that! It's music; it's a phrase of

Beethoven's I was writing up. It means Destiny knocking at the door.'

'Does it?' said the captain, rather low; and he went near and studied the inscription. 'And this French?' he asked, pointing to the Latin.

'Oh, it just means I should have been luckier if I had died at home,' returned Herrick impatiently. 'What is this business?'

'Destiny knocking at the door,' repeated the captain; and then, looking over his shoulder, 'Well, Mr Herrick, that's about what it comes to,' he added.

'What do you mean? Explain yourself,' said Herrick.

But the captain was again staring at the music. 'About how long ago since you wrote up this truck?' he asked.

'What does it matter?' exclaimed Herrick. 'I daresay half an hour.'

'My God, it's strange!' cried Davis. 'There's some men would call that accidental: not me. That ...' and he drew his thick finger under the music – 'that's what I call Providence.'

'You said we had a chance,' said Herrick.

'Yes, *sir*!' said the captain, wheeling suddenly face to face with his companion. 'I did so. If you're the man I take you for, we have a chance.'

'I don't know what you take me for,' was the reply. 'You can scarce take me too low.'

'Shake hands, Mr Herrick,' said the captain. 'I know you. You're a gentleman and a man of spirit. I didn't want to speak before that bummer there; you'll see why. But to you I'll rip it right out. I got a ship.'

'A ship?' cried Herrick. 'What ship?'

'That schooner we saw this morning off the passage.'

'That schooner with the hospital flag?'

'That's the hooker,' said Davis. 'She's the *Farallone*, hundred and sixty tons register, out of 'Frisco for Sydney, in California champagne. Captain, mate, and one hand all died of the small-pox, same as they had round in the Paumotus,[18] I guess. Captain and mate were the only white men; all the hands Kanakas; seems a queer kind of outfit from a Christian port. Three of them left and a cook; didn't know where they were; I can't think where they were either, if you come to that; Wiseman must have been on the booze, I guess, to sail the course he did. However, there *he* was, dead; and here are the Kanakas as good as lost. They bummed around at sea like the babes in the wood; and tumbled head-on upon Tahiti. The Consul here took charge. He offered the berth to Williams; Williams had never had the smallpox and backed down. That was when I came in for the letter-paper; I thought there was something up when the Consul asked me to look in again; but I never let on to you fellows, so's you'd not be disappointed. Consul tried M'Neil; scared of smallpox. He tried Capirati, that Corsican, and Leblue, or whatever his name is, wouldn't lay a hand on it; all too fond of their sweet lives. Last of all, when there was nobody else left to offer it to, he offers it to me. "Brown, will you ship captain and take her to Sydney?" says he. "Let me choose my own mate and another white hand," says I, "for I don't hold with this Kanaka crew racket; give us all two months' advance to get our clothes and instruments out of pawn, and I'll take stock to-night, fill up stores, and get to sea to-morrow before dark!" That's what I said. "That's good enough," says the Consul, "and you can count yourself damned lucky, Brown," says he. And he said it pretty meaningful-appearing too. However, that's all one now. I'll ship Huish before the mast – of course I'll let him berth aft – and I'll ship you mate at seventy-five dollars and two months' advance.'

'Me mate? Why, I'm a landsman!' cried Herrick.

'Guess you've got to learn,' said the captain. 'You don't fancy I'm going to skip and leave you rotting on the beach, perhaps? I'm not that sort, old man. And you're handy, anyway; I've been shipmates with worse.'

'God knows I can't refuse,' said Herrick. 'God knows I thank you from my heart.'

'That's all right,' said the captain. 'But it ain't all.' He turned aside to light a cigar.

'What else is there?' asked the other, with a pang of undefinable alarm.

'I'm coming to that,' said Davis, and then paused a little. 'See here,' he began, holding out his cigar between his finger and thumb, 'suppose you figure up what this'll amount to. You don't catch on? Well, we get two months' advance; we can't get away from Papeete – our creditors wouldn't let us go – for less; it'll take us along about two months to get to Sydney; and when we get there, I just want to put it to you squarely: What the better are we?'

'We're off the beach at least,' said Herrick.

'I guess there's a beach at Sydney,' returned the captain; 'and I'll tell you one thing, Mr Herrick – I don't mean to try. No, *sir*! Sydney will never see me.'

'Speak out plain,' said Herrick.

'Plain Dutch,' replied the captain. 'I'm going to own that schooner. It's nothing new; it's done every year in the Pacific. Stephens stole a schooner the other day, didn't he? Hayes and Pease stole vessels all the time. And it's the making of the crowd of us. See here – you think of that cargo. Champagne! why, it's like as if it was put up on purpose. In Peru we'll sell that liquor off at the pier-head, and the schooner after it, if we can find a fool to buy her; and then light out for the mines. If you'll back me up, I stake my life I carry it through.'

'Captain,' said Herrick, with a quailing voice, 'don't do it!'

'I'm desperate,' returned Davis. 'I've got a chance; I may never get another. Herrick, say the word: back me up; I think we've starved together long enough for that.'

'I can't do it. I'm sorry. I can't do it. I've not fallen as low as that,' said Herrick, deadly pale.

'What did you say this morning?' said Davis. 'That you couldn't beg? It's the one thing or the other, my son.'

'Ah, but this is the jail!' cried Herrick. 'Don't tempt me. It's the jail.'

'Did you hear what the skipper said on board that schooner?' pursued the captain. 'Well, I tell you he talked straight. The French have let us alone for a long time; it can't last longer; they've got their eye on us; and as sure as you live, in three weeks you'll be in jail whatever you do. I read it in the Consul's face.'

'You forget, captain,' said the young man. 'There is another way. I can die; and to say truth, I think I should have died three years ago.'

The captain folded his arms and looked the other in the face. 'Yes,' said he, 'yes, you can cut your throat; that's a frozen fact; much good may it do you! And where do I come in?'

The light of a strange excitement came in Herrick's face. 'Both of us,' said he, 'both of us together. It's not possible you can enjoy this business. Come,' and he reached out a timid hand, 'a few strokes in the lagoon – and rest!'

'I tell you, Herrick, I'm 'most tempted to answer you the way the man does in the Bible, and say, "*Get thee behind me, Satan!*"' said the captain. 'What! you think I would go drown myself, and I got children starving? Enjoy it? No, by God, I do not enjoy it! but it's the row I've got to hoe, and I'll hoe it till I drop right here. I have three of them, you see, two boys and the one girl, Adar. The trouble is that you are not a parent yourself. I tell you, Herrick, I love you,' the man broke out; 'I didn't take to you at first, you were so anglified and tony, but I love you now; it's a man that loves you stands here and wrestles with you. I can't go to sea with the bummer alone; it's not possible. Go drown yourself, and there goes my last chance – the last chance of a poor miserable beast, earning a crust to feed his family. I can't do nothing but sail ships, and I've no papers. And here I get a chance, and you go back on me! Ah, you've no family, and that's where the trouble is!'

'I have indeed,' said Herrick.

'Yes, I know,' said the captain, 'you think so. But no man's got a family till he's got children. It's only the kids count. There's something about the little shavers ... I can't talk of them. And if you thought a cent about this father that I hear you talk of, or that sweetheart you were writing to this morning, you would feel like me. You would say, What matter laws, and God, and that? My folks are hard up, I belong to them, I'll get them bread, or, by God! I'll get them wealth, if I have to burn down London for it. That's what you would say. And I'll tell you more: your heart is saying so this living minute. I can see it in your face. You're thinking, Here's poor friendship for the man I've starved along of, and as for the girl that I set up to be in love with, here's a mighty limp kind of a love that won't carry me as far as 'most any man would go for a demijohn of whisky. There's not much *romance* to that love, anyway; it's not the kind they carry on about in song-books. But what's the good of my carrying on talking, when it's all in your inside as plain as print? I put the question to you once for all. Are you going to desert me in my hour of need? – you know if I've deserted you – or will you give me your hand, and try a fresh deal, and go home (as like as not) a millionaire? Say No, and God pity me! Say Yes, and I'll make the little ones pray for you every night on their bended knees. "God bless Mr Herrick!" that's what they'll say, one after the other, the old girl sitting there holding stakes at the foot of the bed, and the damned little innocents ...' he broke off. 'I don't often rip out about the kids,' he said; 'but when I do, there's something fetches loose.'

'Captain,' said Herrick faintly, 'is there nothing else?'

'I'll prophesy if you like,' said the captain with renewed vigour. 'Refuse this, because you think yourself too honest, and before a month's out you'll be jailed for a sneak-thief. I give you the word fair. I can see it, Herrick, if you can't; you're breaking down. Don't think, if you refuse this chance, that you'll go on doing the evangelical; you're about through with your stock; and before you know where you are, you'll be right out on the other side. No, it's either this for you; or else it's Caledonia. I bet you never were there, and saw those white, shaved men, in their dust clothes and straw hats, prowling around in gangs in the lamplight at Noumea; they look like wolves, and they look like preachers, and they look like the sick; Huish is a daisy to the best of them. Well, there's your company. They're waiting for you, Herrick, and you got to go; and that's a prophecy.'

And as the man stood and shook through his great stature, he seemed indeed like one in whom the spirit of divination worked and might utter oracles. Herrick looked at him, and looked away; it seemed not decent to spy upon such agitation; and the young man's courage sank.

'You talk of going home,' he objected. 'We could never do that.'

'*We* could,' said the other. 'Captain Brown couldn't, nor Mr Hay, that shipped mate with him couldn't. But what's that to do with Captain Davis or Mr Herrick, you galoot?'

'But Hayes had these wild islands where he used to call,' came the next fainter objection.

'We have the wild islands of Peru,' retorted Davis. 'They were wild enough for Stephens, no longer agone than just last year. I guess they'll be wild enough for us.'

'And the crew?'

'All Kanakas. Come, I see you're right, old man. I see you'll stand by.' And the captain once more offered his hand.

'Have it your own way then,' said Herrick. 'I'll do it: a strange thing for my father's son. But I'll do it. I'll stand by you, man, for good or evil.'

'God bless you!' cried the captain, and stood silent. 'Herrick,' he added with a smile, 'I believe I'd have died in my tracks if you'd said No!'

And Herrick, looking at the man, half believed so also.

'And now we'll break it to the bummer,' said Davis.

'I wonder how he'll take it,' said Herrick.

'Him? Jump at it!' was the reply.

The Yellow Flag

THE schooner *Farallone* lay well out in the jaws of the pass, where the terrified pilot had made haste to bring her to her moorings and escape. Seen from the beach through the thin line of shipping, two objects stood conspicuous to seaward : the little isle, on the one hand, with its palms and the guns and batteries raised forty years before in defence of Queen Pomare's capital; the outcast *Farallone*, upon the other, banished to the threshold of the port, rolling there to her scuppers, and flaunting the plague-flag as she rolled. A few sea-birds screamed and cried about the ship; and within easy range, a man-of-war guard-boat hung off and on and glittered with the weapons of marines. The exuberant daylight and the blinding heaven of the tropics picked out and framed the pictures.

A neat boat, manned by natives in uniform, and steered by the doctor of the port, put from shore towards three of the afternoon, and pulled smartly for the schooner. The fore-sheets were heaped with sacks of flour, onions, and potatoes, perched among which was Huish dressed as a foremast hand; a heap of chests and cases impeded the action of the oarsmen; and in the stern, by the left hand of the doctor, sat Herrick, dressed in a fresh rig of slops, his brown beard trimmed to a point, a pile of paper novels on his lap, and nursing the while between his feet a chronometer, for which they had exchanged that of the *Farallone*, long since run down and the rate lost.

They passed the guard-boat, exchanging hails with the boatswain's mate in charge, and drew near at last to the forbidden ship. Not a cat stirred, there was no speech of man; and the sea being exceedingly high outside, and the reef close to where the schooner lay, the clamour of the surf hung round her like the sound of battle.

'Ohé lá goëlette!' [19] sang out the doctor, with his best voice.

Instantly, from the house where they had been stowing away stores, first Davis, and then the ragamuffin, swarthy crew made their appearance.

'Hullo, Hay, that you?' said the captain, leaning on the rail. 'Tell the old man to lay her alongside, as if she was eggs. There's a hell of a run of sea here, and his boat's brittle.'

The movement of the schooner was at that time more than usually violent. Now she heaved her side as high as a deep-sea steamer's, and showed the flashing of her copper; now she swung swiftly towards the boat until her scuppers gurgled.

'I hope you have sea-legs,' observed the doctor. 'You will require them.'

Indeed, to board the *Farallone*, in that exposed position where she lay, was an affair of some dexterity. The less precious goods were hoisted roughly in; the chronometer, after repeated failures, was passed gently and successfully from hand to hand; and there remained only the more difficult business of embarking Huish. Even that piece of dead weight (shipped A.B. at eighteen dollars, and described by the captain to the Consul as an invaluable man) was at last hauled on board without mishap; and the doctor, with civil salutations, took his leave.

The three co-adventurers looked at each other, and Davis heaved a breath of relief.

'Now let's get this chronometer fixed,' said he, and led the way into the house. It was a fairly spacious place; two staterooms and a good-sized pantry opened from the main cabin; the bulk-heads were painted white, the floor laid with waxcloth. No litter, no sign of life remained; for the effects of the dead men had been disinfected and conveyed on shore. Only on the table, in a saucer, some sulphur burned, and the fumes set them coughing as they entered. The captain peered into the starboard stateroom, where the bed-clothes still lay tumbled in the bunk, the blanket flung back as they had flung it back from the disfigured corpse before its burial.

'Now, I told these niggers to tumble that truck overboard,' grumbled Davis. 'Guess they were afraid to lay hands on it. Well, they've hosed the place out; that's as much as can be expected, I suppose. Huish, lay on to these blankets.'

'See you bloomin' well far enough first,' said Huish, drawing back.

'What's that?' snapped the captain. 'I'll tell you, my young friend, I think you make a mistake. I'm captain here.'

'Fat lot I care,' returned the clerk.

'That so?' said Davis. 'Then you'll berth forward with the niggers! Walk right out of this cabin.'

'O, I dessay!' said Huish. 'See any green in my eye? A lark's a lark.'

'Well, now, I'll explain this business, and you'll see, once for all, just precisely how much lark there is to it,' said Davis. 'I'm captain, and I'm going to be it. One thing of three. First, you take my orders here as cabin steward, in which case you mess with us. Or, second, you refuse, and I pack you forward – and you get as quick as the word's said. Or, third and last, I'll signal that man-of-war and send you ashore under arrest for mutiny.'

'And, of course, I wouldn't blow the gaff? O no!' replied the jeering Huish.

'And who's to believe you, my son?' inquired the captain. 'No, *sir*! There ain't no larking about my captainising. Enough said. Up with these blankets.'

Huish was no fool, he knew when he was beaten; and he was no coward either, for he stepped to the bunk, took the infected bed-clothes fairly in his arms, and carried them out of the house without a check or tremor.

'I was waiting for the chance,' said Davis to Herrick. 'I needn't do the same with you, because you understand it for yourself.'

'Are you going to berth here?' asked Herrick, following the captain into the stateroom, where he began to adjust the chronometer in its place at the bed-head.

'Not much!' replied he. 'I guess I'll berth on deck. I don't know as I'm afraid, but I've no immediate use for confluent smallpox.'

'I don't know that I'm afraid either,' said Herrick. 'But the thought of these two men sticks in my throat; that captain and mate dying here, one opposite to the other. It's grim. I wonder what they said last?'

'Wiseman and Wishart?' said the captain. 'Probably mighty small potatoes. That's a thing a fellow figures out for himself one way, and the real business goes quite another. Perhaps Wiseman said, 'Here, old man, fetch up the gin, I'm feeling powerful rocky.' And perhaps Wishart said, 'O, hell!'

'Well, that's grim enough,' said Herrick.

'And so it is,' said Davis. – 'There; there's that chronometer fixed. And now it's about time to up anchor and clear out.

He lit a cigar and stepped on deck.

'Here, you! What's *your* name?' he cried to one of the hands, a lean-flanked, clean-built fellow from some far western island, and of a darkness almost approaching to the African.

'Sally Day,' replied the man.

'Devil it is,' said the captain. 'Didn't know we had ladies on board. Well, Sally, oblige me by hauling down that rag there. I'll do the same for you another time.' He watched the yellow bunting as it was eased past the cross-trees and handed down on deck. 'You'll float no more on this ship,' he observed. 'Muster the people aft, Mr Hay,' he added, speaking unnecessarily loud, 'I've a word to say to them.'

It was with a singular sensation that Herrick prepared for the first time to address a crew. He thanked his stars indeed that they were natives. But even natives, he reflected, might be critics too quick for such a novice as himself; they might perceive some lapse from that precise and cut-and-dry English which prevails on board a ship; it was even possible they understood no other; and he racked his brain, and overhauled his reminiscences of sea romance for some appropriate words.

'Here, men! tumble aft!' he said. 'Lively now! all hands aft!'

They crowded in the alleyway like sheep.

'Here they are, sir,' said Herrick.

For some time the captain continued to face the stern; then turned with ferocious suddenness on the crew, and seemed to enjoy their shrinking.

'Now,' he said, twisting his cigar in his mouth and toying with the spokes of the wheel. 'I'm Captain Brown. I command this ship. This is Mr Hay, first officer. The other white man is cabin steward, but he'll stand watch and do his trick. My orders shall be obeyed smartly. You savvy, "*smartly*"? There shall be no growling about the kaikai, which will be above allowance. You'll put a handle to the mate's name, and tack on "sir" to every order I give you. If you're smart and quick, I'll make this ship comfortable for all hands.' He took the cigar out of his mouth. 'If you're not,' he added, in a roaring voice, 'I'll make it a floating hell. – Now, Mr Hay, we'll pick watches, if you please.'

'All right,' said Herrick.

'You will please use "sir" when you address me, Mr Hay,' said the captain. 'I'll take the lady. Step to starboard, Sally.' And then he whispered in Herrick's ear, 'Take the old man.'

'I'll take you, there,' said Herrick.

'What's your name?' said the captain. 'What's that you say? O, that's not English; I'll have none of your highway gibberish on my ship. We'll call you old Uncle Ned, because you've got no wool on the top of your head, just the place where the wool ought to grow. Step to port, Uncle. Don't you hear Mr Hay has picked you? Then I'll take the white man. White Man, step to starboard. Now, which of you two is the cook? You? Then Mr Hay takes your friend in the blue dungaree. Step to port, Dungaree. There, we know who we all are: Dungaree, Uncle Ned, Sally Day, White Man, and Cook. All F.F.V.'s I guess. And now, Mr Hay, we'll up anchor, if you please.'

'For heaven's sake, tell me some of the words,' whispered Herrick.

An hour later the *Farallone* was under all plain sail, the rudder hard a-port, and the cheerfully-clanking windlass had brought the anchor home.

'All clear, sir, cried Herrick from the bow.

The captain met her with the wheel, as she bounded like a stag from her repose, trembling and bending to the puffs. The guard-boat gave a parting hail, the wake whitened and ran out; the *Farallone* was under weigh.

Her berth had been close to the pass. Even as she forged ahead Davis slewed her for the channel between the pierends of the reef, the breakers sounding and whitening to either hand. Straight through the narrow band of blue she shot to seaward;

and the captain's heart exulted as he felt her tremble underfoot, and (looking back over the taffrail) beheld the roofs of Papeete changing position on the shore and the island mountains rearing higher in the wake.

But they were not yet done with the shore and the horror of the yellow flag. About midway of the pass there was a cry and a scurry, a man was seen to leap upon the rail, and, throwing his arms over his head, to stoop and plunge into the sea.

'Steady as she goes,' the captain cried, relinquishing the wheel to Huish.

The next moment he was forward in the midst of the Kanakas, belaying-pin in hand.

'Anybody else for shore?' he cried, and the savage trumpeting of his voice, no less than the ready weapon in his hand, struck fear in all. Stupidly they stared after their escaped companion, whose black head was visible upon the water, steering for the land. And the schooner meanwhile slipped like a racer through the pass, and met the long sea of the open ocean with a souse of spray.

'Fool that I was, not to have a pistol ready!' exclaimed Davis. 'Well, we go to sea short-handed, we can't help that. You have a lame watch of it, Mr Hay.'

'I don't see how we are to get along,' said Herrick.

'Got to,' said the captain. 'No more Tahiti for me.'

Both turned instinctively and looked astern. The fair island was unfolding mountain-top on mountain-top; Eimeo, on the port board, lifted her splintered pinnacles; and still the schooner raced to the open sea.

'Think!' cried the captain, with a gesture, 'yesterday morning I danced for my breakfast like a poodle dog.'

The Cargo of Champagne

THE ship's head was laid to clear Eimeo to the north, and the captain sat down in the cabin, with a chart, a ruler, and an epitome.

'East a half no'the,' said he, raising his face from his labours. 'Mr Hay, you'll have to watch your dead reckoning; I want every yard she makes on every hair's-breadth of a course. I'm going to knock a hole right straight through the Paumotus, and that's always a near touch. Now, if this South East Trade ever blew out of the S.E., which it don't, we might hope to lie within half a point of our course. Say we lie within a point of it. That'll just about weather Fakarava.[20] Yes, sir, that's what we've got to do, if we tack for it. Brings us through this slush of little islands in the cleanest place: see?' And he showed where his ruler intersected the wide-lying labyrinth of the Dangerous Archipelago.[21] 'I wish it was night, and I could put her about right now; we're losing time and easting. Well, we'll do our best. And if we don't fetch Peru, we'll bring up to Ecuador. All one, I guess. Depreciated dollars down, and no questions asked. A remarkable fine institootion, the South American don.'

Tahiti was already some way astern, the Diadem rising from among broken mountains – Eimeo was already close aboard, and stood black and strange against the golden splendour of the west – when the captain took his departure from the two islands, and the patent log was set.

Some twenty minutes later, Sally Day, who was continually leaving the wheel to peer in at the cabin clock, announced in a shrill cry of 'Fo' bell,' and the cook was to be seen carrying the soup into the cabin.

'I guess I'll sit down and have a pick with you,' said Davis to Herrick. 'By the time I've done it'll be dark, and we'll clap the hooker on the wind for South America.'

In the cabin at one corner of the table, immediately below the lamp, and on the lee side of a bottle of champagne, sat Huish.

'What's this? Where did that come from?' asked the captain.

'It's fizz, and it came from the after-'old, if you want to know,' said Huish, and drained his mug.

'This'll never do,' exclaimed Davis, the merchant seaman's horror of breaking into cargo showing incongruously forth on board that stolen ship. 'There was never any good came of games like that.'

'You byby!' said Huish. 'A fellow would think (to 'ear him) we were on the square! And look 'ere, you've put this job up 'an'somely for me, 'aven't you? I'm to go on deck and steer, while you two sit and guzzle, and I'm to go by a nickname, and got to call you "sir" and "mister". Well, you look here, my bloke: I'll have fizz *ad lib.*, or it won't wash. I tell you that. And you know mighty well, you ain't got any man-of-war to signal now.'

Davis was staggered. 'I'd give fifty dollars this had never happened,' he said weakly.

'Well, it '*as* 'appened, you see,' returned Huish. 'Try some; it's devilish good.'

The Rubicon was crossed without another struggle. The captain filled a mug and drank.

'I wish it was beer,' he said with a sigh. 'But there's no denying it's the genuine stuff and cheap at the money. Now, Huish, you clear out and take your wheel.'

The little wretch had gained a point, and he was gay. 'Ay, ay, sir,' said he, and left the others to their meal.

'Pea-soup!' exclaimed the captain. 'Blamed if I thought I should taste pea-soup again!'

Herrick sat inert and silent. It was impossible after these months of hopeless want to smell the rough, high-spiced sea victuals without lust, and his mouth watered with desire of the champagne. It was no less impossible to have assisted at the scene between Huish and the captain, and not to perceive, with sudden bluntness, the gulf where he had fallen. He was a thief among thieves. He said it to himself. He could not touch the soup. If he had moved at all, it must have been to leave the table, throw himself overboard, and drown – an honest man.

'Here,' said the captain, 'you look sick, old man; have a drop of this.'

The champagne creamed and bubbled in the mug; its bright colour, its lively effervescence, seized his eye. 'It is too late to hesitate,' he thought; his hand took the mug instinctively; he drank, with unquenchable pleasure and desire of more; drained the vessel dry, and set it down with sparkling eyes.

'There is something in life after all!' he cried. 'I had forgot what it was like. Yes, even this is worth while. Wine, food, dry clothes – why, they're worth dying, worth hanging for! Captain, tell me one thing: why aren't all the poor folk foot-pads?'

'Give it up,' said the captain.

'They must be damned good,' cried Herrick. 'There's something here beyond me. Think of that calaboose! Suppose we were sent suddenly back.' He shuddered as stung by a convulsion, and buried his face in his clutching hands.

'Here, what's wrong with you?' cried the captain. There was no reply; only Herrick's shoulders heaved, so that the table was shaken. 'Take some more of this. Here, drink this. I order you to. Don't start crying when you're out of the wood.'

'I'm not crying,' said Herrick, raising his face and showing his dry eyes. 'It's worse than crying. It's the horror of that grave that we've escaped from.'

'Come now, you tackle your soup; that'll fix you,' said Davis kindly. 'I told you you were all broken up. You couldn't have stood out another week.'

'That's the dreadful part of it!' cried Herrick. 'Another week and I'd have murdered some one for a dollar! God! and I know that? And I'm still living? It's some beastly dream.'

'Quietly, quietly! Quietly does it, my son. Take your pea soup. Food, that's what you want,' said Davis.

The soup strengthened and quieted Herrick's nerves; another glass of wine, and a piece of pickled pork and fried banana completed what the soup began; and he was able once more to look the captain in the face.

'I didn't know I was so much run down,' he said.

'Well,' said Davis, 'you were as steady as a rock all day: now you've had a little lunch, you'll be as steady as a rock again.'

'Yes,' was the reply, 'I'm steady enough now, but I'm a queer kind of a first officer.'

'Shucks!' cried the captain. 'You've only got to mind the ship's course, and keep your slate to half a point. A babby could do that, let alone a college graduate like you. There ain't nothing *to* sailoring, when you come to look it in the face. And now we'll go and put her about. Bring the slate; we'll have to start our dead reckoning right away.'

The distance run since the departure was read off the log by the binnacle-light and entered on the slate.

'Ready about,' said the captain. 'Give me the wheel, White Man, and you stand by the mainsheet. Boom tackle, Mr Hay, please, and then you can jump forward and attend head sails.'

'Ay, ay, sir,' responded Herrick.

'All clear forward?' asked Davis.

'All clear, sir.'

'Hard a-lee!' cried the captain. 'Haul in your slack as she comes,' he called to Huish. 'Haul in your slack, put your back into it; keep your feet out of the coils.' A sudden blow sent Huish flat along the deck, and the captain was in his place. 'Pick yourself up and keep the wheel hard over!' he roared. 'You wooden fool, you wanted to get killed, I guess. Draw the jib,' he cried a moment later; and then to Huish, 'Give me the wheel again, and see if you can coil that sheet.'

But Huish stood and looked at Davis with an evil countenance. 'Do you know you struck me?' said he.

'Do you know I saved your life?' returned the other, not deigning to look at him, his eyes travelling instead between the compass and the sails. 'Where would you have been if that boom had swung out and you bundled in the slack? No, *sir*, we'll have no more of you at the mainsheet. Seaport towns are full of mainsheet-men; they hop upon one leg, my son, what's left of them, and the rest are dead. (Set your boom tackle, Mr Hay.) Struck you, did I? Lucky for you I did.'

'Well,' said Huish slowly, 'I dessay there may be somethink

in that. 'Ope there is.' He turned his back elaborately on the captain, and entered the house, where the speedy explosion of a champagne cork showed he was attending to his comfort.

Herrick came aft to the captain. 'How is she doing now!' he asked.

'East and by no'the a half no'the,' said Davis. 'It's about as good as I expected.'

'What'll the hands think of it?' said Herrick.

'O, they don't think. They ain't paid to,' says the captain.

'There was something wrong, was there not? between you and ...' Herrick paused.

'That's a nasty little beast; that's a biter,' replied the captain, shaking his head. 'But so long as you and me hang in, it don't matter.'

Herrick lay down in the weather alleyway; the night was cloudless, the movement of the ship cradled him, he was oppressed besides by the first generous meal after so long a time of famine; and he was recalled from deep sleep by the voice of Davis singing out: 'Eight bells!'

He rose stupidly and staggered aft, where the captain gave him the wheel.

'By the wind,' said the captain. 'It comes a little puffy; when you get a heavy puff, steal all you can to windward, but keep her a good full.'

He stepped towards the house, paused and hailed the forecastle.

'Got such a thing as a concertina forward?' said he. 'Bully for you, Uncle Ned. Fetch it aft, will you?'

The schooner steered very easy; and Herrick, watching the moon-whitened sails, was overpowered by drowsiness. A sharp report from the cabin startled him; a third bottle had been opened; and Herrick remembered the *Sea Ranger* and Fourteen Island Group. Presently the notes of the accordion sounded, and then the captain's voice:

> 'O honey, with our pockets full of money,
> We will trip, trip, trip, we will trip it on the quay,
> And I will dance with Kate, and Tom will dance with Sall,
> When we're all back from South Amerikee.'

So it went to its quaint air; and the watch below lingered and listened by the forward door, and Uncle Ned was to be seen in the moonlight nodding time; and Herrick smiled at the wheel, his anxieties a while forgotten. Song followed song; another cork exploded; there were voices raised, as though the pair in the cabin were in disagreement; and presently it seemed the breach was healed; for it was now the voice of Huish that struck up, to the captain's accompaniment:

> Up in a balloon, boys,
>   Up in a balloon,
> All among the little stars
>   And round about the moon.

A wave of nausea overcame Herrick at the wheel. He wondered why the air, the words (which were yet written with a certain knack), and the voice and accent of the singer, should all jar his spirit like a file on a man's teeth. He sickened at the thought of his two comrades drinking away their reason upon stolen wine, quarrelling and hiccupping and waking up, while the doors of a prison yawned for them in the near future. 'Shall I have sold my honour for nothing?' he thought; and a heat of rage and resolution glowed in his bosom – rage against his comrades – resolution to carry through this business if it might be carried; pluck profit out of shame, since the shame at least was now inevitable; and come home, home from South America – how did the song go? – 'with his pockets full of money'.

> O honey, with our pockets full of money,
> We will trip, trip, trip, we will trip it on the quay:

so the words ran in his head; and the honey took on visible form, the quay rose before him and he knew it for the lamplit Embankment, and he saw the lights of Battersea bridge bestride the sullen river. All through the remainder of his trick he stood entranced, reviewing the past. He had been always true to his love, but not always sedulous to recall her. In the growing calamity of his life, she had swum more distant, like the moon in mist. The letter of farewell, the dishonourable hope that had surprised and corrupted him in his distress, the changed scene, the sea, the night and the music – all stirred him to the roots of manhood. 'I *will* win her,' he thought, and ground his teeth. 'Fair or foul, what matters if I win her?'

'Fo' bell, matey. I think um fo' bell' – he was suddenly recalled by these words in the voice of Uncle Ned.

'Look in at the clock, Uncle,' said he. He would not look himself, from horror of the tipplers.

'Him past, matey,' repeated the Hawaiian.

'So much the better for you, Uncle,' he replied; and he gave up the wheel, repeating the directions as he had received them.

He took two steps forward and remembered his dead reckoning. 'How has she been heading?' he thought; and he flushed from head to foot. He had not observed or had forgotten; here was the old incompetence; the slate must be filled up by guess. 'Never again!' he vowed to himself in silent fury, 'never again. It shall be no fault of mine if this miscarry.' And for the remainder of his watch, he stood close by Uncle Ned, and read the face of the compass as perhaps he had never read a letter from his sweetheart.

All the time, and spurring him to the more attention, song, loud talk, fleeting laughter, and the occasional popping of a cork, reached his ears from the interior of the house; and when the port watch was relieved at midnight, Huish and the captain appeared upon the quarter-deck with flushed faces and uneven steps, the former laden with bottles, the latter with two tin mugs. Herrick silently passed them by. They hailed him in thick voices, he made no answer; they cursed him for a churl, he paid no heed although his belly quivered with disgust and rage. He closed-to the door of the house behind him, and cast himself on a locker in the cabin – not to sleep, he thought – rather to think and to despair. Yet he had scarce turned twice on his uneasy bed, before a drunken voice hailed him in the ear, and he must go on deck again to stand the morning watch.

The first evening set the model for those that were to follow. Two cases of champagne scarce lasted the four-and-twenty hours, and almost the whole was drunk by Huish and the captain. Huish seemed to thrive on the excess; he was never sober, yet never wholly tipsy; the food and the sea air soon healed him of his disease, and he began to lay on flesh. But with Davis things went worse. In the drooping, unbuttoned figure that sprawled all day upon the lockers, tippling and reading novels; in the fool who made of the evening watch a public carouse on the quarter-deck, it would have been hard to recognise the vigorous seaman of Papeete roads. He kept himself reasonably well in hand till he had taken the sun and yawned and blotted through his calculations; but from the moment he rolled up the chart, his hours were passed in slavish self-indulgence or in hoggish slumber. Every other branch of his duty was neglected, except maintaining a stern discipline about the dinner-table. Again and again Herrick would hear the cook called aft, and see him running with fresh tins, or carrying away again a meal that had been totally condemned. And the more the captain became sunk in drunkenness, the more delicate his palate showed itself. Once, in the forenoon, he had a bo'sun's chair rigged over the rail, stripped to his trousers, and went overboard with a pot of paint. 'I don't like the way this schooner's painted,' said he, 'and I've taken a down upon her name.' But he tired of it in half an hour, and the schooner went on her way with an incongruous patch of colour on the stern, and the word *Farallone* part obliterated and part looking through. He refused to stand either the middle or the morning watch. It was fine-weather sailing, he said; and asked, with a laugh, 'Who ever heard of the old man standing watch himself?' To the dead reckoning which Herrick still tried to keep, he would pay not the least attention nor afford the least assistance.

'What do we want of dead reckoning?' he asked. 'We get the sun all right, don't we?'

'We mayn't get it always, though,' objected Herrick. 'And you told me yourself you weren't sure of the chronometer.'

'O, there ain't no flies in the chronometer!' cried Davis.

'Oblige me so far, captain,' said Herrick stiffly. 'I am anxious to keep this reckoning, which is a part of my duty; I do not know what to allow for current, nor how to allow for it. I am too inexperienced; and I beg of you to help me.'

'Never discourage zealous officer,' said the captain, unrolling the chart again, for Herrick had taken him over his day's work and while he was still partly sober. 'Here it is: look for yourself; anything from west to west no'the-west, and anyways from five to twenty-five miles. That's what the A'm'ralty chart says; I guess you don't expect to get on ahead of your own Britishers?'

'I am trying to do my duty, Captain Brown,' said Herrick, with a dark flush, 'and I have the honour to inform you that I don't enjoy being trifled with.'

'What in thunder do you want?' roared Davis. 'Go and look at the blamed wake. If you're trying to do your duty, why don't you go and do it? I guess it's no business of mine to go and stick my head over the ship's rump? I guess it's yours. And I'll tell you what it is, my fine fellow, I'll trouble you not to come the dude over me. You're insolent, that's what's wrong with you. Don't you crowd me, Mr Herrick, Esquire.'

Herrick tore up his papers, threw them on the floor, and left the cabin.

'He's turned a bloomin' swot, ain't he?' sneered Huish.

'He thinks himself too good for his company, that's what ails Herrick, Esquire,' raged the Captain. 'He thinks I don't understand when he comes the heavy swell. Won't sit down with us, won't he? won't say a civil word? I'll serve the son of a gun as he deserves. By God, Huish, I'll show him whether he's too good for John Davis!'

'Easy with the names, cap',' said Huish, who was always the more sober. 'Easy over the stones, my boy!'

'All right, I will. You're a good sort, Huish. I didn't take to you at first, but I guess you're right enough. Let's open another bottle,' said the captain; and that day, perhaps because he was excited by the quarrel, he drank more recklessly, and by four o'clock was stretched insensible upon the locker.

Herrick and Huish supped alone, one after the other, opposite his flushed and snorting body. And if the sight killed Herrick's hunger, the isolation weighed so heavily on the clerk's spirit, that he was scarce risen from table ere he was currying favour with his former comrade.

Herrick was at the wheel when he approached, and Huish leaned confidentially across the binnacle.

'I say, old chappie,' he said, 'you and me don't seem to be such pals somehow.'

Herrick gave her a spoke or two in silence; his eye, as it skirted from the needle to the luff of the foresail, passed the man by without speculation. But Huish was really dull, a thing he could support with difficulty, having no resources of his own. The idea of a private talk with Herrick, at this stage of their relations, held out particular inducements to a person of his character. Drink besides, as it renders some men hyper-sensitive, made Huish callous. And it would almost have required a blow to make him quit his purpose.

'Pretty business, ain't it?' he continued: 'Dyvis on the lush? Must say I thought you gave it 'im A-1 to-day. He didn't like it a bit; took on hawful after you were gone. "'Ere," says I, "'old on, easy on the lush," I says. "'Errick was right and you know it. Give 'im a chanst," I says. "'Uish," sezee, "don't you gimme no more of your jaw, or I'll knock your bloomin' eyes out." Well, wot can I do, 'Errick? But I tell you, I don't 'arf like it. It looks to me like the *Sea Rynger* over again.'

Still Herrick was silent.

'Do you 'ear me speak?' asked Huish sharply. 'You're pleasant, ain't you?'

'Stand away from that binnacle,' said Herrick.

The clerk looked at him long and straight and black; his figure seemed to writhe like that of a snake about to strike; then he turned on his heel, went back to the cabin and opened a bottle of champagne. When eight bells were cried he slept on the floor beside the captain on the locker; and of the whole starboard watch only Sally Day appeared upon the summons. The mate proposed to stand the watch with him, and let Uncle Ned lie down; it would make twelve hours on deck, and probably sixteen, but in this fair-weather sailing he might safely sleep between his tricks of wheel, leaving orders to be called on any sign of squalls. So far he could trust the men, between whom and himself a close relation had sprung up. With Uncle Ned he held long nocturnal conversations, and the old man told him his simple and hard story of exile, suffering, and injustice among cruel whites. The cook, when he found Herrick messed alone, produced for him unexpected and sometimes unpalatable dainties, of which he forced himself to eat. And one day, when he was forward, he was surprised to feel a caressing hand run down his shoulder, and to hear the voice of Sally Day crooning in his ear: 'You gootch man!' He turned, and, choking down a sob, shook hands with the negrito. They were kindly, cheery, childish souls. Upon the Sunday each brought forth his separate Bible – for they were all men of alien speech even to each other, and Sally Day communicated with his mates in English only, each read or made-believe to read his chapter, Uncle Ned with spectacles on his nose; and they would all join together in the singing of missionary hymns. It was thus a cutting reproof to compare the islanders and the whites aboard the *Farallone*. Shame ran in Herrick's blood to remember what employment he was on, and to see these poor souls – and even Sally Day, the child of cannibals, in all likelihood a cannibal himself – so faithful to what they knew of good. The fact that he was held in grateful favour by these innocents served like blinders to his conscience, and there were times when he was inclined, with Sally Day, to call himself a good man. But the height of his favour was only now to appear. With one voice, the crew protested; ere Herrick knew what they were doing, the cook was aroused and came a willing volunteer; all hands clustered about their mate with expostulations and caresses; and he was bidden to lie down and take his customary rest without alarm.

'He tell you tlue,' said Uncle Ned. 'You sleep. Evely man hea he do all light. Evely man he like you too much.'

Herrick struggled, and gave way; choked upon some trivial words of gratitude; and walked to the side of the house, against which he leaned, struggling with emotion.

Uncle Ned presently followed him and begged him to lie down.

'It's no use, Uncle Ned,' he replied. 'I couldn't sleep. I'm knocked over with all your goodness.'

'Ah, no call me Uncle Ned no mo'!' cried the old man. 'No my name! My name Taveeta, all-e-same Taveeta King of Islael. Wat for he call that Hawaii? I think no savvy nothing – all-e-same Wise-a-mana.'

It was the first time the name of the late captain had been mentioned, and Herrick grasped the occasion. The reader shall be spared Uncle Ned's unwieldy dialect, and learn in less embarrassing English the sum of what he now communicated. The ship had scarce cleared the Golden Gates before the captain and mate had entered on a career of drunkenness, which was scarcely interrupted by their malady and only closed by death. For days and weeks they had encountered neither land nor ship; and seeing themselves lost on the huge deep with their insane conductors, the natives had drunk deep of terror.

At length they had made a low island and went in, and Wiseman and Wishart landed in the boat.

There was a great village, a very fine village, and plenty Kanakas in that place, but all mighty serious; and from every here and there in the back parts of the settlements, Taveeta heard the sounds of island lamentation. 'I no savvy *talk* that island,' said he. 'I savvy hear um *cly*. I think, Hum! too many people die here.' But upon Wiseman and Wishart the significance of that barbaric keening was lost. Full of bread and drink, they rollicked along unconcerned, embraced the girls, who had scarce energy to repel them, took up and joined (with drunken voices) in the death-wail, and at last (on what they took to be an invitation) entered under the roof of a house in which was a considerable concourse of people sitting silent. They stooped below the eaves, flushed and laughing; within a minute they came forth again with changed faces and silent tongues; and as the press severed to make way for them, Taveeta was able to perceive, in the deep shadow of the house, the sick man raising from his mat a head already defeatured by disease. The two tragic triflers fled without hesitation for their boat, screaming on Taveeta to make haste; they came aboard with all speed of oars, raised anchor and crowded sail upon the ship with blows and curses, and were at sea again – and again drunk – before sunset. A week after, and the last of the two had been committed to the deep. Herrick asked Taveeta where that island was, and he replied that, by what he gathered of folks' talk as they went up together from the beach, he supposed it must be one of the Paumotus. This was in itself probable enough, for the Dangerous Archipelago had been swept that year from east to west by devastating smallpox; but Herrick thought it a strange course to lie from Sydney. Then he remembered the drink.

'Were they not surprised when they made the island?' he asked.

'Wise-a-mana he say, "dam! what this?"' was the reply.

'O, that's it, then,' said Herrick. 'I don't believe they knew where they were.'

'I think so too,' said Uncle Ned. 'I think no savvy. This one mo' betta,' he added, pointing to the house where the drunken captain slumbered: 'Take-a-sun all-e-time.'

The implied last touch completed Herrick's picture of the life and death of his two predecessors; of their prolonged, sordid, sodden sensuality as they sailed, they knew not whither, on their last cruise. He held but a twinkling and unsure belief in any future state; the thought of one of punishment he derided; yet for him (as for all) there dwelt a horror about the end of the brutish man. Sickness fell upon him at the image thus called up; and when he compared it with the scene in which he himself was acting, and considered the doom that seemed to brood upon the schooner, a horror that was almost superstitious fell upon him. And yet the strange thing was, he did not falter. He who had proved his incapacity in so many fields, being now falsely placed amid duties which he did not understand, without help, and it might be said without countenance, had hitherto surpassed expectation; and even the shameful misconduct and shocking disclosures of that night seemed but to nerve and strengthen him. He had sold his honour; he vowed it should not be in vain; 'it shall be no fault of mine if this miscarry', he repeated. And in his heart he wondered at himself. Living rage no doubt supported him; no doubt also, the sense of the last cast, of the ships burned, of all doors closed but one, which is so strong a tonic to the merely weak, and so deadly a depressant to the merely cowardly.

For some time the voyage went otherwise well. They weathered Fakarava with one board; and the wind holding well to the southward and blowing fresh, they passed between Ranaka and Ratiu, and ran some days north-east by east-half-east under the lee of Takume and Honden,[22] neither of which they made. In about 14° south, and between 134° and 135° west, it fell a dead calm, with rather a heavy sea. The captain refused to take in sail, the helm was lashed, no watch was set, and the *Farallone* rolled and banged for three days according to observation, in almost the same place. The fourth morning, a little before day, a breeze sprang up and rapidly freshened. The captain had drunk hard the night before; and he was far from sober when he was roused; and when he came on deck for the first time at half-past eight, it was plain he had already drunk deep again at breakfast. Herrick avoided his eye; and resigned the deck with indignation to a man more than half-seas-over.

By the loud commands of the captain and the singing out of fellows at the ropes, he could judge from the house that sail was being crowded on the ship; relinquished his half-eaten breakfast; and came on deck again, to find the main and the jib topsails set, and both watches and the cook turned out to hand the staysail. The *Farallone* lay already far over; the sky was obscured with misty scud; and from the windward an ominous squall came flying up, broadening and blackening as it rose.

Fear thrilled in Herrick's vitals. He saw death hard by; and if not death, sure ruin. For if the *Farallone* lived through the coming squall, she must surely be dismasted. With that their enterprise was at an end, and they themselves bound prisoners to the very evidence of their crime. The greatness of the peril and his own alarm sufficed to silence him. Pride, wrath, and shame raged without issue in his mind; and he shut his teeth and folded his arms close.

The captain sat in the boat to windward, bellowing orders and insults, his eyes glazed, his face deeply congested; a bottle set between his knees, a glass in his hand half empty. His back was to the squall, and he was at first intent upon the setting of the sail. When that was done, and the great trapezium of canvas had begun to draw and to trail the lee-rail of the *Farallone* level with the foam, he laughed out an empty laugh, drained his glass, sprawled back among the lumber in the boat, and fetched out a crumpled novel.

Herrick watched him, and his indignation glowed red-hot. He glanced to windward where the squall already whitened the near sea and heralded its coming with a singular and dismal sound. He glanced at the steersman, and saw him clinging to the spokes with a face of a sickly blue. He saw the crew were running to their stations without orders. And it seemed as if something broke in his brain; and the passion of anger, so long restrained, so long eaten in secret, burst suddenly loose and filled and shook him like a sail. He stepped across to the captain, and smote his hand heavily on the drunkard's shoulder.

'You brute,' he said, in a voice that tottered, 'look behind you!'

'Wha's that?' cried Davis, bounding in the boat and upsetting the champagne.

'You lost the *Sea Ranger* because you were a drunken sot,' said Herrick. 'Now you're going to lose the *Farallone*. You're going to drown here the same way as you drowned others, and be damned. And your daughter shall walk the streets, and your sons be thieves like their father.'

For the moment the words struck the captain white and foolish. 'My God!' he cried, looking at Herrick as upon a ghost; 'my God, Herrick!'

'Look behind you, then!' reiterated the assailant.

The wretched man, already partly sobered, did as he was told, and in the same breath of time leaped to his feet. 'Down staysail!' he trumpeted. The hands were thrilling for the order, and the great sail came with a run, and fell half overboard among the racing foam. 'Jib topsail-halyards! Let the stays'l be,' he said again.

But before it was well uttered, the squall shouted aloud and fell, in a solid mass of wind and rain commingled, on the *Farallone*; and she stooped under the blow, and lay like a thing dead. From the mind of Herrick reason fled; he clung in the weather rigging, exulting; he was done with life, and he gloried in the release; he gloried in the wild noises of the wind and the choking onslaught of the rain; he gloried to die so, and now, amid this coil of the elements. And meanwhile, in the waist up to his knees in water – so low the schooner lay – the captain was hacking at the foresheet with a pocket-knife. It was a question of seconds, for the *Farallone* drank deep of the encroaching seas. But the hand of the captain had the advance; the foresail boom tore apart the last strands of the sheet and crashed to leeward; the *Farallone* leaped up into the wind and righted; and the peak and throat halyards, which had long been let go, began to run at the same instant.

For some ten minutes more she careered under the impulse of the squall; but the captain was now master of himself and of his ship, and all danger at an end. And then, sudden as a trick-change upon the stage, the squall blew by, the wind dropped into light airs, the sun beamed forth again upon the tattered schooner; and the captain, having secured the foresail boom and set a couple of hands to the pump, walked aft, sober, a little pale, and with the sodden end of a cigar still stuck between his teeth even as the squall had found it. Herrick followed him; he could scarce recall the violence of his late emotions, but he felt there was a scene to go through, and he was anxious and even eager to go through with it.

The captain, turning at the house end, met him face to face, and averted his eyes. 'We've lost the two tops'ls and the stays'l,' he gabbled. 'Good business we didn't lose any sticks. I guess you think we're all the better without the kites.'

'That's not what I'm thinking,' said Herrick, in a voice strangely quiet, that yet echoed confusion in the captain's mind.

'I know that,' he cried, holding up his hand. 'I know what you're thinking. No use to say it now. I'm sober.'

'I have to say it, though,' returned Herrick.

'Hold on, Herrick; you've said enough,' said Davis. 'You've said what I would take from no man breathing but yourself; only I know it's true.'

'I have to tell you, Captain Brown,' pursued Herrick, 'that I resign my position as mate. You can put me in irons or shoot me, as you please; I will make no resistance – only, I decline in any way to help or to obey you; and I suggest you should put Mr Huish in my place. He will make a worthy first officer to your captain, sir.' He smiled, bowed, and turned to walk forward.

'Where are you going, Herrick?' cried the captain, detaining him by the shoulder.

'To berth forward with the men, sir,' replied Herrick, with the same hateful smile. 'I've been long enough aft here with you – gentlemen.'

'You're wrong there,' said Davis. 'Don't you be too quick with me; there ain't nothing wrong but the drink – it's the old story, man! Let me get sober once and then you'll see,' he pleaded.

'Excuse me, I desire to see no more of you,' said Herrick.

The captain groaned aloud. 'You know what you said about my children?' he broke out.

'By rote. In case you wish me to say it you again?' asked Herrick.

'Don't!' cried the captain clapping his hands to his ears. 'Don't make me kill a man I care for! Herrick, if you see me put a glass to my lips again till we're ashore, I give you leave to put a bullet through me; I beg you to it! You're the only man aboard whose carcase is worth losing; do you think I don't know that? do you think I ever went back on you? I always knew you were in the right of it – drunk or sober, I knew that. What do you want? – an oath? Man, you're clever enough to see that this is sure-enough earnest.'

'Do you mean there shall be no more drinking?' asked Herrick, 'neither by you nor Huish? that you won't go on stealing my profits and drinking my champagne that I gave my honour for? and that you'll attend to your duties, and stand watch and watch, and bear your proper share of the ship's work, instead of leaving it all on the shoulders of a landsman, and making yourself the butt and scoff of native seamen? Is that what you mean? If it is, be so good as say it categorically.'

'You put these things in a way hard for a gentleman to swallow,' said the captain. 'You wouldn't have me say I was ashamed of myself? Trust me this once; I'll do the square thing, and there's my hand on it.'

'Well, I'll try it once,' said Herrick. 'Fail me again ...'

'No more now!' interrupted Davis. 'No more, old man! Enough said. You've a riling tongue when your back's up, Herrick. Just be glad we're friends again, the same as what I am;

and go tender on the raws; I'll see as you don't repent it. We've been mighty near death this day – don't say whose fault it was! – pretty near hell, too, I guess. We're in a mighty bad line of life, us two, and ought to go easy with each other.'

He was maundering; yet it seemed as if he were maundering with some design, beating about the bush of some communication that he feared to make, or perhaps only talking against time in terror of what Herrick might say next. But Herrick had now spat his venom; his was a kindly nature, and, content with his triumph, he had now begun to pity. With a few soothing words he sought to conclude the interview, and proposed that they should change their clothes.

'Not right yet,' said Davis. 'There's another thing I want to tell you first. You know what you said about my children? I want to tell you why it hit me so hard; I kind of think you'll feel bad about it too. It's about my little Adar. You hadn't ought to have quite said that – but of course I know you didn't know. She – she's dead, you see.'

'Why, Davis!' cried Herrick. 'You've told me a dozen times she was alive! Clear your head, man! This must be the drink.'

'No, *sir*,' said Davis. 'She's dead. Died of a bowel complaint. That was when I was away in the brig *Oregon*. She lies in Portland, Maine. 'Adar, only daughter of Captain John Davis and Mariar his wife, aged five." I had a doll for her on board. I never took the paper off'n that doll, Herrick; it went down the way it was with the *Sea Ranger*, that day I was damned.'

The captain's eyes were fixed on the horizon, he talked with an extraordinary softness, but a complete composure; and Herrick looked upon him with something that was almost terror.

'Don't think I'm crazy neither,' resumed Davis. 'I've all the cold sense that I know what to do with. But I guess a man that's unhappy's like a child; and this is a kind of a child's game of mine. I never could act up to the plain-cut truth, you see; so I pretend. And I warn you square; as soon as we're through with this talk, I'll start in again with the pretending. Only, you see, she can't walk no streets,' added the captain, 'couldn't even make out to live and get that doll!'

Herrick laid a tremulous hand upon the captain's shoulder.

'Don't do that!' cried Davis, recoiling from the touch. 'Can't you see I'm all broken up the way it is? Come along, then; come along, old man; you can put your trust in me right through; come along and get dry clothes.'

They entered the cabin, and there was Huish on his knees prising open a case of champagne.

''Vast there!' cried the captain. 'No more of that. No more drinking on this ship.'

'Turned teetotal, 'ave you!' inquired Huish. 'I'm agreeable. About time, eh? Bloomin' nearly lost another ship, I fancy.' He took out a bottle and began calmly to burst the wire with the spike of a corkscrew.

'Do you hear me speak?' cried Davis.

'I suppose I do. You speak loud enough,' said Huish. 'The trouble is that I don't care.'

Herrick plucked the captain's sleeve. 'Let him free now,' he said. 'We've had all we want this morning.'

'Let him have it, then,' said the captain. 'It's his last.'

By this time the wire was open, the string was cut, the head of gilded paper was torn away; and Huish waited, mug in hand, expecting the usual explosion. It did not follow. He eased the cork with his thumb; still there was no result. At last he took the screw and drew it. It came out very easy and with scarce a sound.

''Illo!' said Huish. ''Ere's a bad bottle.'

He poured some of the wine into the mug; it was colourless and still. He smelt and tasted it.

'W'y, wot's this?' he said. 'It's water!'

If the voice of trumpets had suddenly sounded about the ship in the midst of the sea, the three men in the house could scarcely have been more stunned than by this incident. The mug passed round; each sipped, each smelt of it; each stared at the bottle in its glory of gold paper as Crusoe may have stared at the footprint; and their minds were swift to fix upon a common apprehension. The difference between a bottle of champagne and a bottle of water is not great; between a shipload of one or the other lay the whole scale from riches to ruin.

A second bottle was broached. There were two cases standing ready in a stateroom; these two were brought out, broken open, and tested. Still with the same result: the contents were still colourless and tasteless, and dead as the rain in a beached fishing-boat.

'Crikey!' said Huish.

'Here, let's sample the hold,' said the captain, mopping his brow with a back-handed sweep; and the three stalked out of the house, grim and heavy-footed.

All hands were turned out; two Kanakas were sent below, another stationed at a purchase; and Davis, axe in hand, took his place beside the coamings.

'Are you going to let the men know?' whispered Herrick.

'Damn the men!' said Davis. 'It's beyond that. We've got to know ourselves.'

Three cases were sent on deck and sampled in turn; from each bottle, as the captain smashed it with the axe, the champagne ran bubbling and creaming.

'Go deeper, can't you?' cried Davis to the Kanakas in the hold.

The command gave the signal for a disastrous change. Case after case came up, bottle after bottle was burst, and bled mere water. Deeper yet, and they came upon a layer where there was scarcely so much as the intention to deceive; where the cases were no longer branded, the bottles no longer wired or papered, where the fraud was manifest and stared them in the face.

'Here's about enough of this foolery!' said Davis. 'Stow back the cases in the hold, Uncle, and get the broken crockery overboard. Come with me,' he added to his co-adventurers, and led the way back into the cabin.

The Partners

EACH took a side of the fixed table; it was the first time they had sat down at it together; but now all sense of incongruity, all memory of differences, was quite swept away by the presence of the common ruin.

'Gentlemen,' said the captain, after a pause, and with very much the air of a chairman opening a board meeting, 'we're sold.'

Huish broke out in laughter. 'Well, if this ain't the 'ighest old rig!' he cried. 'And Dyvis 'ere, who thought he had got up so bloomin' early in the mornin'! We've stolen a cargo of spring water! O, my crikey!' and he squirmed with mirth.

The captain managed to screw out a phantom smile.

'Here's Old Man Destiny again,' said he to Herrick, 'but this time I guess he's kicked the door right in.'

Herrick only shook his head.

'O Lord, it's rich!' laughed Huish. 'It would really be a scrumptious lark if it 'ad 'appened to somebody else! And what are we to do next? O, my eye! with this bloomin' schooner, too?'

'That's the trouble,' said Davis. 'There's only one thing certain: it's no use carting this old glass and ballast to Peru. No, *sir*, we're in a hole.'

'O my, and the merchant!' cried Huish; 'the man that made this shipment! He'll get the news by the mail brigantine; and he'll think of course we're making straight for Sydney.'

'Yes, he'll be a sick merchant,' said the captain. 'One thing: this explains the Kanaka crew. If you're going to lose a ship, I would ask no better myself than a Kanaka crew. But there's one thing it don't explain; it don't explain why she came down Tahiti ways.'

'W'y, to lose her, you byby!' said Huish.

'A lot you know,' said the captain. 'Nobody wants to lose a schooner; they want to lose her *on her course*, you skeericks! You seem to think underwriters haven't got enough sense to come in out of the rain.'

'Well,' said Herrick, 'I can tell you (I am afraid) why she came so far to the eastward. I had it of Uncle Ned. It seems these two unhappy devils, Wiseman and Wishart, were drunk on the champagne from the beginning – and died drunk at the end.'

The captain looked on the table.

'They lay in their two bunks, or sat here in this damned house,' he pursued, with rising agitation, 'filling their skins with the accursed stuff, till sickness took them. As they sickened and fever rose, they drank the more. They lay here howling and groaning, drunk and dying, all in one. They didn't know where they were; they didn't care. They didn't even take the sun, it seems.'

'Not take the sun?' cried the captain, looking up. 'Sacred Bily! what a crowd!'

'Well, it don't matter to Joe!' said Huish. 'Wot are Wiseman and t'other buffer to us?'

'A good deal, too,' said the captain. 'We're their heirs, I guess.'

'It is a great inheritance,' said Herrick.

'Well, I don't know about that,' returned Davis. 'Appears to me as if it might be worse. 'Tain't worth what the cargo would have been, of course, at least not money down. But I'll tell you what it appears to figure up to. Appears to me as if it amounted to about the bottom dollar of the man in 'Frisco.'

''Old on,' said Huish. 'Give a fellow time; 'ow's this, umpire?'

'Well, my sons,' pursued the captain, who seemed to have recovered his assurance, 'Wiseman and Wishart were to be paid for casting away this old schooner and its cargo. We going to cast away the schooner right enough; and I'll make it my private business to see that we get paid. What were W. and W. to get? That's more'n I can tell. But W. and W. went into this business themselves, they were on the crook. Now *we're* on the square, *we* only stumbled into it; and that merchant has just got to squeal, and I'm the man to see that he squeals good. No, *sir*! there's some stuffing to this *Farallone* racket after all.'

'Go it, cap'!' cried Huish. 'Yoicks! Forrard! 'Old 'ard! There's your style for the money! Blow me if I don't prefer this to the hother.'

'I do not understand,' said Herrick. 'I have to ask you to excuse me; I do not understand.'

'Well, now, see here, Herrick,' said Davis. 'I'm going to have a word with you anyway upon a different matter, and it's good that Huish should hear it too. We're done with this boozing business, and we ask your pardon for it, right here and now. We have to thank you for all you did for us while we were making hogs of ourselves; you'll find me turn-to all right in future; and as for the wine, which I grant we stole from you, I'll take stock and see you paid for it. That's good enough, I believe. But what I want to point out to you is this. The old game was a risky game. The new game's as safe as running a Vienna Bakery. We just put this *Farallone* before the wind, and run till we're well to looard of our port of departure and reasonably well up with some other place, where they have an American Consul. Down goes the *Farallone*, and good-bye to her! A day or so in the boat; the Consul packs us home, at Uncle Sam's expense, to 'Frisco; and if that merchant don't put the dollars down, you come to me!'

'But I thought,' began Herrick; and then broke out: 'O, let's get on to Peru!'

'Well, if you're going to Peru for your health, I won't say no!' replied the captain. 'But for what other blame' shadow of a reason you should want to go there gets me clear. We don't want to go there with this cargo; I don't know as old bottles is a lively article anywheres; leastways, I'll go my bottom cent, it ain't Peru. It was always a doubt if we could sell the schooner; I never rightly hoped to, and now I'm sure she ain't worth a hill of beans; what's wrong with her, I don't know; I only know it's something, or she wouldn't be here with this truck in her inside. Then again, if we lose her, and land in Peru, where are we? We can't declare the loss, or how did we get to Peru? In that case the merchant can't touch the insurance; most likely he'll go bust;

and don't you think you see the three of us on the beach of Calloa?'[23]

'There's no extradition there,' said Herrick.

'Well, my son, and we want to be extraded,' said the captain. 'What's our point? We want to have a consul extrade us as far as San Francisco and that merchant's office door. My idea is that Samoa would be found an eligible business centre. It's dead before the wind; the States have a Consul there, and 'Frisco steamers call, so's we could skip right back and interview the merchant.'

'Samoa?' said Herrick. 'It will take us for ever to get there.'

'O, with a fair wind!' said the captain.

'No trouble about the log, eh?' asked Huish.

'No, *sir*,' said Davis. '*Light airs and baffling winds. Squalls and calms. D. R.: five miles. No obs. Pumps attended*. And fill in the barometer and thermometer off of last year's trip. "Never saw such a voyage," says you to the Consul. "Thought I was going to run short ..." ' He stopped in mid career. ' 'Say,' he began again, and once more stopped. 'Beg your pardon, Herrick,' he added with undisguised humility, 'but did you keep the run of the stores?'

'Had I been told to do so it should have been done, as the rest was done, to the best of my little ability,' said Herrick. 'As it was, the cook helped himself to what he pleased.'

Davis looked at the table.

'I drew it rather fine, you see,' he said at last. 'The great thing was to clear right out of Papeete before the Consul could think better of it. Tell you what: I guess I'll take stock.'

And he rose from the table and disappeared with a lamp in the lazarette.[24]

' 'Ere's another screw loose,' observed Huish.

'My man,' said Herrick, with a sudden gleam of animosity, 'it is still your watch on deck, and surely your wheel also?'

'You come the 'eavy swell, don't you, ducky?' said Huish. 'Stand away from that binnacle. Surely your w'eel, my man. Yah.'

He lit a cigar ostentatiously, and strolled into the waist with his hands in his pockets.

In a surprisingly short time the captain reappeared; he did not look at Herrick, but called Huish back and sat down.

'Well,' he began, 'I've taken stock – roughly.' He paused as if for somebody to help him out; and none doing so, both gazing on him instead with manifest anxiety, he yet more heavily resumed. 'Well, it won't fight. We can't do it; that's the bed-rock. I'm as scrry as what you can be, and sorrier. But the game's up. We can't look near Samoa. I don't know as we could get to Peru.'

'Wot-ju mean?' asked Huish brutally.

'I can't 'most tell myself,' replied the captain. 'I drew it fine; I said I did; but what's been going on here gets me! Appears as if the devil had been around. That cook must be the holiest kind of fraud. Only twelve days too! Seems like craziness. I'll own up square to one thing: I seem to have figured too fine upon the flour. But the rest – my land! I'll never understand it! There's been more waste on this two-penny ship than what there is to an Atlantic Liner.' He stole a glance at his companions: nothing good was to be gleaned from their dark faces; and he had recourse to rage. 'You wait till I interview that cook!' he roared and smote the table with his fist. 'I'll interview the son of a gun so's he's never been spoken to before. I'll put a bead upon the——!'

'You will not lay a finger on the man,' said Herrick. 'The fault is yours, and you know it. If you turn a savage loose in your storeroom, you know what to expect. I will not allow the man to be molested.'

It is hard to say how Davis might have taken this defiance; but he was diverted to a fresh assailant.

'Well,' drawled Huish, 'you're a plummy captain, ain't you? You're a blooming captain! Don't you set up any of your chat to me, John Dyvis: I know you now; you ain't any more use than a bloomin' dawl! O, you "don't know", don't you? O, it "gets you", do it? O, I dessay! W'y, weren't you 'owling for fresh tins every blessed day? 'Ow often 'ave I 'eard you send the 'ole bloomin' dinner off and tell the man to chuck it in the swill-tub? And breakfast? O, my crikey! breakfast for ten, and you 'ollerin' for more! And now you "can't 'most tell"! Blow me if it ain't enough to make a man write an insultin' letter to

Gawd! You dror it mild, John Dyvis; don't 'andle me; I'm dyngerous.'

Davis sat like one bemused; it might even have been doubted if he heard, but the voice of the clerk rang about the cabin like that of a cormorant among the ledges of the cliff.

'That will do, Huish,' said Herrick.

'O, so you tyke his part, do you? you stuck-up sneerin' snob. Tyke it then. Come on, the pair of you. But as for John Dyvis, let him look out! He struck me the first night aboard, and I never took a blow yet but wot I gave as good. Let him knuckle down on his marrow-bones and beg my pardon. That's my last word.'

'I stand by the captain,' said Herrick. 'That makes us two to one, both good men; and the crew will all follow me. I hope I shall die very soon; but I have not the least objection to killing you before I go. I should prefer it so; I should do it with no more remorse than winking. Take care – take care, you little cad!'

The animosity with which these words were uttered was so marked in itself, and so remarkable in the man who uttered them, that Huish stared, and even the humiliated Davis reared up his head and gazed at his defender. As for Herrick, the successive agitations and disappointments of the day had left him wholly reckless; he was conscious of a pleasant glow, an agreeable excitement; his head seemed empty, his eyeballs burned as he turned them, his throat was dry as a biscuit; the least dangerous man by nature, except in so far as the weak are always dangerous, at that moment he was ready to slay or to be slain with equal unconcern.

Here at least was the gage thrown down, and battle offered; he who should speak next would bring the matter to an issue there and then; all knew it to be so and hung back; and for many seconds by the cabin clock, the trio sat motionless and silent.

Then came an interruption, welcome as the flowers in May.

'Land ho!' sang out a voice on deck. 'Land a weatha bow!'

'Land!' cried Davis, springing to his feet. 'What's this? There ain't no land here.'

And as men may run from the chamber of a murdered corpse,

the three ran forth out of the house and left their quarrel behind them undecided.

The sky shaded down at the sea-level to the white of opals; the sea itself, insolently, inkily blue, drew all about them the uncompromising wheel of the horizon. Search it as they pleased, not even the practised eye of Captain Davis could descry the smallest interruption. A few filmy clouds were slowly melting overhead; and about the schooner, as around the only point of interest, a tropic bird, white as a snow-flake, hung, and circled, and displayed, as it turned, the long vermilion feather of its tail. Save the sea and the heaven, that was all.

'Who sang out land?' asked Davis. 'If there's any boy playing funny-dog with me, I'l teach him skylarking!'

But Uncle Ned contentedly pointed to a part of the horizon where a greenish, filmy iridescence could be discerned floating like smoke on the pale heavens.

Davis applied his glass to it, and then looked at the Kanaka. 'Call that land?' said he. 'Well, it's more than I do.'

'One time long ago,' said Uncle Ned, 'I see Anaa all-e-same that, four five hours befo' we come up. Capena he say sun go down, sun go up again; he say lagoon all-e-same milla.'

'All-e-same *what?*' asked Davis.

'Milla, sah,' said Uncle Ned.

'O, ah! mirror,' said Davis. 'I see; reflection from the lagoon. Well, you know, it is just possible, though it's strange I never heard of it. Here, let's look at the chart.'

They went back to the cabin, and found the position of the schooner well to windward of the archipelago in the midst of a white field of paper.

'There! you see for yourselves,' said Davis.

'And yet I don't know,' said Herrick, 'I somehow think there's something in it. I'll tell you one thing too, captain; that's all right about the reflection; I heard it in Papeete.'

'Fetch up that Findlay,[25] then!' said Davis. 'I'll try it all ways. An island wouldn't come amiss the way we're fixed.'

The bulky volume was handed up to him, broken-backed as is the way with Findlay; and he turned to the place and began to run over the text, muttering to himself and turning over the pages with a wetted finger.

'Hullo!' he exclaimed. 'How's this?' And he read aloud. '"*New Island*. According to M. Delille this island, which from private interests would remain unknown, lies, it is said, in lat. 12° 49′ 10″ S., long. 133° 6′ W. In addition to the position above given, Commander Matthews, H.M.S. *Scorpion*, states that an island exists in lat. 12° 0′ S., long. 133° 16′ W. This must be the same, if such an island exists, which is very doubtful, and totally disbelieved in by South Sea traders."'

'Golly!' said Huish.

'It's rather in the conditional mood,' said Herrick.

'It's anything you please,' cried Davis, 'only there it is! That's your place, and don't you make any mistake.'

'"Which from private interests would remain unknown,"' read Herrick, over his shoulder. 'What may that mean?'

'It should mean pearls,' said Davis. 'A pearling island the Government don't know about? That sounds like real estate. Or suppose it don't mean anything. Suppose it's just an island; I guess we could fill up with fish, and cocoanuts, and native stuff, and carry out the Samoa scheme hand over fist. How long did he say it was before they raised Anaa? Five hours, I think?'

'Four or five,' said Herrick.

Davis stepped to the door. 'What breeze had you that time you made Anaa, Uncle Ned?' said he.

'Six or seven knots,' was the reply.

'Thirty or thirty-five miles,' said Davis. 'High time we were shortening sail, then. If it is an island, we don't want to be butting our head against it in the dark; and if it isn't an island, we can get through it just as well by daylight. Ready about!' he roared.

And the schooner's head was laid for that elusive glimmer in the sky, which began already to pale in lustre and diminish in size, as the stain of breath vanishes from a window pane. At the same time she was reefed close down.

PART II

THE QUARTETTE

The Pearl-Fisher

ABOUT four in the morning, as the captain and Herrick sat together on the rail, there arose from the midst of the night in front of them the voice of breakers. Each sprang to his feet and stared and listened. The sound was continuous, like the passing of a train; no rise or fall could be distinguished; minute by minute the ocean heaved with an equal potency against the invisible isle; and as time passed, and Herrick waited in vain for any vicissitude in the volume of that roaring, a sense of the eternal weighed upon his mind. To the expert eye the isle itself was to be inferred from a certain string of blots along the starry heaven. And the schooner was laid to and anxiously observed till daylight.

There was little or no morning bank. A brightening came in the east; then a wash of some ineffable, faint, nameless hue between crimson and silver; and then coals of fire. These glimmered a while on the sea-line, and seemed to brighten and darken and spread out, and still the night and the stars reigned undisturbed; it was as though a speck should catch and glow and creep along the foot of some heavy and almost incombustible wall-hanging, and the room itself be scarce menaced. Yet a little after, and the whole east glowed with gold and scarlet, and the hollow of heaven was filled with the daylight.

The isle – the undiscovered, the scarce-believed in – now lay before them and close aboard; and Herrick thought that never in his dreams had he beheld anything more strange and delicate. The beach was excellently white, the continuous barrier of trees inimitably green; the land perhaps ten feet high, the trees thirty more. Every here and there, as the schooner coasted northward, the wood was intermitted; and he could see clear over the inconsiderable strip of land (as a man looks over a wall) to the lagoon within – and clear over that again to where the far side of the atoll prolonged its pencilling of trees against the morning sky. He tortured himself to find analogies. The isle was like the rim of a great vessel sunken in the waters; it was like the embankment of an annular railway grown upon with wood: so slender it seemed amidst the outrageous breakers, so frail and pretty, he would scarce have wondered to see it sink and disappear without a sound, and the waves close smoothly over its descent.

Meanwhile the captain was in the four cross-trees, glass in hand, his eyes in every quarter, spying for an entrance, spying for signs of tenancy. But the isle continued to unfold itself in joints, and to run out in indeterminate capes, and still there was neither house nor man, nor the smoke of fire. Here a multitude of sea-birds soared and twinkled, and fished in the blue waters; and there, and for miles together, the fringe of cocoa-palm and pandanus extended desolate, and made desirable green bowers for nobody to visit, and the silence of death was only broken by the throbbing of the sea.

The airs were very light, their speed was small; the heat intense. The decks were scorching underfoot, the sun flamed overhead, brazen, out of a brazen sky; the pitch bubbled in the seams, and the brains in the brainpan. And all the while the excitement of the three adventurers glowed about their bones like a fever. They whispered, and nodded, and pointed, and put mouth to ear, with a singular instinct of secrecy, approaching that island under-hand like eavesdroppers and thieves; and even Davis from the cross-trees gave his orders mostly by gestures. The hands shared in this mute strain, like dogs, without comprehending it; and through the roar of so many miles of breakers, it was a silent ship that approached an empty island.

At last they drew near to the break in that interminable gangway. A spur of coral sand stood forth on the one hand; on the other a high and thick tuft of trees cut off the view; between was the mouth of the huge laver. Twice a day the ocean crowded in that narrow entrance and was heaped between these frail walls; twice a day, with the return of the ebb, the mighty surplusage of water must struggle to escape. The hour in which the *Farallone* came there was the hour of flood. The sea turned (as with the instinct of the homing pigeon) for the vast receptacle, swept eddying through the gates, was transmuted, as it did so, into a wonder of watery and silken hues, and brimmed into the inland sea beyond. The schooner looked up close-hauled, and was caught and carried away by the influx like a toy. She skimmed; she flew; a momentary shadow touched her decks from the shoreside trees; the bottom of the channel showed up for a moment and was in a moment gone; the next, she floated on the bosom of the lagoon, and below, in the transparent chamber of waters, a myriad of many-coloured fishes were sporting, a myriad pale flowers of coral diversified the floor.

Herrick stood transported. In the gratified lust of his eye he forgot the past and the present; forgot that he was menaced by a prison on the one hand and starvation on the other; forgot that he was come to that island, desperately foraging, clutching at expedients. A drove of fishes, painted like the rainbow and billed like parrots, hovered up in the shadow of the schooner, and passed clear of it, and glinted in the submarine sun. They were beautiful, like birds, and their silent passage impressed him like a strain of song.

Meanwhile, to the eye of Davis in the cross-trees, the lagoon continued to expand its empty waters, and the long succession of the shoreside trees to be paid out like fishing-line off a reel. And still there was no mark of habitation. The schooner, immediately on entering, had been kept away to the nor'ard where the water seemed to be the most deep; and she was now skimming past the tall grove of trees, which stood on that side of the channel and denied further view. On the whole of the low shores of the island, only this bight remained to be revealed. And suddenly the curtain was raised; they began to open out a haven, snugly elbowed there, and beheld, with an astonishment beyond words, the roofs of men.

The appearance, thus 'instantaneously disclosed' to those on the deck of the *Farallone*, was not that of a city, rather of a substantial country farm with its attendant hamlet: a long line of sheds and store-houses; apart, upon the one side, a deep-verandah'd dwèlling-house; on the other, perhaps a dozen native huts; a building with a belfry and some rude offer at architectural features that might be thought to mark it out for a chapel; on the beach in front some heavy boats drawn up, and a pile of timber running forth into the burning shallows of the lagoon. From a flagstaff at the pier-head the red ensign of England was displayed. Behind, about, and over, the same tall grove of palms, which had masked the settlement in the beginning, prolonged its roof of tumultuous green fans, and turned and ruffled overhead, and sang its silver song all day in the wind. The place had the indescribable but unmistakable appearance of being in commission; yet there breathed from it a sense of desertion that was almost poignant, no human figure was to be observed going to and fro about the houses, and there was no sound of human industry or enjoyment. Only, on top of the beach, and hard by the flagstaff, a woman of exorbitant stature and as white as snow was to be seen beckoning with uplifted arm. The second glance identified her as a piece of naval sculpture, the figure-head of a ship that had long hovered and plunged into so many running billows, and was now brought ashore to be the ensign and presiding genius of that empty town.

The *Farallone* made a soldier's breeze of it; the wind, besides, was stronger inside than without under the lee of the land; and the stolen schooner opened out successive objects with the swiftness of a panorama, so that the adventurers stood speechless. The flag spoke for itself; it was no frayed and weathered trophy that had beaten itself to pieces on the post, flying over desolation; and to make assurance stronger, there was to be descried in the deep shade of the verandah a glitter of crystal and the fluttering of white napery. If the figure-head at the pier-end, with its perpetual gesture and its leprous whiteness, reigned alone in that hamlet as it seemed to do, it would not have reigned long. Men's hands had been busy, men's feet stirring there, within the circuit of the clock. The *Farallones* were sure of it; their eyes dug in the deep shadow of the palms for some one hiding; if intensity of looking might have prevailed, they would have pierced the walls of houses; and there came to them, in these pregnant seconds, a sense of being watched and played with, and of a blow impending, that was hardly bearable.

The extreme point of palms they had just passed enclosed a creek, which was thus hidden up to the last moment from the eyes of those on board; and from this a boat put suddenly and briskly out, and a voice hailed.

'Schooner ahoy!' it cried. 'Stand in for the pier! In two cables' lengths you'll have twenty fathoms water and good holding-ground.'

The boat was manned with a couple of brown oarsmen in scanty kilts of blue. The speaker, who was steering, wore white clothes, the full dress of the tropics; a wide hat shaded his face; but it could be seen that he was of stalwart size, and his voice sounded like a gentleman's. So much could be made out. It was plain, besides, that the *Farallone* had been descried some time before at sea, and the inhabitants were prepared for its reception.

Mechanically the orders were obeyed, and the ship berthed; and the three adventurers gathered aft beside the house and waited, with galloping pulses and a perfect vacancy of mind, the coming of the stranger who might mean so much to them. They had no plan, no story prepared; there was no time to make one; they were caught red-handed and must stand their chance. Yet this anxiety was chequered with hope. The island being undeclared, it was not possible the man could hold any office or be in a position to demand their papers. And beyond that, if there was any truth in Findlay, as it now seemed there should be, he was the representative of the 'private reasons' he must see their coming with a profound disappointment; and perhaps (hope whispered) he would be willing and able to purchase their silence.

The boat was by that time forging alongside, and they were able at last to see what manner of man they had to do with. He was a huge fellow, six feet four in height, and of a build proportionately strong, but his sinews seemed to be dissolved in a listlessness that was more than languor. It was only the eye that corrected this impression; an eye of an unusual mingled brilliancy and softness, sombre as coal and with lights that outshone the topaz; an eye of unimpaired health and virility; an eye that bid you beware of the man's devastating anger. A complexion, naturally dark, had been tanned in the island to a hue hardly distinguishable from that of a Tahitian; only his manners and movements, and the living force that dwelt in him, like fire in flint, betrayed the European. He was dressed in white drill, exquisitely made; his scarf and tie were of tender-coloured silks; on the thwart beside him there leaned a Winchester rifle.

'Is the doctor on board?' he cried as he came up. 'Dr Symonds, I mean? You never heard of him? Nor yet of the *Trinity Hall*? Ah!'

He did not look surprised, seemed rather to affect it in politeness; but his eye rested on each of the three white men in succession with a sudden weight of curiosity that was almost savage. 'Ah, *then*!' said he, 'there is some small mistake, no doubt, and I must ask you to what I am indebted for this pleasure?'

He was by this time on the deck, but he had the art to be quite unapproachable; the friendliest vulgarian, three parts drunk, would have known better than take liberties; and not one of the adventurers so much as offered to shake hands.

'Well,' said Davis, 'I suppose you may call it an accident. We had heard of your island, and read that thing in the Directory about the *private reasons*, you see; so when we saw the lagoon reflected in the sky, we put her head for it at once, and so here we are.'

''Ope we don't intrude!' said Huish.

The stranger looked at Huish with an air of faint surprise, and looked pointedly away again. It was hard to be more offensive in dumb show.

'It may suit me, your coming here,' he said. 'My own schooner is overdue, and I may put something in your way in the meantime. Are you open to a charter?'

'Well, I guess so,' said Davis; 'it depends.'

'My name is Attwater,' continued the stranger. 'You, I presume, are the captain?'

'Yes, sir. I am the captain of this ship: Captain Brown,' was the reply.

'Well, see 'ere!' said Huish; 'better begin fair! 'E's skipper on deck right enough, but not below. Below, we're all equal, all got a lay in the adventure; when it comes to business, I'm as good as 'e; and what I say is, let's go into the 'ouse and have a lush, and talk it over among pals. We've some prime fizz,' he said, and winked.

The presence of the gentleman lighted up like a candle the vulgarity of the clerk; and Herrick instinctively, as one shields himself from pain, made haste to interrupt.

'My name is Hay,' said he, 'since introductions are going. We shall be very glad if you will step inside.'

Attwater leaned to him swiftly. 'University man?' said he.

'Yes, Merton,' said Herrick, and the next moment blushed scarlet at his indiscretion.

'I am of the other lot,' said Attwater: 'Trinity Hall, Cambridge. I called my schooner after the old shop. Well! this is a queer place and company for us to meet in, Mr Hay,' he pursued, with easy incivility to the others. 'But do you bear out . . . I beg this gentleman's pardon, I really did not catch his name.'

'My name is 'Uish, sir,' returned the clerk, and blushed in turn.

'Ah!' said Attwater. And then turning again to Herrick, 'Do you bear out Mr Whish's description of your vintage? or was it only the unaffected poetry of his own nature bubbling up?'

Herrick was embarrassed; the silken brutality of their visitor made him blush; that he should be accepted as an equal, and the others thus pointedly ignored, pleased him in spite of himself, and then ran through his veins in a recoil of anger.

'I don't know,' he said. 'It's only California; it's good enough, I believe.'

Attwater seemed to make up his mind. 'Well, then, I'll tell you what: you three gentlemen come ashore this evening and bring a basket of wine with you; I'll try and find the food,' he said. 'And by the by, here is a question I should have asked you when I came on board: have you had smallpox?'

'Personally, no,' said Herrick. 'But the schooner had it.'

'Deaths?' from Attwater.

'Two,' said Herrick.

'Well, it is a dreadful sickness,' said Attwater.

''Ad you any deaths?' asked Huish, ''ere on the island?'

'Twenty-nine,' said Attwater. 'Twenty-nine deaths and thirty-one cases, out of thirty-three souls upon the island. That's a strange way to calculate, Mr Hay, is it not? Souls! I never say it but it startles me.'

'O, so that's why everything's deserted?' said Huish.

'That is why, Mr Whish,' said Attwater; 'that is why the house is empty and the graveyard full.'

'Twenty-nine out of thirty-three!' exclaimed Herrick. 'Why, when it came to burying – or did you bother burying?'

'Scarcely,' said Attwater; 'or there was one day at least when we gave up. There were five of the dead that morning, and thirteen of the dying, and no one able to go about except the sexton and myself. We held a council of war, took the . . . empty bottles . . . into the lagoon, and . . . buried them.' He looked over his shoulder, back at the bright water. 'Well, so you'll come to dinner, then? Shall we say half-past six? *So* good of you!'

His voice, in uttering these conventional phrases, fell at once into the false measure of society; and Herrick unconsciously followed the example

'I am sure we shall be very glad,' he said. 'At half-past six? Thank you so very much.'

> '"For my voice has been tuned to the note of the gun
> That startles the deep when the combat's begun,"'[26]

quoted Attwater, with a smile, which instantly gave way to an air of funereal solemnity. 'I shall particularly expect Mr Whish,' he continued. 'Mr Whish, I trust you understand the invitation?'

'I believe you, my boy!' replied the genial Huish.

'That is right, then; and quite understood, is it not?' said Attwater. 'Mr Whish and Captain Brown at six-thirty without fault – and you, Hay, at four sharp.'

And he called his boat.

During all this talk a load of thought or anxiety had weighed upon the captain. There was no part for which nature had so liberally endowed him as that of the genial ship-captain. But to-day he was silent and abstracted. Those who knew him could see that he hearkened close to every syllable, and seemed to ponder and try it in balances. It would have been hard to say what look there was, cold, attentive, and sinister, as of a man maturing plans, which still brooded over the unconscious guest; it was here, it was there, it was nowhere; it was now so little that Herrick chid himself for an idle fancy; and anon it was so gross and palpable that you could say every hair on the man's head talked mischief.

He woke up now, as with a start. 'You were talking of a charter,' said he.

'Was I?' said Attwater. 'Well, let's talk of it no more at present.'

'Your own schooner is overdue, I understand?' continued the captain.

'You understand perfectly, Captain Brown,' said Attwater; 'thirty-three days overdue at noon to-day.'

'She comes and goes, eh? plies between here and ...?' hinted the captain.

'Exactly; every four months; three trips in the year,' said Attwater.

'You go in her, ever?' asked Davis.

'No; one stops here,' said Attwater, 'one has plenty to attend to.'

'Stop here, do you?' cried Davis. 'Say, how long?'

'How long, O Lord,' said Attwater, with perfect, stern gravity. 'But it does not seem so,' he added, with a smile.

'No, I daresay not,' said Davis. 'No, I suppose not. Not with all your gods about you, and in as snug a berth as this. For it is a pretty snug berth,' said he, with a sweeping look.

'The spot, as you are good enough to indicate, is not entirely intolerable,' was the reply.

'Shell, I suppose?' said Davis.

'Yes, there was shell,' said Attwater.

'This is a considerable big beast of a lagoon, sir,' said the captain. 'Was there a – was the fishing – would you call the fishing anyways *good*?'

'I don't know that I would call it anyways anything,' said Attwater, 'if you put it to me direct.'

'There were pearls, too?' said Davis.

'Pearls, too,' said Attwater.

'Well, I give out!' laughed Davis, and his laughter rang cracked like a false piece. 'If you're not going to tell, you're not going to tell, and there's an end to it.'

'There can be no reason why I should affect the least degree of secrecy about my island,' returned Attwater; 'that came wholly to an end with your arrival; and I am sure, at any rate, that gentlemen like you and Mr Whish I should have always been charmed to make perfectly at home. The point on which we are now differing – if you can call it a difference – is one of times and seasons. I have some information which you think I might impart, and I think not. Well, we'll see to-night! By-by, Whish!' He stepped into his boat and shoved off. 'All understood, then?' said he. 'The captain and Mr Whish at six-thirty, and you, Hay, at four precise. You understand that, Hay? Mind, I take no denial. If you're not there by the time named, there will be no banquet; no song, no supper, Mr Whish!'

White birds whisked in the air above, a shoal of particoloured fishes in the scarce denser medium below; between, like Mahomet's coffin, the boat drew away briskly on the surface, and its shadow followed it over the glittering floor of the lagoon. Attwater looked steadily back over his shoulders as he sat; he did not once remove his eyes from the *Farallone* and the group on her quarter-deck beside the house, till his boat ground upon the pier. Thence, with an agile pace, he hurried ashore, and they saw his white clothes shining in the chequered dusk of the grove until the house received him.

The captain, with a gesture and a speaking countenance, called the adventurers into the cabin.

'Well,' he said to Herrick, when they were seated, 'there's one good job at least. He's taken to you in earnest.'

'Why should that be a good job?' said Herrick.

'O, you'll see how it pans out presently,' returned Davis. 'You go ashore and stand in with him, that's all! You'll get lots of pointers; you can find out what he has, and what the charter is, and who's the fourth man – for there's four of them, and we're only three.'

'And suppose I do, what next?' cried Herrick. 'Answer me that!'

'So I will, Robert Herrick,' said the captain. 'But first, let's see all clear. I guess you know,' he said, with imperious solemnity, 'I guess you know the bottom is out of this *Farallone* speculation? I guess you know it's *right* out? and if this old island hadn't been turned up right when it did, I guess you know where you and I and Huish would have been?'

'Yes, I know that,' said Herrick. 'No matter who's to blame, I know it. And what next?'

'No matter who's to blame, you know it, right enough,' said the captain, 'and I'm obliged to you for the reminder. Now, here's this Attwater: what do you think of him?'

'I do not know,' said Herrick. 'I am attracted and repelled. He was insufferably rude to you.'

'And you, Huish?' said the captain.

Huish sat cleaning a favourite briar-root; he scarce looked up from that engrossing task. 'Don't ask me what I think of him!' he said. 'There's a day comin', I pray Gawd, when I can tell it him myself.'

'Huish means the same as what I do,' said Davis. 'When that man came stepping around, and saying, "Look here, I'm Attwater" – and you knew it was so, by God! – I sized him right straight up. He's the real article, I said, and I don't like it; here's the real, first-rate, copper-bottomed aristocrat. "*Aw! don't know ye, do I? God damn ye, did God make ye?*" No, that couldn't be nothing but genuine; a man got to be born to that, and notice! smart as champagne and hard as nails; no kind of a fool; no, *sir*! not a pound of him! Well, what's he here upon this beastly island for? I said. *He*'s not here collecting eggs. He's a palace at home, and powdered flunkeys; and if he don't stay there, you bet he knows the reason why! Follow?'

'O yes, I 'ear you,' said Huish.

'He's been doing good business here, then,' continued the captain. 'For ten years he's been doing a great business. It's pearl and shell, of course; there couldn't be nothing else in such a place, and no doubt the shell goes off regularly by this *Trinity Hall*, and the money for it straight into the bank, so that's no use to us. But what else is there? Is there nothing else he would be likely to keep here? Is there nothing else he would be bound to keep here? Yes, sir; the pearls! First, because they're too valuable to trust out of his hands. Second, because pearls want a lot of handling and matching; and the man who sells his pearls as they come in one here, one there, instead of hanging back and holding up – well, that man's a fool, and it's not Attwater.'

'Likely,' said Huish, 'that's w'at it is; not proved, but likely.'

'It's proved,' said Davis bluntly.

'Suppose it was?' said Herrick. 'Suppose that was all so, and he had these pearls – a ten years' collection of them? Suppose he had? There's my question.'

The captain drummed with his thick hands on the board in front of him; he looked steadily in Herrick's face, and Herrick as steadily looked upon the table and the pattering fingers; there was a gentle oscillation of the anchored ship, and a big patch of sunlight travelled to and fro between the one and the other.

'Hear me!' Herrick burst out suddenly.

'No, you better hear me first,' said Davis. 'Hear me and understand me. *We've* got no use for that fellow, whatever you may have. He's your kind, he's not ours; he's took to you, and he's wiped his boots on me and Huish. Save him if you can!'

'Save him?' repeated Herrick.

'Save him, if you're able!' reiterated Davis, with a blow of his clenched fist. 'Go ashore, and talk him smooth; and if you get him and his pearls aboard, I'll spare him. If you don't, there's going to be a funeral. Is that so, Huish? Does that suit you?'

'I ain't a forgiving man,' said Huish, 'but I'm not the sort to spoil business neither. Bring the bloke on board and bring his pearls along with him, and you can have it your own way; maroon him where you like, – I'm agreeable.'

'Well, and if I can't?' cried Herrick, while the sweat streamed upon his face. 'You talk to me as if I was God Almighty, to do this and that! But if I can't?'

'My son,' said the captain, 'you better do your level best, or you'll see sights!'

'O yes,' said Huish. 'O crikey, yes!' He looked across at Herrick with a toothless smile that was shocking in its savagery; and, his ear caught apparently by the trivial expression he had used, broke into a piece of the chorus of a comic song which he must have heard twenty years before in London: meaningless gibberish that, in that hour and place, seemed hateful as a blasphemy: 'Hikey, pikey, crikey, fikey, chillinga-wallaba dory.'

The captain suffered him to finish; his face was unchanged.

'The way things are, there's many a man that wouldn't let you go ashore,' he resumed. 'But I'm not that kind. I know you'd never go back on me, Herrick! Or if you choose to, – go, and do it, and be damned!' he cried, and rose abruptly from the table.

He walked out of the house; and as he reached the door turned and called Huish, suddenly and violently, like the barking of a dog. Huish followed, and Herrick remained alone in the cabin.

'Now, see here!' whispered Davis. 'I know that man. If you open your mouth to him again, you'll ruin all.'

Better Acquaintance

THE boat was gone again, and already half-way to the *Farallone*, before Herrick turned and went unwillingly up the pier. From the crown of the beach, the figure-head confronted him with what seemed irony, her helmeted head tossed back, her formidable arm apparently hurling something, whether shell or missile, in the direction of the anchored schooner. She seemed a defiant deity from the island, coming forth to its threshold with a rush as of one about to fly, and perpetuated in that dashing attitude. Herrick looked up at her, where she towered above him head and shoulders, with singular feelings of curiosity and romance, and suffered his mind to travel to and fro in her life-history. So long she had been the blind conductress of a ship among the waves; so long she had stood here idle in the violent sun, that yet did not avail to blister her; and was even this the end of so many adventures? he wondered, or was more behind? And he could have found it in his heart to regret that she was not a goddess, nor yet he a pagan, that he might have bowed down before her in that hour of difficulty.

When he now went forward, it was cool with the shadow of many well-grown palms; draughts of the dying breeze swung them together overhead; and on all sides, with a swiftness beyond dragon-flies or swallows, the spots of sunshine flitted, and hovered, and returned. Underfoot, the sand was fairly solid and quite level, and Herrick's steps fell there noiseless as in new-fallen snow. It bore the marks of having been once weeded like a garden alley at home; but the pestilence had done its work, and the weeds were returning. The buildings of the settlement showed here and there through the stems of the colonnade, fresh painted, trim and dandy, and all silent as the grave. Only here and there in the crypt, there was a rustle and scurry and some crowing of poultry; and from behind the house with the verandahs he saw smoke arise and heard the crackling of a fire.

The stone houses were nearest him upon his right. The first was locked; in the second he could dimly perceive, through a window, a certain accumulation of pearl-shell piled in the far end; the third, which stood gaping open on the afternoon, seized on the mind of Herrick with its multiplicity and disorder of romantic things. Therein were cables, windlasses and blocks of every size and capacity; cabin windows and ladders; rusty tanks, a companion hatch; a binnacle with its brass mountings and its compass idly pointing, in the confusion and dusk of that shed, to a forgotten pole; ropes, anchors, harpoons, a blubber-dipper of copper, green with years, a steering-wheel, a tool-chest with the vessel's name upon the top, the *Asia* : a whole curiosity-shop of sea-curios, gross and solid, heavy to lift, ill to break, bound with brass and shod with iron. Two wrecks at the least must have contributed to this random heap of lumber; and as Herrick looked upon it, it seemed to him as if the two ships' companies were there on guard, and he heard the tread of feet and whisperings, and saw with the tail of his eye the commonplace ghosts of sailor men.

This was not merely the work of an aroused imagination, but had something sensible to go upon; sounds of a stealthy approach were no doubt audible; and while he still stood staring at the lumber, the voice of his host sounded suddenly, and with even more than the customary softness of enunciation, from behind.

'Junk,' it said, 'only old junk! And does Mr Hay find a parable?'

'I find at least a strong impression,' replied Herrick, turning quickly, lest he might be able to catch, on the face of the speaker, some commentary on the words.

Attwater stood in the doorway, which he almost wholly filled; his hands stretched above his head and grasping the architrave. He smiled when their eyes met, but the expression was inscrutable.

'Yes, a powerful impression. You are like me; nothing so affecting as ships!' said he. 'The ruins of an empire would leave me frigid, when a bit of an old rail that an old shellback leaned on in the middle watch, would bring me up all standing. But come, let's see some more of the island. It's all sand and coral and palm-trees; but there's a kind of a quaintness in the place.'

'I find it heavenly,' said Herrick, breathing deep, with head bared in the shadow.

'Ah, that's because you're new from sea,' said Attwater. 'I daresay, too, you can appreciate what one calls it. It's a lovely name. It has a flavour, it has a colour, it has a ring and fall to it; it's like its author – it's half Christian! Remember your first view of the island, and how it's only woods and woods and water; and suppose you had asked somebody for the name, and he had answered – *nemorosa Zacynthos*.'

'*Jam medio apparet fluctu!*'[27] exclaimed Herrick. 'Ye gods, yes, how good!'

'If it gets upon the chart, the skippers will make nice work of it,' said Attwater. 'But here, come and see the diving-shed.'

He opened a door, and Herrick saw a large display of apparatus neatly ordered: pumps and pipes, and the leaded boots, and the huge snouted helmets shining in rows along the wall; ten complete outfits.

'The whole eastern half of my lagoon is shallow, you must understand,' said Attwater; 'so we were able to get in the dress to great advantage. It paid beyond belief, and was a queer sight when they were at it, and these marine monsters' – tapping the nearest of the helmets – 'kept appearing and reappearing in the midst of the lagoon. Fond of parables?' he asked abruptly.

'O yes!' said Herrick.

'Well, I saw these machines come up dripping and go down again, and come up dripping and go down again, and all the while the fellow inside as dry as toast!' said Attwater; 'and I thought we all wanted a dress to go down into the world in, and come up scatheless. What do you think the name was?' he inquired.

'Self-conceit,' said Herrick.

'Ah, but I mean seriously!' said Attwater.

'Call it self-respect, then!' corrected Herrick, with a laugh.

'And why not Grace? Why not God's Grace, Hay?' asked Attwater. 'Why not the grace of your Maker and Redeemer, He who died for you, He who upholds you, He whom you daily crucify afresh? There is nothing here' – striking on his bosom – 'nothing there' – smiting the wall – 'and nothing there' – stamping – 'nothing but God's Grace! We walk upon it, we breathe it; we live and die by it; it makes the nails and axles of the universe; and a puppy in pyjamas prefers self-conceit!' The huge dark man stood over against Herrick by the line of the divers' helmets, and seemed to swell and glow; and the next moment the life had gone from him. 'I beg your pardon,' said he; 'I see you don't believe in God?'

'Not in your sense, I am afraid,' said Herrick.

'I never argue with young atheists or habitual drunkards,' said Attwater flippantly. 'Let us go across the island to the outer beach.'

It was but a little way, the greatest width of that island scarce exceeding a furlong, and they walked gently. Herrick was like one in a dream. He had come there with a mind divided; come prepared to study that ambiguous and sneering mask, drag out the essential man from underneath, and act accordingly; decision being till then postponed. Iron cruelty, an iron insensibility to the suffering of others, the uncompromising pursuit of his own interests, cold culture, manners without humanity; these he had looked for, these he still thought he saw. But to find the whole machine thus glow with the reverberation of religious zeal, surprised him beyond words; and he laboured in vain, as he walked, to piece together into any kind of whole his odds and ends of knowledge – to adjust again into any kind of focus with itself, his picture of the man beside him.

'What brought you here to the South Seas?' he asked presently.

'Many things,' said Attwater. 'Youth, curiosity, romance, the love of the sea, and (it will surprise you to hear) an interest in missions. That has a good deal declined, which will surprise you less. They go the wrong way to work; they are too parsonish, too much of the old wife, and even the old apple-wife. *Clothes, clothes*, are their idea; but clothes are not Christianity, any more than they are the sun in heaven, or could take the place of it! They think a parsonage with roses, and church bells, and nice old women bobbing in the lanes, are part and parcel of religion. But religion is a savage thing, like the universe it illuminates; savage, cold, and bare, but infinitely strong.'

'And you found this island by an accident?' said Herrick.

'As you did!' said Attwater. 'And since then I have had a business, and a colony, and a mission of my own. I was a man of the world before I was a Christian; I'm a man of the world still, and I made my mission pay. No good ever came of coddling. A man has to stand up in God's sight and work up to his weight avoirdupois; then I'll talk to him, but not before. I gave these beggars what they wanted: a judge in Israel, the bearer of the sword and scourge; I was making a new people here; and behold, the angel of the Lord smote them and they were not!'

With the very uttering of the words, which were accompanied by a gesture, they came forth out of the porch of the palm wood by the margin of the sea and full in front of the sun, which was near setting. Before them the surf broke slowly. All around, with an air of imperfect wooden things inspired with wicked activity, the crabs trundled and scuttled into holes. On the right, whither Attwater pointed and abruptly turned, was the cemetery of the island, a field of broken stones from the bigness of a child's hand to that of his head, diversified by many mounds of the same material, and walled by a rude rectangular enclosure. Nothing grew there but a shrub or two with some white flowers; nothing but the number of the mounds, and their disquieting shape, indicated the presence of the dead.

'The rude forefathers of the hamlet sleep!'

quoted Attwater, as he entered by the open gateway into that unholy close. 'Coral to coral, pebbles to pebbles,' he said, 'this has been the main scene of my activity in the South Pacific. Some were good, and some bad, and the majority (of course and always) null. Here was a fellow, now, that used to frisk like a dog; if you had called him he came like an arrow from a bow; if you had not, and he came unbidden, you should have seen the deprecating eye and the little intricate dancing step. Well, his trouble is over now, he has lain down with kings and councillors; the rest of his acts, are they not written in the book of the chronicles? That fellow was from Penrhyn; like all the Penrhyn islanders he was ill to manage; heady, jealous, violent: the man with the nose! He lies here quiet enough. And so they all lie.

"And darkness was the burier of the dead!"'[28]

He stood, in the strong glow of the sunset, with bowed head; his voice sounded now sweet and now bitter with the varying sense.

'You loved these people?' cried Herrick, strangely touched.

'I?' said Attwater. 'Dear no! Don't think me a philanthropist. I dislike men, and hate women. If I like the islanders at all, it is because you see them here plucked of their lendings, their dead birds and cocked hats, their petticoats and coloured hose. Here was one I liked though,' and he set his foot upon a mound. 'He was a fine savage fellow; he had a dark soul; yes, I liked this one. I am fanciful,' he added, looking hard at Herrick, 'and I take fads. I like you.'

Herrick turned swiftly and looked far away to where the clouds were beginning to troop together and amass themselves round the obsequies of day. 'No one can like me,' he said.

'You are wrong there,' said the other, 'as a man usually is about himself. You are attractive, very attractive.'

'It is not me,' said Herrick; 'no one can like me. If you knew how I despised myself – and why!' His voice rang out in the quiet graveyard.

'I knew that you despised yourself,' said Attwater. 'I saw the blood come into your face to-day when you remembered Oxford. And I could have blushed for you myself, to see a man, a gentleman, with these two vulgar wolves.'

Herrick faced him with a thrill. 'Wolves?' he repeated.

'I said wolves and vulgar wolves,' said Attwater. 'Do you know that to-day, when I came on board, I trembled?'

'You concealed it well,' stammered Herrick.

'A habit of mine,' said Attwater. 'But I was afraid, for all that: I was afraid of the two wolves.' He raised his hand slowly. 'And now, Hay, you poor lost puppy, what do you do with the two wolves?'

'What do I do? I don't do anything,' said Herrick. 'There is nothing wrong; all is above-board; Captain Brown is a good soul; he is a ... he is ...' The phantom voice of Davis called in his ear: 'There's going to be a funeral;' and the sweat burst forth and streamed on his brow. 'He is a family man,' he resumed again, swallowing; 'he has children at home – and a wife.'

'And a very nice man?' said Attwater. 'And so is Mr Whish, no doubt?'

'I won't go so far as that,' said Herrick. 'I do not like Huish. And yet ... he has his merits too.'

'And, in short, take them for all in all, as good a ship's company as one would ask?' said Attwater.

'O yes,' said Herrick, 'quite.'

'So then we approach the other point of why you despise yourself?' said Attwater.

'Do we not all despise ourselves?' cried Herrick. 'Do not you?'

'O, I say I do. But do I?' said Attwater. 'One thing I know at least: I never gave a cry like yours, Hay! It came from a bad conscience! Ah, man, that poor diving-dress of self-conceit is sadly tattered! To-day, if ye will hear my voice. To-day, now, while the sun sets, and here in this burying-place of brown innocents, fall on your knees and cast your sins and sorrows on the Redeemer. Hay –'

'Not Hay!' interrupted the other, strangling. 'Don't call me that! I mean ... For God's sake, can't you see I'm on the rack?'

'I see it, I know it, I put and keep you there, my fingers are on the screws!' said Attwater. 'Please God, I will bring a penitent this night before His throne. Come, come to the mercy-seat! He waits to be gracious, man – waits to be gracious!'

He spread out his arms like a crucifix; his face shone with the brightness of a seraph's; in his voice, as it rose to the last word, the tears seemed ready.

Herrick made a vigorous call upon himself. 'Attwater,' he said, 'you push me beyond bearing. What am I to do? I do not believe. It is living truth to you; to me, upon my conscience, only folk-lore. I do not believe there is any form of words under heaven by which I can lift the burthen from my shoulders.

I must stagger on to the end with the pack of my responsibility; I cannot shift it; do you suppose I would not, if I thought I could? I cannot – cannot – cannot – and let that suffice.'

The rapture was all gone from Attwater's countenance; the dark apostle had disappeared; and in his place there stood an easy, sneering gentleman, who took off his hat and bowed. It was pertly done, and the blood burned in Herrick's face.

'What do you mean by that?' he cried.

'Well, shall we go back to the house?' said Attwater. 'Our guests will soon be due.'

Herrick stood his ground a moment with clenched fists and teeth; and as he so stood, the fact of his errand there slowly swung clear in front of him, like the moon out of clouds. He had come to lure that man on board; he was failing, even if it could be said that he had tried; he was sure to fail now, and knew it, and knew it was better so. And what was to be next?

With a groan he turned to follow his host, who was standing with polite smile, and instantly and somewhat obsequiously led the way in the now darkened colonnade of palms. There they went in silence, the earth gave up richly of her perfume, the air tasted warm and aromatic in the nostrils; and from a great way forward in the wood, the brightness of lights and fire marked out the house of Attwater.

Herrick meanwhile resolved and resisted an immense temptation to go up, to touch him on the arm and breathe a word in his ear: 'Beware, they are going to murder you.' There would be one life saved; but what of the two others? The three lives went up and down before him like buckets in a well, or like the scales of balances. It had come to a choice, and one that must be speedy. For certain invaluable minutes, the wheels of life ran before him, and he could still divert them with a touch to the one side or the other, still choose who was to live and who was to die. He considered the men. Attwater intrigued, puzzled, dazzled, enchanted and revolted him; alive, he seemed but a doubtful good; and the thought of him lying dead was so unwelcome that it pursued him, like a vision, with every circumstance of colour and sound. Incessantly he had before him the image of that great mass of man stricken down in varying attitudes and with varying wounds; fallen prone, fallen supine, fallen on his side; or clinging to a doorpost with the changing face and the relaxing fingers of the death-agony. He heard the click of the trigger, the thud of the ball, the cry of the victim; he saw the blood flow. And this building up of circumstance was like a consecration of the man, till he seemed to walk in sacrificial fillets. Next he considered Davis, with his thick-fingered, coarse-grained, oat-bread commonness of nature, his indomitable valour and mirth in the old days of their starvation, the endearing blend of his faults and virtues, the sudden shining forth of a tenderness that lay too deep for tears; his children, Ada and her bowel complaint, and Ada's doll. No, death could not be suffered to approach that head even in fancy; with a general heat and a bracing of his muscles, it was borne in on Herrick that Ada's father would find in him a son to the death. And even Huish showed a little in that sacredness; by the tacit adoption of daily life they were become brothers; there was an implied bond of loyalty in their cohabitation of the ship and their past miseries; to which Herrick must be a little true or wholly dishonoured. Horror of sudden death for horror of sudden death, there was here no hesitation possible: it must be Attwater. And no sooner was the thought formed (which was a sentence) than his whole mind of man ran in a panic to the other side: and when he looked within himself, he was aware only of turbulence and inarticulate outcry.

In all this there was no thought of Robert Herrick. He had complied with the ebb-tide in man's affairs, and the tide had carried him away; he heard already the roaring of the maelstrom that must hurry him under. And in his bedevilled and dishonoured soul there was no thought of self.

For how long he walked silent by his companion Herrick had no guess. The clouds rolled suddenly away; the orgasm was over; he found himself placid with the placidity of despair; there returned to him the power of commonplace speech; and he heard with surprise his own voice say: 'What a lovely evening!'

'Is it not?' said Attwater. 'Yes, the evenings here would be very pleasant if one had anything to do. By day, of course, one can shoot.'

'You shoot?' asked Herrick.

'Yes, I am what you call a fine shot,' said Attwater. 'It is faith; I believe my balls will go true; if I were to miss once, it would spoil me for nine months.'

'You never miss, then?' said Herrick.

'Not unless I mean to,' said Attwater. 'But to miss nicely is the art. There was an old king one knew in the western islands, who used to empty a Winchester all round a man, and stir his hair or nick a rag out of his clothes with every ball except the last; and that went plump between the eyes. It was pretty practice.'

'You could do that?' asked Herrick, with a sudden chill.

'O, I can do anything,' returned the other. 'You do not understand: what must be, must.'

They were now come near to the back part of the house. One of the men was engaged about the cooking-fire, which burned with the clear, fierce, essential radiance of cocoanut-shells. A fragrance of strange meats was in the air. All round in the verandahs lamps were lighted, so that the place shone abroad in the dusk of the trees with many complicated patterns of shadow.

'Come and wash your hands,' said Attwater, and led the way into a clean, matted room with a cot bed, a safe, a shelf or two of books in a glazed case, and an iron washing-stand. Presently he cried in the native, and there appeared for a moment in the doorway a plump and pretty young woman with a clean towel.

'Hullo!' cried Herrick, who now saw for the first time the fourth survivor of the pestilence, and was startled by the recollection of the captain's orders.

'Yes,' said Attwater, 'the whole colony lives about the house, what's left of it. We are all afraid of devils, if you please! and Taniera and she sleep in the front parlour, and the other boy on the verandah.'

'She is pretty,' said Herrick.

'Too pretty,' said Attwater. 'That was why I had her married. A man never knows when he may be inclined to be a fool about women; so when we were left alone I had the pair of them to the chapel and performed the ceremony. She made a lot of fuss.

I do not take at all the romantic view of marriage,' he explained.

'And that strikes you as a safeguard?' asked Herrick with amazement.

'Certainly. I am a plain man and very literal. *Whom God hath joined together* are the words, I fancy. So one married them, and respects the marriage,' said Attwater.

'Ah!' said Herrick.

'You see, I may look to make an excellent marriage when I go home,' began Attwater confidentially. 'I am rich. This safe alone' – laying his hand upon it – 'will be a moderate fortune, when I have the time to place the pearls upon the market. Here are ten years' accumulation from a lagoon, where I have had as many as ten divers going all day long; and I went further than people usually do in these waters, for I rotted a lot of shell and did splendidly. Would you like to see them?'

This confirmation of the captain's guess hit Herrick hard, and he contained himself with difficulty. 'No, thank you, I think not,' said he. 'I do not care for pearls. I am very indifferent to all these...'

'Gewgaws?' suggested Attwater. 'And yet I believe you ought to cast an eye on my collection, which is really unique, and which – O! it is the case with all of us and everything about us! – hangs by a hair. To-day it groweth up and flourisheth: to-morrow it is cut down and cast into the oven. To-day it is here and together in this safe; to-morrow – to-night! – it may be scattered. Thou fool, this night thy soul shall be required of thee.'

'I do not understand you,' said Herrick.

'Not?' said Attwater.

'You seem to speak in riddles,' said Herrick unsteadily. 'I do not understand what manner of man you are, nor what you are driving at.'

Attwater stood with his hands upon his hips, and his head bent forward. 'I am a fatalist,' he replied, 'and just now (if you insist on it) an experimentalist. Talking of which, by the by, who painted out the schooner's name?' he said, with mocking softness, 'because, do you know? one thinks it should be done again. It can still be partly read; and whatever is worth doing is surely worth doing well. You think with me? That is so nice! Well, shall we step on the verandah? I have a dry sherry that I would like your opinion of.'

Herrick followed him forth to where, under the light of the hanging lamps, the table shone with napery and crystal; followed him as the criminal goes with the hangman, or the sheep with the butcher; took the sherry mechanically, drank it, and spoke mechanical words of praise. The object of his terror had become suddenly inverted; till then he had seen Attwater trussed and gagged, a helpless victim, and had longed to run in and save him; he saw him now tower up mysterious and menacing, the angel of the Lord's wrath, armed with knowledge and threatening judgment. He set down his glass again, and was surprised to see it empty.

'You go always armed?' he said, and the next moment could have plucked his tongue out.

'Always,' said Attwater. 'I have been through a mutiny here; that was one of my incidents of missionary life.'

And just then the sound of voices reached them, and looking forth from the verandah they saw Huish and the captain drawing near.

The Dinner Party

THEY sat down to an island dinner, remarkable for its variety and excellence: turtle-soup and steak, fish, fowls, a sucking-pig, a cocoanut salad, and sprouting cocoanut roasted for dessert. Not a tin had been opened; and save for the oil and vinegar in the salad, and some green spears of onion which Attwater cultivated and plucked with his own hand, not even the condiments were European. Sherry, hock, and claret succeeded each other, and the *Farallone* champagne brought up the rear with the dessert.

It was plain that, like so many of the extremely religious in the days before teetotalism, Attwater had a dash of the epicure. For such characters it is softening to eat well; doubly so to have designed and had prepared an excellent meal for others; and the manners of their host were agreeably mollified in consequence. A cat of huge growth sat on his shoulder purring, and occasionally, with a deft paw, capturing a morsel in the air. To a cat he might be likened himself, as he lolled at the head of his table, dealing out attentions and innuendos, and using the velvet and the claw indifferently. And both Huish and the captain fell progressively under the charm of his hospitable freedom.

Over the third guest the incidents of the dinner may be said to have passed for long unheeded. Herrick accepted all that was offered him, ate and drank without tasting, and heard without comprehension. His mind was singly occupied in contemplating the horror of the circumstances in which he sat. What Attwater knew, what the captain designed, from which side treachery was to be first expected, these were the ground of his thoughts. There were times when he longed to throw down the table and flee into the night. And even that was debarred him; to do anything, to say anything, to move at all, were only to precipitate the barbarous tragedy; and he sat spellbound, eating with white lips. Two of his companions observed him narrowly, Attwater with raking, sidelong glances that did not interrupt his talk, the captain with a heavy and anxious consideration.

'Well, I must say this sherry is a really prime article,' said Huish. ''Ow much does it stand you in, if it's a fair question?'

'A hundred and twelve shillings in London, and the freight to Valparaiso, and on again,' said Attwater. 'It strikes one as really not a bad fluid.'

'A 'undred and twelve!' murmured the clerk, relishing the wine and the figures in a common ecstasy: 'O my!'

'So glad you like it,' said Attwater. 'Help yourself, Mr Whish, and keep the bottle by you.'

'My friend's name is Huish and not Whish, sir,' said the captain with a flush.

'I beg your pardon, I am sure. Huish and not Whish; certainly,' said Attwater. 'I was about to say that I have still eight dozen,' he added, fixing the captain with his eye.

'Eight dozen what?' said Davis.

'Sherry,' was the reply. 'Eight dozen excellent sherry. Why, it seems almost worth it in itself; to a man fond of wine.'

The ambiguous words struck home to guilty consciences, and Huish and the captain sat up in their places and regarded him with a scare.

'Worth what?' said Davis.

'A hundred and twelve shillings,' replied Attwater.

The captain breathed hard for a moment. He reached out far and wide to find any coherency in these remarks; then, with a great effort, changed the subject.

'I allow we are about the first white men upon this island, sir,' said he.

Attwater followed him at once, and with entire gravity, to the new ground. 'Myself and Dr Symonds excepted, I should say the only ones,' he returned. 'And yet who can tell? In the course of the ages some one may have lived here, and we sometimes think that some one must. The cocoa-palms grow all round the island, which is scarce like nature's planting. We found besides, when we landed, an unmistakable cairn upon the beach; use unknown; but probably erected in the hope of gratifying some mumbo-jumbo whose very name is forgotten, by some thick-witted gentry whose very bones are lost. Then the island (witness the Directory) has been twice reported; and since my tenancy, we have had two wrecks, both derelict. The rest is conjecture.'

'Dr Symonds is your partner, I guess?' said Davis.

'A dear fellow, Symonds! How he would regret it, if he knew you had been here!' said Attwater.

''E's on the *Trinity 'All*, ain't he?' asked Huish.

'And if you could tell me where the *Trinity 'All* was, you would confer a favour, Mr Whish!' was the reply.

'I suppose she has a native crew?' said Davis.

'Since the secret has been kept ten years, one would suppose she had,' replied Attwater.

'Well, now, see 'ere!' said Huish. 'You have everythink about you in no end style, and no mistake, but I tell you it wouldn't do for me. Too much of "the old rustic bridge by the mill"; too retired by 'alf. Give me the sound of Bow Bells!'

'You must not think it was always so,' replied Attwater. 'This was once a busy shore, although now, hark! you can hear the solitude. I find it stimulating. And talking of the sound of bells, kindly follow a little experiment of mine in silence.' There was a silver bell at his right hand to call the servants; he made them a sign to stand still, struck the bell with force, and leaned eagerly forward. The note rose clear and strong; it rang out clear and far into the night and over the deserted island; it died into the distance until there only lingered in the porches of the ear a vibration that was sound no longer. 'Empty houses, empty sea, solitary beaches!' said Attwater. 'And yet God hears the bell! And yet we sit in this verandah on a lighted stage with all heaven for spectators! And you call that solitude?'

There followed a bar of silence, during which the captain sat mesmerised.

Then Attwater laughed softly. 'These are the diversions of a lonely man,' he resumed, 'and possibly not in good taste. One tells oneself these little fairy tales for company. If there *should* happen to be anything in folk-lore, Mr Hay? But here comes the claret. One does not offer you Lafitte, captain, because I believe it is all sold to the railroad dining-cars in your great country; but this Brâne-Mouton is of a good year, and Mr Whish will give me news of it.'

'That's a queer idea of yours!' cried the captain, bursting with a sigh from the spell that had bound him. 'So you mean to tell me now, that you sit here evenings and ring up ... well, ring on the angels ... by yourself?'

'As a matter of historic fact, and since you put it directly, one does not,' said Attwater 'Why ring a bell, when there flows out from oneself and everything about one a far more momentous silence? the least beat of my heart and the least thought in my mind echoing into eternity for ever and for ever and for ever.'

'O, look 'ere,' said Huish, 'turn down the lights at once, and the Band of 'Ope will oblige! This ain't a spiritual séance.'

'No folk-lore about Mr Whish – I beg your pardon, captain: Huish, not Whish, of course,' said Attwater.

As the boy was filling Huish's glass, the bottle escaped from his hand and was shattered, and the wine spilt on the verandah floor. Instant grimness as of death appeared in the face of Attwater; he smote the bell imperiously, and the two brown natives fell into the attitude of attention and stood mute and trembling. There was just a moment of silence and hard looks; then followed a few savage words in the native; and, upon a gesture of dismissal, the service proceeded as before.

None of the party had as yet observed upon the excellent bearing of the two men. They were dark, undersized, and well set up; stepped softly, waited deftly, brought on the wines and dishes at a look, and their eyes attended studiously on their master.

'Where do you get your labour from anyway?' asked Davis.

'Ah, where not?' answered Attwater.

'Not much of a soft job, I suppose?' said the captain.

'If you will tell me where getting labour is!' said Attwater, with a shrug. 'And of course, in our case, as we could name no destination, we had to go far and wide and do the best we could. We have gone as far west as the Kingsmills[29] and as far south as Rapa-iti.[30] Pity Symonds isn't here! He is full of yarns. That was his part, to collect them. Then began mine, which was the educational.'

'You mean to run them?' said Davis.

'Ay! to run them,' said Attwater.

'Wait a bit,' said Davis; 'I'm out of my depth. How was this? Do you mean to say you did it single-handed?'

'One did it single-handed,' said Attwater, 'because there was nobody to help one.'

'By God, but you must be a holy terror!' cried the captain, in a glow of admiration.

'One does one's best,' said Attwater.

'Well, now!' said Davis, 'I have seen a lot of driving in my time, and been counted a good driver myself. I fought my way, third mate, round the Cape Horn with a push of packet-rats that would have turned the devil out of hell and shut the door on him; and I tell you, this racket of Mr Attwater's takes the cake. In a ship, why, there ain't nothing to it! You've got the law with you, that's what does it. But put me down on this blame' beach alone, with nothing but a whip and a mouthful of bad words, and ask me to ... no, *sir*! it's not good enough! I haven't got the sand for that!' cried Davis. 'It's the law behind,' he added; 'it's the law does it, every time!'

'The beak ain't as black as he's sometimes pynted,' observed Huish, humorously.

'Well, one got the law after a fashion,' said Attwater. 'One had to be a number of things. It was sometimes rather a bore.'

'I should smile!' said Davis. 'Rather lively, I should think!'

'I daresay we mean the same thing,' said Attwater. 'However, one way or another, one got it knocked into their heads that they *must* work, and they *did* ... until the Lord took them!'

''Ope you made 'em jump,' said Huish.

'When it was necessary, Mr Whish, I made them jump,' said Attwater.

'You bet you did,' cried the captain. He was a good deal flushed, but not so much with wine as admiration; and his eyes drank in the huge proportions of the other with delight. 'You bet you did, and you bet that I can see you doing it! By God, you're a man, and you can say I said so.'

'Too good of you, I'm sure,' said Attwater.

'Did you – did you ever have crime here?' asked Herrick, breaking his silence with a pungent voice.

'Yes,' said Attwater, 'we did.'

'And how did you handle that, sir?' cried the eager captain.

'Well, you see, it was a queer case,' replied Attwater. 'It was a case that would have puzzled Solomon. Shall I tell it you? yes?'

The captain rapturously accepted.

'Well,' drawled Attwater, 'here is what it was. I daresay you know two types of natives, which may be called the obsequious and the sullen? Well, one had them, the types themselves, detected in the fact; and one had them together. Obsequiousness ran out of the first like wine out of a bottle, sullenness congested in the second. Obsequiousness was all smiles; he ran to catch your eye, he loved to gabble; and he had about a dozen words of beach English, and an eighth-of-an-inch veneer of Christianity. Sullens was industrious; a big down-looking bee. When he was spoken to, he answered with a black look and a shrug of one shoulder, but the thing would be done. I don't give him to you for a model of manners; there was nothing showy about Sullens; but he was strong and steady, and ungraciously obedient. Now Sullens got into trouble; no matter how; the regulations of the place were broken, and he was punished accordingly – without effect. So, the next day, and the next, and the day after, till I began to be weary of the business, and Sullens (I am afraid) particularly so. There came a day when he was in fault again, for the – O, perhaps the thirtieth time; and he rolled a dull eye upon me, with a spark in it, and appeared to speak. Now the regulations of the place are formal upon one point: we allow no explanations; none are received, none allowed to be offered. So one stopped him instantly, but made a note of the circumstance. The next day he was gone from the settlement. There could be nothing more annoying; if the labour took to running away, the fishery was wrecked.

There are sixty miles of this island, you see, all in length like the Queen's highway; the idea of pursuit in such a place was a piece of single-minded childishness, which one did not entertain. Two days later, I made a discovery; it came in upon me with a flash that Sullens had been unjustly punished from beginning to end, and the real culprit throughout had been Obsequiousness. The native who talks, like the woman who hesitates, is lost. You set him talking and lying; and he talks, and lies, and watches your face to see if he has pleased you; till, at last, out comes the truth! It came out of Obsequiousness in the regular course. I said nothing to him; I dismissed him; and late as it was, for it was already night, set off to look for Sullens. I had not far to go: about two hundred yards up the island the moon showed him to me. He was hanging in a cocoa-palm – I'm not botanist enough to tell you how – but it's the way, in nine cases out of ten, these natives commit suicide. His tongue was out, poor devil, and the birds had got him; I spare you details, he was an ugly sight! I gave the business six good hours of thinking in this verandah. My justice had been made a fool of; I don't suppose that I was ever angrier. Next day, I had the conch sounded and all hands out before sunrise. One took one's gun, and led the way, with Obsequiousness. He was very talkative; the beggar supposed that all was right now he had confessed; in the old schoolboy phrase he was plainly "sucking up" to me; full of protestations of good-will and good behaviour; to which one answered one really can't remember what. Presently the tree came in sight, and the hanged man. They all burst out lamenting for their comrade in the island way, and Obsequiousness was the loudest of the mourners. He was quite genuine; a noxious creature without any consciousness of guilt. Well, presently – to make a long story short – one told him to go up the tree. He stared a bit, looked at one with a trouble in his eye, and had rather a sickly smile; but went. He was obedient to the last; he had all the pretty virtues, but the truth was not in him. So soon as he was up he looked down, and there was the rifle covering him; and at that he gave a whimper like a dog. You could hear a pin drop; no more keening now. They were all crouched upon the ground with bulging eyes; there was he in the tree-top, the colour of lead; and between was the dead man, dancing a bit in the air. He was obedient to the last, recited his crime, recommended his soul to God. And then . . .'

Attwater paused, and Herrick, who had been listening attentively, made a convulsive movement which upset his glass.

'And then?' said the breathless captain.

'Shot,' said Attwater. 'They came to the ground together.'

Herrick sprang to his feet with a shriek and an insensate gesture.

'It was a murder!' he screamed, 'a cold-hearted, bloody-minded murder! You monstrous being! Murderer and hypocrite – murderer and hypocrite – murderer and hypocrite –' he repeated, and his tongue stumbled among the words.

The captain was by him in a moment. 'Herrick!' he cried, 'behave yourself! Here, don't be a blame' fool!'

Herrick struggled in his embrace like a frantic child, and suddenly bowing his face in his hands, choked into a sob, the first of many, which now convulsed his body silently, and now jerked from him indescribable and meaningless sounds.

'Your friend appears over-excited,' remarked Attwater, sitting unmoved but all alert at table.

'It must be the wine,' replied the captain. 'He ain't no drinking man, you see. I – I think I'll take him away. A walk'll sober him up, I guess.'

He led him without resistance out of the verandah and into the night, in which they soon melted; but still for some time, as they drew away, his comfortable voice was to be heard soothing and remonstrating, and Herrick answering, at intervals, with the mechanical noises of hysteria.

''E's like a bloomin' poultry yard!' observed Huish, helping himself to wine (of which he spilled a good deal) with gentlemanly ease. 'A man should learn to beyave at table,' he added.

'Rather bad form, is it not?' said Attwater. 'Well, well, we are left *tête-à-tête*. A glass of wine with you, Mr Whish!'

The Open Door

THE captain and Herrick meanwhile turned their back upon the lights in Attwater's verandah, and took a direction towards the pier and the beach of the lagoon.

The isle, at this hour, with its smooth floor of sand, the pillared roof overhead, and the prevalent illumination of the lamps, wore an air of unreality, like a deserted theatre or a public garden at midnight. A man looked about him for the statues and tables. Not the least air of wind was stirring among the palms, and the silence was emphasised by the continuous clamour of the surf from the seashore, as it might be of traffic in the next street.

Still talking, still soothing him, the captain hurried his patient on, brought him at last to the lagoon side, and leading him down the beach, laved his head and face with the tepid water. The paroxysm gradually subsided, the sobs became less convulsive and then ceased; by an odd but not quite unnatural conjunction, the captain's soothing current of talk died away at the same time and by proportional steps, and the pair remained sunk in silence. The lagoon broke at their feet in petty wavelets, and with a sound as delicate as a whisper; stars of all degrees looked down on their own images in that vast mirror; and the more angry colour of the *Farallone*'s riding lamp burned in the middle distance. For long they continued to gaze on the scene before them, and hearken anxiously to the rustle and tinkle of that miniature surf, or the more distant and loud reverberations from the outer coast. For long speech was denied them; and when the words came at last, they came to both simultaneously.

'Say, Herrick . . .' the captain was beginning.

But Herrick, turning swiftly towards his companion, bent him down with the eager cry: 'Let's up anchor, captain, and to sea!'

'Where to, my son?' said the captain. 'Up anchor's easy saying. But where to?'

'To sea,' responded Herrick. 'The sea's big enough! To sea – away from this dreadful island and that, O! that sinister man!'

'O, we'll see about that,' said Davis. 'You brace up, and we'll see about that. You're all run down, that's what's wrong with you; you're all nerves, like Jemimar; you've got to brace up good and be yourself again, and then we'll talk.'

'To sea,' reiterated Herrick, 'to sea to-night – now – this moment!'

'It can't be, my son,' replied the captain firmly. 'No ship of mine puts to sea without provisions, you can take that for settled.'

'You don't seem to understand,' said Herrick. 'The whole thing is over, I tell you. There is nothing to do here, when he knows all. That man there with the cat knows all; can't you take it in?'

'All what?' asked the captain, visibly discomposed. 'Why, he received us like a perfect gentleman and treated us real handsome, until you began with your foolery – and I must say I seen men shot for less, and nobody sorry! What more do you expect anyway?'

Herrick rocked to and fro upon the sand, shaking his head.

'Guying us,' he said; 'he was guying us – only guying us; it's all we're good for.'

'There was one queer thing, to be sure,' admitted the captain, with a misgiving of the voice; 'that about the sherry. Damned if I caught on to that. Say, Herrick, you didn't give me away?'

'O! give you away!' repeated Herrick with weary, querulous scorn. 'What was there to give away? We're transparent; we've got rascal branded on us: detected rascal – detected rascal! Why, before he came on board, there was the name painted out, and he saw the whole thing. He made sure we would kill him there and then, and stood guying you and Huish on the chance. He calls that being frightened! Next he had me ashore; a fine time I had! *The two wolves*, he calls you and Huish. *What is the puppy doing with the two wolves?* he asked. He showed me his pearls; he said they might be dispersed before morning, and *all hung by a hair* – and smiled as he said it, such a smile! O, it's no use, I tell you! He knows all, he sees through all; we only make him laugh with our pretences – he looks at us and laughs like God!'

There was a silence. Davis stood with contorted brows, gazing into the night.

'The pearls?' he said suddenly. 'He showed them to you? He has them?'

'No, he didn't show them; I forgot: only the safe they were in,' said Herrick. 'But you'll never get them!'

'I've two words to say to that,' said the captain.

'Do you think he would have been so easy at table, unless he was prepared?' cried Herrick. 'The servants were both armed. He was armed himself; he always is; he told me. You will never deceive his vigilance. Davis, I know it! It's all up, I tell you, and keep telling you and proving it. All up; all up. There's nothing for it, there's nothing to be done: all gone: life, honour, love. Oh my God, my God, why was I born?'

Another pause followed upon this outburst.

The captain put his hands to his brow.

'Another thing!' he broke out. 'Why did he tell you all this? Seems like madness to me!'

Herrick shook his head with gloomy iteration. 'You wouldn't understand if I were to tell you,' said he.

'I guess I can understand any blame' thing that you can tell me,' said the civilian.

'Well, then, he's a fatalist,' said Herrick.

'What's that? a fatalist?' said Davis.

'O, it's a fellow that believes a lot of things,' said Herrick; 'believes that his bullets go true; believes that all falls out as God chooses, do as you like to prevent it; and all that.'

'Why, I guess I believe right so myself,' said Davis.

'You do?' said Herrick.

'You bet I do!' says Davis.

Herrick shrugged his shoulders. 'Well, you must be a fool,' said he, and he leaned his head upon his knees.

The captain stood biting his hands.

'There's one thing sure,' he said at last. 'I must get Huish out of that. *He*'s not fit to hold his end up with a man like you describe.'

And he turned to go away. The words had been quite simple; not so the tone; and the other was quick to catch it.

'Davis!' he cried, 'no! Don't do it. Spare *me*, and don't do it – spare yourself, and leave it alone – for God's sake, for your children's sake!'

His voice rose to a passionate shrillness; another moment, and he might be overheard by their not distant victim. But Davis turned on him with a savage oath and gesture; and the miserable young man rolled over on his face on the sand, and lay speechless and helpless.

The captain meanwhile set out rapidly for Attwater's house. As he went, he considered with himself eagerly, his thoughts racing. The man had understood, he had mocked them from the beginning; he would teach him to make a mockery of John Davis! Herrick thought him a god; give him a second to aim in, and the god was overthrown. He chuckled as he felt the butt of his revolver. It should be done now, as he went in. From behind? It was difficult to get there. From across the table? No, the captain preferred to shoot standing, so as you could be sure to get your hand upon your gun. The best would be to summon Huish, and when Attwater stood up and turned – ah, then would be the moment. Wrapped in this ardent prefiguration of events, the captain posted towards the house with his head down.

'Hands up! Halt!' cried the voice of Attwater.

And the captain, before he knew what he was doing, had obeyed. The surprise was complete and irremediable. Coming on the top crest of his murderous intentions, he had walked straight into an ambuscade, and now stood, with his hands impotently lifted, staring at the verandah.

The party was now broken up. Attwater leaned on a post, and kept Davis covered with a Winchester. One of the servants was hard by with a second at the port arms, leaning a little forward, round-eyed with eager expectancy. In the open space at the head of the stair, Huish was partly supported by the other native; his face wreathed in meaningless smiles, his mind seemingly sunk in the contemplation of an unlighted cigar.

'Well,' said Attwater, 'you seem to me to be a very twopenny pirate!'

The captain uttered a sound in his throat for which we have no name; rage choked him.

'I am going to give you Mr Whish – or the wine-sop that remains of him,' continued Attwater. 'He talks a great deal when he drinks, Captain Davis of the *Sea Ranger*. But I have quite done with him – and return the article with thanks. Now,' he cried sharply. 'Another false movement like that, and your family will have to deplore the loss of an invaluable parent; keep strictly still, Davis.'

Attwater said a word in the native, his eye still undeviatingly fixed on the captain; and the servant thrust Huish smartly forward from the brink of the stair. With an extraordinary simultaneous dispersion of his members, that gentleman bounded forth into space, struck the earth, ricocheted, and brought up with his arms about a palm. His mind was quite a stranger to these events; the expression of anguish that deformed his countenance at the moment of the leap was probably mechanical; and he suffered these convulsions in silence; clung to the tree like an infant; and seemed, by his dips, to suppose himself engaged in the pastime of bobbing for apples. A more finely sympathetic mind or a more observant eye might have remarked, a little in front of him on the sand and still quite beyond reach, the unlighted cigar.

'There is your Whitechapel carrion!' said Attwater. 'And now you might very well ask me why I do not put a period to you at once, as you deserve. I will tell you why, Davis. It is because I have nothing to do with the *Sea Ranger* and the people you drowned, or the *Farallone* and the champagne that you stole. That is your account with God; He keeps it, and He will settle it when the clock strikes. In my own case, I have nothing to go on but suspicion, and I do not kill on suspicion, not even vermin like you. But understand: if ever I see any of you again, it is another matter, and you shall eat a bullet. And now take yourself off. March! and as you value what you call your life keep your hands up as you go!'

The captain remained as he was, his hands up, his mouth open: mesmerised with fury.

'March!' said Attwater. 'One – two – three!'

And Davis turned and passed slowly away. But even as he went, he was meditating a prompt, offensive return. In the twinkling of an eye he had leaped behind a tree; and was crouching there, pistol in hand, peering from either side of his place of ambush with bared teeth; a serpent already poised to strike. And already he was too late. Attwater and his servants had disappeared; and only the lamps shone on the deserted table and the bright sand about the house, and threw into the night in all directions the strong and tall shadows of the palms.

Davis ground his teeth. Where were they gone, the cowards? to what hole had they retreated beyond reach? It was in vain he should try anything, he, single and with a second-hand revolver, against three persons, armed with Winchesters, and who did not show an ear out of any of the apertures of that lighted and silent house? Some of them might have already ducked below it from the rear, and be drawing a bead upon him at that moment from the low-browed crypt, the receptacle of empty bottles and broken crockery. No, there was nothing to be done but to bring away (if it were still possible) his shattered and demoralised forces.

'Huish,' he said, 'come along.'

''S lose my ciga',' said Huish, reaching vaguely forward.

The captain let out a rasping oath. 'Come right along here,' said he.

''S all righ'. Sleep here 'th Atty-Attwa. Go boar' t'morr',' replied the festive one.

'If you don't come, and come now, by the living God, I'll shoot you!' cried the captain.

It is not to be supposed that the sense of these words in any way penetrated to the mind of Huish; rather that, in a fresh attempt upon the cigar, he over-balanced himself and came flying erratically forward: a course which brought him within reach of Davis.

'Now you walk straight,' said the captain, clutching him, 'or I'll know why not!'

' 'S lose my ciga',' replied Huish.

The captain's contained fury blazed up for a moment. He twisted Huish round, grasped him by the neck of the coat, ran him in front of him to the pier-end, and flung him savagely forward on his face.

'Look for your cigar then, you swine!' said he, and b'ew his boat-call till the pea in it ceased to rattle.

An immediate activity responded on board the *Farallone*; far-away voices, and soon the sound of oars, floated along the surface of the lagoon; and at the same time, from nearer hand, Herrick aroused himself and strolled languidly up. He bent over the insignificant figure of Huish, where it grovelled, apparently insensible, at the base of the figure-head.

'Dead?' he asked.

'No, he's not dead,' said Davis.

'And Attwater?' asked Herrick.

'Now you just shut your head!' replied Davis. 'You can do that, I fancy, and by God, I'll show you how! I'll stand no more of your drivel.'

They waited accordingly in silence till the boat bumped on the farthest piers; then raised Huish, head and heels, carried him down the gangway, and flung him summarily in the bottom. On the way out he was heard murmuring of the loss of his cigar; and after he had been handed up the side like baggage, and cast down in the alleyway to slumber, his last audible expression was: 'Splen'l fl' Attwa'!' This the expert construed into 'Splendid fellow, Attwater'; with so much innocence had this great spirit issued from the adventures of the evening.

The captain went and walked in the waist with brief irate turns; Herrick leaned his arms on the taffrail; the crew had all turned in. The ship had a gentle, cradling motion; at times a block piped like a bird. On shore, through the colonnade of palm trees, Attwater's house was to be seen shining steadily with many lamps. And there was nothing else visible, whether in the heaven above or in the lagoon below, but the stars and their reflections. It might have been minutes, or it might have been hours, that Herrick leaned there, looking in the glorified water and drinking peace. 'A bath of stars,' he was thinking; when a hand was laid at last on his shoulder.

'Herrick,' said the captain, 'I've been walking off my trouble.'

A sharp jar passed through the young man, but he neither answered nor so much as turned his head.

'I guess I spoke a little rough to you on shore,' pursued the captain; 'the fact is, I was real mad; but now it's over, and you and me have to turn to and think.'

'I will *not* think,' said Herrick.

'Here, old man!' said Davis kindly; 'this won't fight, you know! You've got to brace up and help me get things straight. You're not going back on a friend? That's not like you, Herrick!'

'O yes, it is,' said Herrick.

'Come, come!' said the captain, and paused as if quite at a loss. 'Look here,' he cried, 'you have a glass of champagne. *I* won't touch it, so that'll show you if I'm in earnest. But it's just the pick-me-up for you; it'll put an edge on you at once.'

'O, you leave me alone!' said Herrick, and turned away.

The captain caught him by the sleeve; and he shook him off and turned on him, for a moment like a demoniac.

'Go to hell in your own way!' he cried.

And he turned away again, this time unchecked, and stepped forward to where the boat rocked alongside and ground occasionally against the schooner. He looked about him. A corner of the house was interposed between the captain and himself; all was well; no eye must see him in that last act. He slid silently into the boat; thence, silently, into the starry water. Instinctively he swam a little; it would be time enough to stop by and by.

The shock of the immersion brightened his mind immediately. The events of the ignoble day passed before him in a frieze of pictures, and he thanked 'whatever Gods there be' for that open door of suicide. In such a little while he would be done with it, the random business at an end, the prodigal son come home. A very bright planet shone before him and drew a trenchant wake along the water. He took that for his line and followed it.

That was the last earthly thing that he should look upon; that radiant speck, which he had soon magnified into a City of Laputa,[31] along whose terraces there walked men and women of awful and benignant features, who viewed him with distant commiseration. These imaginary spectators consoled him· he told himself their talk, one to another; it was of himself and his sad destiny.

From such flights of fancy he was aroused by the growing coldness of the water. Why should he delay? Here, where he was now, let him drop the curtain, let him seek the ineffable refuge, let him lie down with all races and generations of men in the house of sleep. It was easy to say, easy to do. To stop swimming: there was no mystery in that, if he could do it. Could he? And he could not. He knew it instantly. He was aware instantly of an opposition in his members, unanimous and invincible, clinging to life with a single and fixed resolve, finger by finger, sinew by sinew; something that was at once he and not he – at once within and without him; the shutting of some miniature valve in his brain, which a single manly thought should suffice to open – and the grasp of an external fate ineluctable as gravity. To any man there may come at times a consciousness that there blows, through all the articulations of his body, the wind of a spirit, not wholly his; that his mind rebels; that another girds him and carries him whither he would not. It came now to Herrick, with the authority of a revelation. There was no escape possible. The open door was closed in his recreant face. He must go back into the world and amongst men without illusion. He must stagger on to the end with the pack of his responsibility and his disgrace, until a cold, a blow, a merciful chance ball, or the more merciful hangman, should dismiss him from his infamy. There were men who could commit suicide; there were men who could not; and he was one who could not.

For perhaps a minute there raged in his mind the coil of this discovery; then cheerless certitude followed; and, with an incredible simplicity of submission to ascertained fact, he turned round and struck out for shore. There was a courage in this which he could not appreciate; the ignobility of his cowardice wholly occupying him. A strong current set against him like a wind in his face; he contended with it heavily, wearily, without enthusiasm, but with substantial advantage; marking his progress the while, without pleasure, by the outline of the trees. Once he had a moment of hope. He heard to the southward of him, towards the centre of the lagoon, the wallowing of some great fish, doubtless a shark, and paused for a little, treading water. Might not this be the hangman? he thought. But the wallowing died away; mere silence succeeded; and Herrick pushed on again for the shore, raging as he went at his own nature. Ay, he would wait for the shark; but if he had heard him coming! ... His smile was tragic. He could have spat upon himself.

About three in the morning, chance, and the set of the current, and the bias of his own right-handed body, so decided it between them that he came to shore upon the beach in front of Attwater's. There he sat down, and looked forth into a world without any of the lights of hope. The poor diving-dress of self-conceit was sadly tattered! With the fairy tale of suicide, of a refuge always open to him, he had hitherto beguiled and supported himself in the trials of life; and behold! that also was only a fairy tale, that also was folk-lore. With the consequences of his acts he saw himself implacably confronted for the duration of life: stretched upon a cross, and nailed there with the iron bolts of his own cowardice. He had no tears; he told himself no stories. His disgust with himself was so complete, that even the process of apologetic mythology had ceased. He was like a man cast down from a pillar, and every bone broken. He lay there, and admitted the facts, and did not attempt to rise.

Dawn began to break over the far side of the atoll, the sky brightened, the clouds became dyed with gorgeous colours, the shadows of the night lifted. And, suddenly, Herrick was aware that the lagoon and the trees wore again their daylight livery; and he saw, on board the *Farallone*, Davis extinguishing the lantern, and smoke rising from the galley.

Davis, without doubt, remarked and recognised the figure on the beach; or perhaps hesitated to recognise it; for after he had gazed a long while from under his hand, he went into the house and fetched a glass. It was very powerful; Herrick had often used it. With an instinct of shame, he hid his face in his hands.

'And what brings you here, Mr Herrick-Hay, or Mr Hay-Herrick?' asked the voice of Attwater. 'Your back view from my present position is remarkably fine, and I would continue to present it. We can get on very nicely as we are, and if you were to turn round, do you know? I think it would be awkward.'

Herrick slowly rose to his feet; his heart throbbed hard, a hideous excitement shook him, but he was master of himself. Slowly he turned and faced Attwater and the muzzle of a pointed rifle. 'Why could I not do that last night?' he thought.

'Well, why don't you fire?' he said aloud, in a voice that trembled.

Attwater slowly put his gun under his arm, then his hands in his pockets.

'What brings you here?' he repeated.

'I don't know,' said Herrick; and then, with a cry: 'Can you do anything with me?'

'Are you armed?' said Attwater. 'I ask for the form's sake.'

'Armed? No!' said Herrick. 'O yes, I am, too!'

And he flung upon the beach a dripping pistol.

'You are wet,' said Attwater.

'Yes, I am wet,' said Herrick. 'Can you do anything with me?'

Attwater read his face attentively.

'It would depend a good deal upon what you are,' said he.

'What I am? A coward!' said Herrick.

'There is very little to be done with that,' said Attwater. 'And yet the description hardly strikes one as exhaustive.'

'O, what does it matter?' cried Herrick. 'Here I am. I am broken crockery; I am a burst drum; the whole of my life is gone to water; I have nothing left that I believe in, except my living horror of myself. Why do I come to you? I don't know; you are cold, cruel, hateful; and I hate you, or I think I hate you. But you are an honest man, an honest gentleman. I put myself, helpless, in your hands. What must I do? If I can't do anything, be merciful and put a bullet through me; it's only a puppy with a broken leg!'

'If I were you, I would pick up that pistol, come up to the house, and put on some dry clothes,' said Attwater.

'If you really mean it?' said Herrick. 'You know they – we – they ... But you know all.'

'I know quite enough,' said Attwater. 'Come up to the house.'

And the captain, from the deck of the *Farallone*, saw the two men pass together under the shadow of the grove.

David and Goliath

HUISH had bundled himself up from the glare of the day – his face to the house, his knees retracted. The frail bones in the thin tropical raiment seemed scarce more considerable than a fowl's; and Davis, sitting on the rail with his arm about a stay, contemplated him with gloom, wondering what manner of counsel that insignificant figure should contain. For since Herrick had thrown him off and deserted to the enemy, Huish, alone of mankind, remained to him to be a helper and oracle.

He considered their position with a sinking heart. The ship was a stolen ship; the stores, whether from initial carelessness or ill administration during the voyage, were insufficient to carry them to any port except back to Papeete; and there retribution waited in the shape of a gendarme, a judge with a queer-shaped hat, and the horror of distant Noumea.[32] Upon that side there was no glimmer of hope. Here, at the island, the dragon was roused; Attwater with his men and his Winchesters watched and patrolled the house; let him who dare approach it. What else was then left but to sit there, inactive, pacing the decks – until the *Trinity Hall* arrived and they were cast into irons, or until the food came to an end, and the pangs of famine succeeded? For the *Trinity Hall* Davis was prepared; he would barricade the house, and die there defending it, like a rat in a crevice. But for the other? The cruise of the *Farallone*, into which he had plunged, only a fortnight before, with such golden expectations, could this be the nightmare end of it? The ship rotting at anchor, the crew stumbling and dying in the scuppers? It seemed as if any extreme of hazard were to be preferred to so grisly a certainty; as if it would be better to up-anchor after all, put to sea at a venture, and, perhaps, perish at the hands of cannibals on one of the more obscure Paumotus. His eye roved swiftly over sea and sky in quest of any promise of wind, but the fountains of the Trade were empty. Where it had run yesterday and for weeks before, a roaring blue river charioting clouds, silence now reigned; and the whole height of the atmosphere stood balanced. On the endless ribbon of island that stretched out to either hand of him its array of golden and green and silvery palms, not the most volatile frond was to be seen stirring; they drooped to their stable images in the lagoon like things carved of metal, and already their long line began to reverberate heat. There was no escape possible that day, none probable on the morrow. And still the stores were running out!

Then came over Davis, from deep down in the roots of his being, or at least from far back among his memories of childhood and innocence, a wave of superstition. This run of ill-luck was something beyond natural; the chances of the game were in themselves more various; it seemed as if the devil must serve the pieces. The devil? He heard again the clear note of Attwater's bell ringing abroad into the night, and dying away. How if God ...?

Briskly he averted his mind. Attwater: that was the point. Attwater had food and a treasure of pearls; escape made possible in the present, riches in the future. They must come to grips with Attwater; the man must die. A smoky heat went over his face, as he recalled the impotent figure he had made last night, and the contemptuous speeches he must bear in silence. Rage, shame, and the love of life, all pointed the one way; and only invention halted: how to reach him? had he strength enough? was there any help in that misbegotten packet of bones against the house?

His eyes dwelled upon him with a strange avidity, as though he would read into his soul; and presently the sleeper moved, stirred uneasily, turned suddenly round, and threw him a blinking look. Davis maintained the same dark stare, and Huish looked away again and sat up.

'Lord, I've an 'eadache on me!' said he. 'I believe I was a bit swipey last night. W'ere's that cry-byby 'Errick?'

'Gone,' said the captain.

'Ashore?' cried Huish. 'O, I say! I'd 'a gone too.'

'Would you?' said the captain.

'Yes, I would,' replied Huish. 'I like Attwater. 'E's all right; we got on like one o'clock when you were gone. And ain't his sherry in it, rather? It's like Spiers and Pond's Amontillado! I wish I 'ad a drain of it now.' He sighed.

'Well, you'll never get no more of it – that's one thing,' said Davis, gravely.

''Ere, wot's wrong with you, Dyvis? Coppers 'ot? Well, look at *me*! *I* ain't grumpy,' said Huish; 'I'm as plyful as a canary-bird, I am.'

'Yes,' said Davis, 'you're playful; I own that; and you were playful last night, I believe, and a damned fine performance you made of it.'

''Allo!' said Huish. ''Ow's this? Wot performance?'

'Well, I'll tell you,' said the captain, getting slowly off the rail.

And he did: at full length, with every wounding epithet and absurd detail repeated and emphasised; he had his own vanity and Huish's upon the grill, and roasted them; and as he spoke he inflicted and endured agonies of humiliation. It was a plain man's masterpiece of the sardonic.

'What do you think of it?' said he, when he had done, and looked down at Huish, flushed and serious, and yet jeering.

'I'll tell you wot it is,' was the reply, 'you and me cut a pretty dicky figure.'

'That's so,' said Davis, 'a pretty measly figure, by God! And, by God, I want to see that man at my knees.'

'Ah!' said Huish. ''Ow to get him there?'

'That's it!' cried Davis. 'How to get hold of him! They're four to two; though there's only one man among them to count, and that's Attwater. Get a bead on Attwater, and the others would cut and run and sing out like frightened poultry – and old man Herrick would come round with his hat for a share of the pearls. No, *sir*! it's how to get hold of Attwater! And we daren't even go ashore; he would shoot us in the boat like dogs.'

'Are you particular about having him dead or alive?' asked Huish.

'I want to see him dead,' said the captain.

'Ah, well!' said Huish, 'then I believe I'll do a bit of breakfast.'

And he turned into the house.

The captain doggedly followed him.

'What's this?' he asked. 'What's your idea, anyway?'

'O, you let me alone, will you?' said Huish, opening a bottle of champagne. 'You'll 'ear my idea soon enough. Wyte till I pour some cham on my 'ot coppers.' He drank a glass off, and affected to listen. ''Ark!' said he, ''ear it fizz. Like 'am frying, I declyre. 'Ave a glass, do, and look sociable.

'No!' said the captain, with emphasis; 'no, I will not! there's business.'

'You p'ys your money and you tykes your choice, my little man,' returned Huish. 'Seems rather a shyme to me to spoil your breakfast for wot's really ancient 'istory.'

He finished three parts of a bottle of champagne, and nibbled a corner of biscuit, with extreme deliberation; the captain sitting opposite and champing the bit like an impatient horse. Then Huish leaned his arms on the table and looked Davis in the face.

'W'en you're ready!' said he.

'Well, now, what's your idea?' said Davis, with a sigh.

'Fair play!' said Huish. 'What's yours?'

'The trouble is that I've got none,' replied Davis; and wandered for some time in aimless discussion of the difficulties of their path, and useless explanations of his own fiasco.

'About done?' said Huish.

'I'll dry up right here,' replied Davis.

'Well, then,' said Huish, 'you give me your 'and across the table, and say, "Gawd strike me dead if I don't back you up."'

His voice was hardly raised, yet it thrilled the hearer. His face seemed the epitome of cunning, and the captain recoiled from it as from a blow.

'What for?' said he.

'Luck,' said Huish. 'Substantial guarantee demanded.'

And he continued to hold out his hand.

'I don't see the good of any such tomfoolery,' said the other.

'I do, though,' returned Huish. 'Gimme your 'and and say the words; then you'll 'ear my view of it. Don't, and you don't.'

The captain went through the required form, breathing short, and gazing on the clerk with anguish. What to fear he knew not, yet he feared slavishly what was to fall from the pale lips.

'Now, if you'll excuse me 'alf a second,' said Huish, 'I'll go and fetch the byby.'

'The baby?' said Davis. 'What's that?'

'Fragile. With care. This side up,' replied the clerk with a wink, as he disappeared.

He returned, smiling to himself, and carrying in his hand a silk handkerchief. The long stupid wrinkles ran up Davis's brow as he saw it. What should it contain? He could think of nothing more recondite than a revolver.

Huish resumed his seat.

'Now,' said he, 'are you man enough to take charge of 'Errick and the niggers? Because I'll take care of Hattwater.'

'How?' cried Davis. 'You can't!'

'Tut, tut!' said the clerk. 'You gimme time. Wot's the first point? The first point is that we can't get ashore, and I'll make you a present of that for a 'ard one. But 'ow about a flag of truce? Would that do the trick, d'ye think? or would Attwater simply blaze aw'y at us in the bloomin' boat like dawgs?'

'No,' said Davis, 'I don't believe he would.'

'No more do I,' said Huish; 'I don't believe he would either; and I'm sure I 'ope he won't! So then you can call us ashore. Next point is to get near the managin' direction. And for that I'm going to 'ave you write a letter, in w'ich you s'y you're ashymed to meet his eye, and that the bearer, Mr J. L. 'Uish, is empowered to represent you. Armed with w'ich seemin'ly simple expedient, Mr J. L. 'Uish will proceed to business.'

He paused, like one who had finished, but still held Davis with his eye.

'How?' said Davis. 'Why?'

'Well, you see, you're big,' returned Huish; ''e knows you 'ave a gun in your pocket, and anybody can see with 'alf an eye that you ain't the man to 'esitate about usin' it. So it's no go with you, and never was; you're out of the runnin', Dyvis.

But he won't be afryde of me, I'm such a little 'un! I'm unarmed – no kid about that – and I'll hold my 'ands up right enough.' He paused. 'If I can manage to sneak up nearer to him as we talk,' he resumed, 'you look out and back me up smart. If I don't, we go aw'y again, and nothink to 'urt. See?'

The captain's face was contorted by the frenzied effort to comprehend.

'No, I don't see,' he cried; 'I can't see. What do you mean?'

'I mean to do for the Beast!' cried Huish, in a burst of venomous triumph. 'I'll bring the 'ulkin' bully to grass. He's 'ad his larks out of me; I'm goin' to 'ave my lark out of 'im, and a good lark too!'

'What is it?' said the captain, almost in a whisper.

'Sure you want to know?' asked Huish.

Davis rose and took a turn in the house.

'Yes, I want to know,' he said at last with an effort.

'W'en your back's at the wall, you do the best you can, don't you?' began the clerk. 'I s'y that, because I 'appen to know there's a prejudice against it; it's considered vulgar, awf'ly vulgar.' He unrolled the handkerchief and showed a four-ounce jar. 'This 'ere's vitriol, this is,' said he.

The captain stared upon him with a whitening face.

'This is the stuff!' he pursued, holding it up. 'This'll burn to the bone; you'll see it smoke upon 'im like 'ell fire! One drop upon 'is bloomin' heyesight, and I'll trouble you for Attwater!'

'No, no, by God!' exclaimed the captain.

'Now, see 'ere, ducky,' said Huish, 'this is my bean feast, I believe? I'm goin' up to that man single-'anded, I am. 'E's about seven foot high, and I'm five foot one. 'E's a rifle in his 'and, 'e's on the look-out, 'e wasn't born yesterday. This is Dyvid and Goliar, I tell you! If I'd ast you to walk up and face the music I could understand. But I don't. I on'y ast you to stand by and spifflicate the niggers. It'll all come in quite natural; you'll see, else! Fust thing, you know, you'll see him running round and 'owling like a good 'un . . .'

'Don't!' said Davis. 'Don't talk of it!'

'Well, you *are* a juggins!' exclaimed Huish. 'What did you want? You wanted to kill him, and tried to last night. You wanted to kill the 'ole lot of them, and tried to, and 'ere I show you 'ow; and because there's some medicine in a bottle you kick up this fuss!'

'I suppose that's so,' said Davis. 'It don't seem someways reasonable, only there it is.'

'It's the happlication of science, I suppose?' sneered Huish.

'I don't know what it is,' cried Davis, pacing the floor; 'it's there! I draw the line at it. I can't put a finger to no such piggishness. It's too damned hateful!'

'And I suppose it's all your fancy pynted it,' said Huish, 'w'en you take a pistol and a bit o' lead, and copse a man's brains all over him? No accountin' for tystes.'

'I'm not denying it,' said Davis, 'it's something here, inside of me. It's foolishness; I daresay it's dam foolishness. I don't argue; I just draw the line. Isn't there no other way?'

'Look for yourself,' said Huish. 'I ain't wedded to this, if you think I am; I ain't ambitious; I don't make a point of playin' the lead; I offer to, that's all, and if you can't show me better, by Gawd, I'm goin' to!'

'Then the risk!' cried Davis.

'If you ast me straight, I should say it was a case of seven to one, and no takers,' said Huish 'But that's my look-out, ducky, and I'm gyme. Look at me, Dyvis, there ain't any shilly-shally about me. I'm gyme, that's wot I am: gyme all through.'

The captain looked at him. Huish sat there preening his sinister vanity, glorying in his precedency in evil; and the villainous courage and readiness of the creature shone out of him like a candle from a lantern. Dismay and a kind of respect seized hold on Davis in his own despite. Until that moment he had seen the clerk always hanging back, always listless, uninterested, and openly grumbling at a word of anything to do; and now, by the touch of an enchanter's wand, he beheld him sitting girt and resolved, and his face radiant. He had raised the devil, he thought; and asked who was to control him? and his spirits quailed.

'Look as long as you like,' Huish was going on. 'You don't see any green in my eye! I ain't afryde of Attwater, I ain't afryde of you, and I ain't afryde of words. You want to kill people, that's wot *you* want; but you want to do it in kid gloves, and it can't be done that w'y. Murder ain't genteel, it ain't easy, it ain't safe, and it tykes a man to do it. 'Ere's the man.'

'Huish!' began the captain with energy; and then stopped, and remained staring at him with corrugated brows.

'Well, hout with it!' said Huish. ''Ave you anythink else to put up? Is there any other chanst to try?'

The captain held his peace.

'There you are then!' said Huish, with a shrug.

Davis fell again to his pacing.

'O, you may do sentry-go till you're blue in the mug, you won't find anythink else,' said Huish.

There was a little silence; the captain, like a man launched on a swing, flying dizzily among extremes of conjecture and refusal.

'But see,' he said, suddenly pausing. 'Can you? Can the thing be done? It – it can't be easy.'

'If I get within twenty foot of 'im it'll be done; so you look out,' said Huish, and his tone of certainty was absolute.

'How can you know that?' broke from the captain in a choked cry. 'You beast, I believe you've done it before!'

'O, that's private affyres,' returned Huish, 'I ain't a talking man.'

A shock of repulsion struck and shook the captain; a scream rose almost to his lips; had he uttered it, he might have cast himself at the same moment on the body of Huish, might have picked him up, and flung him down, and wiped the cabin with him, in a frenzy of cruelty that seemed half moral. But the moment passed; and the abortive crisis left the man weaker. The stakes were so high – the pearls on the one hand – starvation and shame on the other. Ten years of pearls! The imagination of Davis translated them into a new, glorified existence for himself and his family. The seat of this new life must be in London; there were deadly reasons against Portland, Maine; and the pictures that came to him were of English manners. He saw his boys marching in the procession of a school, with gowns on, an usher marshalling them and reading as he walked in a great book. He was installed in a villa, semi-detached; the name,

'Rosemore', on the gateposts. In a chair on the gravel walk he seemed to sit smoking a cigar, a blue ribbon in his buttonhole, victor over himself and circumstances and the malignity of bankers. He saw the parlour, with red curtains, and shells on the mantelpiece – and, with the fine inconsistency of visions, mixed a grog at the mahogany table ere he turned in. With that *Farallone* gave one of the aimless and nameless movements which (even in an anchored ship and even in the most profound calm) remind one of the mobility of fluids; and he was back again under the cover of the house, the fierce daylight besieging it all round and glaring in the chinks, and the clerk in a rather airy attitude, awaiting his decision.

He began to walk again. He aspired after the realisation of these dreams, like a horse nickering for water; the lust of them burned in his inside. And the only obstacle was Attwater, who had insulted him from the first. He gave Herrick a full share of the pearls, he insisted on it; Huish opposed him, and he trod the opposition down; and praised himself exceedingly. He was not going to use vitriol himself; was he Huish's keeper? It was a pity he had asked, but after all! ... he saw the boys again in the school procession, with the gowns he had thought to be so 'tony' long since ... And at the same time the incomparable shame of the last evening blazed up in his mind.

'Have it your own way!' he said, hoarsely.

'O, I knew you would walk up,' said Huish. 'Now for the letter. There's paper, pens, and ink. Sit down and I'll dictyte.'

The captain took a seat and the pen, looked a while helplessly at the paper, then at Huish. The swing had gone the other way; there was a blur upon his eyes. 'It's a dreadful business,' he said, with a strong twitch of his shoulders.

'It's rather a start, no doubt,' said Huish. 'Tyke a dip of ink. That's it. *William John Attwater, Esq. Sir:*' he dictated.

'How do you know his name is William John?' asked Davis.

'Saw it on a packing-case,' said Huish. 'Got that?'

'No,' said Davis. 'But there's another thing. What are we to write?'

'O my golly!' cried the exasperated Huish. 'Wot kind of man do *you* call yourself? *I'm* goin' to tell you wot to write; that's *my* pitch; if you'll just be so bloomin' condescendin' as to write it down! *William John Attwater, Esq., Sir:*' he reiterated. And, the captain at last beginning half mechanically to move his pen, the dictation proceeded:

It is with feelings of shyme and 'artfelt contrition that I approach you after the yumiliatin' events of last night. Our Mr. 'Errick has left the ship, and will have doubtless communicated to you the nature of our 'opes. Needless to s'y, these are no longer possible: Fate 'as declyred against us, and we bow the 'ead. Well awyre as I am of the just suspicions with w'ich I am regarded, I do not venture to solicit the fyvour of an interview for myself, but in order to put an end to a situyation w'ich must be equally pyneful to all, I 'ave deputed my friend and partner, Mr. J. L. Huish, to l'y before you my proposals, and w'ich by their moderytion, will, I trust, be found to merit your attention. Mr. J. L. Huish is entirely unarmed, I swear to Gawd! and will 'old 'is 'ands over 'is 'ead from the moment he begins to approach you. I am your fytheful servant, John Dyvis.

Huish read the letter with the innocent joy of amateurs, chuckled gustfully to himself, and reopened it more than once after it was folded, to repeat the pleasure, Davis meanwhile sitting inert and heavily frowning.

Of a sudden he rose; he seemed all abroad. 'No!' he cried. 'No! it can't be! It's too much; it's damnation. God would never forgive it.'

'Well, and 'oo wants Him too?' returned Huish, shrill with fury. 'You were damned years ago for the *Sea Rynger*, and said so yourself. Well then, be damned for something else, and 'old your tongue.'

The captain looked at him mistily. 'No,' he pleaded, 'no, old man! don't do it.'

''Ere now,' said Huish, 'I'll give you my ultimytum. Go or st'y w'ere you are; I don't mind; I'm goin' to see that man and chuck this vitriol in his eyes. If you st'y I'll go alone; the niggers will likely knock me on the 'ead, and a fat lot you'll be the better! But there's one thing sure: I'll 'ear no more of your moonin' mullygrubbin' rot, and tyke it stryte.'

The captain took it with a blink and a gulp. Memory, with

phantom voices, repeated in his ears something similar, something he had once said to Herrick – years ago it seemed.

'Now, gimme over your pistol,' said Huish. 'I 'ave to see all clear. Six shots, and mind you don't wyste them.'

The captain, like a man in a nightmare, laid down his revolver on the table, and Huish wiped the cartridges and oiled the works.

It was close on noon, there was no breath of wind, and the heat was scarce bearable, when the two men came on deck, had the boat manned, and passed down, one after another, into the stern-sheets. A white shirt at the end of an oar served as a flag of truce; and the men, by direction, and to give it the better chance to be observed, pulled with extreme slowness. The isle shook before them like a place incandescent; on the face of the lagoon blinding copper suns, no bigger than sixpences, danced and stabbed them in the eyeballs; there went up from sand and sea, and even from the boat, a glare of scathing brightness; and as they could only peer abroad from between closed lashes, the excess of light seemed to be changed into a sinister darkness, comparable to that of a thundercloud before it bursts.

The captain had come upon this errand for any one of a dozen reasons, the last of which was desire for its success. Superstition rules all men; semi-ignorant and gross natures, like that of Davis, it rules utterly. For murder he had been prepared; but this horror of the medicine in the bottle went beyond him, and he seemed to himself to be parting the last strands that united him to God. The boat carried him on to reprobation, to damnation; and he suffered himself to be carried passively consenting, silently bidding farewell to his better self and his hopes.

Huish sat by his side in towering spirits that were not wholly genuine. Perhaps as brave a man as ever lived, brave as a weasel, he must still reassure himself with the tones of his own choice; he must play his part to exaggeration, he must out-Herod Herod, insult all that was respectable, and brave all that was formidable, in a kind of desperate wager with himself.

'Golly, but it's 'ot!' said he. 'Cruel 'ot, I call it. Nice d'y to get your gruel in! I s'y, you know, it must feel awf'ly peculiar to get bowled over on a d'y like this. I'd rather 'ave it on a cowld and frosty morning, wouldn't you? (Singing) "*'Ere we go round the mulberry bush on a cowld and frosty mornin'.*" (Spoken) Give you my word, I 'aven't thought o' that in ten year; used to sing it at a hinfant school in 'Ackney, 'Ackney Wick it was. (Singing) "*This is the way the tyler does, the tyler does.*" (Spoken) Bloomin' 'umbug. – 'Ow are you off now, for the notion of a future styte? Do you cotton to the tea-fight views, or the old red hot bogey business?'

'O, dry up!' said the captain.

'No, but I want to know,' said Huish. 'It's within the sp'ere of practical politics for you and me, my boy; we may both be bowled over, one up, t'other down, within the next ten minutes. It would be rather a lark, now, if you only skipped across, came up smilin' t'other side, and a hangel met you with a B-and-S under his wing. 'Ullo, you'd s'y: come, I tyke this kind.'

The captain groaned. While Huish was thus airing and exercising his bravado, the man at his side was actually engaged in prayer. Prayer, what for? God knows. But out of his inconsistent, illogical, and agitated spirit, a stream of supplication was poured forth, inarticulate as himself, earnest as death and judgment.

'Thou Gawd seest me!' continued Huish. 'I remember I had that written in my Bible. I remember the Bible too, all about Abinadab[33] and parties. Well, Gawd!' apostrophising the meridian, 'you're goin' to see a rum start presently, I promise you that!'

The captain bounded.

'I'll have no blasphemy!' he cried, 'no blasphemy in my boat.'

'All right, cap,' said Huish. 'Anythink to oblige. Any other topic you would like to sudgest, the ryne-gyge, the lightnin'-rod, Shykespeare, or the musical glasses? 'Ere's conversation on tap. Put a penny in the slot, and ... 'ullo! 'ere they are!' he cried. 'Now or never! is 'e goin' to shoot?'

And the little man straightened himself into an alert and dashing attitude, and looked steadily at the enemy.

But the captain rose half up in the boat with eyes protruding.

'What's that?' he cried.

'Wot's wot?' said Huish.

'Those – blamed things,' said the captain.

And indeed it was something strange. Herrick and Attwater, both armed with Winchesters, had appeared out of the grove behind the figure-head; and to either hand of them, the sun glistened upon two metallic objects, locomotory like men, and occupying in the economy of these creatures the places of heads – only the heads were faceless. To Davis, between wind and water, his mythology appeared to have come alive and Tophet[34] to be vomiting demons. But Huish was not mystified a moment.

'Divers' 'elmets, you ninny. Can't you see?' he said.

'So they are,' said Davis, with a gasp. 'And why? O, I see, it's for armour.'

'Wot did I tell you?' said Huish. 'Dyvid and Goliar all the w'y and back.'

The two natives (for they it was that were equipped in this unusual panoply of war) spread out to right and left, and at last lay down in the shade, on the extreme flank of the position. Even now that the mystery was explained, Davis was hatefully pre-occupied, stared at the flame on their crests, and forgot, and then remembered with a smile, the explanation.

Attwater withdrew again into the grove, and Herrick, with his gun under his arm, came down the pier alone.

About halfway down he halted and hailed the boat.

'What do you want?' he cried.

'I'll tell that to Mr Attwater,' replied Huish, stepping briskly on the ladder. 'I don't tell it to you, because you played the trucklin' sneak. Here's a letter for him: tyke it, and give it, and be 'anged to you!'

'Davis, is this all right?' said Herrick.

Davis raised his chin, glanced swiftly at Herrick and away again, and held his peace. The glance was charged with some deep emotion, but whether of hatred or of fear, it was beyond Herrick to divine.

'Well,' he said, 'I'll give the letter.' He drew a score with his foot on the boards of the gangway. 'Till I bring the answer, don't move a step past this.'

And he returned to where Attwater leaned against a tree, and gave him the letter. Attwater glanced it through.

'What does that mean?' he asked, passing it to Herrick. 'Treachery?'

'O, I suppose so!' said Herrick.

'Well, tell him to come on,' said Attwater. 'One isn't a fatalist for nothing. Tell him to come on and to look out.'

Herrick returned to the figure-head. Half-way down the pier the clerk was waiting, with Davis by his side.

'You are to come along, Huish,' said Herrick. 'He bids you to look out – no tricks.'

Huish walked briskly up the pier, and paused face to face with the young man.

'W'ere is 'e?' said he, and to Herrick's surprise, the low-bred, insignificant face before him flushed suddenly crimson and went white again.

'Right forward,' said Herrick, pointing. 'Now, your hands above your head.'

The clerk turned away from him and towards the figure-head, as though he were about to address to it his devotions; he was seen to heave a deep breath; and raised his arms. In common with many men of his unhappy physical endowments, Huish's hands were disproportionately long and broad, and the palms in particular enormous; a four-ounce jar was nothing in that capacious fist. The next moment he was plodding steadily forward on his mission.

Herrick at first followed. Then a noise in his rear startled him, and he turned about to find Davis already advanced as far as the figure-head. He came, crouching and open-mouthed, as the mesmerised may follow the mesmeriser; all human considerations, and even the care of his own life, swallowed up in one abominable and burning curiosity.

'Halt!' cried Herrick, covering him with his rifle. 'Davis, what are you doing, man? *You* are not to come.'

Davis instinctively paused, and regarded him with a dreadful vacancy of eye.

'Put your back to that figure-head, do you hear me? And stand fast!' said Herrick.

The captain fetched a breath, stepped back against the figure-head, and instantly redirected his glances after Huish.

There was a hollow place of the sand in that part, and, as it were, a glade among the cocoa-palms in which the direct noon-day sun blazed intolerably. At the far end, in the shadow, the tall figure of Attwater was to be seen leaning on a tree; towards him, with his hands over his head, and his steps smothered in the sand, the clerk painfully waded. The surrounding glare threw out and exaggerated the man's smallness; it seemed no less perilous an enterprise, this that he was gone upon, than for a whelp to besiege a citadel.

'There, Mr Whish. That will do,' cried Attwater. 'From that distance, and keeping your hands up, like a good boy, you can very well put me in possession of the skipper's views.'

The interval betwixt them was perhaps forty feet; and Huish measured it with his eye, and breathed a curse. He was already distressed with labouring in the loose sand, and his arms ached bitterly from their unnatural position. In the palm of his right hand the jar was ready; and his heart thrilled, and his voice choked, as he began to speak.

'Mr Hattwater,' said he, 'I don't know if ever you 'ad a mother...'

'I can set your mind at rest: I had,' returned Attwater, 'and henceforth, if I may venture to suggest it, her name need not recur in our communications. I should perhaps tell you that I am not amenable to the pathetic.'

'I am sorry, sir, if I 'ave seemed to tresparse on your private feelin's,' said the clerk, cringing and stealing a step. 'At least, sir, you will never pe'suade me that you are not a perfec' gentle-man; I know a gentleman when I see him; and as such, I 'ave no 'esitation in throwin' myself on your merciful consideration. It *is* 'ard lines, no doubt; it's 'ard lines to have to hown yourself beat; it's 'ard lines to 'ave to come and beg to you for charity.'

'When, if things had only gone right, the whole place was as good as your own?' suggested Attwater. 'I can understand the feeling.'

'You are judging me, Mr Attwater,' said the clerk, 'and God knows how unjustly! *Thou Gawd seest me*, was the tex' I 'ad in my Bible, w'ich my father wrote it in with 'is own 'and upon the fly-leaft.'

'I am sorry I have to beg your pardon once more,' said Attwater; 'but, do you know, you seem to me to be a trifle nearer, which is entirely outside of our bargain. And I would venture to suggest that you take one – two – three – steps back; and stay there.'

The devil, at this staggering disappointment, looked out of Huish's face, and Attwater was swift to suspect. He frowned, he stared at the little man, and considered. Why should he be creeping nearer? The next moment his gun was at his shoulder.

'Kindly oblige me by opening your hands. Open your hands wide – let me see the fingers spread, you dog – throw down that thing you're holding!' he roared, his rage and certitude increasing together.

And then, at almost the same moment, the indomitable Huish decided to throw, and Attwater pulled a trigger. There was scarce the difference of a second between the two resolves, but it was in favour of the man with the rifle; and the jar had not yet left the clerk's hand, before the ball shattered both. For the twinkling of an eye the wretch was in hell's agonies, bathed in liquid flames, a screaming bedlamite; and then a second and more merciful bullet stretched him dead.

The whole thing was come and gone in a breath. Before Herrick could turn about, before Davis could complete his cry of horror, the clerk lay in the sand, sprawling and convulsed.

Attwater ran to the body; he stooped and viewed it; he put his finger in the vitriol, and his face whitened and hardened with anger.

Davis had not yet moved; he stood astonished, with his back to the figure-head, his hands clutching it behind him, his body inclined forward from the waist.

Attwater turned deliberately and covered him with his rifle.

'Davis,' he cried, in a voice like a trumpet, 'I give you sixty seconds to make your peace with God!'

Davis looked, and his mind awoke. He did not dream of self-defence, he did not reach for his pistol. He drew himself up instead to face death, with a quivering nostril.

'I guess I'll not trouble the Old Man,' he said; 'considering the job I was on, I guess it's better business to just shut my face.'

Attwater fired; there came a spasmodic movement of the victim, and immediately above the middle of his forehead a black hole marred the whiteness of the figure-head. A dreadful pause; then again the report, and the solid sound and jar of the bullet in the wood; and this time the captain had felt the wind of it along his cheek. A third shot, and he was bleeding from one ear; and along the levelled rifle Attwater smiled like a red Indian.

The cruel game of which he was the puppet was now clear to Davis; three times he had drunk of death, and he must look to drink of it seven times more before he was despatched. He held up his hand.

'Steady!' he cried; 'I'll take your sixty seconds.'

'Good!' said Attwater.

The captain shut his eyes tight like a child: he held his hands up at last with a tragic and ridiculous gesture.

'My God, for Christ's sake, look after my two kids,' he said; and then, after a pause and a falter, 'for Christ's sake. Amen.'

And he opened his eyes and looked down the rifle with a quivering mouth.

'But don't keep fooling me long!' he pleaded.

'That's all your prayer?' asked Attwater, with a singular ring in his voice.

'Guess so,' said Davis.

'So?' said Attwater, resting the butt of his rifle on the ground, 'is that done? Is your peace made with Heaven? Because it is with me. Go, and sin no more, sinful father. And remember that whatever you do to others, God shall visit it again a thousand-fold upon your innocents.'

The wretched Davis came staggering forward from his place against the figure-head, fell upon his knees, and waved his hands, and fainted.

When he came to himself again, his head was on Attwater's arm, and close by stood one of the men in diver's helmets, holding a bucket of water, from which his late executioner now laved his face. The memory of that dreadful passage returned upon him in a clap; again he saw Huish lying dead, again he seemed to himself to totter on the brink of an unplumbed eternity. With trembling hands he seized hold of the man whom he had come to slay; and his voice broke from him like that of a child among the nightmares of fever: 'O! isn't there no mercy? O! what must I do to be saved?'

'Ah!' thought Attwater, 'here is the true penitent.'

A Tail-piece

On a very bright, hot, lusty, strongly blowing noon, a fortnight after the events recorded, and a month since the curtain rose upon this episode, a man might have been spied praying on the sand by the lagoon beach. A point of palm-trees isolated him from the settlement; and from the place where he knelt, the only work of man's hand that interrupted the expanse was the schooner *Farallone*, her berth quite changed, and rocking at anchor some two miles to windward in the midst of the lagoon. The noise of the Trade ran very boisterous in all parts of the island; the nearer palm-trees crashed and whistled in the gusts, those farther off contributed a humming bass like the roar of cities; and yet, to any man less absorbed, there must have risen at times over this turmoil of the winds the sharper note of the human voice from the settlement. There all was activity. Attwater, stripped to his trousers, and lending a strong hand of help, was directing and encouraging five Kanakas; from his lively voice, and their more lively efforts, it was to be gathered that some sudden and joyful emergency had set them in this bustle; and the Union Jack floated once more on its staff. But the suppliant on the beach, unconscious of their voices, prayed on with instancy and fervour, and the sound of his voice rose and fell again, and his countenance brightened and was deformed with changing moods of piety and terror.

Before his closed eyes the skiff had been for some time tacking towards the distant and deserted *Farallone*; and presently the figure of Herrick might have been observed to board her, to pass for a while into the house, thence forward to the forecastle, and at last to plunge into the main hatch. In all these quarters his visit was followed by a coil of smoke; and he had scarce entered his boat again and shoved off, before flames broke forth upon the schooner. They burned gaily; kerosene had not been spared, and the bellows of the Trade incited the conflagration. About half-way on the return voyage, when Herrick looked back, he beheld the *Farallone* wrapped to the topmasts in leaping arms of fire, and the voluminous smoke pursuing him along the face of the lagoon. In one hour's time, he computed, the waters would have closed over the stolen ship.

It so chanced that, as his boat flew before the wind with much vivacity, and his eyes were continually busy in the wake, measuring the progress of the flames, he found himself embayed to the northward of the point of palms, and here became aware at the same time of the figure of Davis immersed in his devotion. An exclamation, part of annoyance, part of amusement, broke from him: and he touched the helm and ran the prow upon the beach not twenty feet from the unconscious devotee. Taking the painter in his hand, he landed, and drew near, and stood over him. And still the voluble and incoherent stream of prayer continued unabated. It was not possible for him to overhear the suppliant's petitions, which he listened to some while in a very mingled mood of humour and pity: and it was only when his own name began to occur and to be conjoined with epithets, that he at last laid his hand on the captain's shoulder.

'Sorry to interrupt the exercise,' said he; 'but I want you to look at the *Farallone*.'

The captain scrambled to his feet, and stood gasping and staring. 'Mr Herrick, don't startle a man like that!' he said. 'I don't seem someways rightly myself since . . .' He broke off. 'What did you say anyway? O, the *Farallone*,' and he looked languidly out.

'Yes,' said Herrick. 'There she burns! and you may guess from that what the news is.'

'The *Trinity Hall*, I guess,' said the captain.

'The same,' said Herrick; 'sighted half an hour ago, and coming up hand over fist.'

'Well, it don't amount to a hill of beans,' said the captain, with a sigh.

'O, come, that's rank ingratitude!' cries Herrick.

'Well,' replied the captain meditatively, 'you mayn't just see the way that I view it in, but I'd 'most rather stay here upon this island. I found peace here, peace in believing. Yes, I guess this island is about good enough for John Davis.'

'I never heard such nonsense!' cried Herrick. 'What! with all turning out in your favour the way it does, the *Farallone* wiped out, the crew disposed of, a sure thing for your wife and family, and you, yourself, Attwater's spoiled darling and pet penitent!'

'No, Mr Herrick, don't say that,' said the captain gently; 'when you know he don't make no difference between us. But, O! why not be one of us? why not come to Jesus right away, and let's meet in yon beautiful land? That's just the one thing wanted; just say, "Lord, I believe, help Thou mine unbelief!" and He'll fold you in His arms. You see, I know! I've been a sinner myself!'

NOTES

The Strange Case of Dr Jekyll and Mr Hyde

1. (p.31) *Juggernaut*: from the Hindi *jagannath*, which means lord of the world, one of the titles of the god Krishna. *Juggernaut* derived from the custom of dragging an idol of the god in a huge chariot, in front of which devotees threw themselves and were crushed. It has come to mean anything which ruthlessly tramples or mows down what lies in its way.
2. (p.33) *Queer Street*: a term that indicates a case of financial difficulty.
3. (p.36) *Damon and Pythias*: *Pythias* should in fact be *Phintias* – it is a common mistake. Damon and Phintias were close friends who were condemned to death by the tyrant of Syracuse, Dionysius. Phintias was allowed out of prison and Damon pledged his life as bail. When Phintias returned Dionysius was so impressed he granted both freedom. The two became a symbol of constant friendship.
4. (p.42) *pede claudo*: on halting foot.

The Beach of Falesá

1. (p.101) *binnacle*: the place where the compass is kept.
2. (p.101) *Falesá* is a fictional place. The word itself means 'sacred house', and was commonly used by Samoans for 'church'. It seems clear that Stevenson knew the meaning of the word and chose it deliberately.
3. (p.102) *copra*: dried cocoanut meat, highly valued for its oil and a staple of South Pacific trade. Wiltshire's success as a trader on Falesá depends on getting copra from the islanders.
4. (p.102) *the beach*: 'South-Sea talk for the complex of interests, proverbs, and gossip emanating from the commercial element of an island. The people involved are either whites or part-whites or natives trying to live in white man's terms.' J. C. Furnas, *Anatomy of Paradise*, New York, 1948.
5. (p.103) *Kanaka*: literally, 'man', but used to denote any native of the South Sea islands.
6. (p.108) *tapa*: bark cloth.

7\. (p. 121) *sawder*: slang, meaning flattery.
8\. (p. 128) *Line Islands*: a group of Polynesian islands.
9\. (p. 128) *Apia*: capital of Samoa.
Papeete: capital of Tahiti.
10\. (p. 130) *sweep*: slang, meaning someone disreputable, a blackguard.
11\. (p. 134) *Blavatsky*: Madame Blavatsky was a well-known spiritualist of the 1880s and '90s.
12\. (p. 149) *sensitive*: sensitive plant.

The Ebb-Tide

1\. (p. 174) *on the beach*: a phrase used to describe destitute whites in the South Seas.
2\. (p. 174) *Eimeo*: one of the Society Islands to the west of Papeete.
3\. (p. 174) *sortes*: *sortes virgilianae*: attempt to foretell the future by dipping at random into a volume of Virgil and reading out the first passage that attracts the eye.
4\. (p. 179) *Freischütz: Der Freischütz, The Marksman*, an opera by Weber, 1821.
5\. (p. 179) *Kaspar* is a character who has sold his soul to the devil, which he can only redeem by enticing another into the devil's clutches.
6\. (p. 180) *Point Venus*: near Papeete, named after the scientific purpose of James Cook's 1765 voyage, to observe the passage of the planet Venus across the sun.
7\. (p. 181) *B-and-S*: brandy and soda.
8\. (p. 181) *growler*: a four-wheeled hackney cab.
9\. (p. 181) *ulster*: a long overcoat.
10\. (p. 186) *Indian Sachems*: *Sachem* is a Narragansett word meaning a supreme tribal chief.
11\. (p. 187) *We twa hae paidled in the burn ...*: the fourth stanza of Robert Burns' 'Auld Lang Syne'.
12\. (p. 189) *Portland*: a major port in the state of Maine.
13\. (p. 190) *Einst, O Wunder*: Beethoven's 'Adelaide', a setting of a poem by Friedrich Von Matthison, a favourite of Stevenson's to which he makes a number of references, in letters and in his essay 'On Falling in Love'.
14\. (p. 194) *Fifth Symphony*: clearly Beethoven's Fifth.
15\. (p. 194) *memor querela*: Merrick is remembering Horace, Odes, Book Three, xi: 'et nostri memorem sepulcro scalpe querellam' – and scratch upon our tomb a lament in our memory.
terque quaterque beati Quies ante ora patrum: Virgil's *Aeneid*, Book One, lines 94–5 translate as, 'O three and four times fortunate, you whose lot it was to die be-

neath the lofty walls of Troy before the faces of your fathers.

16. (p. 194) *Ich trage unerträgliches*: I bear the unbearable.
17. (p. 194) *Du, stolzes Herz, du hast es ja gewollt*: you, proud heart, you have what you desired. Both from Heine's *Die Heimkehr, The Homecoming, Ich unglückselʼger Atlas! Eine welt.*
18. (p. 196) *Paumotus*: a string of islands and very small atolls, also known as the Dangerous Archipelago, and now usually known as Tuamotu.
19. (p. 202) *Ohe lá goëlette*: schooner ahoy.
20. (p. 208) *Fakarava*: one of the Tuamotu atolls.
21. (p. 208) *Dangerous Archipelago*: see *Paumotus* above.
22. (p. 221) *Ranaka, Ratiu, Takume, Honden*: Tuamotu atolls.
23. (p. 231) *Calloa*: Peruvian port.
24. (p. 231) *lazarette*: space between decks used for storage.
25. (p. 234) *Findlay*: Alexander Findlay's 'directory for the navigation of the South Pacific Ocean', first published in 1851.
26. (p. 243) *For my voice has been tuned to the note of the gun...*: I have not been able to trace this. Stevenson was often careless with his quotations: he may even have invented it.
27. (p. 251) *nemorosa Zacynthos*
Jam medio apparet flucto: Virgil's Aeneid, Book Three, line 270: 'Iam medio apparet flucto nemoroso Zacynthos' – now shady Zacynthos appears in the middle of the flood.
28. (p. 254) *And darkness was the burier of the dead!*: Shakespeare, *Henry IV, Part 2* (I, i, 160).
29. (p. 264) *Kingsmills*: the Kingsmill Group of islands, part of the Gilbert Islands.
30. (p. 265) *Rapa-iti*: small volcanic island 300-odd miles south east of the Tubuai Islands.
31. (p. 277) *City of Laputa*: occurs in the third part of Swift's *Gulliver's Travels.* The Laputians are so preoccupied with their own thoughts and speculations that they are totally impractical in ordinary life.
32. (p. 281) *Noumea*: largest town in New Caledonia, with a prison colony.
33. (p. 292) *Abinadab*: there are several Abinadabs in the Bible. Huish is probably not referring to any particular one.
34. (p. 293) *Tophet*: symbolic of the torments of hell. A place where originally Jews were said to have made human sacrifices to outlandish gods, and later used as a rubbish dump where fires were kept continually burning.